EVER WILDE

HK JACOBS

ISBN: 978-1-7358156-8-8

DEDICATION

To the actual Cole's Church, Texas,

Thank you for giving me roots and wings.

CONTENTS

ACKNOWLEDGMENTS

Thank you to the following phenomenal people, without whom, the Alex Wilde Series would be a dream rather than a reality:

Erin for your grace, friendship, talented eye, and penchant for happy endings,
Amy Partain for your editing and polishing,
Angela Wingard for making my vision come to life on all three Alex Wilde covers,
Emily for your literary genius and patient ear,
Rhonda Shepard for shooting the cover of Ever Wilde,
The Grisham family for indulging my obsession with their wooden bridge,
Katie Hagaman for bringing Alex and Ian to life on Audible,
Tammy for your *sexpertise,*
and Rox for inspiring everyone's favorite character

EVER WILDE

ONE

British Virgin Islands, May 2011
"I hope you realize that I'm never moving from right here."

Alex reclined on a chaise, the sun permeating her skin with the most luxurious warmth. From Ian's cottage overlooking an inlet beach, the only thing they could see for miles was turquoise water and white sugar sand. Her black bikini, almost dry from their latest foray into the water, clung to her curves as she shifted to swipe her hair, stiff from the salt spray, from her shoulders.

Ian playfully nipped the prominence of her pelvic bone, earning a quick yelp. "Let's go in town and grab some lunch."

Alex groaned and scrunched her eyes shut. Her entire body felt heavy and sedate. It had been a phenomenal few weeks in Virgin Gorda. They had barely left the villa. Her cheeks filled with heat, remembering the intensity of perfect wedded bliss.

"What are you thinking about?" Ian teased.

The tingling rush coursing up her arched spine catapulted her body from horizontal to semi-vertical. She pushed her sunglasses to the top of her head, her eyes level with Ian's calf and the puckered red scar running from knee to ankle. He had a matching one on his other leg—a permanent reminder that their life together had nearly been over before it started.

Ian grunted as he used the chaise to push himself upright then extended a hand in her direction. "I know a great little ceviche place."

Alex reluctantly shoved her arms into her white linen shirt and allowed herself to be pulled upright by his outstretched hand. The momentum sent her colliding into his shirtless chest, the simple act of reconnecting with his skin causing her head to buzz and her heart to pound. She tipped her face upward to the sun and the ocean's sky, her hungry lips finding Ian's. She took her time tasting the salt there and the luxurious essence of time. Unhurried, precious time. He broke away from her when her stomach rumbled.

"I knew you were hungry," he accused.

"Hungry for you," she replied, biting her lower lip to entice his interest.

He brought her hand to his lips and kissed her knuckles before tugging her behind him. "Come on. We can't survive on saltwater and sex." He turned back to give her a delightful smirk. "As much as I would like to try."

Grumbling to herself, Alex finally relaxed into a smile when Ian led her out to the canary yellow Jeep parked in front of the house. She loved this house, a stucco cottage with its stone-tiled roof of burnt orange and faded turquoise pots overflowing with bougainvillea. The green tendrils and delicate pink blossoms arced lovingly into the air before diving to the ground in a snarl of tangled vines. The second-floor windows had been thrown open, white linen curtains fluttering around wooden shutters like a gull's wings.

In the passenger side of the Jeep, Alex tilted her head back and let the wind whip through her beachy waves and pummel the thin linen of her shirt. They drove parallel to the beach, past a stretch of land richly verdant from the recent rains and unoccupied except for a few feral goats ripping the grass up from the roots. It was a paradise so thorough that Alex could scarcely remember her reality.

A few miles down the single lane road, Ian whipped the vehicle through a patch of sand into a surprisingly full parking lot. The ramshackle building next to them was painted flamingo pink with a thatched roof that looked like it wouldn't survive the next strong gust of wind.

"I haven't been here in years," Ian said, gesturing to the screened-in shack.

"When was the last time?" Alex asked, floating a hand over to stroke the inner surface of his forearm.

"Five years ago or so. My dad took me sailing, and we ate here just about every day. Well, I ate, and he delivered not so subtle hints about how I needed to get my life straightened out."

Alex smirked. "And did you?"

"I did." A faraway look entered his eyes. The same one he always got when he conjured the past. But Alex had a feeling that this time, he was thinking about the future. *Their future.*

They chose to sit outside on a covered patio at a corner table apart from the rest of the crowd where Alex could sit in a slice of sun. She admired the way it made her skin seem even more golden brown, twisting her hand to let the light shimmer over the slim diamond band on her finger.

"It suits you," Ian said without looking up from the menu.

"What does?"

"The beach...time off...the ring...all of it."

His voice had grown husky and now she caught him staring at her, a quiet yearning growing in his eyes. Like what they had was temporary and would run like sand through their fingers if they weren't careful. She wondered if he suspected the restlessness in her—a tiny niggling at her conscience to return to reality. To being a doctor and saving kids' lives. To living her greater purpose. So far it had been surprisingly easy to keep it at bay.

"It suits you too," she said and studied his face.

In the months since the accident, the gaunt lines in his face had softened and the pallor of his skin had been replaced by a lovely shade of bronze. He had always been beautiful to her. But lately, his eyes had never been brighter, his lips fuller, his chest more solid as he pressed against her back every night when they fell asleep.

The arrival of a waiter in khaki shorts and flip flops, a pencil and pad in hand, broke her trance.

"Any idea what you want to order?" Ian asked her.

"Everything," she mused, flipping through the multi-page plastic menu.

"I'll come back in five," drawled the pimpled youth, pocketing the pen and scurrying over to the next table.

Ian glanced up from his menu then abruptly thrust his hand up in the air in greeting. Alex turned her head to find an amicable man, deeply tanned with a short peppery buzz cut, motioning for Ian to join him at the bar.

"Friend of yours?" Alex asked, smiling.

"Yeah. Eddie, my dive instructor. I can't believe he remembers me. Good guy. He moved here from London about thirty years ago and never left." Using the table to push to a stand, he leaned over and kissed the top of Alex's head. "Mind if I go say hi?"

"Of course not but bring me something with an umbrella when you come back."

"Your wish is my—"

3

Alex absorbed the rest of his sentence into her mouth and pressed her lips to his. "And don't forget it," she whispered.

He groaned lightly before shuffling over to the bar, leaning to the right to take the pressure off his left leg. That side hadn't healed as well as the other one after surgery even though it had been over a month. Alex furrowed her brow. They would need to get him back into physical therapy when they got home.

Home. That was a construct she hadn't dared let herself imagine. Since the wedding, they hadn't discussed anything beyond their next meal, but soon, they would be faced with the logistics of their life. His job in London. Her job in Botswana. And their mutual commitment to the hospital in Mongolia that Ian had built, and Alex had promised to support. She had chosen a life with Ian—with this man who loved her irrevocably. They would figure out what home meant. Together.

Her eyes drifted over his tall silhouette leaning over the surface of the bar as his dive buddy gesticulated into the air. The wind blew across his frame, thinner than it used to be, yet still muscular in all the right places. His linen shirt flapped sideways, and she caught a slice of his back right above the waistband of his khaki shorts. He was laughing freely, his head tilted back and bathed in sunlight. He looked positively vibrant. Not at all like someone who had been stranded in northern Mongolia for three months with multiple injuries. Luckily nothing that wouldn't heal over time.

When Ian returned, he plunked down a glass of pink liquid in front of her, a cherry floating lazily on the top, skewered by a nifty paper umbrella. Alex sipped it through a straw as Ian slid into the seat next to her. A sickly-sweet nectar coated her palate as the vapors struck her in the nose.

"Whew." She blew out a breath, wiping her lips with the back of her hand. "What's in this?"

Ian eyed his own glass of pink and swirled it a few times. "Rum punch. A special blend of Eddie's, I think."

"If I drink this, I'm going to either be curled up under the table or dancing on top of it," Alex joked.

Ian raised his eyebrows and put his drink to his lips. She plucked the cherry from the toothpick umbrella and popped it into her mouth. After mashing the fruit between her teeth to release its juice, she began absentmindedly flipping the stem around with her tongue. When she looked across the table, Ian's eyes were on her.

4

"Can you——?" he asked.

Alex furrowed her brow in concentration, coaxing her oral muscles to manipulate the cherry stem into a solid knot. It was hardly the first time she had done this—usually it occurred under the duress of competition—but it was the first time in long time. She caught Ian's wide-eyed expression as his tongue darted out onto his lower lip. Wearing an expression of pure smugness, she plucked the knotted stem from her teeth and laid it next to her glass.

"That was insanely hot."

"Too bad we didn't stay at the beach house." Alex narrowed her eyes and flicked them over Ian's chest.

"We can be back there in exactly two minutes, and I can have your clothes off in one." He held up his index finger then tapped her on the nose, sending her stomach into a delicious flip.

Eddie's gravelly voice punctured their lust bubble before Alex could nod.

"Pardon me everyone. No need to panic, but is there a doctor here today?"

Alex hesitated, giving anyone else the chance to push back a dining chair. *Damn.* She regarded Ian as he casually sipped a drink while raising an arm into the air.

"Right here, Eddie," he called, pointing a finger at Alex.

As the wizened divemaster weaved through the seated guests, Alex stood up, tugging her denim shorts farther down her tanned thighs.

"I'm Eddie," he said, thrusting out a hand covered in flat brown sunspots.

"Alex." Alex took his hand and gave him a wide smile.

"Follow me, Doc." He pivoted on his heel and motioned for Alex to accompany him.

"I'll save your seat, cherry pie," Ian whispered as she bent down for a swift kiss.

Alex trailed behind Eddie down a set of wooden stairs leading to the beachfront where blue and white striped chaise lounges sat in a neat row. One of the chairs was occupied by a woman in the recumbent position, hands folded neatly over her abdomen, a large white umbrella shading her face from the glaring sun.

"One of our regulars—snowbird from up north somewhere who owns a house not too far from here," Eddie explained. "She nearly passed out walking up the stairs to the restaurant, and our hostess made her lie down."

"What's her name?" Alex asked as she approached the still form.

"Margaret Levine," clipped a prim voice from inside the cocoon of the umbrella.

"I've brought you a doctor, Margie," announced Eddie. "Now be a dear and tell her what's going on with you."

"There is absolutely nothing 'going on with me,' Edward," she replied. "The sun was too hot for my walk this morning, and I got dizzy. End of story."

Alex edged around the umbrella to get a better view of her patient. She was dressed in white linen pants and a long-sleeved black blouse. A set of pearls adorned her neck, and a wisp of dark bangs fluttered beneath a black silk scarf tied over her hair. She looked to be in her late fifties, elegant and refined, with perfectly polished red fingernails and skin as creamy as alabaster despite living in a beach community. Alex knelt at the edge of the chaise, her bare knees sinking into the sugary sand.

"Hello, Ms. Levine. My name is Dr. Wilde, but you can call me Alex."

Margaret remained in her reclined position, her face covered by a pair of Chanel sunglasses. "You, my dear, look nothing like a doctor."

Alex gritted her teeth but smiled. "I'm sure I don't, but I am a doctor. I work in the intensive care unit. Can you tell me what happened?"

"I already told you." Margaret's thin lips tightened into a singular red line, deepening the grooves around her mouth.

Alex ignored the woman's tartness and donned the placid yet concerned face of a medical professional. "Have you felt dizzy before?"

"Of course, who hasn't?" she snapped.

"Did you have chest pain?"

"No."

"Shortness of breath?"

"No."

"Nausea?"

"Only since this conversation started."

This was going nowhere. "May I take your hand?"

"If you must."

The woman thrust her hand toward Alex, an enameled bracelet spinning on her bony wrist. Alex enveloped the hand that was cool despite the warm day. She slid her fingers under the bracelet where she felt a thrumming pulse that was regular but not quite strong enough.

"Have you had enough to drink today?" Alex asked softly.

"Hardly," the woman answered, the hint of a smirk forming at the corners of her mouth.

"Can we get you something?" Alex asked and lifted her brows at Eddie.

"I'll take a whisky sour made with Macallan's, Edward," the woman said, pulling her hand from Alex's grasp.

Alex sighed and narrowed her eyes. Her expensive taste in whiskey matched the rest of her.

"You need some water first," Alex said as Eddie chuckled in the background.

"I will have water," she said, smoothly removing her sunglasses and turning her head toward Alex. "It will be frozen and surrounded by whiskey."

The eyes that cut into her like glass were blue—ice blue—and startlingly familiar. Alex was mesmerized by her face; though aged, it was finely boned and beautifully symmetric. A movement near the stairs caught her eye, and she spied Ian making his way down, his linen shirt flapping in the breeze.

"Need anything?" he called.

Alex stood up and cupped her hands around her mouth. "Can you bring some water?"

He nodded and, a few minutes later, carefully limped over with two glistening bottles.

"Thanks," Alex said, brushing the hair out of her face before reaching for both bottles. Margaret remained still, hands clenching the frame of her sunglasses.

"You're really getting better at stairs," Alex said.

"It helps living with a doctor." He smiled brilliantly and ruffled her hair.

"Here you go," Alex said to Margaret, offering her one of the bottles.

What little color that existed in her complexion drained as she stared at Ian, her pupils dilating until only a rim of blue existed.

"Ms. Levine, this is my—"

"Hello Ian," Margaret interrupted.

Ian jerked his chin down to fully take in her features, his face turning stony and expressionless.

"Hello, Mom."

Mom?

TWO

"Are you going to say anything?"

Ian may have glanced at her. Alex couldn't tell through his blacker than black aviators.

"No."

His foot slipped off the brake and they lurched into the driveway of the beach house. *His mom.* Alex never thought she would even lay eyes on this woman's face. And after almost two decades of silence, she imagined Ian hadn't either. Alex remembered the faded Polaroid Ian had shown her once. A carefree woman with dark hair peeking from under a kerchief tied beneath her chin, a pair of sunglasses covering most of her face. She had been beautiful. She *was* beautiful now. Beautiful like high class art. Captivating yet completely inaccessible. Was this who Ian had been before he met her?

The Jeep skidded to a halt amidst a spray of gray and white pebbles. Ian didn't move from his seat, his fingers gripping the steering wheel until his knuckles turned white.

"What is she even doing here?" Alex asked.

"I have no idea."

"Do you think she knew you were on the island?"

"I don't know." His chin dropped to his chest.

"What are you going to do?" Alex moved a tentative hand over to his shoulder and began using her fingers to knead his neck muscles stretched as tight as a drumhead. The more her fingers worked, playing a minuet into his skin, the more he slumped into his seat. She knew his eyes were closed behind his sunglasses. Finally, he sighed. Heavy and brief.

"Does your earlier offer still stand?" he asked quietly.

"Which one?"

"The one where I become the cherry stem."

9

Alex replied without hesitation. "It does."

He removed his glasses, the usual flare of intensity in his eyes dulled by a sheen of anguish. A shard broke from her heart when she saw his face and her body liquefied into willingness—the willingness to do anything to ease his suffering.

"You look lost," she murmured, using her hand to cup his cheek. He twisted his lips into her palm.

"I'll be okay." He drew her fingers into his mouth and bit them playfully. "The only thing I want right now is to forget."

"Forget what?"

"Where I end and you begin."

They tumbled into the house in a flurry of lips and tongues and limbs, discarding articles of clothing with abandon. Alex paused to jerk her shirt over her head and watched the muscles ripple up Ian's flanks as he bent to drag his shorts over his ankles. He widened his stance to fix his balance and Alex's heart surged again. Of course, he didn't want to talk about her. The mother who had abandoned him as a teenager.

When he darted a salacious glance her way, she felt licks of flame on her inner thighs. He had always used women as a distraction. As a balm to his childhood pain. And now that pain had manifested in an ironic twist of fate that felt like steel piercing her gut.

Ian backed away from her one precarious step after another until the backs of his calves met with the sofa and he sat down, motioning for her to follow. Her bare feet slid across the tile floor, and she stopped within a short reach of his knees. Her fingers reached back to gently tug the strings of her bikini top and then, once it fluttered to the floor, she hooked her thumbs under the waistband of her bottoms and pushed them past her thighs. With one flick of her foot, they landed in the corner. As she climbed onto Ian's lap, fully drinking in the heat of his eyes, the parting of his lips, the welcoming grip of his hands, she settled into the moment, vowing to be what he wanted. What he needed. His distraction.

Waking up next to Ian's warm shape had become such a frequent event over the last few weeks that Alex startled when she found herself naked and alone under a blanket. Wrapping the throw around her shoulders, she sat upright and lolled her head along the sumptuous back of the couch. She could smell Ian's lingering scent of seawater and fresh linen, inhaling him in sharp intakes of breath while staring out the glass windows overlooking the inlet bay. Only a few stars were visible, a harem to a stately full moon cushioned by a world of black. The back door had been left open and a warm breeze fluttered across her temple like dove's wings. He would be out there somewhere along the beach, losing himself in the pounding of the ocean waves. The shard from earlier wedged itself deeper into her heart muscle when she thought of him out there, bearing his burdens alone like he had always preferred. But he wasn't alone. Not anymore.

Shrugging off the blanket, her eyes searched the floor for her clothing and instead found Ian's button down. She slipped it on. The linen, soft with wear, was luxurious against her bare skin. Tugging on the black shapeless mass of her bikini bottoms, she stepped toward the door, closing her hand around the slim neck of a glass bottle before exiting. She took the stairs one at a time until her toes met sand and immediately headed toward the ocean, turning to walk along the gentle curve of the inlet where the sand changed from sugary to firm.

Other than a few moonbeams bouncing off the crested waves, the path ahead of her was pitch black. But even in the dark, she was able to direct her course toward the mound of boulders in the distance. She had sunbathed on them yesterday, lying on a surface eroded to the sheen of a gemstone and close enough to the water that her face had been flecked with foam. That was where Ian would be.

The wind lifted her hair in greeting as she walked barefoot, the pads of her feet rubbing against an abandoned shell or a wayward strip of seaweed every now and again. It reminded her of being young. Of growing up near the Texas coast and exploring the microcosms of nature that flourished there every summer with their mix of vertebrates and invertebrates.

Ian had grown up near the coast as well. In modern luxury compared to her simplicity. As the privileged son of a Hollywood actress and the executive of a mining conglomerate. He had taken her to his childhood home once, a pristine white stucco with a tiled roof and a lavish view of the Pacific along the craggy Malibu coastline. It was the home that had watched him grow up; a home that had once been filled with voices and movement but now sat silent like a curated museum to document a happier time. A time before his parents had separated, before Ian's brother had died, before his mom had abandoned him at age fifteen.

His mom. What an unexpected ripple in their hard-earned bubble of happiness. *She* was the reason Ian had spent the better part of a decade indulging himself. It had been his way of staunching the wellspring of grief he contained. Grief and suffering and regret tainted Alex's past as well. And somehow, in a miraculous gift of fate, she and Ian had found a way to be each other's solution. To find a love that transcended sacrifice and suffering. To choose hope and each other.

Margaret Levine, on the other hand, had been given an opportunity to choose Ian and she had abandoned him.

A shape emerged from the darkness, perched atop the largest rock when she rounded the bend in the shoreline. Even in silhouette, he was perfection. His hair ruffling in the wind, so dark that it blended with the night, the angular lines of his face, and the tautness of his posture. She noticed the lines of tension radiating down his back and reached out to put a hand on his bare knee.

"You forgot something," she teased, sloshing the contents of her other hand.

He took it from her, using his teeth to pull out the stopper. His thyroid cartilage bobbed when he put the bottle to his lips.

"Thanks," he said and leaned over to nestle the bottle into the sand.

"It's beautiful out here," Alex said as a fresh gust of wind filled the space between her and Ian's torsos. He continued staring at the water without responding. Alex's pulse pounded in her ears, matching the waves pummeling the sand. "Penny for your thoughts." She slid her hand into his lap and interlaced his fingers with her own.

"They're not even worth that."

"Then I'm getting a bargain. Which is good since I have no current source of income."

He snorted lightly. "You have more money than you can imagine."

Oh. Being married to the heir of Devall Mining was going to take some getting used to. Releasing her grasp on his fingers, she climbed astride the rock like she would straddle a horse and positioned herself behind Ian. Sending her legs forward, she cocooned his body between her thighs and tugged on the back of his shirt until he leaned back onto her chest. Alex wrapped her arms around his middle and rubbed her cheek on the silk of his hair. His chest heaved and then relaxed into a blissful exhale. They sat there with the wind whipping around them and waves crashing in front of them, a delicate salt-infused spray coating Alex's cheeks and forehead. The longer Ian remained silent, the further her mind wandered. It was in these quiet moments Alex struggled to process the tumult of last year.

Nearly five months ago she had been tumbling down a grief spiral with no bottom in sight. Ian had been in a freak accident at one of the Mongolian mines and everyone thought he had died. Eventually Alex had too. And then random chance and fierce determination and unbelievable luck had brought them back together. She would never forget pulling back the felt flap of a tent in the Mongolian *taiga* to find Ian lying there under a pile of blankets. Injured and hungry but alive. Unable to walk because of two fractured legs but otherwise completely intact. Cared for by the *Tsaatan*—the reindeer people—for all those winter months until she found him. They had overcome peril and heartache and distance to be together. Surely, they could navigate the wounds of Ian's childhood. Wounds that cut deep. Wounds that scarred over but never truly healed. She understood. She had some of her own.

Ian's back muscles tensed against her front before he spoke. "My mom asked us to breakfast in the morning."

Alex let the words settle between them before she answered. "Do you want to go?"

"Not really." Alex didn't respond. Instead, she tightened her arms protectively around his middle. "I'm tempted to tell her to just go to hell but..."

"She's your mom."

"Yeah." He took one finger and began drawing circles on the back of her hand.

"What else did she say?"

Alex had excused herself into the restaurant at Ian's request and, from her vantage point on the deck, hadn't been able to derive much from their lack of body language.

"She asked about my father. Where I was living. What I was doing."

"She didn't apologize? Or try to explain what happened? Why she left?"

He shook his head. "Nope. Not a word."

"Maybe that's what breakfast is for."

"I doubt it." His voice had turned bitter and hard. "I think she wants to make herself feel better. If she knows that I'm successful and happy, she doesn't have to feel a bit of guilt about what she did."

"How can she not feel guilty?"

"Because she's the most selfish person I've ever known. Other than me. I guess that's where I get it from."

Alex leaned her lips down to his ear. "You are not selfish."

"Oh, I am," he replied. "I want what I want."

Deliciously warm fingers stroked her bare calf, and a tingle snaked its way up her spine to her hairline. Brushing the shell of his ear with her lips, Alex felt satisfaction settle deep into her belly when Ian groaned.

"So do I," she whispered, her words made nearly inaudible by the crashing surf.

By the time the bright notes of morning crept toward their intertwined legs, tangled in a mass of sheets, Alex made herself remember where they had to be today. Rolling away from Ian, she squinted at the accusatory face of her phone. Eight o'clock. The prone shape next to her groaned into the mattress.

"What time do we need to be there?"

"She said nine and requested that I not be late, which of course makes me want to do exactly that."

An arm snaked out for her waist, but Alex dodged it and swung her feet over the edge of the bed. A handful of bedsheet followed her, one that she deftly tugged and exposed Ian's glorious nudity. He didn't move.

"I'll be in the shower," she said, smiling at the sight of him dressed in sunlight and nothing else.

The drive westward to Nail Bay only took fifteen minutes. Not nearly long enough for Alex to calm her nerves or to think of anything that would assuage Ian's. She smoothed the white linen shift dress for the hundredth time and reached up to tuck a strand of hair behind her ear then reached her fingers behind her earlobe to adjust the back on her diamond earring.

"Are you nervous?"

"I don't know. Yes?"

He reached over to caress the bare spot above her crossed knee.

"We'll make this as short as possible and then I don't plan to ever see her again." He said it with such resolve that Alex almost believed him.

The house was nothing short of majestic. Towering white stucco walls joined by a tiled roof and a thick wooden front door flanked by a set of round windows. Before Ian had a chance to knock, the door opened and a squat woman in a crisply ironed navy dress with salt and pepper hair and skin the color of caramel beckoned them inside. She pointed to the rear of the house where sliding glass doors opened onto a covered patio.

"Mistress Levine will be with you shortly."

Her accent reminded Alex of ripe mangoes and steel drums. And then she was gone, disappearing into a hallway that probably led to the kitchen.

"After you," Ian prompted as they stepped out onto a grand patio with a rectangular table covered with floral patterned dishes and glassware of various heights. A cream linen runner swept down the middle, dotted with rose colored candles and bunches of freshly cut hibiscus. They seated themselves in the tightly woven bistro chairs, behind which fluttered white swathes of fabric hung between Roman-style columns. A sliver of sky was visible between the gaps in the material.

Alex dared a glance at Ian who was on a visual tour of his own, his face placid and betraying nothing. A heavy silence that contrasted the gentle swish of linen and the call of gulls overhead settled between them like a stone. She reached out for Ian's hand, curling her fingers around his. They remained cool despite the warmth of the day.

When Margaret entered the patio, Alex trained her eyes on the statuesque woman in black linen pants and cream top, a wide brimmed black hat placed artfully over her ebony bob. Her expression was unreadable.

She rested knobby fingers on the back of her chair, three of which bore jewels the size of small eggs. Alex studied her eyes. They were exactly the color of Ian's. As blue as an ocean's sky. But instead of warmth and flame, Alex found something cold and hard and bitter. Those eyes daggered toward Ian.

"Ian?" Her voice was like shards of glass. Alex felt a tug on her hand as Ian pushed back from the table and stood. Alex stood with him. "I would hate to think you lost all your manners." Margaret continued staring at him while she seated herself at the head of the table, crossing her legs at the ankles.

"Jacinta!" she shouted, shattering any peace offered by the beautiful day. The woman who had greeted them appeared at the table bearing a large silver bucket. Champagne was poured into flutes. Alex stared into the golden liquid, watching the bubbles dance to the surface and then disappear. Pop. She wished she could disappear as easily.

"A toast," Margaret said, lifting a bony arm. Her lips, painted blood red, moved with precise elocution. "To new beginnings."

A nerve exploded somewhere deep in Alex's brain. *She was moving right to the future when they had never even dealt with the past?* Tipping her glass to her lips, she caught Ian's expression—angst swimming underneath a visage of calm.

"Tell me about yourself, Alexandra, and how you came to know my son."

The words grated against Alex's thinning film of patience. Yet, interestingly, Ian seemed unfazed as he sipped his champagne. She willed stability into her voice. "I'm a doctor...for kids. I work with a hospital in Botswana. That's where I met Ian." He squeezed her fingers with his unoccupied hand.

"Alex is more than a doctor. She saves children all over the world."

"That must be a consuming career."

"It can be but it's what I'm meant to do with my life."

"Hmm." Margaret unfolded her napkin and spread it into a perfect equilateral triangle onto her plate before moving it to her lap. "Now that you're married to Ian, it seems like the children will need to find a new savior."

Alex jerked her head back and resisted the tartness coating her tongue. "I don't see why." Her fingers tightened on Ian's, sensing the tension vibrating there. Or maybe it was her own.

"You will find, dear, that marriage into this family comes with certain...requirements."

"I don't plan on giving Alex requirements," Ian growled, his voice slicing into the conversation like a serrated knife.

"You have a lot to learn about marriage, Ian."

"I'm sure I do but I won't be learning it from you."

Margaret's face didn't change at all. It remained unbreakable, like a mask of cured porcelain. And then despite eyes the consistency of steel, her face broke into a wide smile nearly stretching to her pearl ear bobs. "Perhaps not." She picked up a silver knife and fork when Jacinta slid a neatly folded omelet onto her plate, the hilts glinting in the sunlight. "But when Alex struggles to deal with the loss of her life as she knows it, I'll be happy to offer my advice."

The simpering smile that she directed toward Alex stayed with her for the remainder of the meal and taunted her when she closed her heavy lids that night.

As she replayed the conversation, no matter how she tried to shake the feeling of dread, the words had done their job and settled into her marrow.

THREE

"I'm sorry for the change of plans, baby," Ian said, as he leaned in and planted a kiss on her sunbaked lips, ducking to avoid the brim of her baseball hat. He looked relaxed for the first time in several days. Most likely because they were boarding a plane to extract them from a lifetime of sour memories associated with Alex's rather fashionable monster-in-law.

"It's okay." Alex leaned into the seatback of the private jet, its sumptuous backrest cushioning her shoulders and her disappointment. She stared out the window as the island faded from view and watched the ocean transition from cerulean to teal to an ominous navy. "We had to go back to reality eventually."

"About that..." He paused to crack the top of his laptop open, the screen light reflecting off his corneas. "We're not going back to London. Not yet."

Alex sat up straighter, wondering if her ears had heard wrong. The plan had always been to spend their honeymoon at the house in Virgin Gorda then head back to London where Ian would begin the transition of replacing his dad as chief executive officer of Devall Mining.

Alex's future held a boxcar of question marks. She technically still had a job in Botswana as a pediatric critical care doctor. For the last two years, she had slaved away alongside local pediatricians to upgrade the care provided to critically ill children. Until she had taken a leave of absence three months ago. She had been an emotional wreck when she left Africa for Ulaanbaatar. She had gone to keep a promise and had ended up staying. To mourn. To heal. To carry out Ian's vision with the new children's hospital. And then her world had spun into madness when she stumbled on a clue that led her into the depths of the *taiga* on horseback to attempt the impossible—to find Ian. And she had found him. And resurrected herself in the process.

Once Ian had healed from his injuries, they had gotten married, partly out of the desperation to cleave to one another after such an ordeal. The last few weeks at Ian's beach cottage had been a life of dreams. But it seemed that paradise had finally reached its expiration date.

"Where are we going?" Alex asked.

"To enjoy my father's wedding present."

Alex screwed up her face in confusion and Ian smirked.

"After what happened, he thought we needed a summer of, well, freedom. To travel. To make memories. To just...be."

God bless that man; that selfless gargantuan-sized man. Tears pricked Alex's eyes.

"We can figure out what's next for you, for your job, your life."

"My life is with you, Ian," she said quickly, using the neckline of her t-shirt to dab under one eye.

"I know," he said smoothly. "But I want you to have everything you want. I want you to be a doctor and my wife and whatever else it is you want to be."

Emotion welled up in her throat and she was only able to nod tightly in response.

"So, I thought we'd start at the beginning."

"Which means?" Alex asked

"We'll be landing in Gaborone in about—" he glanced down at his watch "—eighteen hours."

The view was exactly as Alex remembered it. The rainy season had passed, leaving the air with a crisp dusty bite when she inhaled. The mumbling lilt of rich voices speaking Setswana floated through the milieu as she and Ian jostled for a position on the sidewalk. A line of impatient taxis honked and screeched their way through the pickup lane as she adjusted the bag on her shoulder. She lifted a hand to signal one and Ian pushed it down.

He cocked his head toward the black SUV creeping through the line. "We have a car. Company perk," he said and planted a kiss on the side of her head.

When the vehicle approached, Ian slid a hand under the handle and tugged the door open so Alex could slide into the back. Being married to Ian had its benefits.

"Where would you like to go first?" he asked as the car put distance between them and the bustling airport.

A reel of places clicked through her brain in succession—her rental house, still containing the entirety of her belongings; Mary Lou's where her Rhodesian Ridgeback was probably sniffing under the table for bacon; Ex-Pats, the bar where she and Ian had first met; and the hospital where she worked, a cluster of white-washed stucco buildings connected by outdoor corridors bustling with activity. A slow smile parted her lips.

"Take me to Princess Marina."

When the car came to a stop outside the hospital, there was only one word to describe how Alex felt. Giddy. As she stepped out of the car, her shoes grinding into the sediment of the parking lot, part of her expected the building to gesture in welcome. Instead, when she entered the building, bustling ladies in starched white uniforms pushed patients through the corridors without looking up. A man with tawny skin and a long white coat strode past her, trailed by a cluster of young students, their heads bent over clipboards. The grass crackled as a stiff wind blew through, carrying the scents of linen drying on the clothesline and antiseptic.

Straightening her shoulders and quelling the tumult in her stomach, she wrenched open the double doors to the pediatric ward. Three months had passed since the soles of her shoes had touched the faded linoleum, so yellowed with age that she never could decide what its original color had been. She stopped in the antechamber to observe the two halves of the ward, separated by a partition.

Children huddled under cotton blankets, connected via transparent cords to a life source of IV fluids. Nurses soothed in rich, hushed tones. A woman in a white coat, black rubber stethoscope draped over her shoulders, jotted notes onto a metal clipboard as she glanced thoughtfully around the horseshoe configuration of cribs. Her sandalwood eyes flicked upward and met Alex's, recognition spreading through her finely boned face. Fastening the clipboard to a nearby bedrail, she strode toward Alex with arms outstretched.

"Dr. Alex." The woman's voice was warm and familiar and a touch more confident since Alex had seen her last.

"Lucia," Alex said warmly, inviting her former intern into a quick embrace. "It's so good to see you."

"And you," she responded. Her gaze moved over Alex's shoulder and her eyebrows rose together.

Ian extended a hand. "Hello, I'm Ian."

"Lucia," she responded, a smile tugging the edges of her lips as she grasped his outstretched hand. Her eyes riveted to Ian's face, studying it.

"Lucia is one of the pediatric trainees from the University of Botswana. She's a fantastic doctor."

Her eyelashes fluttered downward at the compliment, and she dropped Ian's hand. "I must be going," she said. "It's nice to have you here again, Dr. Alex." She tiptoed past them, stealing one last look at Ian over her shoulder before exiting through the faded pea-green double doors.

"You still have it," Alex teased, squeezing his hand affectionately. "What's that?"

"The ability to make women swoon."

He cocked a brow and parted his lips before whispering into her ear. "I know." She dug an elbow into his ribs. He grunted in response.

"You're also still the cockiest person I've ever met."

Mischief exploded in his irises. "You weren't complaining on the airplane when I showed you just how co—"

"Ian!" Alex clapped a hand over his mouth. "There are children listening." She jerked her head toward one curious toddler who was holding a sippy cup between two chubby hands, quietly regarding their interplay. To her surprise, Ian stepped toward the child, extending a tentative hand toward his bare head. She watched him caress the top of the boy's head gently under his palm and her heart twisted.

Ian hated hospitals. The first time she had seen him here at Princess Marina, he had spent the entire time on his phone, refusing to look her in the eye. At the time she thought he was a self-important jerk, not yet knowing him well enough to recognize the tension in his posture or the slight tremor to his hands. It was only later that she found out why.

When he was a teenager, his younger brother Ryan had been hospitalized with heart failure after a viral infection. Ian spent an entire summer in a hospital room to keep his brother company. The last complete summer of Ryan's life. He died that next year. And then Ian's mother had a breakdown and abandoned him. It had taken him a long time to begin the healing process.

And now—Alex feared this happenstance appearance of Margaret Levine would unravel him. She watched as Ian took his index finger and tapped the little boy on the end of his nose, eliciting a soft giggle. Ian did it again with the same result and a smile crept across his face. Not just any smile. A smile that weakened Alex's knees and sent a pang through her chest at the same time. A smile that she would trade anything to see.

A hand came to rest on her shoulder as a presence rumbled behind her. "Welcome back, Dr. Alex."

She rotated her head over one shoulder to find Dr. Kenosi—or Dr. K, as he preferred—standing behind her. His eyebrows shot up as she rotated fully so that she could wrap him in an embrace. "It's great to be back."

He patted her between the shoulder blades then released her to adjust his pair of black rimmed glasses. Peering down at her he said, "I hear congratulations are in order."

A pink blush bloomed in her cheeks, and she glanced over at Ian, now engrossed in a serious game of peek-a-boo. "I'm sorry I haven't had a chance to update you. Everything happened so quickly." For a moment, her mind relished in a treasure trove of memories. A beautiful day at the cusp of a Texas spring. The luxurious feel of sun-drenched wood under her feet as she stepped toward Ian in a flowing white dress.

"I am sure it is an incredible story. I would love to hear it some time."

Alex nodded. *Incredible barely covered it.*

"Ian looks well," Dr. K continued.

"He does," she agreed, motioning for Ian to join her. Amidst a few protesting whines from the child, Ian cleaned his hands then extended a ropey forearm to Dr. K.

"Good to see you, Dr. Kenosi."

"Good to see you as well, Ian. And please, it's Dr. K."

Ian dipped his chin as he gripped Dr. K's hand. "The hospital seems like it's doing well." He gestured to the group of nurses parading from the supply room with a stack of syringes.

"It is. We are. Thanks to the Devall foundation."

Ian flung an arm around Alex and pulled her into his side. "More like thanks to this one."

Alex rolled her eyes as a warmth spread through her chest.

"Yes. She is quite special to us."

A perceptible blanket of silence settled over them. Alex watched Dr. K rock back on his heels, and a stabbing feeling replaced the warmth in her chest. The time had come to organize her priorities. To establish her life plan. She had dreaded this moment, stuffing it away many times a day since she and Ian had said their vows. Ducking under Ian's arm, she met his eyes with summoned strength. "Can you give me a few minutes alone with Dr. K?"

He kissed her quickly on the top of her head. "Of course. Take all the time you need."

She turned her attention to the attentive brown eyes and clasped hands. "Could we get some tea?"

A short time later, she and Dr. K were seated on a stone bench in the courtyard, each swirling a thick blood red concoction of bush tea. A loud sipping noise interrupted the train of Alex's thoughts, and she gripped the warm edges of the cup tighter between her palms. She inhaled to speak but Dr. K beat her to it.

"My wife and I met at university." He paused, smiling and closing his eyes. "She was a rare creature. Smart and beautiful. She still is." Alex waited, wordless, while he sipped his tea. "There isn't anything I wouldn't do for her." His coffee-hued eyes hardened into resolve.

"Dr. K, I..." Alex hung her head, staring into the depths of the steaming liquid and inhaling its vapors. "I don't know how to make this work. My commitment is here," she said, rubbing a finger along the curled paper edge of her cup, "but it's also with Ian. He's still recovering from his injuries and he's taking over the Devall company when his dad retires." She didn't mention the sudden reappearance of his mother, but they were dealing with that, too. "I've never put anything above my profession or my commitment to my patients. Not my friends, not my family, not myself."

He nodded slowly and Alex soon felt the heaviness of a hand on her slumped shoulder. As they regarded one another, she noticed the additional sprigs of white in his hair since she had seen him last.

"In life, nothing is more important, Alex."

"More important than what?"

"Family. And Ian, he is your family."

Alex sat quietly, staring out the window as the black SUV navigated the afternoon Gaborone traffic. The thick glass silenced the frenetic honking and churning bus engines. Her eyelids began to droop, heavy with jet lag and emotional exhaustion. Ian's fingers slid along the back of her neck, massaging the tense muscles there.

"How was your conversation with Dr. K?"

Her eyes popped open and noticed the giant billboard outside the town's only multistory shopping center. It had changed from Nic's picture to some rugby player she didn't recognize.

"It was...hard."

"I thought so."

The air between them shimmered with her stress.

"Basically, he fired me."

"He did what?" Ian's hand stilled over her cervical spine.

Alex's throat clogged with words. Words she didn't want to say out loud. "He seemed to be convinced that I wouldn't be able to keep working in Botswana and—"

"And be married to me."

Alex nodded, not bothering to wipe away the slip of tears down her cheek. Her nose burned as she kept talking. "He said he didn't want me to be put in a position of having to choose. That there was only one right choice."

"Is there?"

"Is there what?"

"Only one right choice?"

She paused a beat before she answered. Ian was her choice—he always would be. Everything that had happened over the last few months had proven that.

"Of course." She slid a hand over his knee. "But it still hurts."

The car halted abruptly, their driver rolling down the window to fling out his hand in protest. Alex's face broke into a grin at the familiar Setswana gesture and then noticed they were in Masa square.

"Are we going somewhere else before we go to my house?"

Ian looked down guiltily. "I had some of the ladies here at corporate pack up your house weeks ago." In response to Alex's wide eyes, he continued. "I wasn't sure we'd make it back before your lease was up. Everything is in boxes in storage and ready for us to ship it to London. Whenever you're ready."

Sniffing, she nodded. It made absolute sense that he would do that, but no matter how kind the gesture, she felt a rapidly tumbling sense of loss. A disconnect with her life here. In fact, a disconnect with her life anywhere. Like she had zoomed upward on a rocket starship of happiness. Yet now, on the descent, she didn't quite know where to land.

He tucked her into his side, the pungent scents of leather and sandalwood loosening the tightness in her nose. "You need some rest. Tomorrow we can start sorting through our life and how we want to spend the rest of our summer."

Alex opened her lips to speak but Ian's finger was there to block the words.

"Tomorrow," he repeated firmly, and she had no choice but to swallow the words and kiss him instead.

FOUR

Tomorrow came and went and then came and went again. Rain had pummeled the windows of their hotel room for the better part of two days before it slowed into a dribble. Cold air seeped through the cracks between the wall plaster and the windowsill, running its invisible fingers over Alex's flesh as she clacked away on her laptop. Ian had rolled out of bed before dawn to resume his physical therapy in the hotel gym. The long bones in his legs had neatly knit themselves back together with the help of titanium plates and a few screws. Even with a mild residual limp, he was intent on making the most of his newfound stability by working on his cardio. She didn't blame him. He had extra energy to burn these days. Without a company to run or any foundation responsibilities, he longed for a creative outlet. And they could only have so much sex.

The door creaked open, splintering the silence. Ian's face appeared in the entry hall of their suite, raven colored hair plastered to his temples. Alex drank him in—every sculpted sweaty inch of him. He caught her stare and then rid himself of his gray t-shirt to expose a thoroughly etched midsection. The shirt flew past her head.

"Is that really necessary?" she said, trying and failing to sound mollified.

"It is absolutely necessary." He removed his shoes next then his socks. Alex's stomach prepared for a delicate back flip as a pair of mesh shorts landed on the bed next to her. Ian stretched his fingertips to the ceiling, nearly brushing the fan blades as Alex unashamedly counted the rippling hills of his obliques.

"See anything you like?"

Her head lolled to one side as her eyes slid down his midsection. Past the beckoning bulge of his boxer briefs to the linear scars, now faded into a delicate pink, running down the sides of both his legs.

"I'm very impressed by your healing ability. I can barely see your scars."

He sauntered over to the bed and flopped onto his back next to her. "Are you—" He took his index finger and trailed it along the bare surface of her collarbone. "Impressed with anything else?"

"I am," she whispered, closing her eyes to indulge a microsecond of lust. "But right now, you are distracting me." Her eyes flew open, and she tapped him on the end of the nose. "I just typed sex instead of self."

He shrugged and laughed silently. "What are you working on?"

Alex bit her lip thoughtfully. "A curriculum, of sorts. I thought if I came up with something good enough, I could pitch it to Dr. K. It would be a way for me to teach and stay involved while living, you know, not here."

"Is that what you've been talking about in your sleep the last few nights?"

She pinched his arm right above his elbow. "I don't talk in my sleep."

"You're right. It's more of a moan."

She pinched him harder, and he yelped before snapping the lid to her computer shut and pulling her down on top of him. His bare hands snaked their way inside her t-shirt, and he flattened his palms against the skin of her back. She met his sky-blue eyes, expecting to find wicked humor, but, instead, apprehension lurked there.

"Can I ask you something?" He traced gentle lines down her flanks.

"Anything."

His brows furrowed, the right one with a slightly more acute arch than the left. "Is it too much?"

"Is what too much?"

"This life. Me. Are you going to be happy giving up the things you love?"

A pain that had become too familiar burned inside her chest.

"I will be happy if it means having other things that I love." She kissed him on the tip of the nose then flicked her eyes to his before moving to his lips. He didn't move as she continued moving downward, past the stubble on his chin to the smooth skin of his neck. He tasted like salt and something smoky and rich. His throat bobbed against her lips, and she stilled as whispered words settled into her ears.

"Am I worth it?"

Her head jerked upward, her hand settling on the soft skin over Ian's sharp cheekbone.

"Look at me," she commanded softly. His lids fluttered open. A pulsing warmth started in the epicenter of where her pain rested, growing until it spilled over into her veins, spreading outward, farther, into the tips of her fingers. Her face tingled with it as she drew a breath.

"You are worth everything." She searched his face for a sign of acceptance. "Every disappointment. Every success. Every bad day. Every good. Every heartache." She leaned in to press blooming lips against his. "You." She kissed him again. "Are." And again. "Worth it."

The following day, Ian was leaning on the hood of their midnight blue rental car when Alex skipped down the sidewalk toward the gravel parking lot of Princess Marina. Although the sky remained overcast, a few fractured beams of sunlight found their way to his silhouette. Droves of people clad in starched lab coats filtered through the lot to their automobiles and the crisp air soon became tainted with bursts of exhaust. Ian held up a hand as she approached and then stuffed his phone into his coat pocket.

"How did it go?"

Alex couldn't get the words out fast enough. "Dr. K loved the idea. He's going to look over the curriculum tonight, but he thinks we can make a virtual option work...when I can't be here in person." Alex finished slowly, studying his face.

Ian remained unfazed by the last comment and held out his arms, which she slid into with ease. His face beamed, reflecting some of her own joy. *This could work.* It wouldn't be as effective as working here, but it was something. A way she could stay connected. The other details, like when and how long she could be in Botswana, could be worked out later. Ian sent his gaze skyward.

"I think the rain's done with us. Want to go celebrate?"

Alex's heart thumped in response and she cocked her head. "Ex-Pats?"

"Where else?" He tugged her after him as they jostled for position inside the suave low-slung two-seater.

Ian gunned the engine to enter the fray of Friday evening Gaborone traffic, headed toward a tucked away expatriate bar on the edge of town. Alex sighed with contentment as they whipped around Tlokweng circle, the centripetal force of the car tugging them into orbit.

"When was the last time you were there?" Ian asked over the blare of Afro-pop beats bumping up from the radio.

Alex settled into her black leather jacket, hugging it around her middle. "I don't know. Probably after I found out about you."

The air in the car became uncomfortably cold, unmitigated by the dry heat seeping from the vents. Ian stared straight ahead at the road, braking behind an omnibus overflowing with passengers.

"I never asked," he said softly. "I'm not sure why I didn't. Maybe I was too afraid to know how much you were hurting."

Alex quelled the images bubbling up to the surface of her consciousness. The months after the accident when they had searched for Ian and hadn't found him. When everyone had believed he was gone and she, eventually, had to accept it. His hand found hers, solid, warm fingers that contrasted her chilled ones. She relaxed, willing the warmth to seep inward, but it couldn't quite reach the bone level cold of her digits. Ian had suffered enough these last few months. He never needed to know the extent of her grief and the things she had done because of it.

"We can talk about it," he offered, sky blue eyes flicking to hers in concern. She realized how still she had become.

Clearing her throat, Alex squeezed his hand and lost herself in the fiery orange hues of the sunset. "I don't need to." She would rather toss herself into the sun than tell Ian what had happened during those devastating few months he was gone.

By the time they arrived, Ex-Pats had yet to start revving up for the evening. The crisp winter air whooshed through the door behind them as they stepped over the threshold into the welcome warmth of hardwood floors and leather upholstery and the scent of spiced breath. Jeff, the bald, portly bartender squinted his eyes as the glass he was filling overflowed with beer. Even more splashed onto the floor as he juggled the stein onto the polished wood of the bar to wave a hand in greeting. Ian strode over and they grasped forearms, one thick and meaty, the other sinewy.

"Hey man, I heard you was back from the dead," Jeff barked in his thick South African accent.

"It didn't suit me," Ian laughed, clapping Jeff on his broad shoulder.

"Welcome back, mate. Good to see you...and you." He turned to

Alex, winking, and she slid her arm around Ian's waist.

"It's good to be back."

Jeff cleared his throat and dipped under the bar to retrieve a menagerie of glassware, the bald spot on his head gleaming a lobster red. "What'll it be tonight, love?" Alex blushed pink at the term of endearment. "I would say it's on the house, but I suppose now you are the house." Jeff made a quick downward glance at the ring on Ian's left hand and chuckled, swinging out a thick hand to smack him on the arm.

Once Jeff had served the drinks, Alex tucked herself in a shadowed corner, warmed from the gas fireplace next to it, and gratuitously sipped a blood red pinotage. Ian's bourbon glass, empty apart from a few shards of ice, sat across from her. Across the room even though his back was turned, she could feel their connection, like a vibrating cord of air stretching between them. He grasped the hand of a friend from the Devall warehouse who had come to Ex-Pats with a group of co-eds, head tossing in laughter and recognition. This was her Ian. Beautiful. Full of life. *And hers*. For a lifetime.

His long, tapered fingers gestured in conversation. Talented fingers that changed lives with a few keystrokes on a laptop. Smiling into her wine, she allowed heat to bloom southward between her thighs. She knew exactly what those fingers could do. It was strange being at Ex-Pats as she closed one chapter of her life and rested on the page turn of a new one. Pivotal moment after pivotal moment could be traced back to this bar. Nearly three years ago, she had come here with Rox for the first time; her beautiful, devoted best friend who lit up every room with her own sunlight. And the year after that, she had met a sultry stranger dressed in black and sipping bourbon. And then through tragedy, they had lost one another. She would never lose him again.

Sighing, Alex tucked her braid over one shoulder, fingering the silky end and then drained the last few droplets clinging to the bottom of her wineglass. Across the room, another acquaintance of Ian's vied for his attention. He twisted around mid-conversation, blue eyes heating her with his gaze, and motioned her over with two fingers. The wine had warmed her blood, its effects coursing lazily through her consciousness, rounding out the stressful edge of the past few days.

Parting her lips, she pointed at her empty glass then mouthed "want anything?" The fire in his eyes escalated to an inferno and one eyebrow arched suggestively. Silently, he mouthed, "you." Any remaining chill on Alex's body flooded with the most decadent warmth. Her heart skipped erratically as she rose and sidestepped her way to the curved wooden edge of the bar. She tried—and failed—to tame her lopsided grin as Jeff stepped over to serve her.

"Can I get you more of the same, love? That one's an excellent vintage." He pointed to her empty glass.

Before she could answer, a familiar honey-toned voice with a hint of Texas twang rang out behind her.

"Actually, the lady prefers tequila."

FIVE

No. No. No. The universe was not that cruel. Alex turned slowly, carefully, the heady feeling she had just a moment ago evaporating at the sight of the amber eyes and chestnut hair. The neatly trimmed facial hair. The charcoal jacket over a gray sweater. Or maybe the universe was a vindictive bitch.

"Hello there, Alex."

Logan's full lips were upturned at the corners in a notable quirk. Golden hued eyes flowed down her silhouette like a caress. A boom resounded in her head as she stared, unblinking, while two separate spheres of her universe crashed into one other. He stepped closer— too close—crowding out all the other scents in the room except for his. Fresh laundry and vanilla and a bite of something citrus when he exhaled.

"Hi," she croaked. It was a miracle that she managed words at all.

"How you been?" he asked, cocking his head to one side. His face was near enough that she could see where he had cut himself shaving earlier. The tiniest droplet of dried blood stained the undersurface of his jaw. "How's Ian?"

At the mention of Ian's name, a spark of electricity raced through her middle, grounding her to the space between her heels. "He's good."

"I can see that."

She crossed her arms and watched his eyes linger on the diamond band glinting in the overhead light. Mischief flashed behind those heated honey eyes along with a splinter of hurt. Her hand reached out to grip his bicep.

"What are you even doing here?" she hissed.

"What does it look like?" He gestured to the glass shelves of liquor that took up most of the back wall. "Getting a drink. Care to join me?"

Irritation flared. She knew he was baiting her. "No, that's actually the last thing I care to do."

"Hmm, that's not what it seemed like last time I saw you." She physically felt her pupils dilate. "Or the time before that."

Alex's eyes darted wildly around the room. She didn't see Ian anywhere in the vicinity. Suddenly the cramped space they occupied became even smaller when a leggy brunette in clinging black jeans and a lush cream turtleneck nearly stepped on Alex's toes in her designer booties. Her finely boned face stretched into a heavenly smile when she saw Logan.

"This place has gotten seriously overcrowded." She tugged on the neck of her sweater and Alex watched Logan slip a finger into the loop of her jeans. Without waiting for an introduction, she stuck out a slim hand. "Hi, I'm Erin."

Alex couldn't place her accent. American, for sure, with the hint of a southern drawl that made her sound refined and delicate. Though, there was nothing delicate about her grip.

"I'm Alex."

"So nice to meet you. Logan's mentioned you. You're with the mining guy. Ian, right?"

"That's right," Alex said in a voice that sounded strange to her own ears.

Erin regarded her with chocolate-drop eyes that were rich with personality. "I'm going to get a drink." As she stepped past Alex, she held up a hand, the gold in her hair seeming to catch fire in the overhead lighting.

Logan smirked like a cat who had just lapped up the richest of the cream. Alex's stomach tightened into a snarled knot.

"I see you've moved on just fine," she bit out.

"As have you." The edge of Alex's hardness softened when a tendril of hurt flickered in his eyes. "But I guess I can't compete with someone who comes back from the dead."

He chuckled but the humor didn't reach past his mouth. That mouth. The same one that had been all over her a few months ago when she had been grieving over Ian. She had been insane and desperate. Desperate for anything to dull the pain. It seemed like eons ago.

"Can I talk to you?" she whispered, staring at the toes of his polished boots.

"We're talkin' right now," he drawled.

"Somewhere more...private." She gestured to the small room that was an offshoot to the main bar.

"Whatever you like, Alex."

Though acid dripped from his words, she could tell he was following her as she shuffled through the crowd. Alex entered the beckoning silence of the private alcove used for small gatherings. And perhaps a few transcontinental trysts. It smelled musty, a thick layer of dust coating the curved arms of the animal hide chairs. Logan flopped down into one of the chairs, propping his feet up on the nearest table.

"Well, you got me here. What do you want to say?"

Alex fidgeted, running clammy palms over the back pockets of her jeans. "I just wanted to say I'm sorry."

"For what?"

"For—" The words tumbled around her mouth and tasted sour on her tongue. "For kissing you and then—"

"Never talkin' to me again?"

Alex studied the stripes in the rug. "Basically." A wave of guilt rippled through her.

"We kissed. It was fun. End of story." Logan stared as if he saw right through her and then let his shoulders slump into the zebra hide chair. "Look, Alex." He sighed heavily. When she lifted her head, she noticed the softness of his features in the candlelight and the red-gold of his perfectly coiffed hair. "It's not like you made any promises to me. I knew what I was doin' and I did it anyway."

"I know but—" She chewed on her lip. "It's no excuse but I wasn't in a good place then and I did things that—"

"Do you regret it?"

The question smacked her in the chest with a force she didn't expect. *Did she? Should she?* He uncrossed his feet and planted them on the floor, rocking forward with his elbows propped on his knees as he regarded her in perfect silence.

"No," she whispered hoarsely.

"Regret what?"

Ian emerged through the shadowed doorway. A static charge crackled through the room as Alex's head whipped up. With a casual smile, he ran a hand through already ruffled hair and strolled to where Alex stood rooted to the wooden floor. When he was close enough, he snaked an arm around her waist, planting a kiss on the top of her head.

"Logan," he rumbled, sending a nod to the occupied animal hide chair. "What are you doing in Botswana?"

Alex's stomach did a nosedive and her posture stiffened against Ian's still hand on her back. A tendril of tension developed between them. She darted a silent, pleading look to Logan.

"You know," he said lazily, stretching to his full height and adjusting the sleeves of his dinner jacket, "I needed to move on from Tanzania and try something...different."

"Did you find anything here that interested you?"

The sensual timbre of Ian's voice had been replaced by something reminiscent of cold steel.

Logan grunted. "That would be my cue." He dipped his chin, running a hand through his hair. "Alex, good to see you again."

Ian stalked behind him to the doorway and pushed closed the heavy wooden door, blocking out the undercurrent of voices from the bar. The forceful click of the lock made Alex clench any remaining muscles that weren't already tense. Ian didn't look at her as he strode over to the bar and poured a finger's worth of bourbon into an empty glass. He threw his head back, emptying the contents into the back of his throat before pouring another. Slowly, he turned to face Alex, his face now smooth, eyes devoid of emotion. No anger. No hurt. Just a haunted vacancy. Alex's throat bobbed until she felt like she was choking. He knew. He had to know. But he needed to hear it from her.

"Ian," she began, her voice shaky but controlled.

He interrupted before she could continue. "Why is Logan looking at you like he knows you better than he should?"

Parchment had replaced the inside of her mouth and her tongue had become nothing but a thick tuft of wool. "Because he does."

Ian's eyes iced over. "What happened?"

"A few months ago, when I thought you were...when you were gone, I went through a rough time." Alex paused, expecting Ian to interject, but he remained unnervingly silent. She watched the undulating waves of amber in his glass. Her words felt weak, swallowed up by the monster of tension in the room. She tried to turn off her thoughts. The memory of the sweet smell of hay and the taste of champagne. The raw edge of grief and the soothing feel of lips against her skin. Lips that had not been Ian's.

"Rox and I went to Uhuru for the Devall foundation event and

Logan was there." She stared ahead, willing Ian to bridge their distance with understanding. "I went out to the barn to be alone, but he found me there and we...kissed."

"He wouldn't look at you the way he does after one kiss."

"It was more than that," Alex admitted. A wave of fury shadowed Ian's face. "No." She shook her head vehemently. "Not that. We never even got close to that point."

"That information should bring me some relief but surprisingly, it doesn't."

He stared at the wall over her head and Alex rotated to see what had caught his attention. The head of a mounted okapi. An okapi she wouldn't mind trading places with at the moment.

"Before Tanzania, I ran into him in Austin when I was in Texas for a conference. I was grieving and desperate and—"

"That desperate, Alex? Seriously?"

The contempt in his tone shook something loose in her and reared its ugly head.

"I thought you died, Ian."

The rest of his bourbon sloshed onto the counter as he gesticulated with his hands.

"I did!" He set down the glass and ran a hand through the back of his hair. "About five minutes ago when I found out about you and Logan."

His eyes darted toward the door, and he took a step toward it. Every muscle in her body burned to be put into motion yet she willed herself into the inertia of being stationary. The lock clicked open and then he was gone.

Indecision paralyzed her. Follow him? Wait for him to come back? Would he come back? She walked over to the bar and took a swig from the open bottle of bourbon. Her throat erupted in a line of flame. Down it went. She imagined it burning a hole all the way through her chest. She plunked down the bottle and less than a minute later found herself weaving through a packed bar, the air thick with laughter and exhaled liquor. Skirting the edge of the crowd, she slipped out the door into the parking lot.

Every step Alex took cleared her head of all extraneous sensory input. She focused only on her momentum. The gravel crunched under her boots as the ambient light from the windows faded until there was only night. A swathe of silver moonlight bathed a figure leaning against the side of a car, head tilted upward like he was simply enjoying the beauty of the night sky. Alex knew better.

"I forgot how much I love the nighttime here," she said.

The outdoor chill had seeped into her hands. She shoved them into the sleeves of her jacket for warmth.

"It's stunning," he agreed then hooked his fingers under the doorhandle, pulling it wide open. "Why don't you take the car back to the hotel."

Confusion flooded her face and she blinked, opening her eyes in time to watch Ian reach in and insert the keys into the ignition. Two perfectly round headlights popped up from the hood.

"Are you coming?" Alex asked, her hand reaching out to grip the car door.

He shook his head.

"Where are you going then?"

He jerked his head toward Ex-Pats. "Jeff needs me to go over the bar finances and returns." Sighing, he pushed away from the car, widening the distance between them. Each foot felt like a mile. "I won't be too much longer," he said slowly.

Panic surged through Alex's middle. "I don't mind waiting," she said, her voice thin and ragged.

"I'll see you back at the hotel, Alex."

His voice was steady, too steady, and it dismayed and irritated her at the same time. An irritation that sent her flopping into the driver's seat as she watched Ian disappear through the front door of Ex-Pats.

"So let me get this straight, you found Ian and now you've lost him again?"

"I haven't lost him," Alex grumbled, her hands trying to block out the sun rising over Mary Lou's back porch. Her head ached, like a dull blade slicing through her left eye all the way to her occiput. The citrus scent from her glass beckoned. She took a swig, coughing when the orange liquid sent fumes into the back of her nose.

"I didn't ask for vodka," she croaked.

Mary Lou cackled and shrugged, a troupe of dancing geishas on her pashmina following the movement of her shoulders. "You looked like you could use it."

"Probably." Alex took a tentative sip that burned all the way down her esophagus.

McCartney paused his investigation of the yard's perimeter and tucked a wet nose into Alex's lap, whining softly. She stroked the gentle curve of his ears with two fingers then scratched the undersurface of his neck, his russet head squirming in delight under her hand. Mary Lou remained purposefully silent. At least with spoken words. One glittering blue eye sent streams of conscious thought to pierce Alex's brain.

"I made a mistake...or twelve." Alex took another sip and let the words roll past her tongue before she lost her courage. "I had never loved anyone like I loved Ian and when I thought he was gone, I fell apart. My way of coping has always been to martyr myself for work until I was too tired to think, to feel. But I think once I had been in love, that part of my life was just as hard to say goodbye to as Ian, and I did some things I regret."

"Like?"

"I kissed someone. The same someone. On several occasions."

"Pshaw," Mary Lou scoffed and flapped a braceleted arm in the air. "You're too hard on yourself."

"It was more than that," Alex admitted. "I let him see me. My vulnerability. And then I ran away because I knew I liked him too much and I still wasn't over Ian."

"And you told Ian?"

"Not on purpose. We sort of ran into the other guy last night and Ian realized something was wrong, so I told him."

"That sounds dramatic. What did he say?"

"Not much. He sent me back to the hotel and he stayed at the bar."

Alex closed her eyes thinking of the text she had received around two in the morning—*Closing up now. Don't wait up.*

Of course, she had waited up. Waited until her eyes burned from exhaustion. When she had woken up this morning, she had been alone, sprawled over a hotel pillow. Desiccated tears had left a neat linear trail along her cheek. And the only sign of life from Ian was another text message.

Taking care of a few things at the Devall office. Let's talk later.

"Everything feels wrong now. I feel like I cheated and lied about it, even though technically I didn't do either. And I want to make this right but how can I when Ian is avoiding me."

Mary Lou rested her chin on a bejeweled hand, wisps of blonde and gray hair coaxing the lines in her forehead. "I ain't got answers for you."

"I can see you haven't lost your brutal honesty." Alex's mouth twitched into a brief smile.

"And you ain't lost your waistline and those long legs," she snapped back. The words smacked Alex in the face. "Some things," Mary Lou continued, "can't be fixed with words. He's off sulkin' somewhere questionin' his manhood."

Alex snorted. "Ian's ego is not that fragile."

"You'd be surprised." Mary Lou narrowed her eyes. "Especially when it comes to matters of the heart or a man's...potency."

Alex clapped a hand over her face to stifle inelegant laughter. McCartney startled awake and slunk over to the edge of Mary Lou's chair where she was waiting with a strip of bacon.

"Ian is as potent as they come," Alex giggled before downing the rest of her drink in a smooth gulp.

"Then you know exactly what to do, my dear. Go remind him of that."

SIX

Alex had no idea where the Devall offices were located. The downtown buildings of Gaborone loomed like fateful spires into the midday sky. Like totems to the sun. She weaved in and out of their shadows as she skirted the business district, peering up now and then to catch a glimpse of block letters above glass doorways. The security officer in the lobby of the University of Botswana had pointed her in this general direction and told her to find the tenth floor of the tallest building in downtown. From her vantage point on the street, every building appeared the tallest.

She crossed the street to a sleek, modern structure of cement gray brick and glass. A placard on the outside listed the names of several offices. She ran her finger down the block lettering etched in faint gold trim. And at the very bottom of the list traced her fingers around the words *Devall Mining Cooperative*. Jackpot.

A nervous twinge coursed through her chest as she clipped through the lobby in a pair of heels beneath her favorite skinny jeans. Reconciliation was coming for Ian. Even if he didn't realize it. Her finger reached out and pressed the button to call the elevator. It answered in approval with a resounding ding. The sleek silver doors closed lazily right before the elevator lurched upward. It was empty except for her. In fact, the entire building was devoid of humans except for a surly lady in a navy uniform manning the front desk. She had barely looked up from the surveillance camera feed when Alex had clomped past.

When the elevator stopped and the doors slid open, a plush cream carpet softened the sounds of her steps as she strode forward. Twin rows of walnut doors lined each side of the hallway. She stopped at the one bearing a familiar crest—a jumping springbok with a mountain in the background. Ignoring the nervous twinge in her gut, she twisted the metal knob and pushed open the door.

Transparent cubes of enclosed offices lined both sides of a main thoroughfare. Richly colored rugs had been expertly placed underneath pairs of mixed-media chairs. Alex rounded the corner and was met with an entire wall of black and white vintage photographs. She leaned in to study one—a young George Devall, Ian's father, his arm around a Masai chief, the landscape dotted with cattle in the background. Then she let her eyes roam the wall of photos—enlarged shots of giraffes and okapi and one of a hippopotamus opening its mouth in protest. And in one of the photos a teenage Ian, wild and windswept, stood with his father in front of a mining site, holding a rock the size of a baseball. Even in shades of gray, Ian was beautifully vibrant, the wide smile on his face belying the mountain of pain she knew he was living under by the time that photo was taken.

"That was the summer after I graduated high school."

Alex both stilled and startled at the decadent voice that was like a balm to her soul. She turned around slowly. It wasn't enough time to quell the frantic pace of her heart.

"Hi."

Tense as a coiled spring, she waited for him to look at her. His eyes would tell her what his lips could not.

"Hi," he murmured. The tension radiated between them as Ian ran a hand through his hair, leaving a row of ebony tufts pointing in all directions. A fine row of stubble had popped up on his jawline and purple shadows had invaded the spaces under his eyes. "What are you doing here?"

The words stung like barbs on the surface of her skin.

"You didn't come back last night," Alex whispered hoarsely.

"I know."

"I came to find you."

"Maybe I didn't want to be found."

The sound of Alex's chest cracking was audible in her own ears. Even as the first tear stung her lower lids, she lowered her voice an octave and said, "Maybe I didn't care."

Her words were unexpected. She knew it as soon as Ian's face softened into something raw and tragic and bittersweet. He extended his thumb, shaking as he brushed it over her bottom lip. His eyes followed, dancing over her mouth, before he leaned in. She swallowed expectantly, her lips parting in a quick intake of breath before they were covered with warm, softness.

Tension melted into a forgotten puddle on the floor as remorse was translated into exquisite kissing. Alex rose to her tiptoes and was overtaken by a furious cyclone of lips and tongues and teeth. She moved her arms to the back of his neck and up into his hair so that her fingers could dig into its soft pieces. A warm pulsing light grew out of the crack in Alex's chest until it reached the tips of her fingers, her toes, and back up her thighs to the tingling that grew between them. She slid her mouth across the fullness of Ian's bottom lip once more before forcing herself to break away.

"Wait—" she breathed.

"No. I will not wait."

Hands tightened on her hips, the intensity of his grip sending minor shockwaves into her lady region. She wrapped her fingers around his wrists and leaned away from pursuing lips.

"We need to talk."

"I know," he groaned, "but that's what afterward is for."

She schooled her expression and jerked her head toward the office door at the end of the hallway. "Is that your office?"

"One of them," he said, sending his mouth into the shell of her ear.

Pulling back, she twisted toward the partially open doorway, tugging Ian along by his sweater. "Come on."

The walls of the corner office were actually gargantuan-sized windows with a view that extended to the outskirts of town. If she squinted, she could even make out the green roof of Princess Marina from here. A massive mahogany desk was situated in front of one of the windows, shafts of afternoon sun highlighting a barrage of papers and Ian's open laptop. Alex pushed the screen closed with a click and pointed at the leather wingback chair behind the desk.

"Sit."

Alex quickly surveyed the room, soaking in the details of neat shelves lined with dusty volumes and a few hand-drawn maps of southern Africa. "Why is the building empty today?" she asked.

Beside her, Ian reclined into the chair, hands gripping the arms too tightly to feign relaxation. "It's Friday. Most people head home early."

"I have no idea what that would be like," Alex mused, staring thoughtfully at one of the drawings, the initials *I.D.* scribbled in the lower right corner. "Did you do this?"

"Do what?" Ian asked innocently.

"Did you draw this map of Botswana?"

He shrugged, full lips rounding into a boyish smile. "I had an obsession with cartography when I was younger."

"This is good." She traced her fingers on the glass, imagining a young Ian dragging a pencil along a thick sheaf of paper and shading the Okavango Delta. A delicious shiver skittered up her back, bringing the hairs of her neck to attention. A soft moan escaped her lips and she glanced sharply at Ian when he chuckled deeply into his chest.

"God, this turns me on," she admitted as he snaked a hand around her waist and pulled her onto his lap. A wicked hardness met her rear, and she released another soft moan.

Indulgence would be so easy right now. Like taking a bite of cake. Basically harmless. Inconsequential. Except that it wasn't.

Twisting in Ian's lap, she spun like a top then threw her legs to either side to straddle him like a horse. A wicked grin spread like warm sunshine over his face and his eyes half closed in bliss.

"Even better," he murmured.

Alex grabbed his wrists before his twitchy fingers made it to her shirt buttons.

"We need to talk," she repeated.

The sparkle in his eyes flattened to a dull shine. "I know. I just don't want to."

"Me neither...but I'll make you a deal."

He narrowed his eyes into slits. "What kind of deal?"

Alex rolled her hips forward until she was completely flush with Ian's pelvis. His breath hitched, and she smiled at the heave of his chest as a gentle wave of shyness lapped at her throat.

"When you answer a question, I'll start removing articles of clothing."

His eyes flared with heat. "What happens when you're out of clothes?"

"I guess we'll just have to see when and if that happens."

She closed the minute distance between them and placed a feather-light kiss on his lips.

A hint of a smile tugged at his mouth. "By all means, let's begin."

Alex screwed her face up in concentration and mentally urged her words forward. "Where did you go last night?"

Ian slumped into the supple leather. "I stayed at the bar."

"All night?"

"Yeah." He averted his gaze to the V of skin showing above her blouse and then popped the first two buttons open with his fingers.

"Where did you sleep and shower?" Alex inhaled the fresh scent of clean linen and body wash.

"There's a backroom at the bar for employees with a shower and I slept in one of the chairs in our sex den." He smirked and inserted his fingers through the folds of silk and traced the curve of her cleavage. Her blood hummed with his touch, but she forced the gentle buzzing in her head into quietude.

"I was worried."

"I know."

"Why didn't you come back this morning?"

"I don't know."

"Yes, you do." Alex bit down hard on her bottom lip as his fingers tugged on her third button. "Are you still mad?"

"Not at you."

A good bit of her chest was now exposed. Enough that she could feel the chill in the room. Gooseflesh erupted over her breasts and her nipples hardened under the ebony silk of her bra.

"Then who are you mad at?"

"Myself." He bit the word out like it was something ugly and distasteful.

"Why?"

He grew so still that his breath even ceased. "Because I acted just like *her*."

The words were coated in so much bitterness that Alex could almost taste it. "Who? Your mother?"

His face said everything with the tension along his jaw and the way his eyes hardened into chips of blue ice. "Yes," he said quietly.

"What are you talking about?"

The fringe of hair along his forehead almost covered his eyebrows when he hung his head forward.

"Before, when I told you what happened when I was fifteen, I didn't tell you the whole story."

"Tell it to me now." She urged his chin up with her fingertip and he swallowed hard.

"I got home from soccer practice one night. My mom was half a bottle in. She was just sitting on the couch staring into space. I asked her what was wrong, and she said..." His voice cracked and he cleared his throat to try and hide it.

"What did she say?"

"You." He sighed through his nose, averting his eyes to Alex's bare shoulder. "She said that everything wrong always came back to...me." The weight of those words settled into Alex's gut and made it hard to breathe, to think. "She told me to leave—that she couldn't stand to look at me anymore—that every time she did, all she wanted to see was Ryan instead."

"Ian," Alex said, his name a plea, a prayer for solace on her lips.

"It wasn't anything she hadn't said before, but this time I called her bluff. I left. I walked five miles to a friend's house and stayed away. If she wanted to be alone, then that's exactly what she would get. We had argued before, but she had never been so cruel and unapologetic about it."

"How long were you gone?"

"It was two weeks before I got the courage to go back there. I knew she hadn't meant it, but I wanted to punish her. I knew she was struggling, probably depressed. And she definitely had a drinking problem but I didn't care. I knew once I walked through the door, she would probably cry and say she was sorry." A heaving sigh rocked his chest. "But, when I got home, she was gone. And I never saw her again. She must have called my dad because he got there the next day and told me she was going to be gone for a while and that I was going to live with him in London. A while turned out to be seventeen years." A rueful smile crossed his face.

"Why did you say you're like her? You're nothing like her."

"Last night—I was hurt and angry but instead of talking to you, I pushed you farther away." He tried to look away, but Alex held him firmly by the chin. "I don't want you to ever feel like I can only love you during the good moments."

"Is that how your mom made you feel?"

He nodded slowly. "I think that's part of the reason she left..."

"What reason?"

"She knew she couldn't love me anymore."

"I can't imagine anyone not loving you." Alex tugged the hem of her silk shirt from her jeans, finishing off the last few buttons. She shrugged the material off her shoulders and let it drop to the floor.

"God, you're beautiful." He traced a finger under the lace of her bra and circled her nipple. Alex clenched her thighs around Ian's hips as a ripple of pleasure swept through her.

"I would never leave you." She cupped his face in her hands, his stubble abrading the surface of her palms. "Never," she repeated. "Even if you asked me to."

Her other bra strap slipped from her shoulder, her chest heaving so much that her nipples began to peek above the fabric.

"Considering you don't ever do anything that you don't want to do, I believe you." A genuine half-smile cracked the solemn contour of his face. He slid his fingers down her bare side with feathery strokes then dug them into the fabric of her jeans around her hip bones. When he pulled her forward, heat pulsed underneath her. Alex reached behind her back and unhooked her bra. It slithered off her arms and joined the silk shirt.

"No more talking." Her voice was strained, laced with desperation and longing when her nipples grazed the cashmere of Ian's sweater. An ache had been building low in her pelvis, a throbbing heaviness that required release.

Her lips found Ian's and they moved together in a frenzy of heat and desperation. Ian buried his head in her neck, scraping his teeth along the skin just below her jawline before planting his lips there. Alex yanked Ian's sweater over his head and watched his muscles ripple as he picked her up and plopped her down on the desk. And then his hands disengaged her zipper before they rolled her jeans over her hips, past her thighs, until they pooled underneath her feet. He stood in front of her, statuesque with a cutting hardness to his torso, and her breath caught in the tangled web of emotion in the back of her throat. He sent a finger skating along the rim of her panties before hooking it underneath and tugging. She gasped as the fabric grazed the bundle of nerves in her core and pressed her fingertips into the woodgrain of the desk. He knelt at her feet then. She felt his breath, warm and resplendent, but nothing compared to the hot lick of flames that followed. There would be no waiting. No gentle teasing or lighthearted banter. This was about forging reconnection—reminding him of what they were to each other. Partners. Soulmates.

He rose to his feet. In a clash of teeth and tongues, roving lips, and frenzied hands, they moved on each other in an artful dance of passion intermixed with remorse. He filled her in every way possible. An electrical current spread to the periphery of her being when he moved inside her. Marking her. Claiming her. Waves of pleasure drowned out any other unpleasant emotion. Coherent thought wasn't possible when her entire being had sharpened to a single spot. An epicenter of pure pleasure. She felt him everywhere. And in the moment she cried out and he groaned into her neck, she knew that everything was going to be fine. It would always be fine when they were together. *I would never leave you, Ian. Even if you asked me to.*

SEVEN

Sky blue eyes peered down at her and then a hand tucked a blanket tightly around her back. The sun hung low in the sky, its final rays dancing off the mirrored panels of the cityscape. Alex shifted to close the distance between her body and Ian's, soft tufts of fur brushing her bare skin.

"What are we lying on?" she mumbled as Ian drifted his gaze to her mouth. Her lips were swollen and her body ravaged in the most luxurious way. The kind of exquisitely satisfying ravaging that happened only under duress.

"Faux sheep, I think."

"Oh, it feels real," she said, running her hands over the luxurious pelt.

"So do you," Ian murmured as he traced idle circles over her lower back and then down the crease of her bottom.

"I am real." She tucked her head under his chin and shivered against his warmth, feeling the rumble in his chest as he sighed into her hair. "Ian, I'm sorry."

He didn't respond and continued the slow circles on her back that had become comforting instead of arousing. Inhaling a shaky breath, she continued, "Right before I went to Austin in February and ran into Logan, I thought I was...pregnant."

His hand froze against her skin. "Were you?"

"No, I wasn't. It was a mistake." Alex paused to remember the combined terror and wonder she had felt while the ultrasound had probed her belly, searching but not finding a tiny human inside her. "But I thought you were gone and for a moment, I imagined having our baby and it was the first time I felt any hope at all about the future."

His arms trembled as they moved to encase her.

"And then that was gone too, before it ever actually was, and I think I lost it for a while."

In all the weeks since Ian's rescue, after his surgery and recovery and the wedding and then seeing his estranged mother on their honeymoon, Alex had forgotten how grief had gripped her life last winter. On New Year's Eve, she had been ready to say yes to his marriage proposal. Instead, she had found out he was missing and assumed dead after an explosion at a mining site in Mongolia.

"What happened then?" Ian resumed long arcing strokes below her shoulder blades.

"I went to Austin for a medical conference and ended up rip roaring drunk on Sixth Street." Alex dipped her chin and focused on the soothing curve of Ian's pectorals. "I ducked into some fancy bar where I ran into Logan." She chewed the inside of her lip, wondering if the details mattered. Maybe they didn't. But the moment had come to purge her secrets. Nothing belonged between her and Ian. She studied his bare chest, damp and glistening with sweat. Not even clothes.

"He took me to a spot overlooking the river where I channeled my grief into chucking rocks."

Ian's chest vibrated against her as he chuckled silently.

"And then he kissed me, and I let him, and then I freaked out because I let him and ran away. In the rain."

Ian stilled. "He let you run through downtown Austin drunk and in the rain?"

"I don't think he could have stopped me."

By the time he grunted in response, Alex's mind had flitted elsewhere. To another time she had run wildly through city streets next to a witty billionaire, rain coursing over his face as he laughed.

"Are you thinking about Paris?" Ian asked and Alex startled.

"I was," she answered slowly. "I was thinking how that weekend changed everything. It changed the entire course of my life."

"Mine too," he whispered into her hair. "I'm sorry, baby. None of this was your fault. If it wasn't for you, I would have been stuck in a Mongolian *ger* with two broken legs until someone with cell phone service passed through." His lips found her forehead and then the tip of her nose. "I wish you would have told me." He used his lips to push a pleasant but insistent kiss on her downturned mouth. "But it's no excuse for me running away from you like I did."

"Well, it's a good thing I'll always be there to run after you."

"I hope so," Ian murmured, his melancholy soft against her cheek.

She pulled away from him, searching out the familiar eyes. Eyes the color of the sky at its bluest. A raging inferno of flame when he was aroused and the coldest chips of ice when he was angry.

"Hey, it's just you and me. No one else matters. No one comes between us. You..." She placed a palm flat against his chest; his heart reverberated in response. "And me."

When Alex searched for evidence that her words had settled into him, there was a flicker of certainty in his eyes among the doubt. It was enough for now.

"You have no idea how good this feels."

Alex cranked down the window of the official Princess Marina truck as Lucia navigated a desolate highway out of town. Her lips widened into a smile as they neared a row of straw and cinderblock homes tucked behind a cluster of acacia trees. They parked under the nearest one, a few thorns grating the hood in a high-pitched squeal when they crawled to a stop.

"Oops," Lucia muttered and Alex laughed. The day was clear and crisp, the sun barely bobbing over the horizon, the moon not yet slumbering. Alex hopped out to unload the coolers stacked bricklike in the back of the truck.

"Have we ever been this far out before?" Alex asked.

"I don't think so," Lucia said as she raised a hand in greeting to the woman in an orange turban toting a baby on each hip. Alex hauled the coolers to the ground and flipped them open, the painful gust of dry ice dusting her fingertips as she reached in to retrieve a bandolier of syringes and a box of vials.

"Where is Ian today?" Lucia edged around the back of the truck and put out her hand to collect the box.

"He's at the office catching up on work for the foundation."

A smile grew and stretched the entire width of her face. Every time she pictured his office, a collection of shivers skittered down her spine. Their steamy tryst on Ian's desk had magically transformed everything into a version of perfect again. Her heart stuttered with the love blooming there. She would have to thank Mary Lou.

"Dumela ma," called a throaty voice and Alex stood up from

behind the truck to extend a hand in greeting.

"Dumela ma," she replied, regarding the wide-eyed children bouncing on the ample hip surfaces of a woman with a wide toothless smile. One of the babies stretched out a hand and wrapped her sticky fingers around Alex's. Lucia launched into flawless Setswana, pointing to the vaccine vials then at each of the children. The mother shifted her weight between sandaled feet and nodded, interjecting a few questions.

"She said okay to the vaccines," Lucia announced when a break occurred in the conversation.

"Fantastic," Alex replied, reaching out a finger to tickle the infant's exposed abdomen. "One baby for each of us?"

Lucia palmed her a syringe, and they performed a coordinated dance of simultaneously plunging glinting silver needles into little thighs.

Despite the crispness in the air, the sun beat down on them for the better part of the day while they worked. By the afternoon, an uncomfortable sheen of sweat coated Alex's hairline.

"Was that the last house?" Alex asked, rubbing the back of her neck with a hand that came away not only sweaty but covered in a layer of grime.

"I think so." Lucia heaved the final cooler into the back of the truck and then fished out two silver cans from the bottom, handing one to Alex.

"I always knew you were smart, but this is a new level of brilliance. I never thought to stash the diet soda at the bottom of the vaccine cooler."

"Cheers," said Lucia, smiling enough that the tiny gap between her front teeth became visible.

The fizzy burn coated Alex's throat and she internally sighed as she leaned against the tailgate. "We're officially off the clock, although I guess I no longer have a clock." Alex frowned into the open hole atop her soda can. "Dr. K sort of fired me."

A laugh bubbled up from the base of Lucia's throat, a deep, throaty laugh that shook the slender shoulders under her white coat. "He did not actually fire you. He just realized that you can afford to work for free now."

Working for free. Growing up in a small town and living on pennies and resourcefulness had not prepared her for this life with Ian. A life where she could choose how she spent her time apart from needing to provide for herself. She wasn't accustomed to it. Maybe she never would be.

"How long are you staying in Botswana?"

"I don't know." Alex took another gulp of her soda. "Ian's dad gave him the summer off, but I doubt we'll be able to stay the entire time."

"We miss you at the hospital."

"I miss you too, everyone really."

"Dr. K offered me a permanent position in the pediatric ward."

Alex's eyebrows shot up. "Really? Lucia, that's—" A spike of envy flashed and then it was gone, replaced by sincere excitement. "That's fantastic. You'll be perfect."

"I hope we can stay in touch."

"Of course." Alex's voice broke mid-word.

"What are you planning to do?" Lucia asked, regarding her with calm brown orbs for eyes.

"About what?"

"Your medical work."

"I don't know yet." Alex chewed on the inside of her cheek. "Right now, I'm planning to stay involved here with teaching."

"What about clinical medicine? You will still practice, yes?"

"I'll have to figure that part out."

Lucia nodded, satisfied with her answer even though she hadn't really given one.

Practicing medicine. It was Alex's dream. Her life. But now her life wasn't only hers any longer.

"Hi there," Ian said smoothly, tucking his hands between the collar of her jacket and the thin skin of her neck. "How was your day?"

Alex shivered at the difference in their temperature. "Good and your hands are freezing." She sandwiched his frigid digits between the warmth of her neck and her palms. "Where have you been?" she asked, cocking her head to one side. Squinting into the sun as it set over the whitewashed stucco of Princess Marina, she inhaled the scents of disinfectant mixed with sweat and something she couldn't place, something that reminded her of—

"The operating room," he said proudly. "They needed some help transporting patients to and from their rooms. I didn't have anything better to do while I waited for you."

Alex faltered while she searched for words, a vise of emotion squeezing her chest. "That was...incredibly kind of you."

"Oh?" His eyebrows shot up.

"And generous."

Hands slipped around her waist like they belonged there, and she settled into the firm chest beneath the soft wool of his sweater.

"How generous are you feeling today?" He nuzzled the chilled exterior of her ear.

"Very," she whispered, skimming her lips over the stubble on his jawline. He groaned and tucked her farther into his jacket where her head swam in the overpowering scent of leather. "But," she said and received a loud groan of protest into her hair, "we have dinner tonight with Mary Lou."

He stilled as if taming the momentary surge of arousal and pulled away to wrench open the car door. "Raincheck," he rasped, a salacious smile on his face as he gestured for her to get in. "And I do plan on collecting."

The outside of Mary Lou's fawn colored one story beamed with twin windows alight with a warm, buttery glow. Alex interlaced her fingers with Ian's and rapped on the door with her other hand. A brusque bark followed by sharp words broke the silence of the moonlit night. As the door swung open, a gargantuan shape wriggled out of the opening and a wet nose investigated the intertwined hands. A morose whine started deep in McCartney's throat, reaching a crescendo by the time it exited his lips. Ian slid his hand from Alex's to lay it on the flat head, earning a shiver of delightful recognition.

"I missed you, boy," he said, using two fingers to scratch behind the floppy ears.

Mary Lou stood in the doorway behind the over-excited canine. She was dressed in an emerald green sweater and matching pants, amethyst slippers peeking from beneath her hemmed cuffs. Alex watched her sweep a critical eye over Ian and pause on the wrapped package tucked under Ian's arm.

"Mary Lou, this is Ian. Ian, Mary Lou Steiner."

"It's lovely to finally meet you, Mary Lou," Ian purred. "This is for you." He handed her the glass bottle wrapped in layers of gold tissue paper.

Mary Lou cradled it in the crook of her elbow, the lines around her eyes crinkling deeper into paper thin skin.

"Come on inside," she commanded.

Alex exchanged a look with Ian before crossing the threshold that emptied into her living area. A delicious aroma of richly braised meat wafted through the air and Alex inhaled deeply.

"What is that amazing smell?" she asked, settling onto the vintage bottle green sofa with Ian. Mary Lou eased down into a floral-patterned armchair before answering. "Coq au vin. Old family recipe."

"I thought your family was from Kentucky," Alex teased, watching McCartney curl up at Mary Lou's feet right on top of the purple silk slippers.

"You think people in Kentucky are all backwoods hicks that can't read a recipe book?"

"No, but I don't imagine many of them know how to make French food."

"And what do Texans know how to cook? Besides tacos."

Mary Lou's stern visage shattered into laughter that was punctuated by a dry, staccato cough.

"That cough doesn't sound good." Alex said, frowning.

"Nothin' a little bourbon can't fix." She ceremoniously ripped the gold paper from her gift to reveal a bottle that sloshed with richly hued amber liquid.

"I knew I was going to like you," said Ian as Mary Lou reached over to a sideboard for glasses.

"Likewise," she replied, splashing bourbon into three glasses.

Alex ping ponged glances between the two of them, not surprised that Ian's charm had buffed shine into Mary Lou's cheeks. Three glasses clinked in midair.

"To kindred spirits," crowed Ian.

Three sets of lips sucked down a mouthful of fiery spice.

"To epic love," said Alex, receiving whoops of agreement before she tipped up her glass once again. She stared expectantly at a newly pensive Mary Lou.

"To livin' like tomorrow ain't a promise." Her voice caught around something in her throat, the final words sounding strangled. Alex watched her quickly drain the remaining liquid in her glass and begin to refill it. "And," she drawled, "to cheatin' death a time or two...or three." She stared pointedly at Alex past the bottom of her bourbon glass.

"Three?" Alex squeaked and the smirk on Ian's face faded.

"The flood," Mary Lou clipped, holding up her index finger. A second finger followed. "That fire." And then a third finger. "And fallin' into that frozen river in Mongolia."

Ian cut his eyes to Alex. "Don't forget the earthquake in Haiti when part of a school fell on her head."

Mary Lou cackled and pushed out of her chair with surprising agility. "That's four," she called, her voice echoing from the kitchen.

Alex poked Ian in the ribs.

"You're the one who almost died in a mining blast."

"But I didn't." He batted his lashes over crushing blue eyes and smirked for an instant before his face sobered.

"What fire is she talking about?"

Alex rubbed the edge of her glass with her thumb. "I'll tell you about it some time. It happened a long time ago." *To a much different girl.*

"Dinner's ready," Mary Lou called at the same time Ian's phone jangled in his pocket.

He furrowed his brows as he retrieved it, his frown deepening when he saw the number on his screen. "I need to take this." He brushed her forehead with a kiss before springing to his feet and putting the phone to his ear.

Alex floated into the kitchen amidst Ian's murmuring into the phone, her steps light and airy courtesy of the whiskey. Mary Lou had pushed her sweater sleeves up to her elbows and was dipping a ladle in a pot, sending tendrils of steam into the air as she stirred. Emotion curled around her heart as she watched the spidery veins of Mary Lou's hands, the nimble fingers, each one crowned with a different jeweled ring.

"What's got you smilin' like you just won the Triple Crown?"

Alex hadn't realized she was smiling. "I'm just...happy. Maybe for the first time ever. I don't know...everything just feels right. And I can just enjoy it."

Mary Lou split her lips into a grin, the tip of her nose reddening against the steam from the pot. Or maybe it was the alcohol.

"You're very unconflicted these days," she said slowly, spooning a mixture of beef and carrots onto a porcelain plate.

Alex shrugged, mulling over the observation. "I almost lost the love of my life. But I didn't and here we are. Together. Married." She glanced down at the winking diamond band on her left hand. "What else could I even want?"

Mary Lou opened her mouth to speak but the words that entered the air were Ian's.

"Alex." His voice had taken on a wispy quality like it was smoke in the wind and nothing more. When she turned to see his face, it was pale and drawn.

"What is it?"

"We have to go to London. My dad..." The words stopped mid-sentence, swallowed up by a wave of cresting anguish. Ian cleared his throat and tried again. "That was Anne. He's on his way to the hospital in an ambulance."

EIGHT

The plane's twin engines roared as they ascended over Botswana, the twinkling lights of downtown winking out one by one as they gained altitude. Alex glanced over at Ian, hunched over across from her, scrolling and texting, perhaps to disengage his grip on what had just happened.

There had been no time for goodbyes. A hug to Mary Lou, a gentle swipe of McCartney's tongue across her nose, a hand on her back pushing her into a waiting car and then another tugging her onto a foggy strip of tarmac. Their bags had even been waiting for them as they boarded the plane, neatly packed and zipped up. Alex had inspected the contents before takeoff and whomever had been tasked with packing had even found the silk nightclothes shoved under her hotel pillow.

Ian's features appeared sharp against the shadows of the dimming cabin lights. Sharp enough to cut stone and carve a fortress around his emotions. She reached over to caress the back of his knuckles, brushing them lightly with her fingertips.

"Tell me again what Anne said." Alex could imagine Anne, the elegant live-in housekeeper, in her navy slacks and faded brown bun speaking in a clipped British accent.

Ian pocketed his phone, dragging a hand through the tousled pieces of his hair. "He had been at the main office in London all day at some meetings and when he walked in the door, she said he looked pale and was sweating." Alex nodded to encourage him to continue. "She thought it was the heat and took him into the library to sit down and went to get him a glass of water. When she came out of the kitchen, he was breathing hard and clutching his chest."

A tear as sharp as a cactus barb stung the corner of Alex's eye when she imagined George Devall—always the largest man in the room, both in stature and generosity—now vulnerable and in pain.

"She called the medics right away and they rushed him off to the hospital." Ian's fingers started to tremble, and she knew he was thinking of his brother. A calm spread through her, steadying her hands, her voice.

"He's going to be okay. This is not the same as what happened to Ryan."

"Isn't it though?" he bit out. "Once again, I'm not there."

"You have a good reason for being gone." He eyed her without responding so she continued. "Older people have heart attacks all the time, and the medical care in London is the best there is." She inhaled, still able to smell the sweet spice of Mary Lou's bourbon on his breath. "He will be okay."

"I have to do better, Alex. He's...he's all the family I have."

The shadows from inside the darkened plane cabin danced across his face, making him look wild and desperate. She curled her fingers tighter into his hand.

"You have me."

Their steps echoed in the pristine hallway, the squares of hospital flooring polished so brightly that Alex could see a smudged version of her reflection. Everything around them was starkly white; white walls, floor, ceiling. Even the tactful chairs in the waiting room were white—a blank canvas for patients and their families to paint their personal journey. A version of the future. Would it be the peace of pastels or as black as night, as dark as death, or a triangular wedge of supple yellow that colored a path of hope?

When she and Ian rounded the corner, a formidable set of double doors guarded the entry to the cardiac ICU. Alex nearly reached for her hospital badge before realizing two things: she hadn't worn one for quite a long time and this was not her hospital.

The black card swiper sneered at her, unraveling a bit of her composure. Ian sent out a shaky finger and pressed the round button next to it.

"May we help you?" crackled through the speaker.

Ian cleared his throat. "We're here to see George Devall."

A lock disengaged and Alex pushed on the horizontal bar to release one half of the door. On the other side, a horseshoe shaped conglomerate of glass enclosed rooms surrounded a central nurses' station. A giant monitor hovered above the oblong desk, rows of green and red blips traversing the screen with the up-down cadence of a Christmas carol. Women and men in monochromatic gray scrubs moved about like ants. Alex's pulse slowed into a steady thrum as she wound her fingers though Ian's, her eyes scanning the screen.

"He's in room fifteen," she announced and tugged him toward the rightward bend of the horseshoe. This might not be her hospital, but it was her domain.

A tall, lanky nurse with shoulder length hair pulled back from his face with a rubber band typed on a workstation outside the closed door of room 2115. An erasable white board clung to the wall next to the door.

Name: GD Dx: Myocardial infarction

Ian's breathing had become heavy, labored even, his movements slow and leaden. His hand was clammy inside Alex's.

"Excuse me," Alex said, attempting a glance through the curtained window of the hospital room. The smooth faced man glanced up from his computer screen, fingers stilling on the keyboard when he laid eyes on Ian. "We're family of George Devall. Can we go in?"

"Password?" the man drawled in a smooth British accent.

"Clementine," Alex answered without breaking eye contact. The name of Ian's Jack Russell Terrier.

The man nodded curtly and leaned over to push the handle of the door so that it swung inward. They were swallowed up by a cocoon of heavy silence punctuated by intrusive beeping. Alex's eyes swept the room, absorbing every detail, every piece of data flashing from the bedside monitor. Heart rate. Blood pressure. Oxygen saturation. They greeted her like long lost friends waving reassurance.

George Devall slept in the reclined position, his face sagging and pale without its usual vigor, without its natural steadfast cheer. Oxygen tubing entered his nose with a whoosh of high velocity air. A central line protruded from his right neck, the surrounding skin bearing a vicious purple bruise. Ian's grip tightened on her fingers until it became painful, and she tugged him forward so she could lay a hand on George's exposed arm.

Her fingers slid to the inside of his wrist as she observed the steady rise and fall of his chest. His skin was cool and papery thin, but when she found his pulse, it tapped against her fingers. Weak but steady. A door clicked behind them, and they turned in unison. A woman with stick straight hair and steel for eyes stood there, her hands clasped at the waist of the pristine white lab coat that swallowed her small frame. A pair of kelly green scrub pants emerged from the bottom hem and ended in sneakers.

"Good morning. Are you family?"

Ian didn't speak. Alex wasn't sure if he even breathed.

"We are." She slid her arm across his back, melding their sides together. "Son and daughter-in-law."

"Excellent. I'm Doctor Gilani, one of the cardiologists. Your father suffered a heart attack, but we were able to intervene in time. We placed a stent in one of his coronary arteries to relieve the blockage."

"Which one?" Alex asked.

"The left anterior descending."

"How much blockage?"

"About eighty-five percent. He was lucky."

"How's his heart function?"

"Not perfect but improving. We'll get another echocardiogram tomorrow."

The woman slipped a stethoscope out of her pocket and toyed with the end. Alex itched to get her hands on it. To hear the confirmation of her words from George's heart itself. To hear the reassuring thump in her own ears. Instead, she tightened her grip on Ian who had begun to sag with relief. She tipped her head up to glassy, unseeing eyes. And although his face was still beautiful, anguish rippled under his skin.

Doctor Gilani wound the black rubber around her neck and rocked back on her heels. "I'll give you a moment and come back to check on him later."

Alex swallowed hard. "Thank you for taking care of him."

Once the door closed behind her, Alex directed Ian into the supple vinyl of the yellow club chair shoved in the corner of the room. When he was seated, she palmed his face and tipped it up to her own, feeling the prick of his stubble under her fingertips. She rubbed it gently with her thumb.

"He's going to be okay."

His throat bobbed and he closed his eyes. "Really? You're sure?"

"I am."

Balancing his hands on her waist, he buried his head into her stomach. "Alex...I...thank you. I'm not good at this."

Alex reached up to smooth the hair from his forehead, noticing the lines gathered around the corners of his eyes and the purplish hue underneath them. "You don't have to be. That's what I'm here for."

She had never seen him this unraveled, his smooth exterior a spiderweb of fine cracks. The cunning businessman. The generous philanthropist. The loyal friend. The charming flirt. The inexorable lover. Her husband.

"I'll go find some coffee." She leaned down and brushed her lips across his forehead.

Separating from her, he settled back into the chair, reclining his head in a gesture of exhaustion.

There was a cafeteria on the first floor, a cafe really, that comprised the corner pocket of the lobby. Alex collected two steaming cups of espresso from a dour woman in a white apron who seemed to have absorbed the cumulative grief of the entire hospital.

While waiting for the elevator, she cast a critical eye over her surroundings. The early morning sun sent shafts of light through oversized circular windows, framing clusters of people littering the nondescript modular furniture. Somewhere she could hear water tinkling from a fountain behind thick fronds of green. No colorful carpets or lively art. No hand painted murals in primary colors or therapy dogs in smart green vests. No wagons bearing children connected to IV poles.

Adult hospitals were bleak and emotionless compared to pediatric ones. Still, Alex felt comfortable here. It was a universe she could easily navigate, and, most importantly, could use her prowess to alleviate the burden on Ian. She would do anything to spare Ian any more pain.

Balancing the paper cups between her palms, she passed the ICU waiting room, glancing inside the rectangular window to find a familiar silhouette using the vending machine as a backrest. Her breath caught and she pressed her shoulder into the door to open it.

Rox's head snapped in her direction. Alex only had a moment to appreciate her—the navy blue scrubs hugging her growing midsection, the chopped pieces of straw-colored hair brushing the delicate angle of her jaw. The tired, worried look on her face when she wrapped Alex in a hug.

"I came as soon as I got off work." She smelled like a night in the hospital, stale with a hint of yesterday's floral perfume. Rox pushed Alex away from her, surveying her up and down. "You look great by the way and very tan."

"So do you. I've missed you." Alex flicked her eyes to the basketball-sized swell in Rox's abdomen.

"How's George? Is it bad?"

"I'll tell you everything, but can we sit first?" She gestured to the row of connected plastic chairs. When they sat, Rox grasped both of her hands and tucked them against the lump in her lap.

"So, what happened?" she asked.

"He had a heart attack, but they got him to the cath lab quickly and placed a stent." Alex paused to draw a shaky breath. "I think he's going to be okay."

Rox sagged in relief and gripped her hands even tighter. "That's good news."

"I know," Alex replied.

"How's Ian?"

"He's...in shock...I think. He's barely said anything since we left Botswana."

"Botswana?" Her best friend arched a brow. "I thought you were in the Virgin Islands on your honeymoon in the very epicenter of irony."

"We were," Alex started slowly, "but we sort of left when we ran into Ian's mother."

Rox's pupils grew to the size of grapes. "I thought she died when he was a teenager."

Alex fidgeted, unsure of how much of Ian's story to reveal. "Long story short...she didn't but he hasn't seen her for seventeen years."

"What the actual fuck?" She pressed the heels of her hands into her abdomen like she was covering a pair of tiny ears.

"Yeah." Alex couldn't think of a better way to sum it up.

Rox suddenly cringed and pulled Alex's hands to rest atop the mound that was her abdomen. In a few moments, she felt the gentlest of nudges and then another one. A thrill coursed through Alex's arm, all the way to a warm spot inside her chest.

"Was that—?"

Rox began to stroke the sides of her abdomen. "Yep. As soon as I get off my feet and stop moving, she gets feisty."

Alex gingerly pressed against a hard bulge.

"And as soon as I lie down, forget it. Parties all night, this one." Rox continued to stroke her belly in slow loving arcs.

"How are you feeling?" Alex asked, mesmerized by the tiny protrusion of feet underneath her hand.

"Beyond tired. And fat. I feel like a stuffed sausage. But ten more weeks, and this gal is getting evicted." *Ten weeks? How was it time already?*

"Your baby shower—" Alex groaned.

"Will get sorted. Don't worry."

Alex folded her hands into her lap. "I've been so consumed with Ian that I forgot. Well, Ian and other things like an estranged mother-in-law, and running into Logan, and getting fired by Dr. K, and then this." She gestured toward the ICU.

Rox's expression morphed into shock, and she narrowed her eyes. "We have a lot to catch up on."

"I know."

"Go be there for Ian and call me tomorrow." Rox enveloped her in another hug. "We'll have loads of time now that you're in London for good."

Rain slashed across the sky from heavy, foreboding clouds that coalesced above the city. A fine spray of gritty water coated the lower half of Alex's jeans as she stood on the sidewalk. A nondescript black sedan halted in front of her and a bearded man in a newsboy hat bounded out of the driver's seat.

"Madame Devall?" he said in a lilting Scottish brogue. She hadn't changed her name but there was no point in correcting him.

"Are you Hamish?"

"Aye, miss."

Alex turned and reentered the sliding glass doors of the hospital, motioning to a hefty gentleman in scrubs. When he pushed passed her with a wheelchair, she reached out a hand to squeeze George Devall's shoulder. "Our ride's here."

He nodded, eyes dim but perceptive and remained quiet as he was wheeled under a porte-cochere. Between the three of them, they were able to maneuver George's six-foot-five frame into the back of the car.

"Thank you," he grunted.

The ride to Waltham Abbey was cloaked in silence punctuated by the pattering of rain on the windshield. The car's motion had lulled Ian's father into a deep sleep and Alex took the opportunity to rifle through the manila folder of discharge instructions. Her phone vibrated under her thigh, and she raised it to her ear.

"We're on our way home," she whispered.

"Good. How does he look?" Ian asked

Alex shifted her eyes to the sleeping form beside her. "Tired but decent despite what he's been through." Alex heard Ian breathe a sigh of relief.

"I have some meetings at the London office and then I'll drive over to the house." He paused for a beat. "I love you, Alex."

"I love you, too. Don't worry about a thing. I've got this."

When they entered the front door of the countryside estate, Anne, in her prim navy suit with arms folded across her chest, was stationed in the entry hall like a sentry. Despite an unsettling stagger, George had insisted on walking into the house. Alex cupped her palm under his elbow anyway, though she had no idea how she would keep him upright if he decided to slump. Anne swept into motion, stabilizing a tottering George from the other side and guiding them into the library. Alex saw her eyes flick to the stairs, frown lines forming on an already etched forehead.

"Is there a bedroom on this floor?" Alex asked.

Anne bristled in response. "Yes, but it won't do for Master Devall."

"It will, Anne, and it will be far better than tumbling down the stairs. And possibly taking you with me." He winked at her, a lazy lid closing over the mischief in his eye.

Anne huffed in indignation but began urging them toward a back hallway, an offshoot of the kitchen that led into the bowels of the house. When they arrived at a mahogany door, Anne twisted the faded brass knob to reveal a modest bedroom with a simple four poster bed along one wall and a matching chest of drawers on the other. An upholstered wingback chair and footstool had been shoved in a corner near a window that looked out onto the back garden where a neat row of hedges bordered a carriage house. The remainder of the space was filled with stacks of cardboard boxes labeled in a neatly printed script.

Anne marched straight into the room to fluff the pillows and pull back a cornflower blue duvet, her heels quieted by the luscious rugs covering the floorboards.

"This used to be her room," George whispered secretively as Anne threw the silk drapes open in a flourish. "Before we moved her to her own house." He gestured out the window at the carriage house.

Alex turned up her lips, allowing George to wield her as a human cane as he shifted and came to rest on the bed.

"What's in all the boxes?" Alex said breathlessly as his weight lifted off her shoulders.

His chestnut eyes clouded for a moment. "Oh, this and that."

"I can move them out of here if you like," Alex offered.

"That would be lovely, Alexandra. If it's not too much trouble. Perhaps to one of the spare rooms on the second level." He swung his legs onto the mattress then leaned against a mountain of throw pillows.

"Can I get you anything?" she asked gently, daring to place a hand on his shoulder. Anne swiftly moved to George's other side and began tucking a velvet lined quilt over his legs.

"You can move along now. I'll tend to things here, dear."

Dear. That was the first endearment that Anne had ever afforded her. A warmth heated her cheeks and she turned toward the row of boxes.

A few minutes later she was ascending the stairs behind a precarious tower of cardboard. Her footfalls were nearly silent on the Persian runners as she trudged down the hall in search of a proper storage place. When the toe of her sneakers caught an uneven fold in the rug, she cursed as the boxes tumbled to the ground, contents spilling from the top one.

"Crap," Alex muttered, noting the barrage of envelopes, scraps of paper, and a pewter frame, discolored with age. She flipped it over. It was a black and white photograph of a woman with long dark hair smiling unabashedly at the man next to her. A man with an equally dazzling smile. In her arms she cradled an infant with a shock of dark hair in a pair of overalls, his chubby arms reaching for the camera, mischief in his eyes. Joy and love radiated from them. A perfect family. She peered at the date inscribed at the bottom. 1977.

Grief tore at her gut as she stared at the picture and watched their future play out in her mind. The death of a child. The dissolution of a marriage. And then a mother, once lovely and endearing, who would abandon her oldest son without a word.

NINE

"So, what are you and Ian doing for the Fourth, sweetie?"

Alex tucked the phone underneath her ear to slice open a cardboard box. "Mom," she chastised, "I'm pretty sure England doesn't celebrate Independence Day."

"Oh, well then," she said, and Alex could imagine her twisting the phone cord between her fingers. The Fourth of July had always been a spectacle in her hometown—a day of food, friendship, fireworks. The entire town would coalesce under the night sky, families and couples gathered on blankets sharing food and laughter until the sky exploded into vibrant colors. It held some incredible memories. Some terrible ones as well.

"Ian is taking me to some charity event tonight."

"How is Ian?"

The question was casual but purposeful. Alex paused as her mood sunk into a quagmire of melancholy.

"He's...busy," she replied carefully. And although her mother didn't press further, she found herself drawing breath and lifting the lid on a box of inappropriate thoughts. "I haven't seen him much lately. George officially stepped down from the company and Ian is trying to fill some very large shoes." She thought of the last several nights eating dinner by herself in Ian's townhouse in London. Of climbing into cool sheets and falling asleep with the bedside lamp burning brightly, curled on her side at the very edge of an oversized bed. And waking to rumpled sheets and a head shaped indention in Ian's pillow but no Ian.

But she understood. The situation could easily be reversed when she found a job and went back into the fray of ICU medicine. Her mother's high, tinkling voice continued on the other end of the line. Alex realized she had only been paying half attention.

"I was so sorry to hear about George. How is he? And what exactly happened to him?"

"He had sort of a mini-heart attack, Mom. Not the kind that leaves permanent damage. Luckily, he got to the cath lab, and they placed a stent in his coronary."

"Oh, I hope he's doing all right."

Alex's face broke into a smile thinking of the giant man with the gentlest soul she had ever known. She had seen him yesterday after braving the London traffic to pay a visit to Waltham Abbey. He had been seated in his private library, settled into a leather chair by the window reading a recent copy of the *Economist*. Anne had fussed over them while they talked and delivered a tray of tea and miniature biscuits. The color had returned to his cheeks under his neatly trimmed facial hair, the bright perception to his eyes. He had even tried to return to the office, but Ian wouldn't stand for it. The transition was inevitable, he said. There was no sense in delaying it. Despite the kink it made in their plans, and in her career path, protecting George from further stress was the right thing to do.

"He's doing fine, Mom. And he'll continue to be fine as long as he takes care of himself."

"That's good to hear. Did you know that...."

Her voice filled up the distance between them with a soliloquy of the latest town gossip. Alex relaxed into the sound of her lilting speech, listening but not absorbing, until a familiar name jerked her out of a mental haze. The skin on the back of her arms prickled.

"What did you say?"

"Oh, that the dime store was closing down."

"No, before that."

"Oh, I read in the paper the other day that Terry's land is up for auction next month."

It was like a swift wind had suddenly stolen Alex's breath.

"Why?" Her voice sounded strangled.

"Because," Janie paused, "she died last year without a will so the state took possession of the property."

"I didn't know."

"I don't think anyone around here did either. You remember how private she was." Alex didn't comment as her gut churned. "Peter and I are planning to go. You should come with us, honey." An innocent request without agenda or guile. Janie was anything but surreptitious.

"I don't think I can, not with Ian's schedule."

"All right. You know where we live if you change your mind." Her mom's carefree laughter was drowned out by raucous barking on the other end of the phone. She heard a screen door slam and the low, gravelly tone of Peter, her mom's new husband.

"What was that, dear?" Janie asked and Alex wondered if she had been thinking out loud.

"Nothing, Mom. I'll talk to you soon."

Alex checked her reflection in the bathroom mirror, sending her forefinger up to tame a few errant eyebrow hairs. Straightening the jacket of her navy suit, she noticed the deeper furrows on her forehead and the suggestion of crow's feet at the outer corners of her eyes, right where her black eyeliner ended in a smudge. The golden hue of her skin had faded in the weeks they had been in London. A woman in blue scrubs hurried into one of the stalls behind her. Alex checked her phone for the tenth time.

Out in the hallway, her heels made definitive clicks onto the polished floor as she passed a brightly colored mural and then a set of windows showcasing a garden in full bloom. A young girl sat outside, clutching a silver IV pole. Her owl eyes followed Alex with curiosity. Alex adjusted the leather portfolio case in her arms to give her a tiny wave.

When she reached a set of glass doors at the end of the hall, she tugged on one of the handles and entered a tranquil space lined with open doorways and the sound of keystrokes. A woman was seated at a modular cherry desk, her faded ginger hair cropped short. Sharp green eyes assessed Alex while a pointed chin held the end of a telephone receiver.

"Your name, miss?" she asked, fluidly scribbling a message on a pad.

"Alexandra Wilde. I'm here to see Dr. Moretti."

"Ah yes. The American." She rose from her seat, barely taller than the counter she sat behind. "Right this way."

Alex followed her down the hall to a corner office. Mellow shafts of sunshine illuminated the man who sat behind a thick oak desk. He rose in greeting and Alex grasped the smooth olive-toned hand thrust in her direction. His hair was jet black but tempered with streaks of gray, his eyes the deepest shade of brown, like the brown of freshly tilled earth. He immediately reminded her of Dr. K.

"Welcome to Great Ormond Street Hospital, Dr. Wilde," he said, gesturing to the leather club chair accompanying his desk.

"It's my pleasure." Alex sat, smoothing her shirt over shaking knees, crossing her legs at the ankles. "Thank you for meeting with me."

"The pleasure is truly mine," he crooned, settling back into his desk chair with the grace and ease of someone who ruled over the very air she breathed. An uncomfortable stiffness throbbed in her back. She tried to ignore it. He folded long shapely fingers behind his head and then said, "Tell me about yourself."

Alex launched into a prepared monologue describing her academic history as she removed a thick sheet of vellum from a black leather folder borrowed from Ian. Dr. Moretti scanned the paper as she talked, and then placed his palms flat on either side of her curriculum vitae.

He interrupted her in mid-sentence.

"Fellowship at CHOP. That's impressive. How's Mona Gibson?"

Alex gave a wan smile at the mention of her former program director with her muddy brown eyes and no-nonsense multi-tasking. "She's—" Before Alex could finish, he interrupted her again.

"Still living her life inside the hospital walls, I imagine."

The stiffness returned to Alex's spine with a jolt and spread until she felt surrounded by an invisible shield of defensiveness.

"You finished fellowship last year?" he asked, wetting his lower lip with his tongue.

"Yes."

"And then you took a job in Botswana?"

"Yes."

"And now you've moved to London. Why?" His eyes lifted to hers, deep pools of earthy brown with flecks of chestnut that sparked with amusement.

"My husband's work is here."

"And he wasn't willing to move to Botswana for you? I would have."

A crawling sensation encircled Alex's neck until she felt like she might choke. "It's...complicated."

"These things usually are," he murmured. He tilted his head to one side as if staring out the window onto the congested street below.

Alex had the fleeting desire to throw herself out of said window onto the upper level of a double decker bus. It would almost be worth the bodily injury to avoid the rest of this interview.

"I regret that I haven't any job openings at the moment. However," he paused and swiveled around to face Alex across the desk. She nearly recoiled at the feline expression on his face. "If you can spend the next few months padding your CV—" His eyes dipped down to Alex's top half. She wished she had worn a turtleneck instead of the silk chemise under her blazer. "I'll see what I can do."

Pad her CV? Without a job? What could she possibly accomplish in the next few months besides learning to drive on the left side of the road?

The conversation floated through her brain like a slimy piece of seaweed as she stalked down the street and ducked into the nearest coffee shop. By the time the barista handed her a chai tea, she was certain the temperature of her blood matched what was in the cup.

Within the span of an afternoon, Alex peered at her reflection for a second time. The kohl on her lids was thicker and her lips deepened to a blood-red hue. The swirl of sparkling shadow made her eyes pop an unnatural hue of ocean blue. The porcelain of her skin was offset by the dark as night garment form fitted to her frame. A gift, Ian had said, from the most up and coming couture designer in London. A *quid pro quo* since she would be photographed wearing this dress at the charity event this evening.

Ian hadn't even mentioned which charity they would be supporting tonight. Lately it seemed that she lived in a shadow as depthless as the color of this dress. Tonight would be different though. After weeks of missing each other, she would finally spend an evening seeing, hearing, touching, and hopefully tasting, her magnanimous husband. A car horn sounded outside, and she hurried down the stairs with a smile playing at her lips.

"Good evening, Mark," she said, sliding into the jet black sedan.

"Evening, Mrs. Devall."

Her nerves, made raw by her interaction at the hospital, irked at the title.

"Please, Mark. It's just Alex." As he closed the door behind her, she traced the stitching of the empty seat cushion next to her.

"Mr. Devall sends his apologies." Mark hesitated. "He's running a bit late and will meet you at the event."

Alex nodded tightly, gripping the sequined clutch in her lap. "Of course."

Alex had no idea where Mark had driven her, but they passed through a gated entrance ensconced in shadows and up a private driveway into the front yard of nothing less than a manor. Warm white lights encircled stone pillars flanking the entrance to a home that rivaled royalty. When Alex stepped out of the car, guided by Mark's sure elbow, she gasped at the nearby cluster of ladies gilded with a menagerie of diamonds. Their faces as flawless as Grecian statues. She trailed behind them up a set of stone steps toward a flung open pair of ornate doors as soft notes of orchestral jazz beckoned her inside.

To the left, a sweeping staircase led to a second level and to the right, an archway opened into an ornate ballroom. The smells hit her first—the sweet aroma of spiced meat and baking bread swirling amidst the expensive scents dabbed onto bare skin. Men in black jackets paraded through the crowd holding trays of edibles, whirling and disappearing like whisps of smoke.

The dance floor was already packed with glamorous couples laughing between sips of expensive champagne. Alex glanced at the banner strung above the stage where a band would assemble later. *Great Ormond Street Hospital for Children Charity Ball.* A solid ball of ice began to form in her stomach, and she snagged a glass from the first tray that came within arm's reach. Her eyes roved the room, pausing on anyone in a tuxedo with overly shiny dark hair and copper skin. *Please don't be here...please...don't...ugh.* There he was—his arm snaked around the waist of a petite girl with endless blonde hair who flashed him a courtesan's smile. Alex downed the remainder of her drink in one fluid swallow. *What a—*

"What's got you all hot and bothered?"

A silky voice reverberated in her ear. Her knees went weak and nearly buckled before she turned into the arms awaiting her. Ian tucked her against his chest, the solid sound of his heartbeat soothing every aberration, every deranged nerve.

"I missed you," she murmured against the ebony silk of his tuxedo jacket. His lips roved over the shell of her ear and lower onto the bare recess of her shoulder.

"I missed you, too."

The scent of him, the mixture of bourbon and spice, was too much. It flooded her veins with liquid heat and her breath hitched.

"You look ready to be ravaged," he whispered.

"More than ready." And she meant it, even if he asked her to start stripping in the middle of the marble ballroom floor.

"Come on," Ian said, stepping back to grasp both of her hands. "I'll teach you how to donate. You're already a decent dancer and a more than decent drinker." Alex smacked him lightly on the arm as they began to navigate the crowd.

After a solid hour of being guided through the melee with Ian's hand on her bare back, thanks to the plunging V of her dress, Alex's blood sang with vibrant warmth. A whirlwind of faces and names had blended into Ian's laughter. She was content to sip her drink and smile, offered up as the woman who had stolen Ian's heart. Behind her fluid words and smiles, she imagined being home and stepping out of her heels...and then everything else.

"Good evening, I don't believe we have met." A hand, the same hand she had grasped earlier that day, was thrust in Ian's direction. Copper skin contrasted against Ian's alabaster tone. Similar grace and purpose in their grips.

"Ian...Ian Devall."

"I've heard much about you, Mr. Devall," said the smooth, caramel rich voice. "I'm Devon Moretti from Great Ormond Street Hospital."

"Nice to meet you." Ian shifted to incorporate Alex into their circle. "This is my wife."

Wife. Not Alex. Not Dr. Wilde.

"Enchanted."

Slim fingers extended in her direction and Alex took them, the back of her hand crawling when he kissed it. She waited, balancing on the precipice of the inevitable. Surely, he would recognize her. But after a solitary downward glance, a cursory assessment of her attributes, he turned to Ian. "Join me at the bar for a drink?"

Ian hesitated before Alex heard a dreaded "sure" being uttered over her head. She balked against the pressure on her lower back.

"I'll catch up with you in a bit," she said, not waiting for him to respond before she whirled out of his embrace.

One day, she would learn to walk in heels so that her ankles didn't wobble and her toes didn't practically extrude through the structured satin. She was a lone bee in a hive alight with sparkling reverie as she zigzagged through the ballroom to a destination unknown. An alcove strung with rich purple curtains drew her attention and she stepped into the welcoming darkness without a second thought. The interior was lit with dozens of flameless candles, a suffused glow outlining a vanity counter and a row of sturdy wooden doors. A ladies' room worthy of the queen herself. With shaky hands, Alex opened her clutch, the contents erupting onto the marble counter.

"Damn." Her lipstick tube rolled down the marble-topped counter and she snatched it up before it fell to the floor.

"Such language," drolled a practiced voice.

One of the heavy oak doors opened and an elegant figure with dark upswept hair and an emerald gown stepped into view. Alex watched her pupils dilate in the vanity mirror as the rest of her body froze. Her tongue thawed first.

"Ms. Levine?"

Lily white hands fluttered in the air as she joined Alex at the sink. "Please Alexandra, it's Margaret. I am your mother-in-law, after all."

Alex's hands drifted over the counter, retrieving her phone and keys, gum wrappers and errant scraps of paper, stuffing them haphazardly into her purse.

"What are you doing here?"

"Supporting the children's hospital of course."

"Were you hoping to see Ian?"

"Only if he wants to be seen." She began twisting one of the many rings adorning her bony fingers. Alex watched a large emerald catch the candlelight as it spun. "Actually, I was hoping to speak with you."

"I don't think we have anything to talk about."

Crystal blue eyes as hard as gemstones pierced her with a look that dripped condescension. She opened the clasp on a satin and crystal purse and procured a business card.

"I think you'll find, Alexandra, that we do." She held out the card. "Don't you ever wonder what your life will be like? What awaits you in your union with Ian? Haven't you ever asked yourself if you will be truly happy?"

"How would you know the first thing about happiness?"

A saccharine smile swept across her face. "Why don't you ask George? We are still married after all."

Alex barely placed one peep-toe in the door that evening before reaching for the zipper along her lower back and yanking it. Black satin fell into a heap on the floor, and she stepped out of the dress like she was stepping out of a literal black hole. Rage and guilt and denial thrummed through her bloodstream as she stalked up the stairs. When she heard Ian following, a smile softened the hard lines of her mouth.

Once in the bedroom, she backed into the far wall and motioned Ian to her. Wicked wanton lust drove her hands as they shed the layers of Ian's clothing. Shirt then pants then nothing remained between them but the midnight lace of her lingerie. Fingers curled around the rim of her panties, and she shook her head.

"Leave them on," she whispered, her voice guttural and strained. She needed him. Needed his scent, his body, his presence to drive out every negative experience from her day. He did exactly that.

When Ian was sated and snoring lightly, Alex slipped into the bathroom. Her face, a deconstructed version of the one from earlier, was bright, her cheeks flushed and her lips swollen. She reached over to her bag and unclipped the clasp, reaching in to check her phone. A text message from an unknown caller.

I'll be at Burbage's next Friday at 11 am. ML

TEN

Every shade of pink from ballerina to fuchsia was permanently melded to Alex's retinas. Her ears rang from the titillating sighs of unwed females and the cackling laughter of mothers free from their brood for a few hours. The air reeked of vanilla cake and diaper cream long after the last guest had parted. Alex watched Roxanne balance a pinstriped plate of confections on her swollen belly, her feet propped on a cushion.

"It should be against the law to be this pregnant in the middle of July."

Alex reached under Rox's chair to pick up a discarded stack of paper napkins and then proceeded to fan her with them. "Want me to ask Ian if we can borrow the jet for a quick trip to Iceland?" she joked.

"Could you?" Rox's eyelids snapped open.

"You're too close to your due date, otherwise, I totally would."

"Rats." Rox affectionately patted the bulge in her side. "Maybe after I push this one out."

Alex stood, brushing the crumbs off her bare knees. "Have you and Nic come up with a name yet?"

"No," Rox groaned, rolling her eyes heavenward. "We can't agree. He's vetoed all my favorites and I've vetoed his."

"What about a family name?"

Rox ticked off her fingers. "Bertie, Doris, and Maria Magdalena. I don't think so."

Alex snickered and plopped down on a floor cushion.

Rox massaged her belly in long arcing strokes. "What about you and Ian?"

"What *about* me and Ian?"

Rox sighed through her nose and cocked her head toward her

midsection. Alex scoffed and it sounded harsher than she meant it to.

"We barely see each other these days so we don't actually have time to make one of those."

"Is he still trying to run the company and the foundation?"

"Yep. It's become a vendetta. His dad managed to do it and Ian always feels the need to do as much, or more, than George."

Rox clicked her tongue against her teeth. "Any luck with a job?"

Alex shook her head. "No one seems to be hiring. That or maybe no one wants to hire me."

It was Rox's turn to scoff. "Please. Any of these places would be lucky—more than lucky—to have you on staff."

Alex's lips turned upward in a wry smile. "I'm supposed to hear from the director at Brompton today."

"Is it—" Rox bit her lower lip "—hard for you? Not working, I mean."

Alex cast her gaze downward, raking it over the woodgrain in the floorboards of Rox's living room. Her chest cracked open a little and she committed to its honesty. "A little."

Rox snorted.

"Okay, a lot." The crack widened and a gush of emotion leaked out. "It's nothing I didn't expect but..."

"You're not happy."

"No. I'm not. And I have no idea what to do about it."

The house was dark by the time she arrived home, the only sound her own soft footfalls on the stairs up to the main level. The kitchen island was illuminated by an overhead fixture of black iron and soft light that cast a perfect moon shape onto the marble countertop. Alex snagged a bottle of wine from the fridge and a glass from the shelf. She poured and kept pouring until the glass was nearly full. Settling onto a barstool, she cracked open her waiting laptop. A sleek silver companion with a glimpse into the outside world. To her old life. To her old self.

As she sipped, she scrolled, noting a slew of new emails since this morning. One from Tim, her best friend from fellowship training titled "fun in the sun." She clicked open the attachment and a picture of Tim, golden haired and tan, balancing on a paddleboard, filled up her screen. Smiling she moved on to the next one. Sip and click.

Read and delete. One from her mom reminding her about the auction next month and how "fitting" it would be if she were there to see what happened to Terry's land. One from Royal Brompton Hospital caught her eye and she opened it.

Dear Dr. Wilde,
Thank you for your interest in Royal Brompton Hospital for Children. Your curriculum vitae is most impressive. However, we regretfully have no openings for positions in the pediatric critical care department.

Alex scrubbed a hand down her face and took another gulp of wine. It wasn't a surprise. But still, disappointment reigned in every fiber of her being. As she tapped her fingers on the mousepad, an email from Lucia caught her eye.

"Alex," she read aloud, "I hope you are well. Everything is great at PM." Alex's eyes scanned down the page. "A new ICU doctor from Australia joined the staff and has volunteered to take over our educational programs." Alex felt the twinge in her gut like someone had punched her. Hard. She drew in a breath—a ragged, shaky breath—and reread the email. And then drained her glass of wine for the sole purpose of pouring a second one.

When she heard a key in the front door and the scrape of Ian's shoes on the staircase, Alex was in a search engine rabbit hole. Dr. Anthony Turner. From Melbourne. She clicked his name on the hospital website. The photograph of a man with square spectacles and untamed golden-brown hair and a bow tie. A wide smile on his face to showcase his innocence. She scowled at the man who was usurping her. Whatever cavernous hole had developed inside her chest deepened into an abyss.

"Hey you. Sorry I got held up. Should I order us some takeout?"

"I'm not that hungry," Alex snapped, shutting her laptop. Ian's hand dragged along her shoulders as he shuffled around to the refrigerator. It felt heavy rather than comforting.

The light from inside the fridge highlighted the shadows under his eyes. He turned toward her, mouth suggestive of a question. "Want a beer?"

She tilted her head toward the half full wineglass in her hand.

Twisting off the cap to an amber bottle, Ian slumped into the seat next to her in a disheveled heap. He took a long draw of his beer then exhaled a slow, measured breath. "What are you working on?"

The question struck her like a barb. Later she would realize that it was unintentional but at that moment her skin stung with a prickling sensation.

"Nothing," she replied flatly. "Nothing, actually." She rubbed her temples, scrunching her eyes closed against the soft glow from the overhead light. "I never thought it would be this hard to get a job."

Ian glanced at her sideways as he took another swig of his beer. "You know," he said, "you don't have to get a job. Not if you don't want to."

It was the wrong thing to say. Another barbed arrow hit the bullseye of her despair.

"Why would I not want to?" The alcohol in her bloodstream pushed her, taunting her emotions. "I didn't train my entire life to run errands and plan baby showers and wait for someone else to get home."

Anger surged and she swallowed another mouthful of wine to quell it. It mixed with the acid on her tongue before going down. Ian arched a brow and drank in silence. She studied his face, noting the weighty fatigue, the worry etched there.

"I'm...sorry," she mumbled. "I don't know what's wrong with me tonight."

He didn't look at her, instead studying the label on his bottle, a lion's crest of red and gold and midnight blue. His face hardened into a mask. "Do you think this is a mistake?"

The words were no more than whispered syllables but their meaning so dreadfully heavy that they sunk like stones to the bottom of Alex's stomach.

"What? No." She reached out a hand, curling her fingers over his wrist. "Don't ever think that."

"You're not happy."

"I am," she said, her voice wavering. "You make me happy." She drew in a steadying breath over her quivering lips and found his eyes on her. Disbelief churned behind them. "I'm just having a bad night. I found out that the other children's hospital in London isn't hiring and Dr. K found someone for my position at PM. It was just a lot at once."

His face relaxed and his eyes softened. She went to him, pressing her face into the hollow of his neck and inhaled. After a moment, she felt his hands run up her back.

"I want you to have everything you ever dreamed of."

"I already do."

As soon as the words left her lips, she tasted the lie. But she didn't care as long as Ian believed her. Did it really matter if she was lying to herself?

Alex adjusted her scarf, the thin creamy silk and spun gold nearly weightless on her skin. She fidgeted, raising up on the balls of her feet and then down again, the heels of her flats coming to rest on the black and white marble floor splayed out like a giant chessboard. Convenient. She might as well be playing a game of chess. When she left the house earlier, she told herself that she was doing this for Ian. History would not repeat itself. She would succeed where Margaret had failed.

"May I help you, miss?" A black suited man with the hint of a mustache peered down at her.

"I'm meeting someone for lunch. Margaret Levine?"

With a flourish of his hand, he waved her toward a tucked away atrium, its iron doors crawling with vibrant green vines. "She's waiting for you inside."

Of course, she was. Alex tucked a strand of hair behind her ear and steeled herself for what was coming next. The ceiling of the room was all glass, coaxing every bit of sunshine from the overcast sky to fill up its crevices. Like an oversized bubble, the room was round and annoyingly iridescent. Crystal glassware adorned every white tablecloth and diamonds adorned every hand that held that crystal. A few pairs of catty eyes paused amidst their important conversations to slide a glance her way.

At the far side of the room sat Margaret, dressed in a black and white pantsuit, the thread so exquisitely woven that the two colors merged but also remained separate. A triple strand of pearls wound around her neck, and she wore a midnight black straw hat adorned with interlocking C's. When Alex approached the table, she spared an upward glance, no surprise registering on her face.

"Have a seat, Alexandra." She returned to perusing the menu. "The seared tuna is particularly good here if you like raw fish."

Before Alex could respond, the waiter approached the table. "Anything to drink, madame?"

Margaret handed over the leather-bound menu. "We'll have a

bottle of Veuve, the brut please, as well as the soup of the day and the seared tuna."

Alex pressed her lips into a line as Margaret ordered for her. They regarded one another without speaking until the champagne arrived, the pop of the cork shattering through Alex's last intact nerve.

"Why are you so interested in my happiness?"

"I'm not," Margaret said flatly, lifting her champagne glass to her lips. Alex mirrored her gesture, if only to wash away the sting from the words. "But I am interested in Ian's happiness."

"The only thing that makes Ian unhappy is you."

Her casual laughter grated on Alex's eardrums. "Oh, I doubt very much that is true."

"What happened between you and George?" Alex asked pointedly.

The air around her dropped a few degrees as Margaret pursed her painted lips. "That was a long time ago. He was an executive in the company when we met."

"How did you meet?"

"I left home when I was seventeen and moved to Los Angeles. Until I got my first acting job, I had three sometimes four jobs at a time. One of those was delivering coffee and rolls to the Devall office downtown."

"And you met George there?"

She nodded, throat bobbing as she sipped. "He invited me to dinner and life was never the same."

"So, what happened?" Alex probed gently. "Why did everything fall apart?"

"You know Ian's version of the story I assume?"

Alex nodded, thinking back to the scraps of information Ian had revealed over the last few years. When George Devall had taken over the company, Margaret had refused to move to London because of her budding acting career. Then two years after his brother died, she had left him without a word. He hadn't seen her since.

"George was not the first choice to take over the company."

A fragrant bowl of lobster bisque landed in front of her in a white porcelain bowl, but Alex barely acknowledged it.

"His much older brother had agreed to replace their father when the time came, and George had agreed to oversee the operations in California to be close to me and the boys."

Alex noticed she wouldn't say Ryan's name. "Why didn't he?"

"He's a Devall."

Alex narrowed her eyes in confusion. "I'm not sure what that means."

"The Devall men are meant for greatness. It is their legacy. Their fate."

"Greatness comes in many different forms," Alex countered.

"Not in the Devall family."

Alex silently begged her to elaborate as she swirled her spoon through her soup.

"It consumes them and leads them to sacrifice things...and people." Margaret paused to sip her soup from a silver spoon. "All under the guise of the greater good."

"That doesn't sound like Ian at all."

"Then you don't know my son very well."

"I think I know him better than you."

Margaret's nose flared and her upper lip twitched. "How easy do you think it is to run a company? And not just any company, one that cares about its people from the highest paid executive to the most meager mine worker. How easy do you think it is to provide equal opportunity? To fairly consume resources yet turn a profit?"

Alex furrowed her brows as a sickly unease grew in the pit of her stomach. "I have no idea."

"It requires nothing less than a miracle. And for the Devall company that miracle was George, and now it's Ian. You need to realize, Alexandra, that many people, entire families and villages, now depend on Ian to continue the work his father started. And he will not let them down. You need to understand your place in all of this. And that what you want—what you need—will always come second. You," her lips rounded with the word, "will always be second."

"And you didn't want to be second? That's why you let your children grow up without a father. That's why you abandoned your fifteen-year-old son."

"No, I didn't want to be second." Margaret paused and drained the rest of her champagne. "And neither do you."

"Ian and I are not you and George. And Ian has never made me feel like my dreams are insignificant."

Until lately whispered a traitorous voice. Alex ignored it.

"Ian knows what is at stake, but in addition to that, Ian is too much like me. He won't stay in love with someone who is unhappy."

"Ian is nothing like you."

Margaret cocked an overplucked brow.

"He's not the person you think. He's different. He's changed." Alex glared at Margaret, but it took more effort than it should have.

"People don't change, Alexandra. They simply try something new for a while."

Her unease had morphed into a sea monster that churned and whacked its tail against her from the inside. "How are you and George still married?" She lowered her gaze to her hands as they drummed a silent concerto.

"We never got around to divorcing. And in exchange for leaving Ian be, George provides me with a comfortable living arrangement."

"George pays you to stay away from Ian?"

"I think he was always afraid that I would do him more harm than good."

"Does Ian know?"

"No, of course not."

Stomach roiling, Alex stood from the table. "I think I should be going."

Margaret's mouth tightened in a thin line, and she picked up a silver knife that she sliced through the rectangle of pink flesh on her plate.

"Ian wants what he wants, Alexandra, and he will do anything to get it."

"What he wants is me."

"He already has you. Now he is free to direct his attentions elsewhere."

Alex swallowed the bitter pills that were her words. "Thank you for lunch, Ms. Levine."

As she turned from the table, her face stung like it had been slapped. Heat rushed into her cheeks and the clinking of glassware and utensils against porcelain was drowned out by the roaring in her ears. She wouldn't let this happen. She wouldn't let the past failure of his parents come between them. She wouldn't let the words of a fork-tongued serpent of a mother-in-law poison her view of Ian.

Suddenly, she needed air—fresh, cleansing air that would clear her head and slow the frenzy in her heart. Her feet had barely met the first black square of porcelain when she collided into a trim navy suit. Hands flew to her shoulders to steady her recoil.

"I'm sorry...so sorry," she stammered.

Sky blue eyes peered down at her. "Alex? What are you doing here?"

ELEVEN

Frozen in place, Alex willed her mouth to start moving. "I was—"

"Alexandra and I were having lunch," said a brittle voice behind her. Ian's fingers stiffened on her upper arms. She turned into the placid face of her mother-in-law. "You forgot your bag."

Alex's powder blue shoulder bag dangled from Margaret's tautly held wrist. Alex removed it and threw the strap over her shoulder.

"Thank you." She felt Ian's stare burrowing through the back of her skull. When she turned around, he refused to look at her. His eyes were completely riveted on his mother.

"Care to join me, Ian, dear?"

"I'd rather not."

Alex nearly wept as she tipped onto her toes to kiss his cheek. It was like placing her lips on a statue. "I'll see you at home." She stepped around Ian into the gloom and drizzle of downtown London and didn't look back.

Ian wasn't home by dinner or by the time Alex showered and changed into silk pajamas. She trolled the internet on her phone then picked up a novel, the spine cracked and weathered with age, and read the same page until her eyelids fluttered closed. When she woke after midnight, the bedside lamp had been switched off and a still form lay beside her, chest rising and falling with enough irregularity that Alex spoke.

"Are you awake?"

"Unfortunately."

Alex smelled the bourbon when he exhaled. "Penny for your thoughts."

"It's going to cost you more than that."

The deathly quiet of his voice chilled her blood and she scooted closer. Closer to his radiant warmth and the scent of his vanilla bodywash.

"I'm sorry I didn't tell you. She texted me and I wasn't planning to go, and then..."

"Then what?"

Meeting Margaret had been an impulsive decision driven by what? Curiosity? Boredom? Discontent? Fear? She slid a hand between the cotton sheets and Ian's bare chest, running her hand over its taut smoothness. She swallowed past the knot unfurling in her throat.

"I thought I could stop history from repeating itself if I understood more about her. About her and George."

Ian rotated his head toward her, studying her through the darkness. "What did she tell you?"

"That greatness is part of who you are. That people depend on you to be great and that I would always come second. And the reason she stayed in California when your dad went to London was because she wasn't meant to be second."

And neither are you. Margaret's words reverberated through her head.

"The reason she stayed in California was because she's a selfish bitch."

Alex closed the distance between them, molding her body against Ian's torso and sliding a protective arm over his chest. "Did you know that she and your dad are still married?"

"I never asked but I guess he never could bring himself to divorce her."

"Out of guilt?"

"Maybe. Who knows."

Alex wondered if she should tell him about the agreement; Margaret would stay away from Ian and George would assuage himself by monthly deposits in her bank account. She decided against it. A hand began absentmindedly stroking her hair.

"Things will get easier, Alex, but not for a while."

"I know," she said.

"This isn't the life you dreamed of."

So many images flashed through her head that a distinct ache began behind her left eye. A long-forgotten phrase floated somewhere in her brain. *Maybe dreams choose us, not the other way around.* She cleared her throat but failed to keep her voice from sounding strained as she willed the tears to retreat. "Maybe I can find a new dream."

The following week, a forkful of eggs had barely reached her mouth when a brisk knock resounded on the door. Wrapping herself in a cashmere throw she snatched from the couch, she hurried downstairs and twisted the knob. A portly man, deeply rouged with thinning brown hair, waited with a box wrapped in brown paper.

"Delivery for you, miss. Sign here please."

He presented her with a clipboard and then, satisfied with her scribble, traded her for the package. Once upstairs, she set it on the island and began slicing through the tape with her breakfast knife. When the lid popped open, a card lay on top of a menagerie of tissue wrapped items. She opened the card first.

A little something to brighten your day. Mom

Removing the items one by one, she laid them on the counter and surveyed the unexpected treasures. A locally made candle. Texas-shaped tortilla chips and a can of spicy bean dip. The old horseshoe she used to keep on her dresser. A stitched throw pillow that read "Home is where the heart is." And a copy of the local newspaper.

"What's all this?" Ian padded downstairs in bare feet, his hair still dripping from the shower.

"I think this is a not-so-subtle way for my mom to let me know she misses me."

A fleeting smile crossed Ian's face as he reached into the cupboard for a mug. "I remember promising her the holiday season this year."

"I didn't know if you would remember."

"Of course, I do."

"We don't have to promise anything. I know this year may be hard for us."

Ian didn't answer as the Italian coffee machine whizzed and puffed steam. Once he filled a mug, he stirred in the cream, brows knit together in thought.

"I have to go out of town tomorrow," he announced. "It's just a quick overnight trip to Paris for a bunch of foundation meetings. I won't have time for much but if you wanted to come with me, you could explore the city. Maybe do some shopping?"

Paris. They had been there together when their love wasn't even love yet. It was where she and Ian had laid each other bare in the most exquisite ways possible. It was where love had started to unfurl. Tender and new and precious.

"Okay," she said without hesitation and Ian's face relaxed into a smile. A full, boyish smile that she hadn't seen him wear in quite some time. She shed the cashmere blanket and skipped into the kitchen, sending her arms snaking around to his front.

"Are you sure you won't have any time for fun?"

He pulled her fingers up to his mouth and began sucking on the tips. "I have time now."

Heat coursed up her thighs and into her middle. *This.* This is what they needed. What *she* needed. Pulling her hands from his grasp, she hooked her thumbs into his waistband, forcing his track pants to the floor. Her chuckle caught in her throat. "I didn't realize you were going commando today."

He pivoted in her arms to face her. "I didn't plan on someone accosting me in the kitchen."

"I'm hardly just someone."

"No, no, you're not."

Lips found hers—full, welcoming lips rapt with desire. Alex slid out of her silk shorts and Ian groaned into her mouth as hungry hands found her bare bottom. He pulled away to say something and she silenced him with a press of her lips. "Talk later."

A shudder swept through him and when his tongue dove into her mouth, she intertwined hers with his in a permanent embrace. They melded together in frenetic grace as he swept her onto the island. His chest heaved against the thin ballet pink silk of her top and she struggled out of it, breaking their kiss only long enough to shrug it over her head. Hands sliced between her thighs and pushed them apart.

"Oh God," she breathed as an intense spasm coursed through her.

"No, just me," Ian laughed into her ear.

He lowered his head and wet tendrils of hair tickled her lower abdomen as he dove lower and lower. Ian's tongue ignited a riptide of flame. Alex threw back her head. Pressure built in her thighs until she trembled and morphed into something wild. Something uncontrolled and volatile. When Ian lifted his head, she groaned into his waiting mouth right before he moved on her. In her. Demanding yet patient. Pushing her. Coaxing her. Willing her upward. With every thrust, she matched his intensity. His tenacity. And for the briefest of moments, when pleasure clouded her head and Ian's ragged breathing drowned out her thoughts, she forgot why she had ever been unhappy in the first place.

"So, what are you going to do in Paris while Ian is working?"

Alex folded a crisp white shirt into a small rectangle and stuffed it into her suitcase. "Sightseeing, I guess. Maybe some shopping."

"That sounds like a dream." Rox emitted a low-pitched whine.

"I wish you could come."

"Me too, but you'd have to roll me down the street in a wagon."

"For you, I would." Alex smirked.

"Being pregnant sucks."

"Not all of it, right?"

"I've transitioned from cute pregnant to uncomfortable pregnant to looking like I swallowed a beach ball. None of my shoes even fit."

"Only a few more weeks."

"Seven weeks and four days."

"Tell her that Auntie Alex can't wait."

"Thanks, love. Gotta go, they're calling me into surgery."

"Okay. Bye Rox."

"Have fun." Her voice trilled until the phone disconnected.

Alex transferred a stack of t-shirts into her roller bag. Rox was headed into the operating room while she was packing for Paris to go shopping. When she reached up to scrub a hand down her face, she was surprised to find tears. Fat, globular tears that welled up at the outer corners of her eyes and spilled over onto her cheeks. Her nose burned with emotion. *What was she doing?*

This life—her life—didn't resemble anything that she'd dreamed up. Anything she'd worked for. It was loose and purposeless and at times, overwhelmingly frivolous. No matter how much she had tried to convince herself, she knew this wasn't the happily ever after she had expected. She gritted her teeth against the taste of salt. It wasn't Ian's fault, but he would feel responsible. So, she wouldn't tell him. He couldn't know the extent of her despair—the longing to be part of something so big and so great that she got lost in it. She would figure out another way forward.

The scalding water of the tub soaked into all of her crevices, and she released a light groan. The white porcelain tub in the guest bathroom was so immense that Alex could barely stretch her toes and touch the other side. A lavender bath ball fizzed under the stream of the faucet, filling the air with luscious scent.

Alex hooked her big toe around the copper faucet handle and pulled it down until the stream became an occasional droplet. *Bloop. Bloop.* She closed her eyes. *Bloop.* And waited. In the stillness amidst the tendrils of steam and damp warmth, she waited for something to pull her into its gravity. To give direction to her orbit. Life had pushed her off a cliff. Or maybe it had been love. Either way, she had expected to fall on solid ground, not hover with clipped wings above a life where she had yet to grow roots.

Wrapped in a towel, hair clinging to her temples, she stepped out of the steam of the bathing room so lost in thought that her large toe collided with the jutting corner of a cardboard box.

"Holy...ouch," she yelped, bending to shove it to the side.

The newspaper her mom had sent lay on the top and she ran the tips of her damp fingers over her towel before bending to pick it up. The Brazos County News. Every Sunday morning it had been delivered to their front door with ten glorious pages of local happenings. She spread it open on the bed and sat cross legged to thumb through it.

Two entire pages devoted to a recent fishing tournament and a small column about school board re-elections. An entire half page of obituaries illustrated with grainy black and white photos. And on page eight in the lower right corner, a comic strip. She smiled at the canned humor of a stuffed tiger before turning to the back page where a heading caught her eye: Upcoming Events. Ladies quilting circle at the public library. Outdoor movie night in a local park and the Thirteenth Annual County Auction. Her stomach tightened as she skimmed the items: estate furniture and livestock. A few pieces of jewelry and a classic car. And there it was in black and white. Twenty-nine acres of undeveloped property with barn along Cedar Creek from the estate of the late Teresa Hawthorne.

When Ian poked his head in the bedroom door several hours later, Alex had worn a groove in the floorboards from her pacing. His shirt was unbuttoned, tie already cast off somewhere between the front door and the bedroom. He regarded her thoughtfully, cocking his head to one side as he pulled the tail of his pressed dress shirt from his trousers.

"Once, when I was a kid, my dad took me on a business trip, and we went to the San Diego Zoo."

Alex stopped in midstride. "And?"

"And there was a caged tiger that looked less frantic than you. What's up?"

Her hands dropped to her sides, limp and pointless. And then every thought in her head came out in a rush. "I wouldn't change one single second of the past two years. I became a critical care doctor. I travelled. I took care of really sick kids that didn't have anyone else. I fell in love." A smile graced her lips. "I fought for that love, fought hard and risked everything for it."

Ian had stopped moving, stopped breathing. His hand rested in suspended animation on the cuff of his shirt.

"And now I'm living a life I didn't expect to have."

"And you don't want this life?"

She went to him then, snaking her trembling fingers around his wrist and pulling his hands to her chest. Their solidity rested against the pounding of her heart inside her chest.

"I want you." The briefest of smiles tugged at his lips. "But I need to understand how the other pieces of me can fall into place so we can be happy together. And I think before I can go forward, I need to go backward." He eyed her with puzzlement. "I need to revisit a girl that existed once. Before medicine. Before you."

Ian nodded tightly as storm clouds gathered in the sky of his eyes. "So, what are you saying?"

"When we get back from Paris, I need a...break."

"A break from us?" His voice was deathly quiet.

Alex shook her head violently. "No, not from us. From everything else."

"And what does that involve exactly?"

"I want to go to Texas for a while."

Ian pulled his wrists out of her grasp, sending his fingers to attack the remaining buttons on his shirt.

"You're not happy," he said, his words cutting through her like cold steel.

"Ian, I—" Alex bit her bottom lip so hard that a droplet of blood welled up. She smeared it away with her thumb.

"Don't deny it, Alex." He ripped off his shirt and flung it into the closet.

She'd never wanted to deny anything so badly as hot anger welled up inside her. "I'm doing this for us," she said as a tear leaked down her face. "So, we don't end up like your parents."

Her words hit the unmovable stone of Ian's face and bounced right off. His eyes flitted to the corner of the room and her packed suitcase.

"I think you should go to Texas. Today."

"What about Paris?"

"I'm asking you to go to Texas instead."

"I'm not leaving you."

A stream of tears paraded down her face, past her flushed cheeks and into the corners of her mouth. A hiccupping sob erupted from her throat and Ian's face softened. He pulled her into an embrace, coaxing her cheek into the softness of his white undershirt.

"Go home, Alex," he whispered into her ear. "And find whatever it is you're looking for."

Ian's words burned into every sensory cell Alex had. She could see them on the backs of her retinas when she closed her eyes. She could hear Ian's voice in the depths of her inner ear. She could taste his worry like bitter ash coating her tongue. The weight of his discontent, as heavy as granite, pressed into her muscles. Alex rolled her shoulders against the curved seatback of her mom's groaning pickup. *Go home, Alex.*

In the window, a city skyline emerged, a neat array of buildings protruding from what used to be coastal swampland. The truck veered away from the city on a long slow arc that would take them east and then south. *Go home, Alex.* She had thought she was already there. But who was she kidding? London wasn't home. London apart from Ian didn't draw her into its gravity. It didn't call her heart with its promise of hope. Of clarity. It didn't even know her. Not the real her. Not the girl whose bare feet brushed along the earth. Not the girl kissed by moonlight and graced by the stars. Not the girl who grew into something formidable and unreachable under its careful watch. Not the girl who was birthed by flood and fire and freedom.

"Hey, mom?" Her throat was raw after the dry air of the airplane cabin. "Can we take the long way?"

"Of course, honey."

When their ribbon of highway ended at a blinking yellow light, they turned right onto a two-lane road, golden yellow paint long ago scrubbed away by the grit in the wind. Alex rolled down the window, a rush of heated air slamming against her face. Closing her eyes, she let it envelop her and tried to dissect the individual scents and sounds rushing past her. Birds cawing an argument. Something dry and salty like fish bones replaced quickly by clean linen. And then, when the truck slowed around a curve, gentle waves slapped along a barren coastline. She no longer existed in two worlds. Only one. Only this one.

TWELVE

Cole's Church, Texas, Summer 1997

The minute the window came down, a warm gust of air, pregnant with salt water, wrapped its palms around her face. The incessant cawing of a seagull, flapping its wings to hover above a dropped morsel reverberated through the car. Alex reached over to silence the radio. Everywhere around her, life abounded, nurtured by the elements, from the tiniest crab scuttling along the foaming shoreline to the children shrieking as the waves lapped their ankles. She could taste it, could inhale its divinity until her blood felt thick with its promises. Like the promise of freedom. Three long months of freedom. The sweet innocent freedom that came with being seventeen and on the cusp of adulthood minus the weight of responsibility. It was heady.

"Do you see anywhere to park?" Alex asked, spinning the wheel of Natalie's cherry red Acura. The leather steering wheel burned underneath her grip. She abandoned guiding the car to flick her hand in front of the air conditioning vent.

"We should have gotten here earlier," Natalie complained, adjusting her white cat-eye sunglasses then rolling down her window to let more of the air, heavy and salt speckled, into the car.

The Acura crept through a thin strip of bare sand bordered by a row of cars on one side and a dense pulsating beach crowd on the other. Alex caught Natalie scanning the passenger side window.

"He's not here." She tightened her lips to suppress a chuckle. "He had a shift at the Farm and Ranch today."

Natalie bristled as she pushed her sunglasses onto the pile of strawberry blonde hair artfully swept onto the top of her head. "I wasn't looking for *him*."

"Mmm," Alex replied. "Like you haven't been looking for him

the last six months. Every single time we're out driving."

"He's old news. He wasn't interested and I've moved on." She continued her search of the crowd but with far less zeal than before.

Alex spied a dreadfully narrow spot between a blue convertible and a forest green hatchback. She swerved into the spot with the nose of the car, inching forward until its length was even with its neighbors. Cutting the engine, she tossed the keys in Natalie's direction. They landed with a clang in an empty seat. Natalie already had half her body out the door and was examining her reflection in the side mirror. She applied a coat of lip balm before glancing sharply at Alex.

"What are you waiting for, girlfriend? Christmas?"

"I can't believe I let you talk me into wearing this," Alex grumbled, glancing down at her own attire. A blue gingham two piece with tiny red ricrac ribbon lining the edges. Her first bikini. And the first time she would be showcasing her entire midsection to half of Cole's Church High School.

Natalie poked her head back into the passenger side window. "You look amazing."

Alex fussed with the underwire of the bikini top, praying it didn't reveal too much of her alabaster white décolletage. Her pale skin wouldn't last too much longer in the coastal Texas sun. By the end of the weekend, the pink blush of her first sunburn would deepen into a golden tan. Not like her mom. Janie Wilde's skin remained stubbornly pale despite the hours she spent hovering over a vegetable garden. Her bare arms were nothing but a coalescence of muddy freckles.

Through the rearview window Alex watched the multitudes gathering behind them on a wide stretch of coarse beach. Endless exposed skin moving to the thumping bass from a boombox. Someone had put up a volleyball net and a tight group of abnormally tall co-eds were smacking a ball back and forth. She fidgeted and tugged on the hem of her denim shorts once more. Maybe she could trade places with the volleyball. *Smack!*

"C'mon, Alex. All the best spots are going to be taken!"

With a resolute nod, Alex grabbed a canvas tote bag brimming with towels with one hand and pulled open the door handle with the other.

The wind whipped across her face as she and Natalie trudged down a sand dune, her bare feet sinking into the soft sugar. The sun emerged from behind a lost cloud, and she tipped her face up to meet it. This was how she and Natalie had started every summer from the time they had become friends in seventh grade. Although this version, where they drove themselves, was highly preferable to the one where they got dropped off and picked up. Inhaling deeply, she filled her lungs with air coated with the scents of sunscreen and newfound freedom.

"I can't believe we're finally seniors," Natalie huffed as she reached the bottom of the dune.

They surveyed the scene in front of them. Bare flesh everywhere in a spectrum of neutral colors. Gleeful screams and animated voices mixed with the crash of waves. A radio perched on a nearby lifeguard stand dropped the notes of a guitar solo. She turned to Natalie and smiled. Despite her discomfort with her wardrobe choice, this would be their last summer together and she didn't want to miss out on a minute of it. After graduation, everything would change. She planned to accept her diploma with one hand and close the door on her small-town life with the other.

"I can," Alex said, surveying the row of towels for a bare patch of sand.

"You're always so anxious to get out of here."

Alex snorted. "Aren't you?"

"Sure, but I don't have my entire life already planned like you do," Natalie countered.

"I don't have my entire life planned." *Just the next eight years.* Alex kept the crisp white letter on extra thick paper folded neatly in a copy of Sally Swift's Centered Riding. *"Dear Miss Wilde, We are pleased to accept you for early admission into Texas University's accelerated degree program for veterinary medicine..."*

Her childhood dream was less than a year from becoming true.

Alex felt rather than saw Natalie's eyes rolling behind her white rimmed sunglasses.

"Let's focus on the now! On senior year. We have to make memories...or at least make bad decisions and not get caught." Natalie flung her arm around Alex, steering her toward a group of guys clustered around the wooden frame of a lifeguard stand.

When they had almost reached the water's edge where the sand became firm and loamy, Natalie eased the tote bag off Alex's shoulder and plopped it down. Her skin tingled where a few pairs of eyes regarded her from behind. She reached into the bag and grabbed a towel, allowing the wind to unfurl the embroidered outline of a palm tree.

"Can you hand me the sunscreen?" asked Natalie, who had already flopped onto her back.

"Sure." Alex dug into the bag and tossed her the tube. Out of her peripheral vision, she noticed two shirtless guys in board shorts edging toward them. "Here comes our bad decisions," she muttered as Natalie sat up to squirt a thick puddle of white paste into one hand. Alex's hands went immediately to the hem of her denim cutoffs.

"Who is that?" Natalie hissed as she frantically rubbed sunscreen onto her bare arms.

"No idea." Alex blew out a breath and cast a furtive glance in their direction then downward while she feigned digging around in her bag. Maybe they were headed out for a swim.

"I think I know them from somewhere." Natalie craned around Alex's calves to get a better look.

"I'm not surprised. You know everyone in this entire county."

"True." Natalie grinned. Like mother like daughter. Natalie's mom was nothing short of a social butterfly. She owned the only bridal shop in a thirty-mile radius. With an endless supply of gossip from her patrons, Eloise Ashwell was as well informed as anyone in their corner of the world. A trait she had passed on to her bright-eyed, loquacious daughter.

"I think they're from Brazosville," Natalie mused, snatching a *Seventeen* magazine out of her bag and distractedly flipping the pages.

Brazosville was the next town over from Cole's Church and only slightly bigger than their community of three thousand. A rival town where sports were concerned. Friday nights in southeast Texas were infamous. A veritable battleground between longtime foes under stadium lights generation after generation after generation.

When Alex spied two pairs of bare feet inching precariously close to her towel, curiosity got the best of her, and she looked up at the sun-kissed males that owned them. Both were tall and well-proportioned—athletes by the look of their mid-sections. One with short sandy brown hair and liquid chocolate for eyes. The other with blue-black hair that fell artfully over his forehead, partly shielding a piercing pair of crystal blue eyes.

"Hi," said the dark haired one, lips rising into a smile.

Alex eyed him warily. Her lips parted subtly before she spoke.

"Hi," she said evenly, standing to her full height and brushing sweaty palms over the rear of her shorts.

He assessed her. Blatantly. Without bothering to hide it. His gaze roved and dipped over the twin braids resting on her shoulders to the barely filled out bikini top to her long legs emerging from the frayed ends of her denim cutoffs.

"I'm Jake and this is Cory."

"You guys are from Brazosville, right?" Natalie piped from her towel perch. She had removed her sunglasses and was biting on one of the earpieces.

The one called Cory flashed her a grin. "Yeah. You've seen us around?"

Us. Like they came as a package. And then a factoid clicked in Alex's brain. Two cousins from their rival school. A real force of nature on the baseball field. Their names had been plastered all over the paper this past spring as they led their team to district championship victory. Cory Cobb and Jake Brady.

Natalie gave a delicate snort. "Maybe."

Alex observed Jake with fleeting glances. Tall and broad-shouldered, a hint of grace in his posture, assuredness in his gaze. A guy accustomed to being talented, popular, and desired.

"Maybe you can plan to see us around later," he drawled.

"Oh yeah?" Natalie said, an octave higher than usual.

"There's a party tonight," Cory explained, "at the old McCoy land."

The McCoy land was an abandoned barn in the middle of an overgrown field shielded by a ring of evergreens right off Cedar Creek. Old Mrs. McCoy had died a few years ago, leaving the land to her only surviving relative, a wealthy nephew in Chicago who couldn't be bothered with it. The property had sat desolate and unused until the local teenagers had gotten brave enough to start repurposing it for pasture parties. Alex had never been to one. The writhing crowds. The smell of debauchery and unrequited hormonal instinct. The thought of navigating that scene made her nauseous.

"So, we'll see you there?" Cory asked, dragging a foot through the sand.

Natalie tilted her head to the side and slid her sunglasses back in place. "Maybe you will."

Alex daggered a look in her direction but not before she caught the salacious grins spreading across the boys' faces. Shit-eating grins,

Natalie called them.

"Later," Jake said, raising a palm to Alex before they turned as a pair and trudged toward the volleyball game.

Alex whipped her head toward Natalie who lazily flipped the pages of her magazine. "Are we really going to that party tonight?"

"Hell yes, we are. I haven't been out there yet, and I want to see what the fuss is about."

"Are you sure you don't want to see what *that* fuss is about?" Alex asked, cocking her head toward the boys, who were thankfully out of earshot.

"Well..." Natalie drawled, settling back into her magazine.

"They didn't even ask our names," Alex said. She flicked her eyes to the boys disappearing into the distance, but she couldn't for the life of her figure out why.

On the car ride home, Natalie drove with the windows down, letting the breeze cool their sun-soaked skin. Alex shifted in her seat, feeling the chafe of a sunburn on her backside. As they accelerated over the river bridge, the muddy brown ribbon below churned from the recent rains. Her head lolled into the passenger window letting the wind steal her breath one molecule at a time. The smell was intoxicating—fresh and clean with hints of cedar. Natalie drummed her nails on the steering wheel as she hummed along to a lilting pop song.

A peaked roof the color of pine needles came into view and a massive two-story red facade followed. A few pickup trucks lingered in the parking lot, loaded up with bales of freshly cut hay. A pair of sweat-slicked, shirtless guys were stacking square bales into neat pyramids on the back of one of the trucks. The silhouette of the taller one caught her attention.

"Pull in here right quick," Alex blurted, the dimly lit bulb of an idea flicking on in her brain.

"Why?" Natalie asked warily but swerved into the parking lot anyway at a velocity that startled the cowbirds fussing for bugs among the discarded straw.

"Be back in a minute," Alex called, pushing one foot out of the passenger door before it had quite come to a stop. She hopped over the oil spots and through the crumbling asphalt until she reached a long flatbed trailer. She hoisted herself up by the rim of the tire.

The broad back closest to her swiveled around and sea green eyes peered down at her. His deeply auburn hair was plastered to his skull with a mixture of sweat and dirt, little bits of hay clinging to the ends. It had grown out this past spring so that the front hung down past his eyes. He had developed the habit of sweeping it over with one hand when he was thinking...or flirting.

"Nice pigtails, Lex," he drawled, tugging one of the ends with fingers enclosed by thick leather work gloves.

Alex wrinkled her nose as a few beads of his sweat landed on her cheek. "You're a sweaty mess, Justin."

"Oh, I'm sorry," he said, glancing around dramatically. "Let me just find something to wipe it on."

Alex shrieked as he grabbed the bottom of her white t-shirt and ran the length of his forearm across it.

"Not cool," she yelped, springing back a few feet before he could try again.

He chuckled and removed his own t-shirt from the waistband of his Levi's and ran it over his chest. Alex eyed him behind her sunglasses. She could see why half the girls in Brazos County, including Natalie, had become smitten with him during junior year. Her childhood pal, and for a few years, her only friend, had shot up like a cornstalk over the last two years and now stood an entire foot taller than Alex. High school had become his kingdom. Basketball star. Disgustingly popular. Friendly and easygoing. And even though he always spoke his mind, for some reason, the words came out sounding sweet with his slight Texas twang.

Justin's mom was military and she deposited him at his grandparent's house around the time he was seven to give him a semblance of a stable home between her tours of duty. The Robbins' tan brick house sat a quarter mile down the road from Alex's white one. When they were little, summers were spent chasing fireflies in her backyard and licking ice cream cones on his grandparent's porch swing. He was her first friend after everything happened. Her first reason to smile.

"Sweat is just the body's way of cooling itself off," he teased.

Alex lifted the neckline of her t-shirt to wipe the beads collecting on her brow. "Not when it's someone else's," she grumbled but smiled when Justin offered her a half-full bottle of orange Gatorade. "Thanks." She tipped the edge to her lips. His scent lingered there, the scent of male and freshly cut hay and something sweetly tart.

"What have you been eating?" she asked warily, sniffing the edge of the bottle once more.

"Cherry pie." He picked up a wedge of golden crust dripping with jewel-toned goodness from a paper plate balancing on the edge of the trailer bed. "Want some?" he asked, winking as he stuffed the crusted rim into his mouth.

"You know I hate pie."

"I know," he said quietly, sunlight sparkling in his green eyes. "But I keep asking anyway."

"I don't know why you do," Alex mused, rolling her eyes.

Justin checked the digital watch face strapped to his impossibly long forearm. "Two more hours of slave labor and I'm all done. Whatcha up to tonight?"

Alex averted her eyes to the red Acura where Natalie peered over the glossy front of a magazine. She let out an uncertain breath. "I got invited to a...party."

"And you're actually going?" Justin scoffed, snatching the Gatorade from Alex's hand and guzzling the remainder of the contents.

"Maybe." Alex crossed her arms. "It's my last summer in Cole's Church. I'm allowed to have a little fun." She caught a subtle furrow in Justin's brow before he chucked the empty plastic bottle over the side of the truck. "I was wondering if you wanted to come."

Justin cocked one thick brown eyebrow. "Maybe I already have plans."

Of course, he would have plans. If not with the athletic clique, it would be with some girl he was seeing three counties over. And she would hear about it after church on Sunday, like she had for their entire adolescence.

"I thought you and Brittany broke up." Alex wasn't going to miss Justin's last girlfriend. She was a shade too perky, and too blonde, and she made his Jeep smell like the inside of a hair salon on pageant day.

Justin shrugged. "We did."

"Then it's unlikely you have plans tonight. Come with us. It's a perfect time for you to—" Alex paused and tilted her head in the direction of the cherry red Acura, "—get back out there."

Justin crossed his arms over his chest, a chest that was thicker and more muscular than Alex remembered. Having a part-time job heaving giant bales of hay had to help. Alex pushed her sunglasses onto her head and sent the willpower of her ocean blue eyes into his green ones.

"I will if you will," he teased.

Alex rolled her eyes. "Please. Between school and work and getting ready for college, I don't have time for..."

She trailed off, her words drowning in a sea of uncertainty. Could she really know what she was missing if she had never actually had a date? The boys in Cole's Church had never interested her. But even if they had, she had a feeling that Justin's unnerving presence would have scared them off. Her mind jumped to today and Jake Brady, and an interaction that could have been mistaken for flirting. She averted her eyes to her bare toes, their hastily painted tips peeking out from the ends of her sandals.

"Fine," she heard Justin mutter. "I'll try to swing by. For you."

Alex beamed a smile at him before hopping off the trailer, landing neatly in a pile of discarded straw. "It's at the old McCoy place— the one with the barn."

"Cool. Later, Lex."

As Alex pulled open the passenger door of the humming car, he saluted them both with a raise of his sinewy arm. Natalie ducked farther behind a full-length fold-out of Nikki Taylor.

This summer was going to be epic.

THIRTEEN

"Turn your brights on," Alex instructed as she and Natalie crept along a winding country road. Only a faint remnant of golden paint suggested that it was once two lanes instead of one big one. Every hundred feet the headlights caught a break in the fence line where someone's private shale driveway started. Gates stood in metal fortitude over rusty cattleguards.

Alex despised cattleguards—long metal bars embedded into the ground and spaced far enough apart that an animal's leg would become wedged there if it tried to pass. Cows would survive unscathed; horses, on the other hand, would scream and struggle until their limbs were fractured by the unforgiving metal. For a horse with a broken leg, the only treatment was a bullet to the forehead.

"How many driveways did they say it was after the curve?" Natalie asked, scanning the roadside as she slowed the car to a crawl.

"It's that one right there. The one with the 'M' on the gate."

Alex grabbed the console as Natalie swerved into the drive, a fine spray of pebbles mowing down the overgrown weeds flanking the entrance. As they clanked over the cattle guard, she rolled down her window to let in the night air, thick with humidity and filled with the scent of cedar. The sky was peppered with stars that blinked in ignorance of whatever might be occurring under their watch.

"Are you sure this is it?" Natalie asked. She navigated through several turns. The grass was so tall it nearly overtook the driveway.

The hum of summer cicadas filled Alex's ears and they vibrated with the delicate rhythm.

"I'm mostly sure," she replied after a moment.

A shiver of anticipation coursed through her middle and settled into a heap in the pit of her stomach. It was a familiar feeling. One she always experienced before any kind of social event. She wondered if this awkwardness would linger as she got older. Would she ever feel comfortable in her own skin? Confident and unwavering.

Natalie had certainly mastered that skill. She stared at her friend's strawberry blonde locks gently curled in waves around her oval face. Her face with neatly plucked brows and carefully applied lipstick in a shade of cherry red. A pristine white skirt fluttered around her golden-brown thighs, muscular from her hours on the tennis court. The boys here tonight had no idea what they were in for.

Natalie always had a string of potential boyfriends waiting in the wings, but she was choosy, and after her last breakup, had set her sights on Justin. They would be perfect together—a tall, insanely attractive, athletic power couple with every shade of red coursing through their perfect hair. But, despite Natalie's best efforts, including a tight-fitting emerald dress worn to junior prom, Justin hadn't bitten. Alex observed her friend whose nose was scrunched up in concentration, her chin barely clearing the steering wheel. Who knew? Maybe tonight was the night. In matters of the heart, timing seemed to be everything.

When the car cleared the next group of cedars, its twin beam headlights carved a path through a clearing toward a beautifully constructed barn, its doors thrown wide open in welcome. Although it bore signs of disuse, the angular beams and paneled exterior appeared solid. Alex imagined curious equine heads poking over the double row of stalls lining a wide central thoroughfare.

Natalie squealed in excitement as she braked into a swathe of empty grass. Droves of people emptied out of the hazard of automobiles, moths to the incandescent flame of the overhead light at the barn's entrance. Alex fell into the queue behind Natalie.

As they walked, she nervously tugged on her denim shorts that didn't leave much of her legs for the imagination. After today, she had the beginnings of a subtle summer glow on her thighs. She lifted her arms to adjust the band in her ponytail and her t-shirt hovered above her navel. She had to remember to keep her arms down.

Raucous laughter and the final notes of a Mariah Carey song dissipated into the night as they stepped into the fray. Natalie pulled Alex over to the glinting cylinder in the middle of the floor where a few guys pumped beer into red plastic cups.

The sandy haired one flashed a dazzling smile. "You made it," Cory said, beaming at Natalie. His gaze darted over her tightly fitted white button down.

"It's Cory, right?" Natalie asked in a sing-song voice. Alex rolled her eyes. Like Natalie didn't already know. Like she hadn't memorized every feature of his face at the beach earlier today.

"Want a drink?" He proffered a cup brimming with foam in her direction.

"Hell yes," she said, taking the cup and putting it to her cherry red lips.

"How 'bout you?" he asked.

"Sure. Why not?" Alex shrugged, accepting the cup and wincing at the smell. A smell that reminded her of stale breath on her cheek right before her eyes stung from being slapped. Alex took a quick gulp before she was folded into a side-hug with Natalie.

"Can you believe we're seniors?" Natalie crowed. "Here's to making memories!" Natalie clinked her plastic to Alex's before guzzling half the contents. Cory eyed her appraisingly, his hand already outstretched to provide a refill.

"And bad decisions," Alex muttered, before taking another gulp.

Beer really did taste like horse piss.

Over the next hour, every spare breathing space inside the barn was filled with a body. A portable stereo perched on the seat of a rusting tractor vibrated with bass notes. A few girls Alex didn't recognize began writhing to the music. Girls in tight fitting shorts and even tighter fitting t-shirts, beer bottles held aloft in a salute. A few guys were seated on hay bales around an ice chest, ensconced in a lively game of Texas hold 'em.

"You're a dick, dude," drawled a scratchy voice.

Jake Brady ran a hand through his dark hair as Cory reached around Natalie's waist to collect a pile of crumpled dollar bills. She giggled as Cory shifted under her. At some point she had ended up tucked into his lap, nursing a peach wine cooler. Alex flicked her eyes periodically around the crowd hoping to spy a shock of reddish brown hair towering above everyone else.

"A dick who wins," taunted Cory.

As the group around the ice chest laughed, Alex edged farther away. Her lungs craved the freshness of night air and the gentle caress of the wind. Ignoring Natalie's scowl and beckoning fingers, she exited the barn door, dumping warm yeasty beer into the tall grass as she walked into the night. She made it to the edge of the clearing, stopping only when met with a formidable wall of cedar and pecan trees. Like giant sentries they guarded the interior of the property, land that had seen minimal footfalls over the last few decades.

A light bobbed in the distance. A bouncing cluster of photons that grew brighter with every passing second. Alex stared into it, her heart racing, thumping inside her chest like a drum. She edged closer to the tree line, pressing into the ragged trunk of the nearest cedar. And then it disappeared.

"Boo!" rattled a hoarse voice and Alex's stomach dropped into the soles of her feet. She whirled, her outstretched palms meeting with a solid chest wall, and then pushed hard enough that she stumbled backward landing on her own behind. He was completely bent in half, his wheezing laughter filling the heavy night air.

"Justin!" Alex screeched. "You scared the stuffing out of me." She pulled a clump of grass and tossed it in his direction.

"You should have seen your face," he cackled.

"You're a..." Alex huffed, pushing up to her feet and brushing off the dirt from the back of her shorts.

"Superstar?"

"Ass," Alex countered but couldn't help the smile that quirked up the edges of her mouth.

"What are you doing out here?" he asked, pulling his baseball hat lower over his forehead.

"I saw something."

"What was it?"

"Some kind of light."

Justin wrinkled his forehead. "Maybe it was old Brit Bailey."

Alex snorted. The story of Brit Bailey was legendary in their part of Texas. "Yes, I definitely think it was the ghost of a kooky pioneer with a drinking problem whose lantern haunts Bailey's Prairie."

"Doesn't Bailey's Prairie start somewhere around here?"

"I don't know." She cringed. He was exasperating.

"Remember when we were ten?" Justin began solemnly.

"I would think so," Alex replied tartly, enunciating every syllable as the memory came flooding back. They had decided to camp in his aunt's backyard for Halloween and had been lying on blankets, arms folded under their heads as they picked out constellations. A fog rolled in. A fog that wove its way through the Spanish moss hanging from ancient oak trees. And in the middle of the river, surrounded by a dense blanket of sublimated water, they had seen the gentle flickering of a light.

"You were so scared," Justin teased, holding his hands over his abdominals.

Alex folded her arms across her chest and then unfolded them to tug down her shirt. It wasn't the light she had been frightened of.

"I got over it," she hissed.

"Got over what?" Natalie appeared from the shadows with two other figures in tow. Alex's eyes widened when she recognized one of the figures as Jake.

"Her deepest fear," Justin mumbled enigmatically. "I don't think we've met. I'm Justin." He proffered a hand to the two boys who took turns clasping it.

"Cory."

"Jake Brady."

Jake's eyes grazed over Justin to where Alex stood. "We're going up the road to buy some more beer. Wanna come?"

A rush of surprise gripped her and words become parchment in her mouth.

"She'd love to," piped Natalie.

When Jake extended a hand, an internal nudging found Alex extending her own. As he began to lead her through the thick grass toward his car, she felt a pair of eyes boring into the back of her skull. She turned to see Justin watching her, arms folded across his chest. In a moment of pure childishness, she stuck her tongue out.

"After you."

Jake opened the door to a silver two door coupe and Alex crouched down to slide into the worn leather seat. The interior of the car was blood red and smelled faintly of aftershave and something like aerosolized teenage male hormones. Jake settled into the driver's seat and cranked the ignition, the engine roaring to life as twin headlights cut through the underbrush. A beady pair of possum eyes skirted behind a tree.

"I'm Alex, by the way."

Jake quirked a dimpled grin in her direction. "Yeah, I know." Alex parted her lips in surprise as Jake added, "Natalie likes to talk."

"She does," Alex said nervously, fingering the hem of her cropped white t-shirt.

The car emerged from the gravel driveway, bits of rock crunching under their tires as Jake accelerated onto the two-lane road. Alex quietly observed Jake's easy posture, the way he reclined far back in the leather seat, easily controlling the car with the smooth motions of one hand. He reached toward the radio, a secretive smile on his face as he twisted the knob. The light from the dashboard cast shadows over his face; a face that was clean cut with a strong jawline and thin lips that hid a row of straight teeth.

Two dimples sunk into his cheeks as he turned to her and said, "I hope you like Radiohead."

Alex was pretty sure it didn't matter if she hated them. Luckily, she didn't. She began humming along as Jake expertly guided the car through the twisty backroads.

"Are you having fun tonight?" he asked above the blare of *Creep*.

"Yeah...definitely." A slight sheen had developed on her palms, and she brushed them down her shorts to hide it.

"First time?" He cut his gaze to her, winking one perfectly lashed eyelid over the crystalline blue hue of his eye.

"What?" Alex croaked, realizing how dry her throat had become.

"At the barn?"

"First time at that one," Alex answered, the gleaming eyes of a raccoon perched on the side of the road catching her attention.

"I haven't seen you out much," Jake said, accelerating as they entered the main highway that connected Cole's Church with the rest of the universe.

Alex snorted lightly. "That's because I don't get out much."

"What do you do instead?"

She shrugged her shoulders. "I study a lot or read or..." Her voice trailed off under the waves of music building from the speakers.

"What about in the summertime?"

"I work at a barn."

"A real one? With horses and shit?" Jake had been ogling her every few seconds. She couldn't figure out if it was from genuine interest or freakish curiosity.

"A real one," she replied, thinking of the neat green metal roof and whitewashed walls. The scent of fresh hay and the gentle whickering of the occupants—five gorgeous equines who were as different as they could be. "And there's a lot of...shit."

She wrinkled her nose to be socially appropriate but honestly, she had never minded the smell. It reminded her of raw wet earth and sent her imagination somewhere more primitive, somewhere simpler, like a Jane Austen novel set in the English Highlands. Maybe she would go there someday. Maybe she would even fall in love with some British lord who owned stables. And she would be ceremoniously deflowered in a lust-filled sundrenched afternoon surrounded by hay...

The car was silent, and she realized Jake had been talking. Her cheeks pinked. "I'm sorry. What was that?"

"I said, 'that's cool.'" He reached up to change the station, his fingers brushing the exposed edge of Alex's kneecap. Their broad tips were smooth and cool and, although brief, the touch sent an unexpected shiver up Alex's spine.

"How about you?" Alex blurted. "What are you doing this summer?"

He flashed her a grin. "Baseball. Cory and I are playing with a select team in Houston. You should come to a game some time."

Alex nodded before she could stop herself. "I like baseball."

It was the only sport she had ever played, mostly because Justin's grandmother had insisted he join Little League when he was nine and had dragged Alex along. She had a choice of either being eaten by mosquitoes while sitting in a patch of blue grass or being applauded for sending projectiles at Justin's face. She had happily chosen the latter.

Jake looked the part of high school baseball phenom. From his haircut to his long arms and V-shaped torso to the silver chain tucked beneath his t-shirt bearing a set of numerals that were probably his jersey number.

"There's one tomorrow night," he said as he guided the car into a parking lot cast in darkness except for neon signs in the storefront window. Rusty pick-ups lined the storefront, a few of which had fishing poles and tackle boxes spilling from the truck beds. He smiled at her as he killed the engine. A full-on wide smile. Dimples and all. For the first time in her life, Alex felt gripped by a strange warmth spreading through her middle.

"Okay," she said.

"Cool." His gaze narrowed on her face, and she could tell he was looking at her lips. Good grief, his eyes were so blue. He jerked his chin toward the convenience store, shadows dancing across his sculpted cheek bones. "Do you want anything?"

"Diet Coke?" Alex stole another glance at him from under her lashes to gauge his reaction.

"You got it," he said, opening the car door and swinging his long legs out onto the concrete in one motion.

When she was alone in the car, Alex ran her hand along the worn leather. It reminded her of the saddle her boss let her use at the barn. She loved the smell of leather. The pungent spice of it spoke to some part of her brain. She had buried her face in the flaps of her English saddle more than once and let her imagination run wild. As wild as when she galloped across the meadow astride George, the seventeen-hand chestnut thoroughbred who was her favorite. An ex-track horse, he knew how to accelerate from a walk to a gallop in the span of a few seconds. And once he caught his stride, he became almost impossible to stop. It had taken a few years, but Alex had figured out how to maintain the upper hand.

Four-legged males had never been an issue for her. The two-legged variety, on the other hand, were a different story. She glanced through the convenience store window where Jake huddled near a pudgy bald guy in overalls, peeling dollar bills into his hand. The beer supplier, she guessed. Jake gave him a clap on the shoulder then scooted over to the massive cooler where he began studying soft drinks behind the transparent door. He reached in and retrieved a bottle of Diet Coke. Alex's mouth began to water with the anticipated effervescent burn.

Jake sidled up to the front counter behind the man in overalls. He really was nice to look at. Especially the way his backside held up his jeans. Was he really interested in her? It seemed...possible. And it was far past time that she go on a date or two. Even if it was nothing more than a summer fling.

Third wheeling with Natalie had occupied her for the past two years. She had watched from the sidelines while Natalie ran the dating gauntlet. And had spent more than one weekend watching *Dirty Dancing* and eating takeout pizza when she had had her heart broken. Or had done the breaking herself.

Alex released a breath she had been holding and made a promise to herself. If the door opened with Jake, she would see where it took her. What did Natalie's mom always tell her? *Mistakes were for the young.*

Jake glanced into the car, and she offered a wave. He was throwing out the baited hook. She decided to gobble it up with a smile that let the summer glow shine beneath her skin. He was a distraction that she was gifting herself. A distraction she hadn't expected. And one she knew wouldn't last.

A truck pulled into the spot next to Jake's car and Alex startled when a door banged shut. A stooped man in a fishing vest, a shock of dirty brown hair protruding from the back of a netted trucker's hat, dragged a hand along the hood as he limped toward the curb. Once the neon lights cast an orange hue over his face, Alex's blood turned to ice in her veins. The familiar profile. The face snarling down at her while she cowered in a corner. A slap echoed in her ears followed by the scents of cheap beer and sweat.

Her father occasioned a glance into the rolled down car window as he passed. Alex watched his eyes widen in confusion then recognition. Without thinking, she thrust open the car door and started to run. Every muscle screamed in panic, and it was several hundred yards before her mind finally caught up with her feet. And still, she continued to run.

FOURTEEN

Alex shoved a pitchfork into a pile of hay, tossing the golden strands into the widely open doorway of a vacated stall. A trickle of sweat worked its way down the back of her neck, mixing with the aerosolized dirt that hung in the air. She had never been more grateful for barn chores. Anything to distract her from last night.

In her hasty exodus from the convenience store parking lot, she had caught Jake's face in the storefront doorway. His expression bore several versions of shock as she lengthened her stride into an all-out sprint before cutting down a side street and disappearing into the night. At the time, she hadn't cared where her feet took her. As long as it was away from the man in the blue truck. Away from her father.

Alex swatted at a gnat that buzzed the shell of her ear. Jake probably thought she had lost her mind. Maybe this would be the shortest summer fling in history. An entire relationship that unfolded during a car ride and ended in a convenience store parking lot under the neon lights of a Budweiser sign.

"This place smells."

Alex pivoted on the heel of her boot and spied Natalie picking her way down the barn corridor in sandals.

"I kind of like it," she said, dropping the handle of the pitchfork into the pile of straw.

"Where are all the horses?"

"In the pasture. Terry likes to let them out while we deep clean the place."

Natalie plopped down on an overturned five-gallon bucket and erupted in a fit of sneezing. Alex girded herself for what was coming once Natalie finished digging around in her purse for a tissue.

"Jake said you ran off last night. Like literally jumped out of his car and ran down the street."

Alex regarded her hands. They were covered in a spiderweb of fine scratches from squeezing through rows of thorny hedges.

"I...got nervous." Although it wasn't a complete lie, the words felt sour on her tongue.

"Nervous about what? Was he a creep or something?"

Alex's lips spread into a wry smile thinking of the song blaring from Jake's radio last night. "No, nothing like that." She lifted the hem of her t-shirt to wipe the sweat, and the deception, off her face. "You know me..." She shrugged and averted her eyes toward a slice of sunlight streaming through the east facing windows. "Awkward on my best day. A little crazy on my worst."

Natalie's features softened and then sharpened on Alex's profile. "Did you just freak out?"

She avoided the piercing gaze from her friend. "No...yes...I don't know."

"Would it be so terrible?"

"What?" Alex asked.

"To let someone in. To have a little fun. You might surprise yourself...and someone might surprise you."

Alex considered her words. Natalie was treading carefully along a subject that she rarely broached. Her unease in her own skin. The fear that lived like a writhing creature right underneath her composed facade. Natalie had no idea what it was like to live in Alex's head. Her interactions were effortless, natural and composed. She possessed a gravitational pull for every other person in the universe.

Alex still remembered the first day of seventh grade. Natalie had sat in the lunchroom with her hair pulled into a high ponytail with a white scrunchie, surrounded by a gaggle of girlfriends all sipping diet soda and passing around magazines. Alex had clutched her brown paper bag with its apple and turkey sandwich, edging past the laughter and pink fingernails and smell of hairspray. But when she made it to the courtyard bench she and Justin had shared every lunchtime for the past year, he wasn't there.

Her eyes had swept the courtyard as she crumpled the brown bag tightly into her fist, finally spying his chestnut cowlicks in a pack of guys shooting lay-ups. In that moment, she knew everything had changed. She hadn't been ready.

A musical voice had lilted across the cafeteria, pulling her out of her own head. "Hey Alex, come sit with us."

Alex had fingered her long braid as she spied a beckoning hand. A hand connected to a forearm filled with plastic bracelets that twirled and spun with their own rhythm. A smile bloomed on Alex's face as Natalie took her lunch bag and plunked it onto the empty spot next to hers. Her bangs were perfectly curled and completely immobile as she whipped her face toward Alex's. "Want a Diet Coke?" she said, crystal blue eyes swimming with sincerity.

Those same eyes now regarded her with purposeful resolve.

"What are you doing tonight?" Natalie asked, a twitch beginning at the edge of her glossy lips. Alex gestured to the seven stalls that awaited her attention. "No." Natalie shook her head. "You're coming with me to watch Cory and Jake play tonight."

"I seriously doubt Jake wants anything to do with me."

Tiny sparkling lights danced across Natalie's eyes before a full smile stretched over her face. "If you haven't noticed," she purred, "he loves the game. And I'm not just talking about baseball."

Several hours later, an entire layer of barn dust mixed with sweat caked Alex like a second skin. A row of saddle pads lay drying on the grassy carpet behind the barn, permeating the air with wet horse scent. A lazy breeze blew through the main corridor and Alex stretched upward, closing her eyes for a brief second.

With her next exhale, she strode toward the mouth-like end of the barn, underneath rafters rotted from age and filled with knotholes where tiny creatures lived. Her boots scuffed along the ground as she passed each neatly labeled stall full of fresh straw waiting to welcome its occupant back at the end of the day: Sugarfoot, the white-footed bay Quarter Horse used for lessons; Bella, the Arabian mare who was Terry's personal hunter/jumper; Rico, the Dutch warmblood; Wanda, the bright-eyed filly who had been rescued from a slaughter pen last summer. And then there was George, a massive Thoroughbred who hadn't made it on the track and instead became a premier jumper for an East Coast aristocrat. Until he had been downcycled to Terry. He had swagger and intelligence and power. Alex absolutely loved him.

She reached out a fist to rap on Terry's thick office door and then paused when she heard the exchange of voices inside. Alex stepped to the side as the door was flung open and a pink-faced gentleman in a three-piece gray suit stepped out. Alex shrunk into the shadows and pretended to study an outdated calendar hanging lopsided from a nail next to the open doorway.

"Give me a call next week," Terry called in a gravelly voice from inside the office.

"It would be my pleasure," answered the man who turned back once to raise a hand in Terry's direction. With a graceful step, he edged around Alex, giving her a gentle nod before striding around the side of the barn, the sun glinting off a balding patch on the crown of his head.

Alex scurried into the open doorway and was hit with the full force of an arctic wind humming from the window AC unit behind Terry's mousy brown hair. Her hawk-like eyes lifted from the stapled documents splayed across her metal desk.

"How're the stalls comin' along?"

"Much better than when I started." Alex grinned and wiped her palms down the back of her jeans before sitting in the empty metal folding chair.

"Good." Terry looked down and began gathering sheafs of paper back into a folder. "Did you need to ask me somethin'?"

Alex's mind burned with the image of the well-dressed man exiting Terry's office. "Yes, I..."

"Spit it out, Alex. I got somewhere to be."

For all her gruffness, a smile quirked the edges of her lined mouth.

"I was wondering, well, I got invited to a baseball game and—"

"Yep. Go. Get out of here," she interrupted Alex. "I won't be back tonight though. Can you stop by on your way home and put the horses up?"

Alex was nodding before Terry finished. "Of course. Thanks. I really appreciate it."

Terry flapped a sun-spotted hand in her direction. "Go have fun for the both of us."

"I will." Alex tucked a wayward strand of chocolate hair behind her ear.

"Don't look so excited," Terry snorted and reached into her desk to pull out a stoppered bottle. She jerked it out with her teeth and let it fall with a plunk onto the desk. After sniffing the vapors, she took a swig.

"What's the occasion?" Alex asked. Terry rarely drank. Only during the "extremes of life" as she had once explained to Alex.

"Glad you asked." Terry winked before taking another swig from the bottle. She looked practically giddy. "I'm sellin' the barn."

"What?" Alex's throat constricted around the words.

Terry's thin lips split apart enough that her row of crooked bottom teeth emerged. She set the bottle onto the desktop so she could weave her petite fingers together like a web. She leaned back in her leather chair before speaking. "You heard me. It's way past time."

"But what about the horses?" Alex asked in disbelief.

"I've bought 'em a new home." Her lids drew back from her glinting eyes so far that Alex thought they might pop right out of their orbits. "Huge piece of land with a nice stable and room for an outdoor jumpin' ring. And it's right down the road."

Alex released a breath and the knot in her stomach unfurled a bit. "So that man in here earlier?"

"Some big estate lawyer sent over here to work out the details. This place ain't comin' cheap or without its headaches." As if to emphasize her point, Terry tipped the bottle up to her lips a third time.

"Where is the new place anyway?"

"Right off Cedar Creek."

Alex's ears perked and she glanced up sharply at Terry. "That place that's been abandoned for a decade?"

"That's the one. The old McCoy place," Terry said slowly and cocked a thin brow. "You heard of it?"

"Yes, I've heard of it." Her lips twisted up in a wry smile.

Alex was still thinking about her conversation with Terry many hours and miles later as she and Natalie bumped down the road. As they entered the freeway, the Houston skyline popped up from the terrain like the middle of a children's book. After a few wrong turns, they finally eased into a concrete parking lot wedged between a twin set of baseball stadiums.

The elegant *thwack* of leather balls landing inside leather gloves filled the background as she and Natalie scaled the stadium seating to find an empty section near the top. Cheers cascaded through the crowd when Jake and Cory trotted onto the diamond behind their teammates and into their respective positions as catcher and first base. Cory tipped his hat toward their section and Natalie responded with a fervent wave.

Alex eyed her friend speculatively. "I take it you've moved on from Justin."

"Justin who?" Natalie answered. She giggled to herself and crossed her legs, tossing a bouncing strawberry blonde ponytail behind her shoulder.

"What happened after I left the party?" Alex hissed but her words were drowned out by the announcer booming the start of the game.

It was easy to be sucked into the small-scale glamour of the night. The fluorescent stadium lights clicked on after the sun sank lazily into the horizon. The synergistic ooh's and aah's of the crowd accompanied every pitch, every swing of the silver bat, every ascension of the ball into the heavens. More than once, Jake had thrown off his catcher's mask, his face taut with concentration as he trained his eye on the ball arcing above him. And more times than not, he had snatched it up in his glove. Alex had to admit that his hand-eye coordination was impressive.

Once the starlight had supplanted the day, the game drew to a close, and Alex found herself following Natalie, who was swishing her hips inside a pair of white shorts as she sidled up to the chain link fence outside the dugout. The heaviness in Alex's stomach grew as she debated sneaking off to the ladies' room or back to the car or into the nearest bush for that matter. She twisted her fingers together while Natalie interlocked hers with the fence.

"Hey you," Cory murmured, a cocky grin spreading to all corners of his face.

Natalie tipped her face upward, the fluorescence of the overhead lighting reflecting off her corneas between the batting of her lashes. Alex sidestepped away from the love bubble with the intent to settle in somewhere quiet with the book she had toted along in her bag. *Wuthering Heights* would be the perfect distraction for Natalie's post-game flirting.

"Hi Alex."

A deep voice pierced her thoughts. A voice that sent a single line of gooseflesh erupting over the back of her arms. She pivoted slowly and found Jake, still dressed in his catcher's gear, casually gripping the diamond shaped links of the fence, hair fluttering in the breeze like crow's wings. His batting gloves protruded from the rear pocket of his pants. Her treacherous eyes skated over the silhouette of his posterior, and she blew a breath out of her nose. It was more of a snort really. A snort that reminded her of a mare who had just noticed a stallion. Pushing down an uncomfortable shame, she ambled over to the fence to stare straight into the sky blue jersey that matched his eyes perfectly.

His eyes burned a path from the top of her head down past her flushed cheeks to her mouth that she had purposefully set in a stalwart line. Maybe it was true what Natalie had said. Maybe Jake thrived on the chase. Maybe her mad dash from the parking lot had only made him run toward her, not away. She heard his intake of breath and steeled herself for his next words. She had imagined all sorts of things coming out of his cocky mouth but not, "You hungry?"

She flicked her eyes to his in puzzlement and saw an inkling of mischief there. "Maybe?"

"Cool." His eyes under thick dark brows roved over her face once more and settled on her lips. "We'll meet you ladies in the parking lot." He motioned to Cory and they ambled off toward the field house.

Minutes passed, which Alex spent sitting on the hood of Natalie's car under a veil of humidity. Natalie had settled into her front seat with the vanity mirror popped open to apply a second coat of lip gloss and a dab of mascara.

"How do I look?" she inquired, thrusting her head through the open window.

"Perfect." Alex flashed her a smile that faded quickly when she caught site of the two lean silhouettes sauntering in their direction. Her stomach crouched into a backflip while she took in the site of Jake with a shock of damp hair splayed artfully over his forehead and a fitted blue t-shirt tucked into relaxed jeans. Maybe it wouldn't be so bad to be chased after all.

FIFTEEN

Alex watched Jake dip three fat fries into a puddle of ketchup and stuff them into his mouth. All four of them had crammed into a corner booth at a late-night fast-food restaurant. The backs of Alex's bare legs were cemented to the red vinyl bench cushions. She didn't dare move. Any change in position would bring her closer to Jake's left thigh.

Natalie giggled as Cory whispered something in her ear, a rosy blush creeping into her cheeks. Alex concentrated on her half-eaten burger with a half-smile turning up one corner of her mouth. Natalie deserved this. She was vibrant and beautiful and loads of fun. And she always got what she wanted. Except for Justin. He had turned a blind eye to her giggling and hair tossing and arm grazing. Probably because he had several other contestants lined up and didn't know how to choose. It was just as well. Having to be third wheel to her two best friends' summer love affair would have been less than appealing.

The air was thick with the smell of grease and the squeak of straws being pushed and pulled through plastic lids. She took her own straw in her mouth and caught Jake side-eyeing her.

"What?" she asked, not sure she wanted to know.

"You have a little—" he began, running his thumb across the corner of her mouth before uttering, "mustard."

Alex squinched her eyes closed. She really was hopeless. "I guess you can't take me anywhere," she joked. The words hung in the air between them.

"It's not for lack of trying," said Jake as he knit together his thick black brows.

The dimples in his cheeks deepened as he tried to hold the laughter in his cheeks. Alex surprised herself by chuckling loudly and was soon joined by the rest of the table. She clutched her stomach and balled up the napkin she spied near Jake's hand, lofting it at his glossy bent head. Quicker than she would have imagined possible, he inserted a hand between her knees, squeezing her lower thigh. Another involuntary howl left her lips. Her hand flew out, knocking her soda across the table. Caramel colored liquid pooled across the table and streamed in steady rivulets over the side and into Cory's lap.

Alex clapped her hand over her mouth as Cory muttered an expletive under his breath and Natalie hopped up from the booth to avoid soiling her white shorts. Under her hand, Alex's face burned. She began mumbling apologies, wishing her hair was down so that she could bury half her face behind it.

"Don't worry about it," Cory smirked, using a pile of white table napkins to sop up the mess on his jeans.

Alex glanced worriedly at Natalie who was busy collecting wrappers and half cartons of fries and tossing them into the trash bin behind her.

"Yeah. Don't worry about it, Alex," she said casually over her shoulder, giving Alex a solid wink. "We were ready to get out of here anyway."

By "we", Alex didn't think she meant with her.

Once the night air bathed her face outside, Alex relaxed a little. The stars were hidden behind the glow of the parking lot lights and the thick layer of fog that had rolled off the Gulf. She could almost smell the heavy droplets of aerosolized ocean.

The four of them coalesced around Natalie's car. Alex kept glancing into the passenger seat, waiting anxiously for the moment she could hop in and escape the tension of the last few hours. She had had fun, but it wasn't relaxing fun. It was more like running a gauntlet and she was so close to crossing the finish line.

Natalie cut her eyes at Alex, her lids lowered as Cory slid one finger through the beltloop of her shorts and pulled her into his side. Their bodies bumped off one another like a physics experiment. Two objects in motion that rebounded off each other's kinetic energy. Jake was behind her, close enough that she could feel his body heat radiating into the small of her back. A back that was exceptionally sore after mucking out seven stalls at the barn today.

"Natalie," Alex said sharply and her friend twisted around from Cory's embrace. "I have to go. I promised Terry I would put the horses in the barn tonight."

A wave of disappointment shadowed Natalie's face before she answered. "All right. Let me just—"

"I can take you," Jake drawled behind Alex.

Natalie cocked one shapely brow as she eyed Jake over Alex's shoulder. "Perfect," she said before Alex could protest.

Cory was already climbing into the passenger side of Natalie's car by the time Alex realized a sinewy forearm had snaked itself around her waist.

Once inside Jake's car for the second time in twenty-four hours, she resigned herself to sticking this out. This wasn't exactly a date, but it also wasn't not a date. It was practice. A beta test for when she actually went on a real date.

A soulful, grating voice crooned in the background. Eddie Vedder from Pearl Jam. At least she wouldn't have to suffer through crap taste in music.

"So, what are your plans after high school?" Jake relaxed into his leather seat and shifted into fourth as they hit the highway.

Alex twisted her fingers into her long ponytail and swallowed past the parchment that was the roof of her mouth. "College at Texas University."

"Oh really?" He raised his brows in unison. "You think you'll get in?"

Alex stared at her bare thighs under the fringe of her denim shorts. "I already did," she answered quietly, "to the pre-vet program."

She felt Jake's sharp glance. "Really?" Wow. That's—"

"Nerdy, I know."

"Totally cool," he said. "So, you must be wicked smart."

"I've always liked school."

Alex felt his eyes on her again and she gave him a tentative glance. His eyes were so crystalline blue, piercing but amused at the same time. She blinked rapidly in a desperate attempt to re-compose herself. No one had ever looked at her like that before. Like they wanted to devour her. She knew everything about this moment was a bad idea. A trajectory destined to go up in flames. But to hell with caution.

"So, what about you?" she asked, the words catching in her throat as a warm hand drifted off the gearshift and came to rest on the bare spot of her thigh above her knee. His eyes remained riveted on the road while his fingers stroked the sensitive skin there.

"Baseball scholarship," he said firmly, his jaw setting with determination.

Alex nodded appreciatively. If tonight had been an indication of his athletic prowess, she didn't doubt he would get one.

"Where do you think you'll go?" she asked as her skin heated under his touch.

"Hopefully a division one school that needs a good catcher. Texas University maybe?"

He flashed her a grin that deepened the dimples in his cheeks. Something Natalie once said popped into her brain and she had to stifle a giggle. *A smile that would drop a girl's panties.* Well, now at least she knew what that meant. Not that he was getting anywhere close to her dimestore cotton briefs.

"It's right after this curve," she interjected, spying the familiar white fence line contrasting with the inky night.

Jake removed his hand from her leg to downshift and slowly ease onto the gravel driveway. He pulled the car to a halt in front of a steel gate and Alex jumped out to open it. Her hands shook as they fumbled with the combination lock. What was wrong with her? He was just a boy. A human boy with forty-six chromosomes and normal appearing appendages. Blushing, she swung the gate wide enough so Jake could drive his car through it. Appendages that seemed to gravitate to her bare skin. She tingled with a chill that was not borne of night air.

Following the twin red rectangles of Jake's taillights, Alex began walking toward the barn-shaped silhouette in the distance, picking her way along the rocky driveway. It wasn't easy in sandals. She knew exactly how it felt to fall on her face during the trek from the road to the barn. As she walked, she sucked in a mouthful of night air and emitted a low whistle and then clucked her tongue a few times.

A shadowy head popped up, followed by another. She heard the delicate swish of long grass. Two lumbering creatures fell into step beside her across the fence. A soft neigh resounded through the cacophony of a frog quartet and a third horse trotted toward the first two. Alex increased her cadence to a slow jog and the horses picked up their pace, heads swaying in time with their hoofbeats. She heard a soft whicker and a chestnut fell into step with the herd. George. She smiled at the sight of the moonlight dancing off the white star on his forehead. By the time Alex reached the paddock gate, four curious heads strained over the fence, eager for the comfort of their stalls and a belated dinner.

"Sorry guys," she murmured, her fingers fumbling with the latch. She swung the gate wide, they squeezed through it one by one and trotted toward their assigned stalls.

"How do they know where to go?" Jake reclined casually on the hood of his silver car, arms folded onto his broad chest.

"Habit, I guess. Horses are incredible creatures of habit," Alex explained as she loped after them and began sliding closed the stall doors.

George eyed her, his giant brown orb studying her face while burying his muzzle in his water bucket. She stopped short as the latch clicked into place. One stall was empty. Bella, Terry's black Arabian jumper, hadn't come in with the others. Alex groaned. Bella was prone to being spooked by just about anything from a stray dog to an invisible shadow.

Jerking open the door to the feed room, she dipped a rusting metal pail into the giant barrel of sweet feed in the far corner. A troupe of shivers danced across her bare arms. Spiders filled the spaces between the rafters above the feed barrel. Even though she couldn't see them, she knew that huge webs with enormous black and gold spiders in their centers stretched above her.

Alex rubbed a hand over her face a few times to rid herself of the feeling of a cobweb lacing her cheek. She saw Jake near the bay Quarter Horse, tentatively stretching his fingers inside the stall.

"Sugarfoot bites," Alex said and Jake jerked his hand back to his chest.

"Good to know," he said, massaging his fingers with fervor. "Do you?" he asked wickedly.

A startle shuddered between her shoulder blades. Did she hear him correctly? "Only...when provoked." She shifted her eyes down to the grain bucket, her tension escaping in a soft laugh. When she looked up, Jake was standing within reaching distance of her. Her eyes scanned upward to the swell of his chest and the faded blue t-shirt with Bay Area Bluejays written over his pectorals.

"I'll take that as a challenge."

The dimples in his cheeks deepened as a shock of blue-black hair fluttered over his forehead. The air in the stable suddenly felt overwhelmingly thick with dust and humidity. Alex shifted the bucket to her other hand as a rivulet of sweat dripped down her lower back into the landing zone below her waistband.

"I'm not sure you're up for this one." She cracked a sideways grin and the bucket handle slipped from her sweaty palm, landing with a thump in the soft dirt. "Crap," she muttered, squatting down to retrieve the bucket but Jake was faster.

The bucket now hung neatly on his glistening forearm. He waggled the fingers of his free hand. Rocking back on her heels, she grabbed them. They were warm, solid fingers that could fire a baseball from home plate to second in two seconds or less. What would those fingers feel like...? Giving her head an imperceptible shake, she used his inertia to pull herself up.

"I have a question," he said solemnly, and her heart rate ticked up.

"Okay," she murmured and the pounding intensified inside her chest.

"What am I supposed to do with this bucket?" He grinned and began swinging it to and fro.

Alex mentally shoved against the heady anticipation creeping up the back of her throat. "One of the horses didn't come in with the others," she said. "I need to go out and find her. She's a bit...skittish."

Jake passed her a knowing look, a twinkle starting in his eyes. "Lead the way," he drawled, cocking his head into the black hole of night at the back of the barn.

"You want to come along?" she asked, narrowing her gaze.

"Most definitely," he answered, still not taking his eyes from Alex's.

"Okay," she said quietly and took a few steps toward the open end of the barn. Jake didn't make any motion to drop her hand.

They strode into the night, a light breeze lifting the ends of Alex's ponytail as they tromped through an overgrown section of dalisgrass. The sticky seeds deposited themselves on her calves as they walked. She clicked her tongue a few times while Jake brandished the feed bucket but no Bella.

Her senses narrowed to touch and hearing as her vision quickly faded to black. She could feel every contour of Jake's hand in hers. Every worn callus. Every smooth line. The dark made her nervous. Like a thousand butterflies shimmering their wings all at once inside her stomach.

Her ears rang with the chorus of the creek frogs. Straining her eyes, she peered into the darkness. They had almost made it to the tree line before she detected movement near the fence. An undulating form that blended in and out of shadow.

"Bella," she cursed, extracting her hand from Jake's. "Why are you all the way out here, girl?"

She extended her hand into the darkness, reaching until the nothingness became a pair of quivering haunches. As Alex felt her way up the mare's body, past her bony withers and up her silken neck, the white rim of Bella's eye flashed in the moonlight. When Jake slid up beside her, Bella promptly forgot about her terror and shoved her head into the feed bucket.

"Well, I guess she's over whatever spooked her," Alex mused, watching the pony thrust her head as deep as it would go inside the pail.

"She's stronger than I thought she would be," Jake grunted as he tried to keep the bucket upright.

"Looks like you made a new friend," Alex said sweetly as Bella shoved a slobbery muzzle into Jake's arm. "Bella falls in love with anyone who holds the feed bucket." A delicious pause ensued while his lips took form to say something but Alex interrupted. "Just start walking toward the barn. She'll follow you."

"What about you?"

Alex eased into a smile. "I'll be right behind you."

Jake shuffled through the grass followed by the sound of clomping hooves. Easing her hand out to the wooden fence, she pressed her palm into the grain. It creaked under her weight, not entirely collapsing but bending ominously. She and Terry would have to fix that before they let the horses out again. The next stray dog that came along would bark Bella right through the fence. As she turned toward the barn, she caught a glimmer of light in her peripheral vision and whipped back around. Deep in the brush, a ball of light danced between the dense foliage.

"Who's there?" she called shakily. The light halted in mid-air. And then it was gone. She had an eerie flash of déjà vu. Maybe it *was* the ghost of old Brit Bailey out for a jaunt. All the saliva in her mouth turned to cotton before she mentally chastised herself. "I must be a raving lunatic," she whispered, before, heart pounding, she skittered through the grass to catch up with Jake.

She found him stationary in a patch of clover halfway to the barn.

"Why did you stop?" she asked, patting Bella on the hindquarters.

Alex watched the outline of his shoulders shrugging. "I didn't want to get lost out here."

"You won't get lost just follow the light from the..." The teasing died in her throat. "Barn."

Instead of a warm, friendly structure lit up like a Christmas tree in June, the barn was cast in shades of gray, silhouetted against black sky. Its angles and sofits were lost in the dense fog rolling in from the river.

"The power must have gone out," Jake offered.

Alex said nothing. She strode past him, opening the gate to allow Bella into the gaping mouth of the stable. A whicker resounded into the wood as Bella trotted past, her tail swishing between her hind legs. Once Alex had closed the stall door behind Bella's rump, she felt along the wall for the electrical panel. Her fingers closed over the plastic switch, flipping up and then down and then up again. Nothing.

"I guess you're right," she mused, sensing Jake behind her. "It's just really odd." A set of palms settled on her shoulders, their heat permeating through the cotton of her shirt. She startled with the touch and then relaxed as expert fingers began kneading the balled-up muscles between her shoulder blades.

"Feel good?" Jake whispered into the cusp of her ear.

She didn't want to admit it, but it did. It felt more than good. No one had ever touched her that way. His fingers climbed the bare skin of her neck with weighty familiarity and expectation. *A summer of fun*, she repeated to herself. Something she had more than earned. Something she deserved.

Alex sucked in a breath and turned around. Not a morsel of light existed in the shadow of the barn's sloping roof. Jake had become nothing more than a solid, colorless form. His arms draped over her shoulders and when he pulled her closer, close enough that she could feel the heat radiating from his middle and smell the sweetness to his breath, he brought his mouth to her lips. Alex closed her eyes and willed herself to breathe. Willed her heart to slow down its frenetic pace in her chest. The fullness of a bottom lip brushed her own and the cresting noise in her ears calmed into a languid swell as Jake pulled her into his chest and kissed her.

SIXTEEN

Alex stood abruptly with the rest of the congregation as the organist keyed up for the second hymn of the morning. Yawning, she covered her face with her folded church bulletin and snuck a glance down at her watch. It had been after midnight by the time Jake had dropped her off on the front porch. He had kissed her again under the porchlight. A chaste but sweet press of his lips to hers. It hadn't been earth shattering but what could she compare it to? It was only the second kiss of her entire life.

She brought her fingers up to her mouth and gently rubbed her bottom lip. She had promised herself fun. And that's exactly what this summer was turning out to be. Senior year would be gone in a blink between studying and working at the barn to save money for college. And then she would be free. On her own and away from Cole's Church on a high-speed train of academia that would take her exactly where she wanted to go. The promise of independence was so intoxicating she could taste it. And when that day happened, she would really begin to live her life. Leaving Cole's Church would mean leaving all the nightmares behind. It would be so easy to never think of him and his beat-up blue truck ever again.

Out of the corner of her eye she watched a tiny projectile land on the cushioned bench seat beside her. Scowling, she unfolded the butter yellow paper.

Come over for lunch after church.

Alex rolled her eyes. For nearly a decade, she had spent every post-church meal with Justin and his grandparents. They had practically adopted Alex as his surrogate sibling. She reached up to grab the dull bit of pencil stuck in the pew in front of her and scribbled a reply.

I thought you'd never ask.

She smirked and dropped the scrap of paper in the wicker offering basket as it passed by. While Pastor Brian droned about denying the flesh, Alex felt her cheeks pink as her skin remembered the way Jake's lips had lingered there. Another balled-up shred of church program landed in her lap, and she cut her eyes at Justin. He stared into his hymnal like he didn't see her.

"Please open your hymnals to number one forty-nine." Pastor Brian's smooth tenor filled her ears. She opened the scrap of paper.

Whatever you did last night is written all over your face.

The blush in Alex's face deepened into a crimson and she stuffed the paper into the abyss at the back of her seat. She reined in her expression and tried to dilute the annoyance building in her gut. The teasing was a part of their friendship she accepted because they had history. They had grown up together, and, despite the onslaught of adolescence, their loyalty to one another remained. Even though they weren't as close as they once were, she still considered him her best friend.

By the time Pastor Brian drawled the last "amen" Alex had already scooted off the padded burgundy bench and joined the milieu of ladies in their polyester blend dresses and sensible heels. At a snail's pace she edged closer to the double doors and the sunshine coating the steps down to the pavement. The moment her sandaled foot reached freedom, a delicate hand moved to block her path.

"God bless you and keep you, Alexandra," said Pastor Brian, taking her hand in his own.

"Thank you, Pastor Brian," she replied, reflexively glancing down at the hem of her cotton dress.

"Where's your mama today?" he asked, withdrawing his hand but keeping her in place with his stare.

"Working," Alex said quietly. She hated that Janie held two jobs to make ends meet—one at a law office in town and then every other weekend at a department store in the next largest town before Houston.

"Well, make sure and tell her I'm prayin' for her."

"I'm sure she'll appreciate that. If you'll excuse me, Pastor Brian." Alex averted her attention to the two people waiting for her under the towering oak tree that shaded the parking lot. Natalie motioned to her expectantly and she scurried down the stairs before anyone else tried to make small talk.

"Thanks," Alex muttered, not necessarily intending for anyone to hear.

"I'm surprised you're even here," Natalie remarked as she extracted a faded green compact from her purse.

"Why wouldn't she be here?" asked Justin, crossing his arms across his chest and narrowing his eyes.

"She was at the barn really late last night," Natalie said while she dabbed powder on the end of her nose.

"How did you even know that?" Alex asked, her voice cracking like a chicken egg.

"Your mom got a little worried and called mine to see if you were still with me."

"Well, obviously I'm fine. I had things to take care of."

Justin relaxed his stance and reached over to ruffle Alex's hair. "Out there messing around with the horses?"

Natalie snorted so forcefully that Alex thought her breakfast might erupt from her nose. "Among other things," she said casually.

Alex shot her a glare, but Natalie had already turned on her heel and was heading toward her car. "Sorry, gotta run. I'll call you later," she called over one shoulder.

"Do I even want to ask what that was about?" Justin bent his head and focused on her face.

"It's...nothing," Alex muttered. "Absolutely nothing."

Lunch at the Robbins' house on a Sunday was never a simple exchange of food and conversation; more like a multi-act play or a double-header sporting event. When Alex entered the screen door, the smell of roast beef simmering in brown gravy and freshly baked bread drowned her in decadent olfactory bliss. Sunday afternoons, according to Justin's grandmother, were meant for rest. The Bible even said so she had claimed on more than one occasion. And the resting always happened courtesy of nothing short of a five-course meal that left Mr. Robbins draped over an armchair with his eyes tightly shut and his mouth half open. The door banged closed behind her but not before a ball of black and white fur streaked between her legs.

"How's my baby?" cooed Mrs. Robbins, twirling a wooden spoon dripping with brown liquid with one hand while she bent down to rub the other over the feline's arched back. A vibratory purring met Alex's ears when she stepped through the archway into the cheery kitchen and hopped onto one of the painted wooden barstools tucked under the island.

"And how's my other baby?" Mrs. Robbins twisted toward Alex as she wiped her hands on a striped kitchen towel hanging from one of round cabinet knobs.

"I'm fine," Alex answered.

The same question Mrs. Robbins had been asking for almost ten years deserved the same answer. She nodded, her liquid brown eyes absorbing Alex's smile. Lips painted burgundy split into a toothy smile and the lines etched into her face deepened. She kept her hair a natural salt and pepper gray and clipped short enough that it easily set into tight curls the night before church.

"Can I get you some tea?"

Alex shook her head. The tea at Justin's house was like drinking syrup.

"Ice water?"

"Yes, please."

Twin roars erupted from the living room around the corner, drowning out her reply.

"I guess that means the Astros are winning," said Mrs. Robbins as she filled a glass with water from a ceramic pitcher with a faded painting of a rooster. Then she yelled, "Justin, you have a guest in here."

"Alex isn't a guest," he called from the other side of the wall.

She had been in this house more times than she could count but his words still felt like a slight. Tipping the chilled glass up to her lips, she let the ice-cold liquid fall into the back of her throat and gulped.

"Do you need any help with lunch?" she asked, her words now directed at an ample posterior covered by a full length flowered skirt.

"No, I surely don't," she answered, her voice muffled by the confines of the oven. She jerked out a glass dish of macaroni and cheese and settled it on the stove. "Frank, Justin," she shouted, her voice rising over the hum of the television set. "Alex and I are ready to eat."

Winking at Alex, she handed her a porcelain plate lined in blue trefoils and gestured toward the bubbling dishes resting on the stove. Alex scooted off the barstool and paused to inhale the delicious scent of warm, melted cheese before scooping a spoonful onto her plate. A pile of green beans next to a slice of roast beef and a fluffy cat head biscuit filled the entire surface area of the plate. She placed it on the dining table before returning to the kitchen to retrieve her water glass. Her stomach grumbled in protest. She had been so nervous last night that she had barely touched her dinner and breakfast had been an afterthought of a diet soda on the way to church. *Last night.* She hoped it wouldn't be the last time she was kissed this summer.

When she settled into her dining chair, Justin slid into the one next to her, auburn hair properly tousled by the ride home from church in his Jeep. A Jeep that he always refused to put the top on— even when it was raining. More than once, Alex had arrived home from school soaked to the bone because he believed that the weather would align with his will. Justin's eyes remained glued to the screen in the living room as he casually reached over and stabbed Alex's slice of roast beef with his fork.

"Hey, that's—" She watched him shove the entire slab of meat into his mouth. "Mine," she finished.

"I thought you were a vegetarian," he mumbled around a mouthful of beef.

Alex pushed the peppered green beans around her plate as irritation rose into the back of her throat. "I don't always have to be one thing or the other," she grumbled.

Mrs. Robbins plopped down in the seat across from Justin, partially blocking his view of the next pitch. With a pointed glare from her, he swallowed his objection and loped into the kitchen, plate in hand.

"Did you have a nice time last night, dear?" Mrs. Robbins inquired as she slathered a thick layer of butter on a biscuit.

Alex dropped her fork onto her plate with a resounding *ping*. Was it written all over her face in permanent marker? I, Alex Wilde, kissed a boy for the first time last night. Her cheeks heated before she stammered out a reply. "I...I did...it was fun. How did you know?"

Mrs. Robbins lips turned up in a smile, the shafts of sunlight beaming through the single bay window, lighting up the dust motes around her gray curls like a halo.

"How did you know what?" Justin asked, balancing a plate piled high with food, half a biscuit dangling precariously from his lips.

"About Alex's gentlemen caller," Mrs. Robbins said.

Alex nearly choked on the solid mass of macaroni making its way down her esophagus. She snatched up her water glass, gulping down the cold that would offset the heat spreading up the front of her chest.

"Mr. Pickles got out last night and I went down the road a piece to look for him." Mrs. Robbins stared fondly at the cat curled up on the faded yellow linoleum soaking in a patch of sunlight.

Justin looked from Alex to his grandmother then back to Alex, his face an evolution of disbelief. He tore the biscuit from his mouth and dropped it on his plate. "Alex doesn't have time for callers, Grams," he said nonchalantly, plunking his plate down on the gingham tablecloth. "She's either studying or knee deep in horse manure."

Alex bristled before spewing words from her lips like flaming arrows. "Maybe I finally found a better way to spend my time."

She wasn't sure why, but she meant for the words to hurt. Maybe because over the last few years she had become Justin's backup friend for when he got bored with the guys or didn't have plans with a pretty girl. Maybe because she had developed a loneliness that, at times, not even Natalie's presence could ease. And maybe because she was on the precipice of change—of leaving Cole's Church—and when she felt her youth slipping away, it would hurt a little less if she purposefully let it go altogether.

Justin snorted into his tea. "Like what? Jake Brady?"

Alex's vision narrowed to one of the blue flowers encircling her plate. "Maybe."

"He's a player, Lex. He goes for anything with a set of...He's not interested in..." His voice trailed off as Alex pushed back from the table, rocking the glassware with her momentum. She folded her arms across her chest.

"Go ahead. Finish your sentence."

Justin looked down, suddenly engrossed in his food, and Alex noticed something she hadn't seen since he was a kid, a faint pink flush creeping into his cheeks. Justin never faltered much less remained speechless. He refused to look at her as she huffed out a breath.

"You meant to say he's not interested in me."

"Dammit, Lex, I didn't—"

"Language, young man," barked out Mrs. Robbins.

Alex glanced around the table, suddenly remembering she had an audience to her rare display of emotion. The thought extinguished the angst burning a hole through her chest. "I'm so sorry, Mrs. Robbins," she murmured quietly, "about lunch."

Alex heard the scrape of Justin's chair over the linoleum as she pushed open the screen door. Her stride lengthened into a run before she reached the end of the shale driveway. When she dared a glance over one shoulder, she saw that he had stepped onto the porch, arms folded across his chest. She only hesitated a moment before turning left onto the country lane that led toward the white clapboard house with the red begonias out front flanking each side of a porch swing. If he had called out to her, she would have turned around, but he never did.

Alex pushed her bodyweight into the front door, twisting the handle and pulling up slightly to wrench it open. Once inside her house, she collapsed onto the beige sofa, tucking her knees under her dress, and leaning her head back onto the cushion. A beam of warm buttery sunshine from the front window struck her in the face and her eyelids drifted closed. It was the perfect backdrop for the riptide of her thoughts to crest.

It had only been a kiss. An electrostatic attraction between a boy and a girl. Nothing more. She almost believed her own lie. Because what she wouldn't admit to herself—and especially not to Justin—was that she did want more. She always had. Even when she wasn't even sure what more entailed. She only knew in the depths of her soul that someday she wanted more. More than this town and its small-minded gossip. More than studying and working to pay for college so that she could do more studying. She wanted to be seen as more than the quiet girl with her nose between the pages of a book. More than the socially inept adolescent who struggled to exist in her own skin. More than the daughter of a single mom. More than the scared, broken doll who still quaked every time she laid eyes on her father.

A high-pitched noise disrupted the ebb and flow of her thoughts. The yellow rotary phone jangled from its perch next to the kitchen cabinet. She let it ring without moving. Justin could just walk over if he was so inclined. She might open the door. Then again, she might not. The answering machine clicked on and, instead of Justin, Terry's pressured speech met her ears.

"Alex, pick up the phone if you're home. I need you out at the barn."

"Hi Terry, I'm here," Alex interrupted as she pressed the phone into her ear.

Within ten minutes, she had shucked off her dress and pulled on yesterday's jeans and a faded red shirt from last year's county fair. Her running shoes lay askew by the backdoor, and she shoved her feet into them before jumping the distance from the back porch to the ground. She glanced at the empty driveway once before gritting her teeth and setting off at a moderate jog back the way she had just come. To Justin's and to her only source of transportation at the moment.

Before her fist even reached the faded hunter green paint of the front door, it opened. Like he had been waiting for her to return. She quelled her irritation. Justin took up the entirety of the vertical height of the doorway, standing right inside the carpeted living room balancing a plate of poundcake covered in strawberries and whipped cream.

"Want some?" he said, stabbing a section of yellow sponge with his fork and extending it toward Alex's mouth.

Alex folded her arms across her chest. "Is this your version of an apology?"

He shrugged, a smile tempting the corners of his mouth. "I guess it is. Do you accept cake?"

Alex opened her mouth and slid the cake off his fork with her teeth. "Depends on how good it is." Her words were garbled by the buttery goodness soaking into her palate. There were no cakes in the county better than Mrs. Robbins. Alex swallowed and rubbed the back of her hand over her mouth. "You're forgiven," she said, and Justin's smile widened between his perfectly positioned ears. "If you can drive me to the barn."

Her ponytail whipped over the lower half of her face as Justin downshifted to take a sharp curve. "One day this summer, I'm going to teach you to drive a stick," he shouted above the blare of the radio. A nervousness crept into her stomach. Without her own car, she had never driven much, and even though Justin made it look easy, having to think about shifting gears had always intimidated her.

"I don't know," she said, grabbing onto the Jeep's metal frame as they squealed into Terry's driveway.

"Come on," Justin chided. "I promise it's easier than riding a horse."

"Doubtful," Alex muttered as they crept through the open gate.

The Jeep's tires scattered gravel into the flanking grass as they pulled into the space beside Terry's black extended cab truck. Alex hopped out before Justin had even killed the engine and strode into the barn. It was eerily quiet without the normal wickers of greeting or banging of impatient hooves against the wall planking. Despite the expansive gray clouds, pregnant with summer rain, the sun's heat radiated off the pavement.

"Terry?" Alex called into the poorly lit interior.

"In here." Terry's voice sounded thin and ragged as it echoed down the corridor.

Alex sprinted to the rear of the enclosure and the open stall door where she could make out the outline of Terry's boots. Squatting down, she took in the sight of Terry on her knees in the straw cradling Bella's head. The horse's sides heaved with exertion, her breath coming in forced bursts across a bone-dry muzzle. Alex placed a hand on the curve of her cheek.

"What happened?" she asked softly.

"No idea," Terry bit out. "I found her this way when I got here."

"Did you call the vet?"

"Yeah. Right before I called you. He's out pullin' a calf and will get here when he can."

Alex ran her fingers down Bella's forehead. "She was fine when I left her last night. I had to go get her out of the back pasture, but she seemed fine once I got her to the barn."

Terry shook her head, cursing under her breath. "Maybe she got into somethin'. Hell, I don't know."

"Like what?" Alex furrowed her brows. Bella's breathing was becoming slower, shallower. A thick stream of frothy drool dribbled from the side of her mouth.

"Somethin' out in the pasture, maybe," Terry mused, running gnarled hands over the horse's neck as if a clue would present itself. Alex jumped to her feet, half expecting Bella to startle. Instead, she simply lay there without even a flicker of her eyelid.

"Where're you off to, girl?" Terry asked when Alex backed out of the stall, colliding with a formidable shape blocking the doorway. Justin put his hands out to steady her elbows before her knees buckled from the impact.

"Thanks," she murmured and pulled a strand of hair off her sweat-soaked forehead. "I'm going to search the area where I found Bella last night. Maybe I can find something to help the vet figure out what's wrong with her."

"I'll help you," Justin said, his chin dipping in affirmation.

"Okay," said Terry, glancing upward. "Hurry before this sky rips open."

SEVENTEEN

A newly birthed wind struck her in the face as she clambered over the gate in her haste to reach the inside of the pasture. A deep purple hue had spread across the heavens where the clouds coalesced into a single mass. She heard Justin's feet strike the ground behind her and in another two strides he had caught up to her, his legs lengthening into a lazy jog. A peal of thunder resounded over their heads, the air crackling with electricity. Justin cursed and they both picked up their pace.

"Aren't you worried about getting struck by lightning?" he asked.

Alex snickered under her breath. "Nope. Being the tallest thing out here, you'll get struck not me."

He laughed and she barely heard him say, "I guess I deserve that."

Alex motioned her hand for him to follow her to a dense overlay of grass near the fence line. "Over here," Alex wheezed, her lungs burning with effort. She stopped short, peering into the grass with considerable effort, trying to dissect the various fauna displayed before her.

"What are we looking for?" Justin bent down, hands on his knees.

Alex chewed on her lip for a moment before answering. "I don't exactly know. Anything that looks poisonous I guess." She swiped her hand over the smooth green blades of grass that nearly reached her knees.

Justin squatted to the ground and pulled out a few suspicious looking weeds with dangling pods. He squished one between his fingers and a milky substance ran down his hand. Alex wrinkled her nose.

"Disgusting but not poisonous."

Another bolt of lightning illuminated the sky to the west.

"One one-thousand, two one-thousand," Justin counted and

Alex's face broadened into a grin. She held up five fingers. When they were kids, they used to watch the rain come in from Alex's front porch. Whoever guessed how far away the lightning struck could pick the next game. Thunder rumbled across the sky just as Justin said "five one-thousand."

"Every time," he muttered. "Remind me that it's your turn to pick the next game."

"I won't forget," she called over her shoulder as she hoisted herself up onto the fence. It creaked under her weight. She had forgotten about the weak spot and jumped to the ground before one of the planks cracked in two.

"What are you doing over there?" Justin called.

"Something wasn't right last night." In her frantic worry over Bella, the details of last night had evaded her at first. But now they came floating to the surface one by one. "Bella didn't come in with the other horses last night. I found her up against this fence and I swear I saw—"

"What?" asked Justin as he squeezed between the two broken halves of fence.

"A light out there in the woods, like a flashlight or something."

Justin eyed her skeptically. "Maybe it was some people out looking for their dog or, I don't know, somebody out there laying pipe."

"There aren't any pipes that run this far back," Alex said, as she felt the first splatter of rain on her lashes. She heard a noise erupt from Justin's throat that was halfway between a choke and a laugh. "What?" she said, annoyance flaring.

"That means having sex, Lex. Not actually—"

"Okay, fine," she interrupted. "That's all the explanation I need."

Despite the cool rain-soaked breeze, her cheeks heated into twin embers. She felt a sharp tug on the end of her ponytail.

"You're cute when you're embarrassed."

Did Justin say she was cute? He probably felt guilty for earlier.

"Are you ill? Something's definitely wrong with you if you're calling me cute."

He sidestepped around her and began studying the trees. "You're right. You're not cute."

Alex blinked away the rain now sliding over her eyelids and collecting on the bridge of her nose. It shouldn't have mattered; yet, she felt the sting of his words in the deepest part of her chest.

"You're beautiful," he whispered.

What? She momentarily ignored every other sensation as her entire being narrowed down to those words. Words that felt like whispered honey. No one had ever said those words to her before. Her eyes drifted over the tree line as she scrambled for a reply, but nothing broke the surface of her churning thoughts. The air between her front and Justin's back became a reservoir for a sentence that had been tossed into the atmosphere but had no business being there.

"What the hell?"

The words erupted from Justin as he jogged over to a cedar tree several feet into the underbrush. When Alex reached his side, she noticed a frayed rope tied onto one of the lower branches. The end formed a perfect noose and the stiff corpse of a dead possum, its mouth gaping open in a snarl, rotated from the end. Extending a trembling finger to the trunk of the tree, she traced the symbol someone had carved there. A symbol she had never seen before. The prickly bark under the pad of her finger felt wrong, like something evil had carved its way into this natural beauty and tainted it.

"What does this mean?" she asked.

Justin opened his mouth, but his answer was lost in an ear-splitting peal of thunder followed by a barrage of rain.

"We have to get back," he shouted as a hefty gust of wind flipped the rain sideways.

Alex nodded and before another second passed, he grabbed her hand and began running full speed toward the barn. With adrenaline pouring through her system, Alex had little trouble keeping up with him, star athlete or not. By the time they reached the entrance to the barn, fresh rain ran in rivulets down her hair, her back, past the waistband of her jeans and into her socks. Justin let go of her hand to swipe his bangs out of his eyes and slick the longer sections behind his ears. The rain clung to his t-shirt, melding it to his midsection. Alex averted her eyes from the ridges made by his abdominals.

"Did you find anythin'?" Terry called from inside Bella's stall.

"Nothing to explain Bella's condition," Alex answered. "I just don't understand what—" she paused mid-sentence when Terry emerged from the stall, grief etched into her face as if it had been carved there.

"Whatever it was, it don't matter now," Terry choked.

Alex reached for her, holding her thin shoulders in an embrace. Words wouldn't suffice for grief this deep.

The ride back to Alex's house was quiet apart from the lightly pattering rain on the hood of the Jeep and the low undulating tones of the radio in the background. Justin pulled into her driveway and transitioned into neutral before either of them said a word.

"I'm sorry about the horse," he said, placing a large hand on Alex's knee. It rested there, warm and heavy and comforting.

"I know," she murmured, the grief a fresh wound inside her chest. Alex inhaled and blew out a breath laden with the words she couldn't bring herself to say. With gritty eyes focused on her doorstep, she unclicked her seatbelt and wrenched open the door, sliding out from under the warmth of Justin's touch. She needed a shower, the hotter the better, and some time alone to process. Not to mention unravel the icy ball of fear in the pit of her stomach when she thought about what they had seen in the cedar tree.

"Thank you," she said, the water squelching inside her shoes when they struck the ground. "For driving me." For some reason, she hesitated before turning toward her back door and looked up to find Justin's brows knit together over his sea green eyes. "What?"

He parted his lips then closed them then parted them again.

She reached up to grab her dripping ponytail, squeezing a tributary of water onto her chest. "I look ridiculous, don't I?"

For a second, she could have sworn his eyes followed the path of the water dripping lazily over her t-shirt and off the end of her breasts. Then he closed his eyes, leaning his head to rest on the leather seatback. "Yep, that's exactly what I was thinking."

Alex shook her head, flinging water droplets onto the dashboard. In her heightened emotional state, she was imagining things. Of course, he would take this opportunity to pick on her. "You're a butt face," she said calmly, trying to tame lips that quivered with a smile.

Justin's eyes popped open. "I think the last time you called me that was when we were eleven and I pushed you into the river while we were fishing."

Alex screwed up her face. "I think I screamed it at you while looking for something large and hard to throw in your direction."

Justin's shoulders shook with laughter as his head lolled back and forth. A surge of manageable terror ripped through her with the memory. She had always hated the river. Hated the brown, muddy swirl of water and what lied beneath it. Hated the way the water lapped against her skin like it wanted to invade every crevice, every pore, and extinguish the life right out of her.

"I've always hated that river," she said quietly. Justin stopped laughing, training his gaze on her face.

"I know," he said softly.

Alex felt awash in awkwardness with this little piece of her vulnerability exposed. "I need to go inside and change," she said, closing the door with a click. "I'll see you later."

She had only taken a few steps when Justin's voice halted her.

"Hey, do you want to hang out tonight? Maybe watch a terrible movie?"

It had been ages since they had done anything together. An unexpected jolt traveled through her heart.

"Like when we were kids?" she asked, slowly turning back around.

"Sure," he answered, his voice low and serious. Not like the tone he typically used around her. A solitary droplet of rain dangled from the end of his nose.

"Okay." She found herself nodding agreeably. "But there better be cake."

The shower scalded her face when she tipped her head back into the onslaught of rushing water. It ran down through her hair and swished over her lower back. The heat was a salve to her grief. A sublimate to the fear lurking under her skin. When she heard a door slam shut, Alex twisted the handles to turn off the water. She used her fingernail to pick away a line of rust that had formed on the seashell pink tiles of the shower wall.

"Mom?" she called from behind the billowing shower curtain. She heard the clink of keys into the silver bowl they kept on the kitchen counter before a ginger head appeared amidst the shower's leftover steam.

"Hi there, sweetie. I didn't want to scare you. Just wanted to make sure you knew it was me coming through the door."

Alex's face relaxed into a smile. "Thanks, Mom. I figured it was." She accepted the white cotton towel Janie handed her through the space between the shower curtain and the wall. "How was work?"

"It was good. I restocked an entire section of children's shoes and sold a pair of sandals to the nicest young girl. She was from Brazosville and said she was going to be in the fair queen competition this year."

Behind Janie's cheery tone, Alex heard the exhaustion. She hated that her mom worked two jobs. That every hard-earned penny went to caring for her or helping her save for college.

Janie disappeared into the hallway and called, "How was your day, sweetie?"

While she dressed in fresh jeans and a long-sleeved t-shirt, Alex debated what to tell her. A part of her resisted heaping another mound of worry onto her mom's ever-growing pile. She decided to trust her instincts. "It was fine," she said when her bare feet hit the faded flowery pattern of their kitchen linoleum.

"That's good." Her mom's back was to her as she fished around in the pantry and emerged with a jar of sauce. "Spaghetti okay for dinner?"

"You don't need to make me dinner, Mom. I'm seventeen years old. If I get hungry, I can feed myself." Alex wound her dripping hair up into a bun.

"It won't be long before I don't have anyone to cook for. Let me do it while I can." She smiled gently yet Alex noticed the worry lines deepen around her eyes.

"Okay then. Spaghetti is great." Alex pulled a rickety chair from the table and plopped down in it. "And you'll see me all the time next year. Texas University is only two hours away. I'll probably be begging for you to come visit me every weekend."

Rushing water from the faucet struck the bottom of a worn silver pot. "We'll see" was all Janie said in response.

Alex chewed in silence as she mulled over the events of the day. The pasta became a gooey mess in her mouth. She struggled to push it down her throat. Terry would be devastated. She was probably tucked in her office drowning her grief with yesterday's bottle of liquor. Everything that had happened over the last twenty-four hours made absolutely no sense. And what made even less sense was the weird symbol carved into the cedar tree next to a strung up dead possum.

Growing up here in the literal birthplace of Texas, the very spot where Stephen F. Austin had brought the first three hundred settlers, she had heard whispers of folklore from a rougher time. A crueler time when anyone who wasn't a white male was considered a lesser human. Alex knew there were isolated pockets of the county where suspicion and prejudice had been allowed to fester. Like where her father had been raised.

She only remembered visiting her father's parents once in the eight years her parents were together. It had been Christmas time. She had been wearing a red velvet dress that her mom had upcycled from a church hand-me-down and black patent shoes. When they pulled into the yard, it was a forest of old tires and a rusted car with a shattered back window. Her mom had helped her out of the truck and her new shoes had sunk into the red clay up to the white socks that gathered at her ankles. A yellow short haired dog with most of its ribs showing had stalked toward them with hackles raised until a gruff voice from the near-collapsing wooden porch called him off.

"Billy Ray! Come get yur dog and tie it up." The woman spoke with a mouth missing most of its teeth, her voice gravelly, a cigarette bobbing up and down from the outer corner of her lips. Her beady eyes had raked over Alex. "Get up here girl so's I kin see you."

She had smelled stale like dirty laundry. Alex didn't remember much else of the visit, only sitting on a stained sofa until late in the evening, watching her father and grandfather finish a bottle of brown stuff. Their voices had risen as the sun set. First becoming more animated and then angry. When they started scuffling, the dining room table had turned over and Alex's mom had carried her outside to the truck. Her dad came out several minutes later, blood splattered over his gaunt face and one eye almost swollen closed. They never went back after that.

Alex heard that her grandparents died in a housefire several years ago. A fire started by someone's leftover cigarette per the local fire department. A cigarette that had burned long after its owner had drunk herself into oblivion.

The phone jangled from its perch on the wall and Alex's middle involuntarily tightened.

"I'll get it," Janie offered, looking warily at Alex as she wiped her hands on the back pocket of her jeans and pulled the phone from its hook. "Hello. It's Janie Wilde."

Alex absentmindedly shoved another spoonful of pasta in her mouth. It had gotten cold while she burrowed deeper into her thoughts.

"Yes, she's right here," she heard Janie say into the receiver. Alex flicked her eyes upward, noting her mom's bemused expression.

"For me?" she mouthed silently, and Janie nodded. Alex jumped up from the table, nearly toppling over her water glass, and accepted the phone. She strung the cord behind her as she rounded the doorway that separated the kitchen from the hall.

"Hello?"

"Hey there." The husky voice on the line was not the one she had expected.

"Hi, Jake."

"Did I call at an okay time?"

"Yes. Sure...absolutely." Her stomach did a little nervous dip as he chuckled on the other end of the phone.

"Are you busy tonight?"

She trapped her bottom lip between her teeth. Fun and distraction. That's what her summer was supposed to be.

"No, I'm not busy." She inhaled a quick breath and before she could change her mind blurted, "Want to come over?"

When the twin rectangular beams of light from the silver coupe lit up her driveway, Alex was watching from her bedroom window. Janie had already gone to bed, feigning exhaustion and the need for her "beauty sleep." But Alex could tell that she was thrilled for her only daughter to experience a bit of normalcy.

Almost every weekend night of Alex's adolescence had been spent religiously devoted to her textbooks. Strangely, she had never viewed diligence and ambition as flaws. They would be the currency for her ticket out of Cole's Church and into a giant universe of possibility. Nothing else mattered. No sacrifice was too great to achieve her dreams. And she had already sacrificed the carefree existence of being a teenage girl. Of late nights comparing CD collections. First kisses behind the low hanging moss of a willow tree. Slumber parties with pizza and makeovers.

Despite her choices, she had never really felt like she had missed out. Until lately. Something thrummed inside her that she couldn't explain, pushing its way out of her pores. Something that craved recklessness and adventure. Like the way she felt on the back of a horse taking a jump at full speed or when Jake had moved in to kiss her last night. Was it just last night? It seemed ages ago. An entire day of tragedy wrapped in mystery had unfolded since then.

A knock resounded on the front door and her heart leaped into her throat. Tucking a strand of hair behind her ear, she sprinted to the front of the house then willed a wave of calm to wash over her before twisting the knob. Illuminated by the single porchlight, the contours of his face seemed more accentuated, his cheek bones sharper, his jaw more angular, the dimples in his cheeks deeper when he smiled. A smile that she knew she could get lost in, even if just for a while. A smile that would distract her from today.

"Hi there," he murmured.

"Hi." The flush deepened in her cheeks. "Want to come in?"

He nodded once and reached for her hand, allowing her to lead him over to the worn beige sofa. They settled into the dip in the middle facing one another, knee to knee, his fingers winding through hers with smooth precision.

"What did you do all day?" he asked, a callused thumb brushing over her knuckles.

The reel of the last twelve hours played out in her brain. She sifted and edited, forcing her mouth upward into a smile. "I went to church then to the barn. How about you?"

His chin dipped lower so that if she moved her head the slightest bit, her forehead would feel the brush of his hair, silky and dark like seal's fur. "I thought about you."

Alex's stomach dropped into her toes right before a healthy dose of disbelief surged. "No, you didn't," she said as her lips twitched into a smile.

He only smirked in response, the dimple in his left cheek deepening into a proper abyss. "Did you think about me?"

Alex blinked a few times. She had, hadn't she? "A little?" she answered, biting down on her bottom lip with her incisors. She could tell he didn't believe her by the way his lips curled up at the edges.

"Do I need a second chance to make an impression?"

She inhaled the air of his exhale, the taste of spiced mint on her tongue before she even felt his bottom lip connect with the sensitive corner of her mouth.

"You know you really shouldn't leave your backdoor unlocked."

Alex jumped at the sound of Justin's voice emanating from the kitchen. She used the momentum to scoot as far as she could away from Jake, draping her upper body over the rolled arm of the sofa.

"You never know who—" Justin rounded the corner, his face transitioning from smooth to murderous. "Might come in." He paused in the archway between the kitchen and the living room.

A rush of embarrassment filled every inch of Alex's skin. "Hey, I'm sorry I totally forgot we were hanging out tonight," she stammered.

"It's fine." Justin's tone was quiet, belying the angst churning under his skin. "You guys have fun," he said before turning around and retreating the way he had come.

Alex heard the screen door slam and then blew out a breath before turning an apologetic eye to Jake.

EIGHTEEN

Dark water lapped against her thighs, its ominous tentacles sucking her lifeforce with every slap of her skin. It was all around her with no beginning and no end. A darkness that absorbed every photon of light. Yet she continued forward toward a destination unknown, trying to reach somewhere, something, before the darkness swallowed her. The water rose higher. It was up to her chest now and so cold that she couldn't draw breath, and soon, it would be over her head.

Alex snapped her eyes open, the room she occupied as black as the night of a new moon. She felt oddly disconnected, like she existed somewhere between a dream and reality. The only thing exquisitely real was the sweat collecting along the band of her pajama pants. Her next inhale was heavy with heat and humidity. Sitting up, she threw one arm in the air. Nothing. No gentle wind from the air conditioning vent in the ceiling. Groaning, she flopped backward, her mattress squeaking in protest, and shoved her blankets to the end of the bed.

Their air conditioning malfunctioned at least once a year. What a day for it to happen when, despite being on the cusp of summer, the humidity made it seem like the middle of July. Sleep would not reclaim her, either because of the nightmare or the suffocating heat. She wasn't sure which. Maybe both. Sweat began pooling between her thighs. She sat up again, this time twisting her long layers into a bun.

From her bed, she leaned over to the window frame to curl her fingers under the sill and pushed upward until a light breeze kissed her face. Reclining into her pillows, she closed her eyes. In the stillness, a reel of images flashed and disappeared. The swirling water of her nightmare. The rain streaming through the branches of a cedar tree with a strange carving in its trunk. Bella's lifeless eye. Justin's stony expression as he glared at her from the doorway.

Alex had jumped off the couch and chased after him to the backdoor, spouting apologies the entire way. He hadn't responded as he covered the distance of her yard in about four strides.

The bitter taste of guilt filled the back of her throat followed closely by a spike of annoyance. How many times had Justin ditched her because he had a date? He had to understand. It's not like he relied on her companionship. Not anymore. Not like when they were kids. Things had changed. She had accepted long ago that their friendship had entered a dormant phase, spiking in importance every now and then when basketball season was over or Justin was between girlfriends. Their friendship was a constant among a constellation of ever-changing variables. Maybe he couldn't accept that she might be ready for something more.

And the *more* had turned out to be fun and freeing and brilliant. Her index finger traced her bottom lip, still plump and alive from being thoroughly kissed. The memory of it made her skin prickle all over again. Tugging her shirt over her head, she lay there, eyes behind heavy lids, relishing the wind snaking through the open window. She fell asleep imagining that it was something else caressing her bare chest.

As soon as the sun flared over the horizon, Alex popped out of bed and dressed quietly in the pink-tiled bathroom she shared with Janie. She scrawled "went to library. see you later" on a strip of paper and stuck it under a magnet that read "Don't mess with Texas." Swiping the keys from the plaque of hooks by the washer, she edged out of the screen door, closing it softly behind her. Her face scrunched up briefly as she glanced toward the shingled roof of Justin's house that was visible from her backyard.

Only a few cars sped down the narrow-laned highway when she veered her mom's faded blue sedan toward town. A few minutes later she had made it through most of Main Street, past the early morning petroleum plant workers filling up their trucks at the only gas station and the serpentine line of night shifters waiting at the small taco stand. When Alex pulled into a parking spot at the faded brown brick building with white block lettering, a hunched woman in spectacles with tight snow-white curls was inserting a key into the glass doors.

"Hello, Mrs. Vickery," she called out the open window of the car.

A coffee-colored hand fluttered in her direction and Alex skipped over to prop open the door with her foot.

"Thank you, dear," she huffed, adjusting her leather shoulder bag. "I think this door gets heavier every year." Her coral lips parted in a grateful smile. "You're here early, dear. Especially with it being summer vacation." She regarded Alex over the top of wire rimmed spectacles.

"I have some research to do," Alex responded. "It's kind of urgent."

"Oh." Her eyelids peeled back in interest.

Alex followed her into the doorway, relishing in the deliciously cool air carrying the rich odor of shelves and shelves of books.

"Well, that sounds exciting." She drew out the last word, pursing her lips so that the lines etched on her lower face coalesced at her mouth. A light flared in her gray eyes, magnified by the lenses of her glasses. She reminded Alex of a barn owl. A very curious barn owl. Everyone knew that the epicenter of town gossip was the public library.

"Can I help you find something?" Mrs. Vickery plopped her purse onto the counter and flipped a panel of switches, illuminating rows upon rows of neatly shelved book spines with carefully plastered-on barcodes. She eyed Alex expectantly, practically vibrating with interest.

"I'm looking for a book about—" Alex chewed her lip in hesitation, mentally conjuring the crude carving on the cedar tree. "Symbols. Maybe ones that would be specific to this area."

Confusion knit Mrs. Vickery's caterpillar-like brows together. "Take a seat at the table dear. I'll bring you what we have."

Moments later Alex's upper half was hidden behind a stack of decently thick textbooks. Textbooks that had most likely gone years, maybe decades, without being opened. A fine layer of dust imbued the jacket of the first book she opened, its spine cracking under the strain. Flipping open the weighty pages, she traced her index finger down the table of contents. Religious symbols. Symbols for communication. Ancient Greece. The zodiac. Hieroglyphs. Sighing, she left the thick volume open to a page depicting the Sanskrit alphabet and took another book off the stack. Hours passed and dust clogged her nasal passages. Alex rubbed her lower back where it had started to cramp.

"Any luck?" The rumbling voice surprised her. She glanced up to a somber face made leathery by decades of sun exposure. His straw cowboy hat was tipped back so that it revealed a sheen of sweat coating his forehead. A faded plaid shirt was tucked carefully into a pair of jeans held up by a braided leather belt. He held a foam cup in one hand, filled to the brim with aromatic ochre liquid.

"Not so far." Alex eyed him quizzically. How could he even know what she was doing? Over his shoulder, Mrs. Vickery gave Alex a serene smile and then returned to inscribing the inside cover of a paperback. Alex sighed. By now, the entire town most likely knew that Alex Wilde was spending her summer vacation at the community library.

"That mark you're lookin' for?" he drawled. "Can you draw it?"

Alex studied the burnished gold of his belt buckle engraved with a fat letter 'C'. "Sure, I think so."

Reaching down into the abyss of her messenger bag, she extracted a ballpoint pen and a half-crumpled sheet of paper. She smoothed a few of the wrinkles out of the paper before depressing the tip of the pen. Her mind rewound to the tree. The frozen smile of the dead possum hanging from the fraying rope and how her finger had traced the backward letter B cleaved in half by a horizontal line. When she was done, she handed him the paper, breath held as he scanned it with deep-set eyes. Eyes that had probably seen a lot and still didn't miss much.

"Never seen it." He grunted and folded the paper in half. Alex's spirits fell a realistic distance. She hadn't really expected him to know what it was. It might not even be anything.

"But—" He folded the paper in half again and laid it on the table amidst the pile of hardbound books. "It reminds me of a brand."

"Brand?" Alex's mouth turned down into a frown. "Like for cattle?"

"Yep. I believe so."

The wheels in Alex's brain began spinning at high revolution. "How do I find a record of all the brands used in the area?"

"County clerk's office. They'll have a list of everything registered 'round here."

Alex nodded, already planning out the remainder of her day. "Thank you. I really appreciate your help. What was your name again?"

"Jack...Jack Cole."

Alex froze into stunned silence. *Cole? As in Cole's Church?* It couldn't be. She had never even seen the name apart from a few solitary plots in the town cemetery. His mouth turned up in a grin as a hint of amusement danced across his eyes. She parted her lips with a question, but he had already shuffled past her and disappeared behind a five-tiered shelf.

Alex's fingers drummed a beat on the steering wheel as the car wheezed to a halt in a grassy spot in front of the barn. Her brain hurt from the effort of trying to assemble a puzzle without having all the pieces.

She squeezed between a black truck parked on one side and bulky maroon SUV with a notable dent in the hood on the other. Terry was here as well as Dr. Zielinski, the town veterinarian who everyone referred to as Dr. Z.

Despite being well into his fifties, he had a thick chest and fortitude to match. Alex had watched mesmerized while he controlled a flailing horse hoof with a gentle voice and the bulging muscles of his forearms. His face had been permanently bronzed from years under the sun and his hair faded to the color of beach sand. He was attractive for an older man. Alex had caught even Terry lingering a look a few seconds longer than she should have. She had always claimed they were friends, nothing more, but Alex had to wonder if she was the only one sneaking kisses in the twilight of the barn.

"Alex!" The wind carried a gentle tenor voice as her sneakered feet hit the grass.

"Hi, Dr. Z," she called, spying his tall silhouette clad in blue scrubs, standing in the shadowed entryway of the barn. As she drew closer, he extended a hand in greeting, and she took it earnestly.

"How's my favorite future veterinarian? Ready for me to offer you a job?"

Alex ducked her head as a rush of blood pinked her cheeks. "I'm good, but I have a long road before I need a job."

He nodded, amber eyes twinkling with delight. "I heard you already got into TU."

"I did."

"And that there were five people accepted into the fast-track vet program." He paused until she met the bemused expression on his face. "And one of them was you."

Her responding smile kept spreading over her face until it felt like her earlobes touched the corners of her lips.

"If you keep givin' her compliments, she's going to melt like butter on a hot Texas sidewalk." Terry's gravelly voice emerged from behind Dr. Z. She strode toward them, ruddy brown dust puffing up around her boots.

Sobering her expression, Alex pressed her palms together. "I'm so sorry about Bella, Terry," she said. "How are you holding up?"

"How do you think?" Terry ran a hand through her mousy shag hairdo. Alex waited for her to elaborate, but she didn't.

"Did you figure out what happened?" Alex clenched her abdominals in anticipation of another barbed comment.

Terry pursed her lips as Dr. Z's voice filled the void. "I think we did." He turned, motioning for Alex to follow. "Let me show you."

Alex followed Dr. Z to the feed room and watched him plunge his hand into a brimming barrel of sweet feed. He thrust a handful under her nose and, instead of the syrupy wholesome goodness of horse feed, she smelled something rotten like overripe fruit.

"What do you smell?"

"Something...tainted," Alex answered. Dr. Z nodded his approval and tossed the grain back into the barrel.

"I think," he said, rubbing two fingers along his structured chin, "that Bella died from poisoning."

Alex's eyes widened to saucers. "Why do you think that?"

"Terry said she foamed at the mouth right before she collapsed."

Alex nodded at the memory of froth spewing from the mare's nostrils every time she took a breath.

"And this horse feed smells like it's been contaminated with ionophore."

"What's that?" Alex leaned over and took a gentle whiff of the feed barrel.

"An additive they put in cattle feed that slows down certain bacterial growth. Completely safe for cows. Deadly to horses." Dr. Z shook his head and tossed the grain back into the abyss of the barrel. "The only strange thing is why the other horses didn't get sick."

Alex swallowed past the mutating lump in her throat. "Because Bella was the only one that got fed that night."

Terry's slight figure appeared behind Dr. Z. "What do you mean Bella was the only one?"

Alex twisted her hands together and side-eyed Terry who, despite her small stature, filled up the feed room doorway once her hands were parked on her hips. Alex ignored the churning shame in her chest. She had been so wrapped up in first kisses in the moonlight that she had forgotten to feed the rest of the horses.

"Bella didn't come in with the other horses Saturday night so I went out to get her," Alex said weakly. "I found her at the very back of the pasture and thought something had spooked her. She seemed edgy at first but completely fine once I gave her some oats. And then I forgot to feed the others."

Dr. Z's head riveted over his shoulder to exchange a knowing look with Terry. Another piece of the puzzle clinked into place so loudly that it echoed through Alex's brain. Her mind riveted to the whisps of fur becoming airborne as the possum swung side to side like a pendulum. The possum. The carving in the tree. Bella's death. It couldn't be coincidence.

"Can I show you guys something?" Alex managed to ask as her heart thundered in her chest.

Terry kept pace with her as they strode through the pasture toward the fence line. The silence was suffocating underneath the buzz of aggressive gnats in Alex's ear and the swish of Dr. Z's scrubs against blades of stubborn grass. The stench of decay nearly bowled her over when they emerged at the rear fence line. The possum corpse had baked in the sun and was made nearly unrecognizable by the swarm of black flies covering the carcass.

Their trio paused at the slanted boards of the fence. Terry's eyes were shards of stone as she surveyed the scene in front of them. Alex cleared her throat while inhaling the least amount of air possible.

"When Justin and I came out here to look around, we found this." Alex gestured toward the cedar tree.

Dr. Z stared straight ahead and ran a callused hand through his thinning hair. "This was probably just some local kids with nothing better to do."

Alex shook her head honing her gaze on the tree trunk where, if she squinted, the barely perceptible outline of the symbol became visible. "I don't think so," she insisted. "There's a weird mark carved into the tree trunk and when I found Bella the other night..." She frowned, realizing that a few details of that night had involuntarily slipped from her memory. Terry and Dr. Z had grim lines etched into their faces, a pair of bookends hanging on her every word. "I thought I saw a light bobbing through the woods like someone waving a flashlight."

Disbelief crowded out the interest in Dr. Z's eyes. Alex's voice wavered as she continued. "And then when I got back to the barn, the lights wouldn't turn on. I thought it was just a breaker but—"

Terry had remained in stony silence until now when she peered over Alex's crown to catch Dr. Z's attention. "This ain't no coincidence," she seethed and then she whipped her head to Alex. "What did you say that mark looked like?"

NINETEEN

Alex huddled deeper into a pile of pillows, hugging a stuffed brown dog to her chest as she replayed the day's events. Bella's death had been intentional, and not only that but shamefully malicious. The knowledge cut deep through her chest. She had been in denial before. A silly little girl trying to assemble a puzzle without appreciating how horrifying it would look once it was finished.

Earlier today, after searching the pasture for any clues, all three of them had squeezed into the barn office. Alex had watched Dr. Z and Terry pass a stash of bourbon back and forth as she retold the events of Saturday night, careful to leave nothing out. Well, almost nothing. Terry and Dr. Z didn't need to know about her make out session with Jake Brady under the cover of moonlight.

When she had re-drawn the backward B slashed in half by a horizontal line on a sheet of yellowing paper, Terry had squinted at it then shook her head.

"The man at the library seemed to think it was some kind of cattle brand," Alex offered. She eyed the half empty bourbon bottle, tempted to swipe a swig herself.

"Not one I've ever seen," grunted Terry and then put the bottle to her lips.

"Me neither," said Dr. Z, rubbing two fingers across the gray stubble littering his chin.

"But whoever poisoned the feed has to be the same person who left a dead possum hanging in a tree." It all sounded incredibly illogical when Alex said it aloud.

Dr. Z inhaled sharply then drummed his fingers on the desktop. "Someone obviously wants credit for their work," he said wryly, then reached for the neck of the bottle.

Terry snorted. "Maybe they'll come around again so I can give it to 'em." She gestured to her right where a double barrel shotgun sat propped in the shadow of a metal filing cabinet.

Dr. Z swallowed audibly then exhaled so forcefully that the liquor vapors wafted up Alex's nose. "They'd deserve it," he said quietly. "The only reason all your horses aren't dead is because Alex got distracted and forgot to feed 'em." He winked and Alex felt her face go up in flames.

When the telephone rang, Alex relinquished her hold on her stuffed companion and made a move to rise. She didn't bother keeping a phone in her room when the kitchen one with its extendable cord could reach just about anywhere in the house. A light knock brushed against her bedroom door and her poster of Secretariat was suddenly exchanged for her mom's profile.

"It's for you," Janie said, proffering the receiver with one hand while she pulled some slack on the cord with the other.

"Thanks, Mom," Alex mouthed, putting the handle to the shell of her ear and tucking it into her shoulder. "Hello?"

"Hey there," murmured a smooth voice that reminded Alex of dark chocolate chunk ice cream right as it reached its melting point.

"Hi, Jake." The flush was already blooming in her cheeks by the time Janie gently eased the bedroom door closed. "What are you doing?"

"I'm more interested in what you're doing."

The blush turned into crackling flames that licked the edge of her hairline. Wow, he was good. She groaned and reached over to redirect her box fan so that it blew across her face.

"Trying to pretend I'm in the Arctic surrounded by mounds of ice and snow."

"What?" He snorted with laughter on the other end of the phone.

"Our air conditioner is broken right now."

"Whoa that sucks."

"Yeah. Summer is not my favorite season right now."

"Oh? I thought your summer was getting pretty interesting."

"Oh, really? How so?" A delicious rush whooshed up her middle before flipping over and settling in her lower abdomen.

"Come out with me tomorrow and you'll find out," he murmured.

Indecision tore at her and she ground her teeth together. "I...can't. I have plans tomorrow night." She heard the beginnings of a protest building in his throat. "But I'm free next weekend."

"Fair weekend?"

"Yeah, is that okay?"

"It's a date. See you then, Alex."

In the frenetic two weeks since junior year had ended and summer break had descended, Alex had gone to her first pasture party, kissed someone for the first time, and was now sucked into a vortex of mystery regarding an equine tragedy. She had barely thought about the biggest event of the summer—The Day of the Old Three Hundred. Every year since Alex could remember, the entire county set aside the third week in June to celebrate Stephen F. Austin's arrival with the original three hundred families to southeast Texas in 1836. Alex glanced upward at the blue lettered banner spanning the street as she and Natalie slowed to a stop.

"I hate parallel parking," Natalie whimpered, glancing over her right shoulder as she maneuvered the car into an empty space.

"You're good at it," Alex encouraged her, flitting her eyes between the chrome bumpers of the bordering vehicles.

"I know but it gives me hives," Natalie said through gritted teeth as she jerked up the emergency brake.

An elegant woman waved at them through a pane of crystal-clear glass. She wore a yellow belted dress and matching heels, her hair cropped short with a spectrum of gold highlights. The door chimed energetically as she thrust it open.

"Good morning, girls! Come on inside." Her voice was practiced and neat like a perfectly cut square of wedding cake.

"Hi, Mrs. Ashwell," Alex chirped as she watched the finely painted lips plant a kiss on Natalie's crown when they entered the quaint shop.

"Hi, Mom," Natalie murmured before becoming distracted by a tiara set atop the white polyfoam bust of a mannequin. "Thank you everyone," she purred, propping the tiara onto her head. "I'm honored that you chose me as this year's Fair Queen."

A French-manicured hand gently disentangled the combs from Natalie's strawberry blond waves and returned it to the mannequin. "When you win the crown," she said, "you get to keep the crown." A lavender eyelid closed over a cornflower blue iris in a wink.

"There is no way Natalie won't win," Alex said, admiring a set of chandelier costume earrings that dripped with fake diamonds.

Mrs. Ashwell owned the best, and only, bridal shop in a tri-county area, a mecca for blushing brides seeking a pile of taffeta and lace that resembled a well-frosted cake. Alex had always loved the shop since the first time Natalie had brought her here when they were barely fifteen. She loved the faded wood floors scuffed with heel marks and the organized chaos of wedding paraphernalia that sparkled in the gentle light streaming through the glass storefront. Generations of women had bonded here over silhouettes and bodices. Over hair up or down. Over whether a certain dress revealed too much skin or too little. All amidst the rustle of fabric and the clicking of Mrs. Ashwell's heels.

"I assume you're here to try on your fair dress," she said pointedly, shifting a cluster of aluminum hangers to the other side of a metal rod. Yanking a cream garment bag from the back of the rack, she ceremoniously descended the zipper to reveal a swathe of glittery green fabric adorned with gold sequins.

"It's even more fabulous than I remembered," Natalie sighed and floated off to the curtained dressing room. Alex accepted the dress and carried it like an over-sized child to the rear of the store where she passed it to Natalie's twitching fingers.

"Alex, why don't you look around and see if there's anything you'd like to wear for pageant night," Mrs. Ashwell prompted amidst the rustling sounds of Natalie shimmying into the dress.

"Yeah, Alex. Go look for something new. Something that will make Jake drool all over his baseball jersey." Her pale blue eyes, so much like her mother's, suddenly appeared in the gap between the curtain and the wall. She waggled her perfectly plucked brows knowingly.

Alex rubbed the frayed edge of her denim shorts between her thumb and index finger and frowned. "I can't," she said. "I'm trying to save everything I'm making at the barn this summer. It's my last full summer of work before I—"

"We know," Natalie interrupted rolling her eyes. "Your last summer before you rush out of here for college and your big career."

She started to respond but there was nothing to refute. Natalie was right. Alex had said so herself on more than one occasion.

"There's no such thing as can't. There's only won't," chimed Mrs. Ashwell as she floated over to a spinning rack of cocktail dresses.

"Is that what you tell your flustered brides?" asked Alex, a smile tugging her mouth upward.

Natalie's mom responded by pursing her lips and flipping through a ream of dresses in every color of the rainbow from exquisite silver to deepest blue to ballet pink. She extracted a short strapless dress in pale robin's egg blue made from a lightweight spun silk. A dress that would hug her form in all the right places and maybe even create a curve or two. A dress the exact shade of Jake's blue eyes. The dress appeared in front of Alex, swinging from the end of a bony outstretched arm.

"Mrs. Ashwell, I can't afford that."

"Who said you were buying it dear? It deserves a little field trip. Just bring it back in the same condition that it left the store."

"I can't believe your mom," Alex said as the wind from the open car window whipped her ponytail across her face in stinging little lashes.

Natalie adjusted her white cat-eye sunglasses and smiled. "We're going to have so much fun this weekend. I can hardly stand it." She exhaled in a soprano sigh and Alex knew the "we" most likely included a certain sandy-haired baseball player. Alex smiled. *Good for her. And good for me.* She had never realized summer flings could be so invigorating.

"Are we still on for the movies? I can't spend one more night sitting in our house. It feels like a sauna." Two solid hours in the arctic chill of the four screen multi-plex cinema sounded like heaven.

Natalie bit her lip between her teeth. "Oooh."

"What?" Alex asked. "You forgot?"

"I made plans with Cory, but we could totally pick you up and all go see something."

Alex shook her head as she caught sight of a massive billboard with a chaotic herd of cattle followed by men on horseback. "No, actually, that's okay. I owe someone an apology. Can you drop me off at the Farm and Ranch?"

The entire time Alex trekked the length of the concrete aisle to the very back of the Farm and Ranch storeroom, she noticed Justin darting cool glances her way. *Click clack.* It wasn't the first time they had disappointed one another but it was the most recent. Typically, it was Justin doing the apology walk not Alex. She straightened her spine and kept going.

The worst infraction had happened in sixth grade. Before she had any other close friends. Lunchtime had been perfect contentment with Justin and a book for company. One day Billy Watson stole her copy of *The Black Stallion* and tossed it to Justin. Instead of giving it back, he had tossed it to Mark Davis, who had thrown it into the courtyard where it was pouring rain. After a solid week of the silent treatment, a brand-new copy of the book had appeared in her mailbox, and all was forgiven.

"Hi," she said when she could smell the sweetness of hay mixed with Justin's sweat.

"Hi yourself," he grunted as he threw a sack of feed over his shoulder then piled it onto a growing pyramid.

Here went nothing. "Look, I'm sorry. Jake called and I totally forgot we were supposed to hang out the other night. I've been distracted because I really like him. More than I thought I would." She paused, heat flooding her veins as she realized this thing with Jake might have become more than fun and distraction. Justin cocked a thick brow but said nothing. "Anyway, I want to make it up to you. Want to go to the movies tonight? My treat."

Both brows rose in sync then flattened above the steely gleam in his eyes. "If you throw in popcorn—a large popcorn—I'm in," he said flatly but the smile tugging the corners of his mouth gave him away.

"Okay. It's a d—deal," she stuttered. She had almost said date. It definitely was not a date.

"I'm off in ten," he said, glancing at his watch. "I'll go clean up in the back." He reached into his pocket and tossed her the keys to his Jeep.

By the time Justin emerged from the side door of the rust-colored building, Alex was blaring boy band pop music from his radio and moving her shoulders to the captivating rhythm.

"I can't believe you like that song," he chastised her, tossing a black sports bag into the Jeep's back seat.

"I know." Alex wrinkled her nose. "It's just so addictive."

He scoffed in response but didn't move to change the station.

The leather creaked in the seat next to her as he leaped into the vehicle. Other than the sound of gears shifting and tires churning over the soundtrack of a harmonizing boy band, a welcome bubble of silence filled the air. Alex squinted into the horizon as they sped down the highway over the brown snake of a river that divided their county into two halves. A vast expanse of flat land topped with sprouting pecan trees gave shade to the clusters of bovine lounging below the branches. A pair of calves with rust colored fur accented with white patches leaped and bucked through a patch of clover.

Houses divided the expansive tracts of land. Small squatty ranch style homes with shingled roofs transitioned into two-story brick masterpieces surrounded by pristine white fences as they approached the city. City was a generous term to use for Brazosville, but compared to Cole's Church, it was a metropolis. A major thoroughfare to Houston ripped right through the middle of it, filled with the congestion of commuter traffic.

The presence of a major highway had birthed an outcropping of shopping malls and chain restaurants. They passed the diner with red halogen lettering where Alex had eaten her first cheeseburger and the shoe store where Janie brought her every year to purchase new sneakers for school. They passed the gold-painted lettering of the bridal shop. Alex watched Natalie's mom twist the lock on the glass double doors. An entire lifetime of memories had all happened within a twenty-mile radius.

Well, that was about to change. A stirring thrill curled Alex's toes as Justin swung the Jeep around a corner. A thrill that had nothing to do with the change in velocity.

"Are you going?" Justin glanced up at the suspended blue letters that she and Natalie had passed under only hours earlier.

"Yeah," Alex answered absentmindedly. "Jake asked me."

A blush like a rose's vine crept up her neck. She tried to dilute it with her next rush of words. "But I have to be there anyway to help Natalie with her dress. She's in the fair queen pageant Saturday night and…" She babbled on about the dress Natalie's mom had special ordered from New York and the way she planned to do her hair. "I guess I'm going as her lady-in-waiting."

Justin grunted as he eased the Jeep into a parking space. It sailed through Alex's stream of words like a carefully thrown stone.

"What?" she barked. "You don't like her, do you?"

For a second, the cloud of melancholy that Justin had been existing under lifted when he flashed her a wicked smile. "I never said that, Lex."

He stilled for a moment. It was so rare for him to pause for words that Alex caught herself staring. She noticed the lean muscular legs tucked under the steering wheel, so long that they banged the dash every time he shifted gears. The chest that had broadened and the midsection that had flattened over the last several years until even she had to admit he was more a man than a boy now. Not the boy who used to race her home from the bus along their dusty, then unpaved, road. Not the boy who had stuffed his cheeks so full of marshmallows during a campout that she had to pull them out with her own fingers so he wouldn't choke. Not the boy who helped her raise a baby turtle in her bathtub. Her head jerked back with the force of his hand on her ponytail.

"Come on. I'm hungry."

Well, maybe still a boy in some ways.

The aroma of buttered popcorn was carried on a rush of frigid air. Alex sniffed greedily when she breezed through the theater doors ahead of Justin. The multi-plex reminded her of lazy summer days when she was dropped off to watch movies while her mom ran errands. Simple days when she filled up on all the candy that two dollars in loose change could buy and pretended to be Princess Leia when no one was looking.

"Contact or ConAir?" asked Justin scanning the black lettered billboard.

A fresh-faced scientist who discovered the existence of alien lifeforms or a convicted elite soldier who saved the day by foiling the escape plot of a group of prisoners. She knew exactly which movie Justin would choose and sighed. "Two tickets for ConAir please."

A surly teen with a pock-marked face handed them a pair of tickets and directed them toward number four. "It's about to start," he called after them.

As Justin reached out to grasp the silver door handle, Alex tiptoed up to whisper, "You grab the seats and I'll get the popcorn." He froze, his face tightening for a moment before he nodded and disappeared into the black abyss of the theater. By the time she crept inside with the largest bucket of popcorn she could carry, the mournful yet witty dialogue had already started overlaid by the sounds of shifting body parts and crunching.

"What did I miss?" Alex whispered.

Justin said nothing. Instead, his large hand dove into the popcorn bucket and he continued staring straight ahead. As he shoved popcorn in his mouth in handfuls, he smiled, and Alex finally began to relax. Whatever was bothering him seemed to have dissipated. Settling into the threadbare fold-out seat, she welcomed the next two hours of silence and disconnection from the world.

Halfway through the movie while the drama unfolded in a hijacked airplane, Alex crossed her legs and shifted in her seat for the hundredth time. Grinding her teeth to stifle a groan, she edged into the aisle. Justin hadn't looked at her once during the movie, so she startled when his hand snaked out and grabbed her wrist.

"Where are you going?"

Alex cocked her head toward the exit. "Bathroom." Her voice was barely audible, a whisper of words through open lips. She saw him glance at the large diet soda, now empty in her cup holder, and roll his eyes.

Alex entered the aisle and ignored the angry looks daggered in her direction. Letting the door close softly behind her, she paused while her pupils adjusted to the bright lights. A swelling crowd jostled forward at the theater next door and a familiar backside caught her eye. A blue t-shirt tucked into low slung jeans. Hair that gleamed bluish black in the incandescence overhead. A ropey forearm slung over the thin shoulders of a blonde in an indecently short denim skirt. She tipped up her face, a perfectly done face with just the right amount of shine to her lips, and pressed those lips right onto Jake Brady's welcoming mouth.

TWENTY

One thunderous heartbeat pounded into the back of her sternum. Then another. Alex glanced wildly at the archway to the ladies' room that loomed beyond Jake's head and back at the solid doors of the theater and then back to the hand sliding up and down the blonde girl's back. Curse words ping ponged through her brain so forcefully that her gray matter felt sliced into pieces. She twisted to grasp the silver handle of the theater door, but her bladder protested so violently that she hissed under her breath.

"Shit."

Alex whirled back around, keeping pace with the rest of the crowd, willing her eyes to focus on the faded burgundy carpet littered with gum wrappers and flattened popcorn kernels. She reached back and pulled the elastic band from her hair, allowing the waves to cascade over her face and hide it from view. And then she edged past the last place she had seen Jake wrapped around a girl who probably smelled like summer roses. High pitched grating laughter wormed its way into her ears, and she tried to shut it out. Only a few feet to go. The smell of stale paper towels and disinfectant reached her nose and for once she welcomed it.

She was almost there. Mere feet from the arched entrance when her shoe caught on a section of puckered carpet. She pitched forward, her knees slamming into the floor. Twenty pairs of eyes riveted toward her as she slowly rose into a crouch then brushed the lint from her knees. She had to know if he had seen her.

Once her tunnel vision cleared, Alex spotted his raven head craning toward her, his face a mixture of confusion and anguish. He looked sick to his stomach. She held up an awkward hand to wave at his date who stared at her like she was infected with the plague. Disentangling his arm from around the girl's waist, Jake started toward her.

"Alex?"

Move, she commanded herself silently, and her legs darted into the only place Jake couldn't follow her.

"Alex," she heard him shout again before she flung open the door to the first empty stall.

She stayed in there for a long while. Much longer than usual. So long in fact that her senses dulled to the grime coating the floor and the air laden with perfume and aerosolized urine.

Staring at her face in the mirror, she rotated her head side to side examining the minute details of her features. Maybe it was the subtle point to her chin or the size of her eyes relative to her face. Or the ridiculous blemish on her right cheek. Maybe it was her awkward speech or, she looked closer at the bow of her upper lip, the way she kissed. Maybe she was terrible at it.

Under the calm visage that stared back at her, an uncomfortable prickling spread through skin that no longer felt like her own. The rims of her eyelids bloomed a fierce red although she didn't remember shedding tears. She dabbed them with the edges of a roughly spun paper napkin.

He had promised her nothing. Yet, for the price of her first kiss, the first brush of her lips against another human's, the first intimate touches to her giddy skin, she had to admit that she had expected more. *Fun and distraction.* She had lied to herself to conceal the truth growing and spreading through her body like a virus. Something had taken hold of her. A desperation to live. To be reckless and wild. A desperation for something more.

A tall shape entered the bathroom and, in the mirror, Justin's gangly form leaned against the graffitied wall.

"You can't be in here," Alex sniffed, tossing her balled up napkin toward the trash bin. It bounced off the edge and landed at Justin's feet.

He picked it up and, without taking his eyes from Alex, tossed it over his shoulder right into the black hole center of the can. "I forgot how terrible you are at basketball," he teased, quirking his lips in a smile.

"Apparently I'm terrible at a lot of things," she sighed, checking her appearance once more before turning around to see his eyes narrowed into slits.

"I would ask what happened but I already—"

"Saw Jake Brady," Alex finished.

"When you didn't come back, I got worried," he explained, his eyes hardening into malachite.

Alex glanced toward the door, fearing that the vision of him groping his date's behind would be permanently etched into her memory. "It's fine. It's not like we were...it's not like he ever..." Alex stumbled over her words as she trudged toward the doorway. Justin's fingers wrapped around her elbow when she brushed past him.

"It's not fine," he said quietly.

Her eyes pleaded with his to say nothing more. "Let's just go home."

The starlight-infused wind whipped past her eyes, its evaporative effects drying any tears that had defied her and remained. She let the thumping bass replace the ache in her chest until it seeped into her very bones. And then she plucked the precious petals from the flower of her memory and discarded them. His scent. Sugared words and moonlight kisses. There were more important things to focus on. As the Jeep shifted gears, so did her entire being, renewed by exquisite purpose. She leaned forward to turn down Justin's blaring rap music.

"Terry doesn't think Bella's death was an accident."

Justin whipped his head toward her so quickly that the Jeep swerved. "What?"

"Terry doesn't think—" Alex repeated loudly.

"No, I heard you the first time." His lips tightened in a grim line. "I just meant, why? Who? How?"

"I can only answer the how part," Alex replied, squinting into the night as a pair of headlights loomed on the highway opposite them. "Dr. Z thinks Bella was poisoned. She was the only one who got oats that night because I...forgot to feed the others."

"How did you forget to feed the other horses?"

"I was distracted by something stupid."

"You mean *someone* stupid?"

Alex ignored him and pressed on. "Dr. Z thinks that someone put a type of cattle product in the horse feed. A substance that's fatal to horses." Alex shivered with the re-appreciation of what had actually happened to Bella. It was terrifying in a way that only reality could be.

"Any idea who?" Justin asked.

Alex shook her head. "No, but Dr. Z thinks that the person who tripped the electrical breaker and poisoned the feed is the same one who left the dead possum and that weird mark on the tree."

A row of lines appeared in Justin's forehead. "And why? Terry have any enemies?"

"Who knows? She's not the friendliest person but this was extreme. It was...evil."

Justin's chin dipped in solidarity as the first suffused lights of Cole's Church appeared in the veil of black that had descended on them.

"I went to the library yesterday to figure out what the mark could mean."

Justin grinned from ear to ear and a deep chuckle escaped his throat. "Of course, you did."

Alex lightly punched his bicep and he responded by reaching over to squeeze the sensitive area where her thigh met her knee. She squealed as they eased around a curve to enter the downtown stretch of Main Street and pulled to a stop at a rusted porte-cochere. A woman in a knotted pink t-shirt stood cleaning a drive through window with a spray bottle.

"Did you find out anything?"

Alex shook her head. "Not really." The image of a leathery face with deep-set gray eyes flashed through her mind.

Justin regarded her curiously. "I know exactly what we need," he announced, yanking up the emergency brake and swinging out to the ground using the doorframe.

Alex checked her watch and cast a furtive glance at the lady. "I think they're closing up, Justin."

Her words fell on deaf ears as she watched him stride over to the woman in pink, her dyed blonde hair put up in a banana clip, ebony roots visible along her part. She set the spray bottle on the ground and folded her arms across her chest as Justin smiled down at her. Her head cocked in a question. When he nodded vigorously, she casually placed a lily-white hand on his bicep and squeezed. *Oh brother.* He flashed up two fingers and she disappeared back into the building, emerging a few minutes later with two large foam cups. Her cheeks blushed when Justin thanked her before she resumed scraping the outside window.

"You are a shameless flirt," Alex chided when he passed her a drink.

"Never said I wasn't." He settled into the driver's seat.

Alex examined the pink hued liquid undulating beneath the plastic lid. "Is this what I think it is?"

"Cherry limeade. Extra on the lime," he sang, piercing his own cup with swordsman-like precision. Her mouth watered and she leaned down to wrap her lips around the straw. "Hold on there." Justin pressed the heel of his hand to her forehead. "Do you remember the summer after third grade?"

"When your grandmother used to drop us off in town while she got her hair done at the beauty parlor?"

"Uh-huh."

"And we would spend all afternoon walking Main Street?"

"And?" He used his elbow to dig into her ribs.

Scrunching her eyes closed, she reveled in the memory. "We would buy cherry limeades."

It was the summer of 1989. The sun beat down on her forehead until a sheen of sweat stretched from one braided pigtail to the other. She wiped a sweaty palm across the faded rainbow on her tanktop and then used it to wave at the passenger in the blue sedan clunking down the street. She swung her feet off the stone bench, her trainers barely scraping the top of the overgrown grass filling the gentle knoll in the middle of town. Another car honked as it passed her, a cloud of exhaust billowing from its tailpipe like a giant puffed marshmallow.

Waves of heat shimmered up from the asphalt street, partially blocking her view of two stick-like legs sporting long tube socks waiting in line at the drive through window. His red mesh shorts hung off bony hips, the same hips that supported a basketball the size of a juicy pumpkin. He twisted around and split his wide mouth into a smile that showed a row of teeth almost too big for his face.

Offering a hesitant wave, Alex smiled back. Her first one in such a long time. After that one, they came easier and easier all summer until smiling once again become effortless.

Justin's pressured speech interrupted her trip down memory lane. "Same rules apply. Same stakes. Winner takes all." He peered at her so intensely that it stopped her breath just short of exhaling.

"Okay." She steeled herself for what was coming next.

"On three. One...two...three!"

Alex swallowed her laughter as Justin snatched his straw between his teeth and began huffing huge gulps of liquid into his mouth.

Focusing on her own straw, she shoved it into the back of her mouth and began taking long draws of ice-cold beverage, the mixture of sweet and tang and bubbles coating the back of her throat. The sound of aggressive slurping urged her to suck faster until the chill turned to pain behind her sternum.

A lid sailed past her lap onto the floorboard, and she caught sight of Justin digging frantically through a mound of pellet ice until his two fingers emerged with a lime slice and a perfectly round cherry. Removing her own lid, she scooped fingerfuls of ice and hurled them at Justin while he sucked the juice from the lime then popped the cherry into his mouth. As he fist-pumped the air in a flourish of victory, she stuffed her own lime in her mouth, her next words garbled by the thick rind.

"You still have to tie the stem!"

Pursing his lips, Justin spit a neatly tied stem into her lap, along with a delicate showering of saliva droplets. Alex took one last draw from the lime and dropped it into her lap.

"You're disgusting." She attempted a glower but failed and clutched her now dangerously full stomach and laughed.

"There it is," he remarked triumphantly, gesturing toward her with open palms.

"There what is?" She still hadn't managed to find her cherry and shook her cup violently to separate what remained of her ice.

"That laugh." He tucked her grown out layers behind her ear, the tips of his fingers warm against her temple. Her entire body quieted. "I missed it," he admitted.

"I missed you too," she said quietly, watching him stare at the worn spot on his jeans his neat brows combining into one long fuzzy line. A frog bellowed out a croak that sliced through the quiet and Alex blinked. "So, you won, now what?"

If childhood rules still applied, the loser would be required to do the winner's bidding for the rest of the day. A wicked smirk appeared on Justin's lightly stubbled face.

"I'm feeling a need to visit the cemetery."

A moan started in Alex's chest and grew until it left her mouth in the form of a wail. "Nooo!"

"I haven't even said the best part."

"I'm afraid to ask."

"You're going to drive me."

Alex stomped her foot on the clutch and dragged the gear shift into reverse. Looking over her shoulder, she eased backward until she reached an incline in the parking lot that led to the street level.

"You're going to regret this," she gritted as she pressed her foot onto the gas pedal and the Jeep lurched backward.

Justin scrambled to hook his hand onto the metal frame, his head snapping forward when Alex braked. "Probably," he said, yet grinned from ear to ear when she transitioned into first. "Now give it some gas and let off the clutch."

Her feet pulsed in opposite directions, the engine in a constant state of crescendo/decrescendo until the tires spun and jerked them forward.

"Holy hell," Alex cursed as the engine whined in protest when she depressed the gas pedal even more.

"It's time for second, Lex."

Her sweaty palm wrapped the gearshift in a death grip and popped the clutch, the Jeep shuddering in response.

"I hate you," she griped, "and I wish I could—"

"Okay, here comes a stop light," he interjected. "Just let up on the gas, push her into neutral and press the brake."

Alex hit the clutch and shifted but instead of slowing down, the Jeep continued barreling forward.

"What's happening?" she yelped.

"You're in third not neutral."

The stop light flickered from green to yellow when they were several yards away.

"What do I do?" Her brain and her extremities had disconnected in traitorous mutiny. "Justin!" she shrieked.

He glanced up at the light which had just changed to red. "Nobody's on the street. Just run it."

As the Jeep rolled through the red light, the wind stung her lashes. She stole a glance at the gas station on the corner where a man filling up his lawnmower stared at her wide-eyed. Next to her, Justin whooped with laughter. She didn't dare remove her hands from the steering wheel to smack him.

Gritting her teeth, she depressed the clutch once more and jerked the gearshift downward into fourth. Their trajectory smoothed out as they reached a wider portion of the street lined by the winking lights of one-story homes. She veered off a fork in the road that took them down an unnamed street that ran along an intimidating iron fence. The engine groaned as she began to slow, veering around a set of red taillights parked catawampus in the grass, the car windows covered in a light sheen of fog.

"Wonder what they're doin'?" snickered Justin.

Alex ignored him and concentrated on shifting into neutral then braking. The Jeep shuddered as it rolled to a complete stop at the street's dead end. A fitting finale for the entrance to the Cole's Church cemetery. As the last guttural moans of the vehicle transitioned into beautiful silence, Alex leaned her head into the leather seatback and inhaled. The air, sweet and warm, filled her nose with the delicious scent of honeysuckle.

"I did it," she said.

"Yeah. You did. And next time I feel the urge to fly in a fighter jet, I'll just jump in the car with you."

This time Alex did smack him in the chest with her palm. "It wasn't that bad."

"Oh, it was."

In the dark night, his face was a blend of shadow, but she could tell he was smiling.

"Are you ready for your next task?"

"I can't believe you're making me go in there."

She peered into the gaping hole of the cemetery gate, a realm of black except for the ghostly gray headstone silhouettes popping up from the mossy ground. Justin held three fingers close to her face, ticking them off one by one.

"You have to find a fresh daisy, a person buried in 1977, and a headstone with some kind of animal on it."

Alex winced as she unbuckled her seatbelt to slide out of the driver's seat. Justin passed her a flashlight and she scurried through the grass to the entrance before fear won out.

"Just remember," he called, "if you see any supernatural creatures, scream as loud as you can so I can start running away."

The grass, already wet with condensate from the day's humidity, soaked the toes of her sneakers through to her socks on her walk toward the twin oak trees that marked the start of the gravesites. Her heart thundered behind her sternum, a symphony of fear mixed with adrenaline. She hated being scared; she had always hated being scared. The only people that didn't were the ones who had never endured actual terror.

Within a few minutes, her pupils adjusted to the dark and she willed her breathing to slow. Breathe in. Breathe out. No one could hurt her in here. Everyone was already dead. Like poor granny Ashwell. She had died last winter from pneumonia. Alex passed her headstone, her name carved into thick block letters. She couldn't decipher the epitaph written in a ladylike script. She wondered what someone would write on her gravestone when she died. What would she want them to write? Here lies Alexandra Wilde...

When she shook her head to scatter those thoughts to a remote corner of her brain, a shape caught her eye. A vase teetered on the top of the headstone in the next row. Tiptoeing over to the wilting floral arrangement, she reached out and plucked a flower from the bunch. A white petaled daisy with a cheerful yellow center smiled up at her. Jackpot. She stuffed it into her back pocket.

Like a prowling cat, she slunk to the right between a cedar and the giant statue of an angel with enormous, curved wings. As she crept by another row of headstones, the ambient light from town faded into speckles. Her eyes strained as they swept back and forth for anything that looked like the silhouette of an animal. In the distance, along the back corner of the cemetery where the grass hardly ever got trimmed, she spotted something with four legs standing guard over a rock-filled cairn.

Alex started toward it, success humming in her ears, moving silently between gravestones like a specter herself. A gust of wind puffed through the cemetery. She shivered despite the warm night, her heart rate kicking up another notch. She wasn't going to sleep a wink once she got home. A car backfired on the bordering street, the sound zapping her legs into motion until she was in a full jog.

As she closed in on her target, the shape became more familiar. A delicate muzzle and spindly legs emerged from the darkness. A fawn carved from pure alabaster, its feet caught in mid-stride. It was ethereal and captivating. Alex drew closer, heart pounding in her ears, her breath coming in short bursts until her momentum abruptly halted. She catapulted forward in a heap, the toe of her sneaker wedged under a jagged rock.

When she lifted her head, she tasted blood in her mouth, a thick ooze of metallic mixed with earth. Reaching up a shaky hand, she rubbed a finger over the linear split in her lower lip. She used her other hand to search the grass for the flashlight that had tumbled out of her hand when she fell. Finding the reassuring metal, she flicked it back on.

Deep in the grass, buried under an intricate labyrinth of criss-crossing roots, a corner of granite protruded. Putting her t-shirt to her lip to staunch the blood, she ripped away the grassy carpet covering this long-forgotten grave marker. Maybe she would be in luck and it would be the one she needed to complete her trifecta of tasks.

When a pile of weeds lay next to her, she surveyed the surface, smooth and speckled underneath a thick layer of dirt. She flattened her palm to brush away the grime, and a name came into view. A name and a date and a marking. She felt every bit of her next heartbeat slam against her chest as she traced the backward B with a horizontal line slashed through its center.

TWENTY-ONE

Alex stared at her reflection in the round ornate bathroom mirror and touched her lower lip that was now knit back together with a thin seam of dried blood. She rubbed one finger across it. Tender but not exquisitely painful.

When she had arrived back at the Jeep, jittering with adrenaline and blood covering her chin, Justin had jumped nearly three feet in the air and screamed like a drowning cat. He had deserved it.

Alex traced her jawline with her index finger where his hand had clasped her chin and examined the damage. It was different when he touched her these days, even when he was teasing her. It was purposeful. More tentative than she remembered. And something else. What was it? It was no longer comfortable and meaningless. Something lived there between them. A different entity that she had ignored lately and wasn't sure she wanted to explore. *Expectation.*

Reaching into her back pocket, she pulled out the scrap of notebook paper where she had traced the name and the mark from the headstone. J. Powell 1924-1945. She didn't know any Powell's. Not a single person in school or church or anyone in town she had ever met. But it was something. The tiny gift of a clue that she could birddog into fruition.

The day of the fair dawned in the most spectacular way with a swirl of pink and purple pushing its way through the gauzy white curtains fluttering over Alex's open bedroom window. She prayed some of the humidity would wane so her hair might actually last until tonight's pageant. Not that her appearance mattered much. But as Natalie's lady-in-waiting this evening, she did not want to disappoint.

Somewhere in the house a door burst open followed by a vibrant exchange of words. One voice was her mom's lilting Texas twang and the other Natalie's full-throated soprano. She smiled and pulled her shirt over her head. Throwing her hair into a bun, she padded into the kitchen where an ecstatic Natalie in full makeup, strawberry ringlets extending past her shoulders, was accepting a mug of coffee from her mom.

"You're not ready yet?" she squeaked, passing over Alex's rumpled appearance a few times before sipping her beverage.

"I—" Alex yawned, "got home late last night."

"Again," added Janie and Alex shot her a look. She hadn't realized her mom had even noticed. Natalie's full berry red lips parted as her lashes fluttered like a pair of erratic butterflies.

"How's Ja-ake?"

Alex stiffened, her lips tightening into a thin line. "He seemed okay when I saw him at the movies the other night." Natalie's eyes shifted in confusion. "With a very pretty blonde girl."

Natalie gasped and placed a protective hand on Alex's arm. "What an—" Her face erupted into lava red, her lips contorted with the words begging to be spewed.

"I know." Alex cast her eyes at the broken kitchen sconce above her. Summer flings were as fragile as thinly blown glass.

Janie, in her pink terrycloth robe, nursed a mug of coffee between her palms while she stared out the window above the sink. "I think the word you're looking for is asshole."

"Mom!" Alex spat and Natalie cackled. "Come on." She hooked her arm through Natalie's as Janie grinned at them enigmatically. "I'm going to make us late."

Alex sped down the highway in Natalie's red Acura that was filled to bursting with duffel bags, a makeup trunk, and garment bags layered over the seats.

"We're going to make it," Alex reassured her, speeding up to pass a dented brown station wagon flashing its hazard lights. "The parade doesn't start for another—" she glanced at the radio's digital clock, "—half an hour."

"It's going to take me that long to get that damn dress on."

All the contestants in the fair queen contest had to don traditional 1800s attire and stand like cake toppers on a float bearing the likeness of the original Texas capitol building.

"I'll help you. You'll be fine."

"I know." She toyed with the end of a curl. "Are *you* fine?"

Alex shifted in her seat and cast her a side eye. "What do you mean?"

"I mean, it seemed like you really liked Jake and now you've already moved on. I'd be a basket case."

Alex remained thoughtful for a moment. "I guess I've been through worse, and I imagine I'll go through worse again at some point."

"It's just like—"

"Like what?"

"Like you've always known that this life is temporary for you. Almost like it's not real. Like once you leave here, you'll start over and the life you lived before just won't exist. That's why it doesn't affect you."

Alex's insides were suddenly heavy and burdensome. "That's not true," she whispered.

But she wondered if that was a lie.

The first prickle of sweat formed at the nape of Alex's neck as the boom of a bass drum resounded in the distance. She shaded her eyes with one hand while fishing a camera out of her bag with the other. As the high-pitched brassy notes of a school song hurtled through the air, a spangled pair of twirlers pranced down the street to the beat. A clustered grid of band members marched past followed by a red truck pulling a trailerful of boy scouts proudly waving American flags. The president of the Old Three Hundred Society rode in a white convertible draped with crepe. He removed a felt cowboy hat and gestured to the crowd. A horse broke away from a tightly knit pack of trail riders, its owner in chaps and a plaid shirt bouncing up and down with the unexpected momentum.

And then came the fair court atop a flatbed trailer that would have fit at least two full size tractors. Alex cupped a hand around her mouth and whooped as she spotted Natalie in a full petticoat overlaid by a skirt of creamiest silk nipped in at the waist by a matching bodice embroidered with a rim of red. The women representing the seven major cities of Brazos County were artistically placed around a replica of the first capitol building draped in a giant

Texas flag.

Alex stepped onto the street and pressed her eye to the viewfinder on the camera, depressing the shutter button several times in quick succession. Her eyes roved through the swaying silk garments and gloved hands waving to the wildly cheering crowd. A set of blonde curls pinned to the crown of one girl's head caught her eye. A petite silhouette nearly swallowed up by the Victorian era dress. Alex's insides betrayed her by sending a wave of tension down her spine. If a pageant queen was what Jake wanted, he wouldn't be finding it in Alex. It was just as well.

"You looked gorgeous," Alex exclaimed as she helped Natalie step out of the vintage dress, petticoats unfurling like a ship's sail.

"Thanks," Natalie breathed. "If it was any hotter, I was going to start dripping like an ice cream cone."

Alex giggled and hurled the dress onto a faded brown comforter belonging to the Brazosville Inn. They had graciously donated rooms for the day to each of the pageant contestants to use as a place to change, rest, and re-beautify.

"What's next on the agenda?"

Natalie pulled a folder from her bag, color-coded tabs sticking out the side and an elegant script handwriting on the front in embossed gold. "We each have to judge a booth at the fair." She bit her lip as she flipped through the bound pages. "Whoo! I got elementary school art. Thank the good Lord."

"Why does it matter what booth you're judging?"

"Last year Callie Whitehurst got jam. She had to taste like twenty different kinds before she put on her dress for the pageant."

"I'm afraid to ask what happened."

"She put on her dress, and it wouldn't zip. She didn't even walk the stage. It was a total catastrophe."

"Shameful." Alex shook her head and grinned, tilting it to the side when a projectile in the form of a balled-up pair of panty hose sailed past her.

"Don't make fun, Alex. It ruined her life. Her boyfriend broke up with her and she got so depressed that she quit cheerleading, bombed her SAT's and never even got into college." Natalie's voice lowered to a whisper, even though they were completely alone. "She works at the mall now...in the food court."

Alex clicked her tongue sympathetically. The fate of a small town almost pageant queen.

The sun had already peaked in the endless blue of a clear sky before Natalie had perfected her art judging outfit of a white eyelet dress. When they entered the fray of the main fairgrounds, aerosolized dirt from hundreds of pairs of feet shuffling along the main thoroughfare clung to Alex's calves. The smell of fried dough and leather and animal musk all swirled together in a cloud of scent. Laughter blended with screams as they passed a spinning carnival ride.

The Ferris wheel towered above the entire scene. Above the rows of striped tents filled with jam jars, painted pottery, and belts made from bottle caps. She had always wondered what her world would look like from the very top. But she had never been on it. The creaking and swaying of the baskets always convinced her otherwise.

"Here's my stop," announced Natalie as she adjusted her sash. "You should go have fun."

"Okay. I'll meet you back at the room to help you get ready for tonight."

"Tootles," Natalie called. As she turned away, Alex saw Cory waiting for her under the eaves of a tent, its walls hung with hand-drawn dinosaurs and princesses. She swore one of the princesses looked exactly like Natalie.

Alex shuffled along with the swelling crowd, waving to familiar faces from school and stopping to peruse the books on display from a local author. She inhaled deeply and her nose recognized the overwhelming perfume of smashed cherries and browned butter. A woman with a tightly wound gray bun in a gingham apron stood behind the next booth.

"Hello dearie, care to try some pie? It's world famous. Well, at least in our part of the world." She cackled and displayed a row of crooked front teeth.

She stared at the mound of fried dough and the viscous red liquid leaking from its seams. Bubbling and dripping and oozing. Her face felt flammable and something squeezed her sternum like a vise.

"No thank you," she croaked. "I don't...I don't eat pie." She retreated into the crowd as a frown marred the woman's expression and hurried toward the glinting metal roof in the distance.

Terry was bent over a horse's hoof digging out a mound of compacted mud when Alex skidded into the barn.

"Hey there," she said, without looking up. "Can you hand me that other hoof pick?" She pointed to a toolbox with handles and

Alex dug around until she found what Terry wanted.

"Here you go."

"Poor baby got a piece of glass shoved in here," she muttered as she made a few more swipes before releasing the chestnut foreleg. Terry handed the pick back to Alex and wiped her hands on the seat of her pants. "How you doin' over there? You look pale as a ghost."

"Me? No, I'm fine. I just came to see how the judging was going."

"So far so good." Terry straightened up. She was in her usual plaid button down with a badge that read "equine judge." "You need somethin'? I got to get over to the arena."

"I guess not," Alex replied.

Terry moved past her in a blink, the legs of her starched jeans noisily swishing together.

Steeling her senses, she called after her. "Hey Terry, do you know anyone with the last name Powell?"

A rare thoughtfulness shaded her sharp features before she spoke. "No, I don't."

Damn. Alex stuck herself for the second time with a safety pin in the sensitive fleshy part of her thumb. "Why these dresses have to be so high maintenance, I will never understand," she gritted as she tacked Natalie's underthings to the lining of her dress.

"Survival of the most beautiful," Natalie snarked as she flattened her stomach against the upward stroke of the zipper.

Alex swept aside a few curls and clasped the hook and eye at the V of the emerald, green gown covered in gold sequin filigree.

"How do I look?" Natalie rotated in front of the bathroom mirror, the light catching on the sequins and the understated glitter in Natalie's eyeshadow.

"Like a queen," Alex proclaimed and then both girls burst into giggles.

The fair queen contest was held on an outdoor stage in the natural amphitheater created by the rodeo arena to the north, the animal enclosure to the east, and the carnival to the west. Alex stood at the rear of the crowd, perched on a grassy hill in her dress of sky blue, hair pulled back in a high ponytail. From her vantage point, she could see the entire length of the stage and creep forward to take photos once the queen was crowned.

The sun had begun its descent, filling the western sky with the richest of purple hues, lilac and lavender and plum. A light breeze brushed the ends of her hair against her bare back as the master of ceremonies announced the beginning of the pageant. The girls were sparkling jewels come alive, resplendent in fiery reds and golds, richest purple, and inkiest black. The exiting rays of the sun played off the costume jewelry, casting miniature rainbows on the wooden stage.

Alex clasped her hands together when Natalie walked out, bold yet demure, and strutted in front of the rest of the female flock. A hush rippled through the crowd as she turned and cast her most dazzling smile to the front row. In less time than it took to drive through Cole's Church, a crown had joined Natalie's strawberry curls atop her head. She blew kisses and waved to her subjects from an elevated throne wrapped in metallic gold paper.

Alex oscillated between cheering and snapping photographs. She spied Cory, a few yards to her left, resting his elbows on the stage and smiling as big as the broad side of a barn. It sparked some warmth in Alex's heart for him. He genuinely seemed to like Natalie, and she knew the feeling was more than returned. A dark head appeared next to Cory's sandy brown one and her stomach dropped. *Jake.*

Sending a final burst of applause toward Natalie, Alex sidestepped to the edge of the crowd, but she wasn't alone. Behind her, Jake slowly wove his way through the Stetsons and permanent hairdos and balloons toward the spot where she had been standing. Once free of the crowd, she broke into a clumsy jog.

"Alex, wait up."

His voice was sweet, insistent, and she didn't dare turn around. The main thoroughfare had become even more congested as the curtain of night had fallen over them. Glow sticks and sparklers and the lit ends of cigarettes dotted her line of sight. Darting between the ring toss and the funnel cake stand, she followed a serpentine line leading to an explosion of size and light. A familiar backside stepped up to the ticket booth ahead of her. She rushed over, trying to ignore the hateful glares arrowing toward her.

"Justin," she hissed. His eyes flicked down to hers in surprise, widening as he assessed her attire. The borrowed blue silk dress clung to every minute curve, the sweetheart neckline giving her the semblance of a womanly figure that she hadn't known she possessed.

In a half panic, she pointed inside the booth to the man with a bulbous nose and sparse tufts of gray hair sprouting from his temples. "Two for the," she gulped silently, "Ferris wheel."

He nodded curtly and tore two yellow tabs from a rolled-up string of tickets. "Go through the gate. Two people per car. Keep your parts inside at all times," he said sourly. He blew his nose with a threadbare handkerchief.

Alex flattened her palms on Justin's lower back, damp from a day's worth of sweat, and pushed him forward.

"Since when," he drawled, opening the gate to the waiting passenger car, "do you want to ride the Ferris wheel?"

Alex slid into car onto a lacquered bench. The bar groaned as she pulled it as close to her thighs as it would go. "Since Jake Brady saw me at the pageant."

Justin's shoulders shuddered with laughter as the ride jerked into motion. The disturbance to her inertia reached the deepest part of her gut.

"God, I'm going to regret this," she moaned, glancing down once at the quickly disappearing ground.

"Whatever you do, don't barf."

Alex squeezed her eyes closed as the air touching her cheek seemed to thin. "If I do, I need to barf in your direction. If I ruin this dress, Natalie's mom is going to kill me."

She expected a volley of sarcasm, but he was uncharacteristically quiet. Popping one of her eyes open, she caught him staring at her.

"Noted," was all he said in reply before putting his hands behind his head and gazing up at the encroaching sky, voluptuous with stars.

Silence buzzed around them for a few minutes, long enough for Alex to dare a few glances at the fading tent roofs and shrinking people below.

"You're too good for him, you know," Justin remarked, not taking his eyes from the sky overhead.

"Or maybe—" Alex tucked her longest layer behind her ear. "I'm not enough."

This got Justin's attention. His eyes, as green as the waves right before they crested the shore, riveted to hers and held her gaze. "Don't say that. Never say that again or think that again."

Alex shrugged and studied the dust coating her block-heeled satin sandals.

"You're meant to be someone's...everything."

The upward momentum of the wheel lurched to a stop and their car swung back and forth on a creaking axle, suspending them above the earth. Back and forth they swayed with the wind. This was the part she had always dreaded. The groundlessness. The lack of control. The real possibility of mechanical failure. But when she braved a look, it wasn't as horrible as she had feared.

Part of her was terrified but another part, a part that was awakening to life's possibilities, reveled in the thrill. Her skin prickled with excitement at the same time her stomach twisted itself into a pretzel. She willed her eyes to open wider and wider still to take in what the universe offered. Calm began to edge out the fear. Nothing below her mattered anymore. It was amazing how a simple change in perspective could provide so much clarity. When all she could see was night, she pretended to kiss the stars.

"I hear you over there," Justin said.

"I didn't say anything."

"Your brain is loud."

Alex chuckled knowingly.

"What are you thinking about?"

She continued staring into the black. But instead of nothingness, she saw everything.

"Do you ever hope that you see so much of the world that it shrinks down to something small and familiar, and it changes how you view everything? Even something you've known your entire life?"

A summer breeze blew across her face, a breeze warmed by the tropical waters mixing in the Gulf just a few miles away.

"I like my view right now. Exactly how it is." His voice was low and laced with sadness.

An ache throbbed in her chest. A pain that she didn't know how to put into words. She wouldn't be leaving for another year, but it felt like they were already saying goodbye.

The twang of a guitar followed by a drum cadence rippled through the air. From her perch, far above the crowds, Alex could see where a set of string lights and picnic tables had been used to shape a rectangular dance floor on the grass. A few Lilliputian-sized couples were twirling the two-step to the beat of a country song. She barely registered when the wheel began to turn, bringing her closer to the ground and the reality that waited patiently for her down below.

Jake stood by the striped ticket booth, hands tucked into his pockets, a smoldering stare lasered in her direction as Justin helped guide her out of the passenger car. She took a cleansing breath and exhaled through her nose before picking her way through the grass toward the pale blue eyes that perfectly complimented her dress. A hand closed around her elbow.

"Hey, you don't have to go over there."

"I know," she replied. "But the sooner I see what he wants, the sooner I can stop running the other direction every time I see him. My feet are starting to hurt." She flashed him a wry smile that wasn't returned. He nodded, storms churning in his eyes as he turned to let her go.

TWENTY-TWO

"Hi," Jake murmured, so low and husky that she barely heard him over the rising crescendo of the music.

"Hi." Alex smoothed a hand down the front of her, thankfully unmarred, dress.

"You look...amazing," he offered and took a tentative step toward her. So close that she could reach out and touch him if she wanted to. She didn't want to. Or maybe she did. His jeans hugged his hips and sinewy forearms were crossed over the outline of his chest muscles under a royal blue collared shirt.

"Thanks," she said.

He nodded, eyes alight with renewed hope. "Look, about the other night. I've been trying to break it off with Candy for a while."

Candy. So that was the blonde's name. Alex focused all her energies on keeping her face blank. "It didn't really look that way."

"I know and I'm sorry. I wasn't sure about us."

Us? Alex reeled and had to focus on steadying her breathing.

"But I am now. You are what I want."

Alex felt her mind separate from her corpus. Like some mini out-of-body experience when reality became so vastly different from expectation that it was literally mind blowing. "I'm not sure you really know what you want."

The words hung between them. She didn't know if she had said them for Jake's benefit or her own. The music had grown louder, wrapping them in a comfortable shroud of cadence and melody. He held out his hand. A hand with long fingers and calluses that knew the many hours of throwing a baseball. Calluses that had brushed against her face and the sensitive band of skin along her lower back.

"Want to dance?"

She couldn't think of any good reason to say no, so she held out her hand and let him take it.

They swayed off tempo amidst the rhythmic twirling and dipping of the other couples. Neither of them was any good at dancing, but as the song played on, Alex relaxed into the sear of his palm on her lower back. His long arm curved around her side and his smooth fingers interlocked with hers. Out of the corner of one eye, a glimmer caught her attention and a crowned Natalie swept by, encased in Cory. She passed Alex a surprised face that morphed into approval. Alex ducked her head.

"So, there's a big party tomorrow night. Down at Cory's river house."

Alex snapped her eyes up at Jake. "Are you asking me to go with you?" she asked, a skitter of anticipation dancing along her bones. What was so appealing about his crooked smile and those dimples and the way he only seemed to see her?

He cocked his head to the side, a whisp of raven hair brushing his eyebrows. "Of course. I want you there...with me," he added, a sense of desperation in his tone that she hadn't heard before.

"Okay," she agreed, feeling every droplet of sweat collecting under her arms and behind her knees.

His smile turned to dazzling and he pulled her in close enough that her cheek could rest on his chest if she wanted. And she did want it.

When the song was over, Jake tugged her off the dance floor and they weaved through the thinning crowd, bobbing between the incandescent light from food stands that remained open.

"Are you hungry?" Jake asked, stopping in between two booths with bold neon signs hung precariously atop their roofs. A glowing fried crust around a sausage beckoned from one and a bun stuffed with chopped barbecue beef from the other.

"I think I want a corn dog."

"Totally what I was thinking." He smiled and those dimples appeared again making her stomach dip a little.

She and Jake stepped into line as a unit, and he interlaced his fingers with hers. A wave of heat hit her face as they neared the register. Heat that contained the sweet scent of frying batter.

"Two corn dogs and two fried pies." Jake let go of her hand to reach into his wallet and remove a wad of bills.

Her stomach lurched at the mention of pie, but she plastered a smile on her face and gingerly accepted the wooden stick and the paper wrapped around a thick corner of crust. Balancing the food in her arms she trailed behind Jake and began scanning the perimeter for an open table.

"Over there."

He cocked his head toward the end of a long picnic table that was being vacated by a family with three kids in tow. One had fallen asleep in his stroller, dark curls matted to his head. Alex smiled at his cherubic face with his perfectly full lips that complimented a set of dark lashes and thick rumpled hair. His mother had similar hair plaited in a full black braid that fell over her shoulder. A chubby toddler, face smeared with a mixture of sticky coated with a fine layer of grime, yanked on her red crinkled skirt. When she bent over to soothe him, she lost the entire contents of her tote bag onto the ground. Diapers and bottles and little plastic bags filled with dry cereal were scattered haphazard onto the grass.

"Here, let me help you." Alex dropped to her knees. In her haste the pie slipped out of its wrapper and landed in the stubby grass.

"Gracias," crooned the woman, lifting the child up to her ample waist and pushing the stroller away from the table. Quickly collecting the spilled contents, Alex dropped them into the abyss of her wide-open bag.

"That was impressive," Jake snickered as she balanced on the grass with one hand and held the corndog aloft with the other.

As she shifted up to a squat, her heels bobbled and she tipped over, her palm meeting with something soft and squishy. When she lifted her hand, a thick red dribble stained her palm and oozed its way down her inner forearm. Cherry pie. A wave of nausea churned inside her stomach. A tempest rose in her chest as she stared at her hand. Through the roaring in her ears, Jake's words were muffled.

"Oh no! Here." He handed her a stack of table napkins.

"Thanks." She traded him the abused corndog for the napkins.

"I'll get you another pie."

"No, that's okay." Her heart rate spiked and even her hair follicles prickled as she methodically wiped her palm.

"Seriously, I don't mind."

The shaking started as she continued swiping long strokes over her hand and arm. She violently scrubbed as the red seeped into her skin, staining her fingers.

"She doesn't like pie."

The words vibrated behind her, and she twisted around. Justin stood there, fists clenched at his sides, staring down at Jake. Jake raised a brow, stepping around him to address Alex.

"I'll be right back, Alex." And then he puffed his chest out at Justin, turning his palms up to the sky. "Everybody likes pie, dude."

It wasn't until Jake's backside was barely visible that Justin grabbed her by the wrist and pulled her into a vacated artist booth filled with handmade bottle openers.

"What are you doing?"

"A lady dropped her bag. I was helping pick up her stuff." Alex jerked her wrist out of Justin's grasp.

"No. What are doing with him?"

"Nothing."

"It doesn't look like nothing."

"He's...we're talking. That's all."

"I can't believe you'd even consider going out with him again after the other night."

Alex glared at the angular silhouette of Justin's face. "Why not? He likes me. I like him. I'm just having fun."

"This isn't fun. It's reckless." Justin ran a hand through the long top layer of his hair, the reddish gold strands catching fire in the ambient light.

"What about this is reckless? Please enlighten me."

"You don't know what kind of guy he is. What he wants. What he expects."

"He says what he wants is me." Alex's fists clenched at her sides and she shifted her eyes to the packed earth under her feet.

"Do you want him?"

Alex didn't answer.

"Do you want him?" Justin repeated.

"As opposed to what?" Alex crossed her arms across her chest without thinking. And nearly collapsed in a wave of panic when she riveted her eyes to the bodice of her dress and the pink fingerprints ebbing into the fabric. She flung out her hands as if the stain would follow. "To always being *reliable Alex*. Hey, I'm between girlfriends, want to be friends again, Alex? Hey, can you help me study for our chemistry final because I've been too busy playing basketball to pay attention, Alex?"

"You know it's not like that. I just—"

"What?" Alex seethed with a roiling anger that was rare for her. The practiced self-preservation from a childhood of violence and abuse crystallized the air around her until she felt comforted by its presence. Secure behind the protection it offered.

"I can handle Jake. I can handle anything and in case you haven't noticed, I'm not the sad little girl anymore. The little broken doll who cries every time someone raises their voice."

"What are you then?" he asked so quietly that his voice blended with the night.

"I'm something else. Someone else. And I'm still your friend, but I don't need you. Not anymore."

"You don't know what you need."

Alex heard the whisper of his words somewhere in her brain, but she was well beyond earshot by the time she processed them and felt the first sting of moonlight tears.

Alex hugged her plush, tawny-colored dog to her chest, rubbing her nose through his fur and inhaling a decade's worth of subtle odors. Her mom's laundry detergent. Vanilla body spray. Jasmine scented shampoo. He was beyond ragged, but she couldn't bear to part with him. This tattered dog was the only thing that remained from their old house. Her old life. A life she rarely thought about and wished she couldn't remember. But tonight, the veil of her fortitude had thinned. Her vulnerability on display as readily as the queen's crown.

The summer she was five, her mom had won a game of ring toss at the fair. Once the final green ring had clinked over the glass bottle, Alex had bounced with glee, pointing at the brown furry head and molten chocolate eyes suspended at the back of the booth. She remembered her mom in a red dress with white polka dots, ginger hair piled on top of her head in a bun. Her dad had replaced his overalls with a stiffly starched collared shirt and pressed blue jeans. The Day of the Old Three Hundred always brought out the best in everyone; even her father had stayed sober for the better part of an afternoon.

The day had started out perfect. A sunshine sky with enough puffy white clouds to relieve the heat and a breeze to lift the tiny hairs of Alex's arms. The air had sizzled with the scents of all manner of fried delicacies. With her new prize tucked under one arm, she had accepted a slice of cherry pie from a lady in a gingham apron.

"Howdy there," barked her father and raised his arm in the

direction of a group of men in boots and cowboy hats. She trailed behind her mother, her nose wrinkling when the pungent fumes of liquor entered it.

"Come with me, honey," said her mom, tugging her by the hand past the raucous laughter and glinting silver flasks.

Somewhere between the carousel and the petting zoo, a wide smear of cherry red glaze settled on Alex's fingers and all over the bib of her dress. As the sun sank on the horizon, her cheeks matched the pink hue in the sky as she and her mom skipped across the broad lawn still filled with fair goers. A few irreverent balloons fled to the skies after escaping from chubby fists.

When they arrived at their old blue truck, her father was slumped against it, his stubby chin nearly touching the turned down collar of his button down.

"Where you all been?" he drawled, drawing out each syllable.

"Out and about. Having a little fun," Janie replied crisply, tightening her grip on Alex's hand. "We saw the cutest little goat."

Her father glared at them through half-hooded eyes and raised his head. That's when Alex saw the puffy bruise around his left temple and the rivulet of dried blood extending in front of his ear.

"What happened to your face, Daddy?" Alex asked, clutching her hands to her chest.

"What'd you do to yer dress, girl?" he asked, ignoring her question. He reached out with two fingers and poked the dried crimson splash of color across her chest.

"I got pie on it."

He scoffed loudly and Alex stared down at his dingy nails.

"It'll come out in the wash," chided Janie.

"It better. I ain't got money to get you 'nother one."

Alex nodded fiercely, blinking away the fretful tears.

"Less go," he slurred, turning to swing open the truck door.

Alex began climbing in, using both hands to balance on the side rails of the truck. *Her hands.* They were missing something. "Wait," she squealed. "I forgot my dog. I left him at the goat pen."

"I'll get him," reassured Janie and she strode back into the fairgrounds, weaving between the exiting crowd.

As soon as Janie was out of sight, rough hands gripped Alex's arms and a cloud of rancid breath exploded over her face. She started crying then.

"Next time I take you somewheres, keep yerself clean and yer head outta yer ass," he barked and shoved her face first onto the upholstery of the bench seat.

The cherry stain never came out of that dress. No matter how many times her mom washed it.

TWENTY-THREE

Faster. She squeezed the heaving body, slick with sweat, between her calves and bent her head closer to the pumping neck. The howl of the wind and the pounding of hooves in her ears drowned out everything else. She had woken up in a sweat drenched nightgown and it wasn't from the lack of air conditioning. With every ray of sun flung over the horizon, the nightmare was fading into whisps of memory. Mere cobwebs. Every inhale of honeysuckle rich air supplanted the lingering odors of stale breath and tobacco. Every ripple of muscle between her thighs made her feel alive again.

Terry was waiting for her in the awning of the barn when she slid off George's back. Spent from exertion, he didn't even try to snatch a few luscious sprigs of clover from the patch near the gate. Head down, tail swishing forward to flick a fly from his massive haunches, he ambled into the barn and waited, perfectly docile, while Alex put him in cross ties.

"You're a perfect gentleman when you been rode hard," clucked Terry, reaching up to pat the Thoroughbred on his blazed forehead.

Alex grinned in agreement. "And the rest of the time, he does what he wants when he wants."

George, a former racehorse turned jumper, loved to preen and had no qualms about reminding his rider that he could retake control, if he wanted to. Alex wouldn't be the rider she was without his unique challenges. Haughty yet talented. A redeemable prima donna. Turning on the hose, she directed the jet of clean water at his steaming sides.

"What time did you get here?" asked Terry.

"Right before sunrise."

"Last time I checked it was summertime and a Saturday."

"I couldn't sleep," she admitted, then added, "plus it's way too hot to ride if I wait."

"You goin' back out to the fairgrounds today?"

Alex nodded. "I promised Mr. Robbins I'd help with the barbecue cookoff."

She pursed her lips. Her anger with Justin, still fresh from last night, had sunk all the way to her soles. Every step felt twice as heavy as usual. She began to scrape the dirty water from the chestnut's back, the sweat and muck-filled droplets landing on her forearms.

"Somethin' on your mind?" Terry handed her a curry comb.

Alex grabbed it and massaged the curve of George's back in long arcing strokes. His ears flickered once before he bounced his head up and down in contentment.

"No...yes. I don't know."

Terry rubbed her chin thoughtfully. "Where's your gentleman friend?"

"Which one?" Alex replied without thinking and Terry cocked a brow. The frayed ends of her nerves bristled at the sight of Terry's smirk. Instead of responding, she changed the subject. "I saw that crazy symbol again."

Terry's ears visibly perked. Alex could swear she was half-horse sometimes. "Where?"

Alex began untying George who nibbled her fingers searching for a tidbit. "Strange enough, in the town cemetery." As she flung open the stall door and let George rush past her to thrust his head into the feed trough, Terry's weathered hand came to rest on her forearm.

"Why were you flouncin' around in the cemetery?"

"No real reason." Alex averted her eyes to the latch of the stall door and fiddled with it. "Anyway, I tripped over a headstone and underneath the name there was a backwards B with a line through it. Just like on the tree."

Terry ran a hand through her grown-out layers. "I don't know what this means. And I don't have time today to figure it out."

Alex stood in front of her, nearly a head taller than Terry since she turned fourteen. Yet somehow, she had never lost the illusion that Terry towered over her.

"I have to go into town," she finished.

"What for?"

A cautious, rare smile split Terry's mouth. "Signin' the papers for the new land."

Alex smiled back. "I'm happy for you. The horses are going to love it."

"All of us are." Terry's steel irises clouded with emotion for a second, long enough to leave Alex disconcerted. And then she strode outside, the edge of her plaid shirt flapping outside the waistband of her riding breeches. "Check the mail and put it on my desk before you go," she called over her shoulder.

Alex watched her petite frame climb into the extended cab truck and gun the engine forward until a plume of dust was all that remained in her wake. She tromped behind the dust cloud toward the dented silver mailbox stationed at the end of the driveway. The gray filly grazed in the front pasture, lifting her head in brief curiosity as Alex ambled past. She was Terry's newest horse, a spontaneous purchase from the auction block last summer. Bella had been the only one she had brought with her when she moved here from North Carolina.

Terry never talked about her past and Alex knew better than to ask. Over the past seven years, she had picked up clues here and there like misshapen pieces of a puzzle that didn't quite fit together. A hushed phone conversation from time to time. A faded photograph of a young Terry in jockey silks astride a racehorse. A postcard with a return address from Alaska of all places.

At the end of the day, Terry was an enigma. A paradox. Most of the time, she was brash and straightforward about life. Except for her life before she arrived in Cole's Church. Working with animals upward of a thousand pounds had kept her lean and wiry in her middle age. With her feathered hair, preference for bourbon, and stand-offish personality, most of the ladies in town steered clear of her. Except Janie Wilde. Janie had seen Terry's new face lurking at the rear of church after service one Sunday and invited her to lunch. Terry had refused, of course, but after a month or so, Janie had worn her down.

Alex had been in awe of the steely-eyed stranger who never wore anything but pants. And when she had found out that Terry was a horse trainer, she clung to her every word like it was biblical. When she began doing chores around the barn in exchange for lessons, something inside her had awoken. Being around the horses, these magnificent creatures she could control with a bend of her forefinger or a brush of her heels, had started healing a festered wound deep inside her until it was nothing more than a battle scar.

She yanked the lid open to the mailbox and began retrieving the contents. There wasn't ever much. A few catalogues for barn supplies, bills, and the normal advertisement detritus filled most of the interior. But today, behind the regular mail, a thick brown envelope had been shoved into the shadowed rear of the box.

Alex tugged until it came free. *Ugh.* It smelled rotten. She flipped it over and her heart thumped the back of her sternum. There was no return address. Or postage stamp. Deep in thought, she jogged back to the office, heaving open the painted metal door on rusted hinges. Terry's desk was a menagerie of papers, sticky notes with scribbled memos, and usually a candy bar wrapper or two. She had a weakness for chocolate bars that almost matched her weakness for bourbon.

Depositing the regular mail on the only clear section of the battered desktop, Alex stared at the scrawl on the brown envelope: Teresa Hawthorne, Route 2 Box 127, Cole's Church, Texas. She sniffed the thickly woven paper again and nearly gagged. Decision made, she ran a finger under the flap and pulled out the contents. A single sheet of notebook paper with a message written in block letters. Alex's eyes scanned the page, her pulse increasing with each line of text.

we don't want no yankee bitch buyin our land
if you do, you'll regret it

It was signed "the sons of Brit." The mirror image B slashed in half was drawn below the signature line. A fullness remained in the envelope and Alex turned it over and shook until an oblong shape wrapped in cheesecloth plunked onto the glossy cover of *Horse Monthly*. She pulled the edges back. As soon as she saw the pink mound of flesh, she screamed.

The blue swirling lights of a police car had always reminded Alex of the slushy machines at the town's only convenience store. The electric blue spun around and around until it became mesmerizing but without the tangy arctic treat as a reward. Alex sat on an overturned bucket while Chief Maloney scratched notes onto a pad of paper.

"And you say you have no idea who could be behind all this?"

Alex shook her head. She had provided the story, in exquisite detail, starting from the night she found Bella to the opening of the mail. The police officer ran a beefy hand down his crisp blue uniform, a ribbed white undershirt peeking through the spaces between the buttons. She noticed a grease stain on the end of his navy blue tie. His bald head gleamed with sweat. It had transitioned from pale to lobster red during the interrogation.

"Chief Maloney," Alex began, "who are the sons of Brit?"

"I ain't got no idea." He rubbed a sleeve across his sweaty forehead, his eyes darting to the clear plastic bags displayed on the hood of his police car: one containing the note, the other a slice of cow tongue. "Look, it's probably just some backwoods folk lookin' for an excuse to be mad."

Alex didn't think so, but she kept her thoughts to herself. Nothing ever happened in Cole's Church. Nothing except for men who got rowdy at the high school football game or teenagers who got caught toilet papering someone's house. Once a year, the police might catch a few underage drinkers at a party. Nothing like this though.

A crunching sound drew Alex's attention as Terry barreled up the driveway. Her black truck skidded to a stop next to the shiny navy and white police vehicle. Leaping from the truck, she jogged over to where Alex sat upright on the bucket.

"What's this about, Gerald?" Terry crossed her arms over her plaid button down.

"This young lady here—" he gestured to Alex, "—tells me that you been gettin' threats."

"Seems like it." Terry flicked her eyes over to the contents of the police evidence then back to Alex. "She called and told me what she found in my mailbox."

Alex dropped her chin to her chest. Exhaustion had seeped in to replace her adrenaline. Her head throbbed and no matter how much fresh air whiffed past her nose, she still smelled the rot from that envelope.

"Alex, why don't you go see about turnin' out the rest of the horses? I'll finish up here."

"Okay." Edging off the orange bucket, Alex tottered back toward the barn on rubber limbs, turning occasionally to watch as Terry gesticulated in the space between her and Chief Maloney.

Once the horses were romping in the back pasture, Alex returned to Terry's office and stared at the paper chaos. On an impulse, her hands began stacking and straightening, shoving similar sized papers into piles and lining up all the sticky notes into rows. When the door swung open, it rattled her nerves and she knocked over a stack of magazines. Terry entered, slapping a thick white folder onto the center of the desk. She plopped down in the worn leather office chair and immediately began rubbing her temples.

"Sit down, Alex. People make me nervous when they clean."

Alex obeyed, settling into a butter yellow upholstered armchair fraught with linear rips from several generations of kitty claws. She waited until Terry reached over to her lopsided filing cabinet and took out the bourbon from the bottom drawer before casting her line.

"What did Chief Maloney say?"

Terry's throat bobbed as she took a swig of bourbon. "Nothin' useful."

Alex scanned the thick white folder with Charles C. McIntosh, Attorney at Law, inscribed on the front. Her mind reeled with so many questions it took effort to pace herself.

"So, all of this has to do with buying the McCoy place?"

Terry nodded and examined the bottle in her hand like the answers to all their questions rested in its golden depths.

"Who are these people?"

Terry shrugged. "Hell, if I know. Local troublemakers? A couple of misogynistic assholes?"

Alex straightened with a jolt. All the pieces were on the table now. They just needed to make them fit together. "What are we going to do?"

"*We* are not goin' to do anything. I want you to stay out of this, Alex. I mean it. These people, whoever they are, ain't right in the head."

Alex opened her mouth to argue but Terry put a hand up. She quieted despite the tumult building in her chest. No wonder the skittish yearlings calmed when they entered Terry's atmosphere. Her eyes alone could bring a Pegasus to heel.

"Go on to the fairgrounds and don't mention a word of this to anyone."

"I won't," Alex said but her mind was elsewhere, frantically organizing a subset of details that she hoped would equate to answers. Answers that she planned on finding.

"By the way, this was in my mailbox yesterday." Terry reached into a side drawer and withdrew a slim letter-sized envelope and pushed it across the desk toward Alex.

A royal blue college crest caught her eye. She gingerly picked up the envelope addressed to her.

"What's that all about?" Terry pried.

"Nothing," Alex said dismissively. "I just wanted to see if I could get in. That's all."

Terry opened her mouth, but when she said nothing, Alex took the silence as her cue to go. She made it to the threshold before Terry's voice resounded behind her.

"I went to Duke."

Alex whirled around. "You did?"

"Yep, a long time ago. There weren't very many women there in those days. We all fit into one single dormitory."

"What was your major?"

"Engineering, but I never finished my degree."

"Why not?"

"Got bit by the horse bug. It's in my blood." She laughed harshly and took another swig of bourbon. "I had a chance to join the circuit as a junior trainer. Left home and never looked back."

"Was it hard?" Alex swiped a layer of dirt off the threshold with the toe of her boot.

"Which part?"

"Changing your mind about your future? Leaving home?"

"Life is about making big decisions and making one should bring you closer to your destiny, to your true self, not farther away."

Alex felt the words enter her bloodstream and settle somewhere. Somewhere she could revisit later when she was alone with her envelope. When she could block out everything else and think. Reaching out for the doorjamb to steady herself, she focused on Terry's face, worn from age and a life spent outside in the elements. She studied the harsh lines and thin lips that spewed criticism and praise with equal fervor.

"Terry, I'm so sorry about all this trouble with the land."

"Why? It ain't your fault."

"I know, but it's not your fault either."

"The devil was bound to catch up with me someday." She plunked the bottle on top of the slick white folder. "I got too much on my mind to worry about some sons of bitches tryin' to threaten me."

"Don't you mean sons of Brit?"

"No, I really don't."

Apart from the Friday night fair queen competition, the Saturday barbecue cookoff reigned as the favored event of Old Three Hundred week. A grassy lawn transformed into a smoke-filled haven of delectable meats, beer drinking, and lively conversation among friends, some of whom had been sharing insults for decades.

Alex slipped under the knotted rope that sectioned the cooking area from the rest of the fairgrounds and headed toward the silver dragon on wheels, its snout sending puffs of black hickory smoke into the atmosphere. Underneath a makeshift awning, Grandpa Robbins was tilted backward on a kitchen chair in a plaid pearl-snap shirt and faded jeans, pointed toe boots propped up on an ice chest. He guffawed with laughter over something muttered by the man seated next to him, rail thin and in a trucker's hat sporting a thin brown mustache. He lifted an amber bottle with a red label to his lips as Alex approached.

"Howdy there, Miss Alex."

Alex waved shyly and then tucked an errant piece of silken hair behind her ear.

"Want something to drink?" He removed his boots from the ice chest and cracked open the lid to reveal a well-stocked collection of soda cans and beer bottles. She snagged a frosted soda then reached across the beverage cooler to give the elderly gentleman's arm a squeeze.

"Thank you, Mr. Robbins."

His cheeks deepened to crimson. "You sure are welcome. Now, I think Justin is round here somewheres. If you find him, have him bring some more wood for the fire."

"I sure will," Alex answered, her voice sounding steadier than her insides felt.

She roamed through a sea of potbellied men bending over tendrils of sweet smoke and slabs of meat, scanning above their heads for the deep brown shock of hair with hints of reddish gold. She half hoped she wouldn't find him. Their last conversation plagued her with a nagging anxiety-ridden nausea that nothing seemed to quell.

When they were kids, they had fought all the time, bickering over whose turn it was to pull weeds from Janie's garden or what movie they rented from the small selection of titles at the grocery store. No matter what the argument, night would inevitably fall, and any dissent would fade just like the sunlight. She hoped that was still the case.

Eventually she found him. He was sitting on the tailgate of the Robbins' red pickup truck, his long legs swinging back and forth making patterns in the dirt, a long-necked bottle between his palms. The curved brim of his baseball hat was pulled so far over his forehead that it cast a shadow across his face. He didn't look up as she approached.

"Your grandpa needs more wood for the fire. He sent me to tell you."

"Alright."

Alex gripped her soda can so tight that it crinkled. "Are you drinking?"

He saluted her with the bottle instead of answering.

"Aren't you worried you'll get caught?"

"Nope."

She rolled her eyes in exasperation, his arrogance derailing the apology she had been working on since waking up this morning. "Do you want to talk about last night?"

The way he sat hunched over nursing his beer suddenly made him look ten years old again sitting on her front porch swing after his mom left for another tour of duty. His eyes were chips of jade when they finally met hers.

"Not really."

His gaze drifted over her shoulder. Alex half turned to the sound of giggling and the sight of densely sprayed hair. One of them she recognized as Candy, the petite blonde who had been wrapped up in Jake Brady at the movies. A pair of boots hit the ground in front of her and Justin brushed past her.

"I'll see you around, Alex."

Her heart was so far up her throat that she was surprised she didn't choke on it. She lifted her soda and sent a stream of burning cold around it.

TWENTY-FOUR

Toward the end of the afternoon, nimbus clouds in shades of grayish purple overtook the sun's fiery disc. A cool breeze snaked through the densely populated lawn and found its way to the back of Alex's neck. Closing her eyes and inhaling deeply, she could smell the promised rain through the lingering scents of smoke and sweat. The day had been fruitful in the form of a cherry red second place ribbon displayed proudly on the white canvas awning. Grandpa Robbins had not stopped smiling or gloating among his friends for hours. The limited square footage had quickly filled with people wishing their congratulations and hoping to sample a bite of richly smoked meat dipped in sauce.

Alex busied herself with toting around a large black trash bag the size of a pirate's sail and picking up the discarded cans and napkin bits embedded in the grass. As the afternoon stretched on, the conversation ticked up several decibels until shouts mingled with laughter underlaid by a continuous hum of voices. Justin had appeared shortly before the ribbons were distributed with a doe-eyed blonde in tow. Not Candy, thank goodness.

When he stretched out in a camping chair, the girl decidedly perched herself on his thigh, leaning over to whisper in his ear at every opportunity. Her peasant top did little to conceal the bulges of her burgeoning womanhood. Despite her better judgment, Alex kept stealing glances in their direction. Justin caught her once and stared with amusement from underneath his Dodgers baseball hat until she had looked away.

The smoke and heat and emotional churning in her gut had culminated in a pressurized spot behind her right eye that quickly bloomed into a fierce headache. She glanced at her watch. Minnie's hands gestured that it was past time for her to go home and change.

Jake would be picking her up in less than an hour. Dropping the nearly full trash bag near the smoker, she slunk out between two groups of men having words between chews of tobacco.

When she slid into her car, the immediate silence was therapy itself. A temporary cocoon from the rest of the world. As she drove, a gentle patter of rain struck her windshield and she relinquished her hold on the tears. She cried in silence as waves of emotion crashed to shore. She cried for Bella and for Terry. For Justin. For the letter she had found this morning. Grief and fear. And something twisty that could only be jealousy. Curiosity and resolve. Each emotion was as fleeting as the raindrops pinging her windshield. And then they slid away. Down her cheeks, past her chin, dripping onto the stained front of her cotton shirt. She lifted the hem to dab her nose.

What was happening to Terry was evil to the core. Either her boss was living in denial or she knew more than she let on. Either way, the situation had to be dealt with and Alex wasn't sure if the sum total of the four law enforcement officers of Cole's Church were up for the job.

Her mind whirred back to the conversation with Justin last Sunday. The how had been answered, at least where Bella's death was concerned. Dr. Z had confirmed the toxicology screen was positive for ionophore poisoning.

But the why? It seemed specifically targeted to Terry, but it couldn't be because she was an outsider who wasn't from Cole's Church. Or maybe these "sons of Brit" were a backwoods gang that doled out punishment in the form of hate crimes. And who were they anyway? Alex had grown up here and never heard of them.

Her mind conjured the one person she wished would appear in the passenger seat of her mom's vintage sedan. But things had changed. Life had changed. And maybe holding on to a childhood friendship birthed by proximity and mutual loneliness wasn't meant to last. Maybe she needed to let him go.

The nearby crickets performed a symphony of strings as the first stars winked through the violaceous clouds; clouds that had filled to near bursting in the short time Alex had been waiting on the porch swing. When she saw the familiar headlights, she shot off the porch, jumping to the ground and swishing through the freshly mown grass to the edge of the asphalt road. The car rolled to a stop, and she jerked open the door, welcomed by the overpowering scent of cologne and a steady thrum of bass blaring through the speaker system.

"Hi."

The dimples on his cheeks deepened into ravines as he groped her with his gaze, not once but twice. "You look—"

"Thanks," Alex murmured, cutting him off before he could fish an adjective out of his head. Rarely had she put this much effort into her appearance, even dabbing a fingertip of perfume above her collarbones and rubbing a hint of gloss over her lips. When she had called Natalie for fashion advice, she had received a squeal of approval and a borrowed yellow halter top that ended well above her navel. Jake stared at her like he wanted to eat her alive. "You look great too."

The stark white of his polo contrasted with his bronzed skin and dark hair, the ends still damp from showering. Her stomach engaged in a slow, arcing backflip when he leaned over and brushed his lips over her cheek. Momentarily, she forgot about everything except for the sensation that something inside her was melting and seeping into her veins, warming her from the inside.

"Ready to go?" he murmured.

Alex fought past the dizzying spin in her brain before responding. "Yes, I'm ready."

Long considered the most coveted property in all of Brazos County, the Cobb's river house was nestled behind a grove of pine trees on a gentle slope that culminated in an outcropping of land along the water. The grounds stretched into infinity until they disappeared into the black nothingness over the lazy brownish-gray ripples of Cedar Creek. A brightly lit two-story plantation style home towered over a neatly clipped lawn. Alex stared up at the balcony that stretched the entire length of the second floor. The shutters had been thrown open and a row of cheery windows stared back at her.

"This place is unbelievable."

"I know. Cory and I had a blast growing up here."

"Are his parents okay with," Alex surveyed the grocery bags being carried around to the back of the house, "all of this?"

Jake snickered as he undid his seatbelt. "Cory's dad travels a lot for work and his mom decided to go this time." A wave of concern peaked and then ebbed as Jake placed a large hand on her bare thigh.

"Don't worry. We've done this before and had it all cleaned up before they got home. And we're so far out of town the cops don't bother coming out here."

Alex tamped down her rising discomfort and took Jake's hand so he could tug her out of the low-slung car. He tucked her hand into his side as they navigated the dimly lit stone pathway around the house to the backyard, using his other to wave greetings at a dense gathering of people she might have recognized in better lighting.

A firepit blazed in the center of a cluster of mismatched lawn chairs. Like cars from a derailed train, compact ice chests lined the entire length of the yard. Cory cracked open one of the lids, surveying the interior, and as Jake approached, pulled out two silver cans. Jake let go of Alex's hand to accept the beer and after surveying it, punched his cousin in the bicep.

"Come on, bitch, where's your good stuff?"

Cory split his lips apart and laughed as he opened the can. A delicate spray coated Alex's cheek.

"It's in the house. What do you want?"

"Jack and Coke, dude."

Cory loped toward the house and pulled open the backdoor while shooting the finger over his shoulder.

Jake rumbled with laughter then draped an arm across Alex's shoulders. "You want something?"

Debatable. She did want something. What that was remained undecided.

"Not right now." She smiled sweetly into his face, the shadows dancing off the angle of his jawline. He leaned down but stopped before he kissed her, instead brushing his lips along her ear.

"You warm enough?" A single finger trailed across her bare back and slid into one of her belt loops.

"I am," she stuttered.

"Okay, let's go meet some people then."

He took a step and tugged her by the shorts, parading her toward a crowd gathered at the edge of the manicured lawn. Every few feet he threw out a fist bump or a high five while pushing Alex ahead of him to join a tight circle of his friends. Alex elbowed in next to a thin guy in a straw cowboy hat holding a beer bottle. He smirked and passed her a look of appraisal. Opposite him, a brunette with a high ponytail wearing a bikini top sneered at her between sips.

"Guys, this is Alex," Jake announced. "She's from Cole's

Church."

"We've seen her around," said bikini girl. "Don't you live next to Justin James?"

"Yeah, we're—" What were they? Alex struggled for a moment before resolving herself to the truth. "We're friends." No matter how their life trajectories had separated, they were friends. They always would be.

"He's so hot." The girl cast her eyes to the heavens as if they might gift her with his presence.

And then Alex remembered where she had seen her. She had seen that long brown ponytail whipping around a lithe body as it performed a flawless herkie. "You're a cheerleader for Brazosville, right? Whitney?" Alex asked.

"Yeah, that's right. Good memory." She flashed a mouthful of white teeth that contrasted with her sunkissed skin. "Want a drink?"

Reaching down to a cardboard container at her feet, she removed a slim bottle sloshing with peach-colored liquid. Her brown eyes hardened into packed earth when she directed them at Alex.

"She doesn't want anything," said Jake at the same time Alex spouted, "Sure," and closed her fingers around the sweating glass.

Alex twisted off the cap and tilted the rim to her lips, guzzling as much as she could before she needed to breathe.

"You go, girl," said Whitney, eyebrows raising above the swirl of lavender shadow on her lids.

The contents of the bottle tasted like fermented peach pulp and flat soda, but there was no way she was going to make a face. She darted a look at Whitney over the top of the bottle and took another swig.

"What'd I miss?" asked Cory, shoving a plastic cup into Jake's chest.

"We were just talkin' about your mama," shouted a nasal voice from the other side of the circle.

Cory's smile faded and his face hardened before he burst out laughing and shoved the squat, beefy guy in the shoulder. Jake snickered and took a long draw from the cup in his hand. When he spoke, Alex's nose burned with the vapors that clung to his words. "Sorry, these guys have no shame."

Alex smiled and forced down another swallow of peach. "It doesn't bother me."

"Where's your girl?" Jake asked Cory as someone behind them

turned up the volume of a car radio. The thumping groove of Snoop Dogg permeated the summer air through the open driver's side window.

Cory looked at his feet and grinned. "She had fair stuff tonight. She'll be here later."

Alex wished that later would come sooner than it usually did.

Drinking. Laughing at inside jokes. Insulting one another. More drinking. The night had taken on a predictable rotation of activities. When Alex drained the first bottle, another one was thrust into her hand. A pink one this time. At least it didn't taste half bad. Or maybe the magical part of drinking was how it seduced even her taste buds.

"I'm bored," whined Whitney. "Let's play a drinking game."

"What do you wanna play?" slurred the heavy-set guy with the flipped baseball cap.

"Never have I ever." Whitney zeroed in on Alex, who at some point had been pulled down into Jake's lap. He reclined in a lawn chair, eyes at half-mast as his fingers curled into the waistband of her shorts. "I'll say something and anyone who hasn't done it has to drink. Then we'll go around the circle."

Alex steeled herself for what came next.

"Never have I ever," Whitney started, daggering her cat eyes at Alex, "had sex in a car."

Alex tried to go unnoticed as she took a small sip.

"Never have I ever," boomed a gruff twang, "thrown a touchdown."

Most of the circle drank and Alex giggled into her drink in response to Jake's fingers creeping up her flank.

"Never have I ever smoked pot," another voice chimed.

Alex drank again and this time Jake and Whitney shared a laugh instead of guzzling.

"Never have I ever gone streaking," Jake said through a rumble of laughter.

The last of her drink slid down her throat. Her head felt fuzzy. Like a dandelion or a baby duck's wing. Leaning over and embedding her lips in Jake's ear, she whispered, "Isn't this game usually played the other way around?" Jake shrugged and smirked without opening his lids. "I'll be right back," she slurred as a fog settled in her brain.

Wiggling off his lap, she strode toward the back door. Through the transparent glass, she watched a group of guys crowded around a round kitchen table dividing a deck of playing cards. Hoping to remain unseen, she entered quietly and began scanning for anything that resembled a guest bathroom.

"You can use the one upstairs," drawled Cory, who emerged from behind the steel refrigerator door with a jar of salsa in his hand.

"Thanks," she replied gratefully.

Grabbing the smooth wood of the bannister, she lifted one foot at a time on the carpeted stairs. Had it always taken this long to climb a flight of stairs? She was so focused on her feet and not tripping that she felt rather than saw the formidable mid-section at the level of her forehead.

"Oh, I'm sorry," she mumbled then looked up into the wicked gleam from a pair of seafoam green eyes.

"Apology accepted," he smirked, amusement and victory dancing across his face.

Rolling her eyes, Alex tried to edge around him, but he moved with her until she was forced to squeeze between his backside and the wall.

"Don't drink too much," he sang after her.

In a completely uncharacteristic moment of insanity, she thrust her middle finger into the air.

Jake was waiting for her when she exited the second-floor bathroom with its fluffy white hand towels and overwhelming scent of lavender. His hands were spread eagled across the doorjamb, and she stopped short at the sight of him. In the glow of the bathroom light, his eyes were bloodshot. When he exhaled, the alcohol on his breath mingled with something else. Something overripe.

"Do you know," he purred, "how long I've wanted to do this?"

Dipping his chin, his lips found the groove of her neck. She stilled, placing a hand on his chest. Her uncertainty was mistaken for permission. In the span of seconds, he grappled with her bottom lip and walked her backward into the bathroom where he flipped off the light. One hand pressed firmly between her shoulder blades while the other roamed inside the cuff of her shorts.

"Jake," she managed to croak when he paused to catch his breath. She flattened her palms on his pectorals and pushed as he began another assault of her mouth. Clamping her lips closed, she pushed harder. Panic began to seep in. An ancient panic of being pinned down without any control and it fueled the strength in her biceps. She stabilized her legs and pushed again. This time he staggered backward into the open hallway.

"No," she said. "I'm not...just...no."

"Don't be that way, Alex. You're hot. You know you're hot."

She folded her arms across her chest and straightened her spine. This wasn't the something more she was searching for. This was a bad decision wrapped in a layer of regret.

"It's not my fault that I'm crazy about you." He approached her again, extending his arms toward her and grinning. A shit-eating grin Natalie would call it.

"I need some air," she breathed and then regretted inhaling when she was so close to Jake's mouth.

"Okay," he whispered raggedly then leaned over and salivated into her ear. "I'll find you outside." With that, he disappeared in the bathroom, thankfully closing the door behind him.

Despite the unhinging last few minutes, Alex descended the stairs like a mountain goat and escaped out the onto the back lawn and into the anonymity of shadowed faces and drunken howling. She had no idea where to go next. She glanced to her right then her left. Blend into a gaggle of tipsy teenage girls taking shots or hide out between the couples making out in parked cars? Directly ahead of her, a wedge of moonlight outlined the pier, drawing her in with its simplistic beauty. She started toward it. Fun and distraction. Tonight, wasn't turning out to be either of those things.

Sighing, she undid her ponytail and ran a hand through her layers. Kissing was supposed to be poetic. Epic even. Not sloppy advances from a horny, drunk teenage boy. Briefly, she wondered where Justin was and if he might be sober enough to drive her home.

When she cleared the rise of the riverbank and began descending toward the pier, the voices behind her faded into a lull, low enough where she could hear the faint tenor of a frog. The day's pent-up moisture had blanketed the river in a delicate shroud of fog, thick enough to shield her vision from the black churning waters below.

A tremor of terror sparked up her spine when the first board of the pier groaned underfoot. She would have turned back if not for the figure standing on the end with his hands in his pockets. With nearly silent footfalls, she made her way to his side, never taking her eyes from the dense thicket of trees on the other side. Silence became their mediator as all the joy and anguish of the last decade sublimated into the space between them.

"I love being out on the water."

Alex gave a wry smile. "And I hate it."

"I know," he answered quietly, and her breath hitched in her throat. "You ever going to tell me why?"

"No," she answered.

"It's a good thing I'm patient then, Lex."

A warmth surged through her when he said her name. He was the only one who ever called her that.

"Listen, I—"

The whine of a police siren drowned out his next words and, for the second time in one day, Alex became mesmerized by a swirl of electric blue flashing light. Justin swore under his breath while reaching over to a frayed rope knotted over the post at the end of the pier. She watched two policemen exit their vehicle. Alex debated between outright giggling and screaming as hordes of people darted across the yard. Her heart pounded as she realized the depth of her bad decision making. Of all nights to drink ridiculously bad alcohol.

When Justin balanced on the edge of the pier and jumped into the blackness below, her heart nearly stopped.

"Holy...son of a...what the hell are you doing?" she hissed.

A *thunk* resounded and he called up to her. "Come on. Grab my hand."

Glancing back only once at the high school party descending into chaos, she grasped the outstretched hand, scrunched her eyes closed, and jumped.

The night enveloped them like a chrysalis of star studded black. Alex sat in the front of the canoe, her posture rigid, as Justin paddled swiftly upriver. Each dip of the oar striking the water was like music. A sacred melody only for her. The fog grew denser, its thick ropey tentacles weaving through the moss that dripped from overhanging cedar branches. A single amber porchlight appeared on their right and Justin grunted as he veered the canoe into a narrow tributary.

"Where are we going?" she whispered into the blackness.

"You'll see," he whispered back, neither of them willing to disturb the sacred quietude of this elegant microcosm of nature.

To distract herself, Alex blinked up at the sky, not entirely cloudless, but so dense with stars that a few clouds didn't seem to matter. A crescent moon shone its reflection onto the water, and she gasped as something skittered away from the prow of their boat. Not too long after that, a bridge came into view. A wooden bridge spanned the space between a forgotten field and an equally forgotten church—a white clapboard A-frame church, its windows boarded up, the shadows of a few headstones peeking up from the tall grass behind it.

"Hold on," Justin said as the boat made contact with the riverbank just shy of the bridge.

Alex pitched forward but kept her seat. "What is this place?"

"Somewhere that most people have forgotten about," he answered smoothly. He jumped out onto marshy land and deftly pulled the canoe farther onto solid ground, despite Alex being in it. He held out a hand, his face revealing nothing. "Come take a walk with me."

Placing her hand in his, she leaped to the ground, her knees buckling when her feet met the earth. They climbed up the riverbank until they reached a flat plane where the first trestle of the bridge rested. Justin pulled her up to join him. He led her onto the solid wooden beams to the very middle of the bridge. The world was quiet at this hour. Utterly silent and calm.

"Nobody uses that church over there anymore, but people say the cemetery is full of folks with unforgivable sins."

Alex felt a shiver course down her spine. "It's beautiful," she said then slipped her hand out of Justin's to wipe it on the cuff of her shorts. "Is that your Jeep over there on the other side of the bridge?"

He grinned and rubbed the back of his neck. "Yeah. I took the canoe over to the party because I had a feeling the police might show up."

"Is that why you were down at the pier?"

"No." He stared into the depths of the creek water below.

"What were you doing?"

"Thinking. What were *you* doing down there?"

Alex bit her lip almost to the point of bloodshed. "Trying to get away from Jake."

"Why?"

Even in the dark, Alex could see his posture stiffen.

"You were right about him. I don't think I'm the right girl for someone like him."

Justin grabbed her by the arms and spun her to face him. "You are everything that's right. He's the one who has it all wrong."

Alex shrugged. "It's fine. He was just supposed to be a fun distraction. Something different. Something more." Her lips twisted in wistfulness. "But for now, I guess I'm only meant to be who I already am."

"Who you are, who you really are, is pretty damn amazing."

With every word, his face had inched closer to hers until his lips hovered right at the level of her forehead.

"Who am I?" she asked, not expecting him or the night to give her an answer.

"You," he breathed, lowering his mouth until it crested on her upper lip, "are perfect."

TWENTY-FIVE

Alex was too stunned to respond. Too stunned until the tiny electrical current emanating from his touch sparked life into her mouth. And then she was kissing him. It was only a brief brush of lips, but this was what kissing was supposed to be. It was delicate. It was ravenous. This was kissing that inspired novels.

He pulled away to catch his breath, a ragged uncertainty unfolding on his face. So, she snaked an arm around his neck and reached up on her tiptoes to meet his lips once more. They were soft and hard all at once. Tender and receptive and demanding. Enveloping her with the scent of pine and the lingering taste of sweetness.

When she pulled back, her eyes widened. Her pulse thrummed in her lips as he palmed her cheeks between large hands and stared down at her.

"What was that?" she croaked. Her voice barely sounded like her own. Justin smirked down at her.

"What have you been drinking?"

"What?" She freed her face from his hands by grabbing his wrists and jerking backward.

"You taste like an orchard."

Wrinkling her nose, she began to laugh uncontrollably. "Really cheap wine coolers, I think. What about you?" Using two fingers, she poked him in the steel of his abdomen.

"Not a thing," he confessed.

"Really?" Alex stared at him in disbelief. He looked away and rubbed his foot along the rim of the bridge.

"I didn't want to be drunk if I had to kick anyone's ass and then drive you home. In that order."

"Oh."

"But I guess you're all grown up and can take care of yourself."

Running a hand through his hair, he assessed her with intent eyes. Curious and without judgment. Without expectation.

"Not like the time Billy Caldwell tried to kiss me at recess and you pushed him into the ditch."

He barked with laughter and doubled over. "I got detention for that," he pouted.

Alex rolled her eyes. "It wouldn't have been the first time."

"No." He rubbed the dimpled surface of his chin. "The first time was when someone tripped and knocked over Mrs. Brightwell's art cart and yours truly took the blame."

A prickly flush crept into Alex's face. "I forgot about that."

"I didn't," he said smoothly and held out a hand. "Want to make it up to me?"

Alex stared down at the proffered hand. The long fingers that excelled at shooting baskets. The calluses on his palms from tossing countless bales of hay. The wielder of the reigning thumb war champion. She took it without hesitation. He pulled her gently down with him so they could sit on the edge of the bridge together, swinging their legs into the empty air below. Tucking her hand into his lap, he began stroking his thumb over her knuckles.

Alex bit the inside of her lip to stifle the words there but failed. "I have a question."

"Of course, you do."

"What is this?" Alex glanced down at his index finger that was now tracing the chaotic dips and edges of her hand. He didn't answer right away but continued his exploration, flipping over her hand to trace the inside of her wrist. Her stomach felt like a cageful of parakeets all flapping in unison.

"This," he said matter-of-factly, "can be whatever you want it to be."

That was not what she expected him to say. He was giving her all the control. All the autonomy. She didn't necessarily know what to do with it.

"What if I don't want it to be anything?" she challenged.

"Then we'll go back to being just friends. No harm. No foul."

Leave it to Justin to utilize a basketball analogy.

"But we kissed!" Alex sputtered.

"What's a kiss between friends? Hardly worth remembering."

Alex tried to jerk her hand back, but he anticipated her and tightened his grip.

"So, you'll just add me to the disturbingly long list of girls you've kissed?"

He shrugged, his eyes twinkling mischievously. "That depends."

"On what?"

"On what happens in the next few minutes."

He wasn't going to pressure her with expectations or show his own hand. What would be the purpose of risking their friendship if he didn't want more? More importantly, did she want more? The gnawing, pulsing excitement in her gut told her that she did. Oh God, she was terrified. She licked her lips as the moisture sieved from her mouth.

"What do you want me to say?"

"Whatever you're thinking right now."

"I...do."

"You do what?"

"Want more."

"Me too."

The words were whispered onto the cusp of her upper lip as the silken shock of hair that he was always brushing back fell over her forehead in a curtain. At his urging, she parted her lips and let him explore her in hesitant darts of his tongue. She wasn't sure how this was supposed to feel but it set her on fire. She found herself drawn into the sweet intensity, the heady bliss. The entire rest of their conversation happened without uttering a single word. He groaned when she let loose her own tongue to join his. A piece of her heart melted right then as she felt him deep in her bones. Her childhood friend. Her most trustworthy companion. Her protector. Her...what was he now?

Drawing in a ragged breath, Justin reclined backward and settled his shoulders against the formidable wood of the bridge. Feeling his absence, she froze in her seated position and stared down into her lap, tucking a strand of hair behind her ear.

"Sorry, I...I'm not that experienced compared to..."

She felt a tug on the hem of her shirt that pulled her down into his waiting arms. He tucked her into his side and kissed the top of her head.

"Have you ever kissed anyone?"

"Not like that," she replied shakily. "Was it okay?"

"It was perfect, so perfect that I had to take a timeout before the next half." His shoulders shook in silent laughter.

"You and the basketball," Alex groaned.

"It's going to get me where I want to go," he said assuredly.

"And where is that?"

"Texas University," he said quietly, and Alex stilled. "I recently found out my girlfriend got in there." He nuzzled the curve of her ear with his nose.

"Girlfriend?"

"Yes," he explained patiently. "You're a girl and you're my friend."

They lay in silence for a while lost in circulating thoughts while they settled into a new level of intimacy. Her hand had never tingled quite so much as it did when her fingertips cascaded over the lines of his jaw. She could feel every single inch where their bodies were in contact. Every ripple of breath from his chest. Every movement magnified into tendrils of sweet sensation.

"How's your mom? Have you talked to her lately?" she asked while absentmindedly rubbing her nose along the sleeve of his t-shirt. Her head fit perfectly into the crook of his arm.

"No, but she's got some leave coming up around Thanksgiving and she'll be home for a while."

"Where is she these days?"

"Somewhere in Iraq. She can't tell me exactly where."

"Do you think she ever regrets being in the military?"

A sigh left his chest. "I don't think so. And I miss her, but I'm really proud of her. She's great at what she does."

"Would you ever enlist?" Alex laid a flat palm on his mid-section to steady herself.

"I sort of already tried."

"What? When?" Alex pushed up to her elbow, the uneven woodgrain digging into her skin.

"I applied to West Point, but I don't have any hope of getting in and maybe I don't even want to go now."

A terrifying quiet enveloped them and when the thunder resounded overhead, Alex thought her chest had been split in two. A barrage of rain doused her in the face and high velocity pellets stung her legs. Justin leaped to his feet, pulling her up alongside him. Their feet pounded a steady rhythm into the wood crossbeams of the bridge until they reached the twin headlights of the Jeep. Alex, rain streaming down her face and chest, hopped in as soon as Justin threw open her door. In a moment, he was situated next to her in the driver's seat.

"Do you feel like," he said, shaking his head like a wet dog then slicking it back with one hand, "we're always getting rained on?"

The tension burst as easily as soap bubbles as Alex relaxed into a laugh. "You know what they say about Texas weather."

Justin drove her home slowly, avoiding the overflowing gutters and deep potholes, navigating the road carefully as one would a burgeoning love affair. Once the Jeep bounced into Alex's driveway, he cut the engine and they sat inside with nothing but the frantic pattering of rain on heavy duty plastic. Alex's breath fogged up a section of window and she drew a smiley face inside the circle before it faded.

"When did things change for you?" The moment felt as delicate as a night rose opening its bloom for the first time. Alex kept waiting for the petals to recoil into a bud again.

"It's been a while," he admitted, and she twisted in her seat to look at him.

"How long is a while?"

"Months. A year. A few years. I don't know."

"You never said anything. You've basically avoided me since we started high school."

"I know. I wasn't sure if it was real at first and then when I did, I wasn't sure how you would feel and the last thing I wanted to do was lose you, so I focused on sports and believe it or not, school. And other girls."

"That's why you wouldn't go out with Natalie."

"One of the reasons." His brow furrowed and he stared down at his hands. "What about you?"

The question hung in the air, and she debated whether to answer honestly. To lay her own hand on the table. Something inside her churned. A blend of light and heat. Warmth and desire. But something deeper too. Something solid and steadfast. It bubbled under her skin along her veins right to her fingertips. She took a breath to quiet it, to quell it somehow. A repository of memories danced across her consciousness with fleeting images of the boy who held her hand on the school bus on her first day of third grade. Of the gnawing ache she pushed deep inside herself every time she had seen him with another girl. Of the girl who felt most comfortable in her own skin when she was with him.

"Whatever this is...I've never let myself feel it but..."

"But what?"

"I'm feeling it now."

A solitary tear leaked from the outer corner of one eye and joined the rain already coating her face. His thumb reached up and brushed it away in the gentlest caress.

"Why do I feel like the minute I let you out of this car, this is all going to be over?"

Alex grabbed his hand and brought it to her lips, pressing them to the pad of his thumb. "It won't. I promise."

"What's got you all moony-eyed and goosy-goosed?"

Alex startled when Terry's gravelly voice carried through the stall door. She had been spreading fresh straw on the loose earth, but her mind had been elsewhere. Possibly on a bridge in last night's rainstorm.

"Nothing," she answered, rubbing her forehead on her shirt sleeve.

Terry grunted in response. "I hope you chose the tall one. The other one was too pretty for my taste."

A lovely thrill skittered down her spine even though she answered with, "we're just friends."

"Sure, and I'm Glinda the Good Witch." Terry's mousy hair and piercing metallic eyes suddenly appeared through the bars of the stall. "Well, whatever is slowing you down today, speed it up. We need this place spic and span for the buyers. They're expecting us to be outta here in two weeks."

Alex descended into further awareness. "Is that enough time to fix up the new place and move everything over there?"

"It's gonna have to be. Maybe you can get your new boyfriend to help out."

Terry's face softened for a moment, giving Alex a glimpse of the beauty she had possessed in her youth. Sharp high cheekbones that wouldn't be hidden behind decades of wear and delicate, almond-shaped eyes that glittered in the sun. Like fool's gold.

"We're just friends," Alex repeated but Terry had already reached the end of the corridor.

The next two weeks slipped by in a blur. After dodging a few of Jake's late night phone calls, she heard he had moved on to someone else, or maybe he had revived his relationship with Candy. She hadn't had time to notice between readying Terry's new barn for the big move, packing up a decade's worth of artifacts at the old one, and secretly meeting up with Justin for a summer of exquisite, unadulterated fun and distraction.

"I still don't know why we've been sneaking around the past few weeks," he teased, tucking a length of her hair behind her ear.

They had taken a break from barn clean-out at the old McCoy Place, or rather the new Teresa Hawthorne place, and were stretched out on a blanket under a towering oak tree. Alex groaned and flipped over onto her stomach.

"I'm not ready for the town drama. Can you imagine when this gets out?" She held up one finger. "Everyone will know within twenty-four hours." She flipped up a second one. "The ladies at church will already have our wedding planned and our first three children named." She held up three fingers. "And, we'll never have another peaceful moment as long as we live."

"That's extreme."

"No. It's reality. It's where we're from. I just want..."

"What do you want?" He lifted himself onto his elbow and drifted his lips across her cheek.

"Just some time to ourselves to figure this out. To just be."

"Then that's what you'll have." His lips stopped just short of the corner of her mouth. Alex breathed in the scent of honeysuckle and tilted her head so he could kiss her. Her toes danced with the lingering taste of Coca-Cola on his breath. "Can we at least watch the fireworks together tonight?"

"I guess so," Alex said, feigning annoyance, "but only because it'll be dark and no one will notice us."

"I'm starting to love the dark. So many possibilities." His fingers curled around her calf, and she squealed in response.

"Please do not let me forget to check on the horses. They hate the fireworks. Last year George nearly kicked a hole in the wall."

His face sobered and a hardness entered his gaze. "Did the police ever figure out who was sending all those threats?"

Alex shook her head. "No, and Terry hasn't mentioned anything to me if they did. But things have been quiet. Nothing since that last letter. Maybe whoever it was gave up when Terry wouldn't back down."

"Maybe," Justin said but his face radiated disbelief. "Just be careful, okay? There are some mean, prejudiced mother f—"

"Justin!" Alex exclaimed.

"People," he continued, "that live around here."

Alex sat on her bed surrounded by a mound of freshly laundered clothing. She never minded laundry day. Folding different textures into prim shapes and stacking them together was soothing. A pile of denim. A pile of t-shirts. And several bunched-up pairs of socks. One day she would have to expand her wardrobe.

She glanced out her bedroom window at the fading sunshine and felt immediately relieved. Today had been unbearably hot. The kind of hot that made her blood bubble, even with an endless supply of popsicles. Out her window, Alex noticed that their grass had shriveled into nonexistence.

The muscles of her shoulders ached as she reached into the basket for the remaining assortment of mismatched socks. Today at the barn had been especially brutal. She had held a broom above her head for several hours to clear out the most resistant of cobwebs and was rewarded by a black and yellow spindly legged arachnid that plopped to the ground right in front of her. Just thinking of it made the screams well up inside her again. Justin had stomped it to death with the heel of his converse sneaker while muttering an array of expletives.

"Why didn't you let me do that?" Janie *tsk'ed* and claimed the basket from the middle of Alex's bed.

"I can take care of myself, Mom."

"I know. You always have, but you don't always have to."

As Janie scooped up the folded piles and began shoving them into the chest of drawers, Alex's eyes roved over her bedroom. Its treasure trove of objects had grown more special lately: the porcelain unicorn that played *Beautiful Dreamer* when the bottom was wound, a blue science fair ribbon, her favorite picture of her and her mom from their first Christmas in this house. Her mom was in a green velvet dress kneeling on the floor with her arms wrapped around Alex against the background of a plastic tree decorated with silver tinsel.

"You look like your grandmother in that photo," Janie remarked, removing it from her bookshelf.

Alex's mouth dropped open in shock.

"My mother," Janie clarified, "not your dad's."

Alex closed her mouth. "Oh."

A niggling in the back of her brain started and she blurted the question before she could stop herself. "Mom, do you know anybody in town with the last name Powell?" The isolated block of gray granite jutting from the cemetery landscape flashed through her mind.

"I used to," Janie replied slowly, placing the picture back on the shelf and Alex felt her heart rate take off at a wild cadence. "Why do you ask?"

Alex clutched the frame of Justin's Jeep as he rolled to a stop at the rear of the baseball field parking lot. A massive crowd had already gathered at the entrance, keen to claim a square of closely cropped grass for blankets and lawn chairs. A trio of little girls wearing brightly colored hairbows trailed behind their mother who was carrying an overstuffed basket of goodies. One of them waved a fairy wand in the air. Once the engine died, neither she nor Justin moved.

"So, hang on, the Powell with the weird mark on his headstone was your dad's uncle? Your grandmother's brother?"

Alex gripped the armrest even tighter. "Apparently. My mom said he died in World War Two, somewhere in the Pacific."

"And your grandmother died too?"

"Yeah, a few years ago."

"Is there anyone alive who would know what that symbol means?"

The tension in the car thickened and when Alex took a breath, she felt like she was choking.

"No," she answered hoarsely even while images of a dirt-streaked face sneering at her in the lamplight appeared in her mind's eye.

"What about your dad?" Justin spoke softly, gently, like he would talk to a frightened dog.

"I don't..." Alex croaked and closed her eyes, willing the images back into a receptacle in her brain. "There's no one else to ask."

He didn't press further although she heard his jaw pop several times with the opening and closing of his mouth.

"Just because no one talks about it doesn't mean they don't know," he said.

"Know what?"

"The reason you scan every store before you go in. The reason it took you the entire length of third grade to smile. The reason you love water but can't stand to be on the river."

Alex couldn't hear anything above the roaring in her ears or the pounding of her heart against the underside of her sternum. It struck her so fiercely she thought her chest would explode.

Warm fingers under her chin turned her head to the side and her eyelids flew open. Justin's face was a few inches from her own, his eyes flaring with cold heat.

"He's a piece of shit, Alex. Fuck that son of a bitch."

What was left to say after a cursing spell like that?

TWENTY-SIX

Justin gripped her hand tightly enough that eventually, somewhere between the Jeep and centerfield, she stopped shaking. She had reshelved her past back where it belonged. In the permanent rearview.

Despite worrying that the entire town would know the intimate details of her last two weeks with Justin the minute they saw her face, her fears failed to come to fruition. A few amused glances came their way. But not one comment or catcall. By the time they secluded themselves near the outfield chain link fence, she finally let herself relax.

Kids with sparklers in hand ran screaming through the seated guests like miniscule comets zipping through the galaxy. Food wrapped in tinfoil was unpacked onto gingham blankets. A steady din of voices rose and transcended into a cumulative sigh when the first fireworks exploded overhead and the sky rained stars.

Alex reclined shyly into Justin's waiting arms until they wrapped snugly around her middle and he tucked his chin over her shoulder.

"What do you think fireworks look like from space?" she yawned.

"Probably like tiny missiles. Like the entire world could be at war."

"Of course, you would think that." She tried to sit up, but he pulled her farther into his chest.

"I can't help it. It's in my genetics."

"What do you know about genetics?"

"Fruit flies, wild types, et cetera. I already forgot the rest." He nuzzled into her hair which she had pulled back in a bun and she squirmed.

"People are watching us," she gritted but felt the sting of his absence when he pushed her away from him.

"Then I better not do anything crazy. Like this."

Suddenly his head was in her lap, strands of ridiculously thick auburn hair tickling her inner thighs. He curled his fingers around the V of her shirt and pulled her into his parted lips. For a moment, she reveled in the tenderness she found there. The fullness of his bottom lip tasted like honey and mint. And while rockets burst over their heads in their full glory, she let herself enjoy every minute of it.

Once the entire spectrum of the rainbow had exploded overhead, she nudged Justin whose head remained comfortably positioned in her lap. She cocked her head toward the parking lot. "I need to go check on the horses."

With a groan, he catapulted to a stand and held out his hand. One minute she was seated on the grass and the next she was on her feet with the headrush to prove it. Hand in hand, they tiptoed along the back fence until they reached an open gate, quietly leaving the magic behind. The magic of fireworks that could heal any wound, reforge any bond, and spark new ones.

As they walked through the parking lot, she looked, truly looked, at his face. The angular jaw always cast in shadow. The mouth that so easily switched from sarcasm to tenderness. The shock of hair that, at its longest, hung almost to his cheekbones. She had the sudden urge to brush it back out of his eyes. They arrived at the Jeep too soon.

"Ready?" He opened the door for her to crawl in.

Hesitating, she let the full impact of youth and innocence in the sweet pulp of summer bloom in her chest. It filled every bit of her, surging to the tips of her toes and the ends of her fingers. Fingers that she fluttered upward to rest on Justin's cheek. And then she stared into his face, imbibing this memory like it was air or sustenance. She could hear the sea in his eyes and feel the flickering fire in his hair. She could smell the decadence on his breath. And then she rose up to kiss him, running her palm down his face and behind his neck to the damp heat that coated his skin.

"What was that for?" he said breathlessly when their lips parted.

"No reason," she replied and smiled while her flood of feeling condensed down into a shimmering ball of light that she tucked deep inside her.

"Where's Terry tonight?" Justin asked as they swung around a curve too quickly to stay upright without sufficient centripetal force. Their headlights reflected off an armadillo that hissed from the side of the road.

"Probably out at the new place. We're supposed to start moving the horses over there tomorrow."

"Need any help?"

"Don't you already have a job?"

"Yes, but it's missing certain benefits."

He waggled his eyebrows suggestively and she blushed fiercely. Closing her eyes, she let the wind whip across her face, eluting her thoughts until her mindscape was nothing but blurry images. The past, the present, the future. Why did it seem like they were all suddenly colliding? The mysterious incidents at Terry's barn and how they were tied to a family she wanted to forget. A summer of unanticipated romance. Her well planned future whose trajectory had begun to shake.

She took a cleansing breath. There was time to worry about all of this. Tomorrow.

An unexpected acrid scent met her nose and she coughed. Her nostrils flared and she sucked in another breath. The wind carried the fleeting smell of something burning.

"Do you smell that?" She twisted around to Justin.

"Yeah, hopefully someone didn't set their pasture on fire with their fireworks."

Tires crunched as they entered the gravel driveway to the barn and Alex leaped out to open the gate. A breeze blew across her face as she undid the latch and swung it wide. A breeze that was abnormally hot. Not the sundrenched air from the shoreline but something dry that crackled with heat. The scent of smoke grew more potent, and she swung her eyes to the barn where the air seemed to shimmer above its peaked roof. She didn't scream. She didn't hesitate. Before she realized it, her legs stuttered into motion, and she was running.

Faintly, she heard Justin's shouts as he parked the Jeep and barreled behind her. One word pounded through her head every time her feet struck the ground. Faster. Faster. As she rounded the last bend, she saw the cloud of smoke, churning and writhing, over the entire upper half of the stable. As if in a nightmare, she paused at the gaping blackness that was the entrance, long enough to hear hooves pounding a death march inside the cavernous space. She took a step inside and swallowed a scream when the entire ceiling erupted in flames. Rough hands jerked her backward and she lost her balance, landing on a patch of gritty earth.

"You're not going in there." Justin bent down and held her firmly by the shoulders.

"Get off me," she shouted. She tried to scramble to her feet and failed. "We have to get the horses out."

"We need to call the fire department."

"There's no time. You know they won't make it."

"Okay. Let me just think for a second. Look at me."

She met his eyes and then her entire body, which had been shaking like a leaf, suddenly calmed. Her breathing steadied and she felt her pulse rate become slow and steady like the ticking of a clock.

"Horses hate fire. They either run or freeze," she explained, enunciating every word. "First, we'll open all the stalls and then if they don't come out, we'll find something to put over their head and try to lead them out."

He nodded quickly, erratically, and his grip loosened enough that she scrambled to a stand. Grabbing his hand in hers, she reentered the haze of smoke that had now swept through the corridor of stalls.

"You take the right and I'll take the left."

Justin moved mechanically, pulling up metal pins and flinging open doors to the three occupied stalls on the right. As Alex's fingers found the latch to George's stall, a wave of heat consumed her face and a piercing scream split open her skull. The large chestnut Thoroughbred was backed into the corner of his stall, throwing his head from side to side and pawing the air with a solid hoof.

"It's okay, boy. It's okay," Alex repeated in a whisper voice. She edged to his heaving side out of the pathway of his hooves and placed a hand on his neck. Feeling her way to his hindquarters, she gave them a solid smack then waved her arms toward the open door. He wouldn't budge. She smacked him again.

"Come on," she grunted and then shouted, "go!"

Rearing into the air to his full height, George pawed the air with precision, and, for a moment, Alex appreciated just how magnificent he looked. Wild, but not yet free. When he plummeted to the ground, his hoof met with Alex's left foot. She heard the definitive crack of bones inside her head. Sparks of pain shot up her leg and into the marrow of her toes as another pungent plume of smoke forced its way into her lungs.

"We gotta get out of here, Alex," Justin yelled above George's snorts of terror.

Reacting rather than thinking, she yanked off her t-shirt and flung it over the horse's pricked ears. Positioning herself behind him, she shoved into his backside until she heard hooves clattering over the metal railing of the stall. Once George sniffed the fresh night air, he galloped toward it, past Justin who had to flatten himself against the stall door to avoid being trampled. Alex crawled out of the stall on all fours. Justin dropped to his knees in front of her.

"This," he grunted, pulling her up by her waist, "is not how I wanted to see you without your shirt on."

A burst erupted from her chest, a laugh that quickly devolved into a bellow of pain when her foot met with solid earth.

"Did all the horses make it out?" she croaked.

"Yeah, now let's go!" he barked followed by a hacking cough.

Alex glanced over his shoulder down the smoky corridor of the barn where Terry's office door was wide open.

"I have to check Terry's office."

She limped in the direction of the flames licking down the rafters as Justin swore without refrain. He joined her at the door, and they peered into the inky black at a figure slumped over on the desk. Alex lunged inside, dragging one leg behind her and shook Terry by the shoulders. A glass bottle clattered to the ground, splashing its contents on her bare leg.

"Terry!" She shook harder. "Terry!" As her voice devolved into a fit of coughing, Justin was already flinging the petite woman over his shoulder like a ragdoll.

Somehow, they made it to out of the barn, weaving and wobbling, falling against one another amid shared grunts and curses. Alex collapsed onto the grass sucking in oxygen rich air in gulps. As the adrenaline waned, sharp pain throbbed from her left foot. She felt every imperfection inside her shoe.

Justin flopped Terry's lifeless body next to her. Alex willed her eyes open, taking in the sallow skin and slack mouth. Foot forgotten for the moment, she pushed up to her knees and moved her fingers up and down the groove in Terry's neck.

"I think I feel something," she said hoarsely. The rapid cadence of a pulse drummed against the tips of her fingers. "But I don't know if she's breathing."

They exchanged a look and her eyes watered at the soot covering his face, the angry red capillaries in the whites of his eyes.

"Okay." He scrubbed a hand over his face. "I'll go for help. There's a house about a mile that way. I can call the fire department." He hesitated before words began to tumble out of his mouth. "Alex, I can't believe...I'm so sorry."

"Just go," she said. "And hurry."

Grotesque shadows danced around her as the barn was engulfed in flames. She rocked on her knees beside Terry, her hands tipping up her chin like she had learned in CPR class. Counting then breathing into paper dry lips then counting again. Checking for a pulse. Her movements became robotic as her entire existence honed to willing life back into the body that lay before her.

Every breath into Terry's lungs tasted like charred wood. As the minutes ticked by, her ears attuned to every sound. Hoping. Praying to hear the high-pitched whine of an ambulance or at least the spinning tires of a Jeep. What was taking so long? Her stomach clenched in horror at the sound of cracking wood. Was this an accident? Or was it arson? Was it the sons of Brit?

Inhale. Exhale a lungful of air into Terry's mouth.

Her fingers slipped onto Terry's neck but this time, there was no steady thrumming to greet her. Her own heart sped up in response like it was siphoning up Terry's lifeforce as it left her body. Alex spurred into action and pressed her hands onto Terry's breastbone. It was more compliant than she thought it would be. As she started counting and pressing, she finally heard the sound of tires coming up the drive.

"I don't need to go the hospital," she grumbled as Justin drove behind the flashing red lights of the ambulance.

"Your foot disagrees."

Alex had stifled a scream when he had removed her shoe and helped her into the passenger seat of the Jeep. She supposed he had been trying to distract her. An EMS crew was pumping methodically on Terry's chest as they loaded her onto a stretcher then shoved her into the rear of the ambulance, slamming the doors behind them. As they had pulled away from the inferno, Alex watched the arcs of high-pressured water colliding with the flames in the air.

When they arrived at the hospital, Justin cradled her to his chest and carried her inside the one-story brick building through a pair of automatic sliding glass doors. He walked past the information desk and the triage station, both of which were unoccupied, and carefully placed her on a stretcher parked in the hallway outside the one room used for true emergencies. Car crashes and heart attacks. Drownings. Farming accidents. And now Terry.

The overhead fluorescent lights cast an eerie glow over the polished floor. Everything was white. Sterile. Generic. Alex couldn't see what was happening behind the opposed halves of the door, painted an impersonal army green and labeled with white block letters: trauma room. She only caught glimpses every time someone entered or exited.

A ring of nurses was stationed around the bed, creating a blockade to Terry's body. At the foot of the stretcher, a thick chested man in powder blue scrubs gestured to the monitor then at one of the nurses. Medical supply detritus littered the floor and a cerulean balloon positioned at the head of the bed was squeezed in time to an unspoken rhythm. A nurse with snow-white hair exited the doors and shuffled over to Alex with a blood pressure cuff.

"What's happening in there?" she wheezed before coughing.

"Dr. Daniel is doing what he can," the nurse answered matter-of-factly.

"Can I go in?" Alex asked.

"No, you can't." She turned to Justin. "It'll be a while before the doctor can see her."

A while turned into an even longer while. Long enough for Janie to arrive and take up vigil beside Alex's stretcher. Her eyes were rimmed red from crying and her hand shook violently as she reached for Alex's.

"I'm okay, Mom," Alex reassured her.

Janie nodded silently and reached in her shoulder bag for a tissue. A vibratory roaring whirred overhead, and all three of them craned their necks to peer out the single heavy paned window.

"They called Lifeflight," Justin said.

The helicopter blades never even paused a beat, acting as a soundtrack to a frenetic stir as the doors burst open. Terry, completely unconscious, a plastic tube extending from her mouth like a giant straw, was wheeled out the sliding glass doors and into the parking lot.

From her view out the window, Alex saw the bits of grass uprooted by the violent tornado of the helicopter's blades and the seamless way three people in flight helmets loaded the stretcher into the open door. They were gone in less than a minute.

A weary face under a surgical cap greeted her when she turned from the window. Everyone knew Dr. Daniel. For years, he had been the only doctor in town until a younger partner, fresh out of training, had joined him last year.

Alex remembered the first time she had seen him. She had been a frightened, shivering eight-year-old who had just waded through miles of flood water. A violent spring storm and an even angrier river had washed away their house one night while her father had been shooting whiskey at a bar.

Despite the passage of nearly a decade, Dr. Daniel hadn't changed. He wore the same expression of patience and solidity, though the trim beard he kept was now more gray than brown. He took in the sight of Alex flanked by Janie and Justin and released the brake on the stretcher. He surveyed her exposed left foot, swollen to twice its size and boasting an ugly shade of purple.

"I'll be back with Alexandra in a moment," he announced and began pushing her down the short hallway toward a pair of swinging doors labeled "Radiology".

"Can you move enough to put your foot right in this square?"

Alex nodded and obeyed, placing her foot in a square beam of light on the X-ray table.

"Any reason to think you're pregnant?"

"No," she looked down and shook her head while heating with embarrassment.

When Dr. Daniel was satisfied with the pictures he had taken, he came out from behind a glass enclosed booth and popped the radiographs into a lightbox. Alex hacked a cough as he began to speak.

"Well, it's broken." She had already suspected that. He noticed her leaning forward to inspect the films and he pointed with his index finger. "Each of your toes is connected to your foot by something called a metatarsal. This right here. You've broken three of yours." He pointed at the disruption in the bones in succession. "Nothing too serious, but you need to stay off it for a month or so. We need to X-ray your chest too. You inhaled a lot of smoke."

"Dr. Daniel," Alex said, tasting soot as she licked her lips, "how is Terry?"

He stuffed his hands deep into his white coat and took a seat next to her on the stretcher. "She survived. Thanks to you. What you did was really quick thinking, and the EMS crew got her back on the way here."

Alex didn't quite know what to do with the praise, so she let it flutter to the floor. Nothing mattered until she knew the rest of the story. "What will happen now?"

He stilled for a moment as if weighing the impact of his next words. "When we sent Terry's blood to the lab, we found a very high level of carbon monoxide as well as alcohol." Alex wracked her brain to remember what this meant. "When the carbon monoxide is breathed in during a fire, it binds to red blood cells and displaces oxygen. So, the oxygen is unable to get to the tissues. Kind of like a train car that's already full but the passengers aren't getting off."

"What does that mean?" Alex massaged her brain to reconcile the science with how this related to an actual person. Her stomach churned as emotion flooded Dr. Daniel's face and he strained to keep it under the visage of the calm professional.

"Terry will most likely survive, but she has suffered significant brain injury."

TWENTY-SEVEN

Significant brain injury. The words were on a constant loop in Alex's thoughts. As constant as the blades of the ceiling fan she had been staring at for the better part of a morning. It had been two full weeks since the fire. Her foot was on the mend. She could now shove it into a shoe with only minor wincing. Janie had driven her all the way to Houston to see Terry. Terry, who prided herself on independence and wit, was now reduced to a shell of a human, breathing through one tube and eating through another. The fire simmering beneath her eyes had vanished, replaced by a stark vacancy.

No family had come except for the daughter of a distant cousin who stared awkwardly at the machines and tubes and taken possession of the few belongings Terry had on her person. No one called to let Alex know when Terry was discharged. One day she had been whisked away by a transport service to her home state of North Carolina where she would be cared for in a facility. Alex had shown up to the hospital and she had simply been gone, her hospital room taken over by someone with a bleeding ulcer.

"I'm going to the store, honey. Need anything?" Janie poked her ginger head through Alex's doorway.

"No thanks, Mom." She didn't take her eyes from the ceiling. A few minutes after her mom's tires peeled out of the driveway, the telephone rang. She groaned but swung off the bed and limped over to the kitchen.

"Hello?"

"I'm calling to speak to Alexandra Wilde."

"Chief Maloney, you know it's me."

"I know, but this is a formal call. Police business, you know."

"Okay."

Adrenaline surged through her veins in an uncomfortable rush.

"I reviewed your statement on the fire, and we sent some folks out there to poke around."

"It was the sons of Brit...whoever they are. You know they were threatening Terry. They had been there twice before, and they warned her if—"

"Now don't get your dander up, Alex. We know all that. We reviewed the case, and the investigators came to the conclusion that the fire was caused by some faulty wiring that set the hay bales on fire."

Faulty wiring? Alex felt an ice-cold shudder trickle right down her spine. "But why wouldn't Terry have noticed that?"

An uncomfortable silence ensued, and she knew she had asked a question he wished she wouldn't have.

"Well, now, you yourself know Terry was fond of her whiskey."

So, he was saying she was too drunk to notice. Too drunk to smell the smoke and call the fire department. It sounded so easy. A packaged-up explanation for what in reality had been a crime.

"If you have any other questions, you know where you can find me."

He hung up before she could ask the million questions buzzing through her brain.

A knock reverberated through the thin particle board of the back door. She limped over and opened it to find Justin, hair tucked into a worn baseball hat, long arms splayed out past the width of her doorway.

"Hey there, you," he said softly, and her heart quickened.

"Hi," she answered, a swarm of joy and guilt and impatience surging through her all at once.

They had barely seen one another since the fire between his shifts at the Farm and Ranch and her trips to see Terry. Not to mention her exhaustion and inability to hold a conversation most of the time because of her pain medication. But it wasn't just that. Something was changing inside her. Something big. And she both wanted and didn't want it to happen all at the same time.

"Want to take a drive?"

It felt good to be outside. The heat was nearly unbearable as it scorched down on them, but she didn't care. The birds twittering through the nearby trees sang a ballad of hope and the moss hanging from the tree limbs rustled with promises. The timbers of their bridge had soaked up enough morning sun that they felt warm on her backside. Justin sat a few feet away dangling his legs off the side, peering at something in the water that rippled with the tide.

"It's interesting how one small change can affect everything else. All the way down the river." She hadn't realized she was talking aloud until Justin twisted his neck to look at her.

"None of this is your fault, Alex."

"I know," she whispered but inside her brain, shadowy thoughts reared their heads. If she wasn't so afraid of her father, she could have discovered who the sons of Brit were. If she hadn't been wrapped up in a summer love affair, she would have been at the barn that night. If she had simply checked the office first or noticed Terry's truck parked along the fence line. If. If. If. A merry-go-round of guilt plagued her.

But something else lingered there too. The sense of control she had felt when her mind quieted and she pressed downward on Terry's sternum. A moment of chaos that had become rational and calculated. And then watching the coordinated efforts inside the emergency room that were like a choreographed dance. A dance meant to save someone's life. She could do that. Her hands itched to be put on another human. To reanimate their lifeforce. She could do it. She would do it.

"I think I want to go to medical school." The words, said aloud, became real—a living, breathing alternative to her expected reality. And it thrilled her.

"What?" Justin asked, his eyes widening into saucers. "I thought you already had a plan. Texas University and then vet school. You've already been accepted."

"I know."

"With a scholarship."

"I know."

He frowned. "Maybe you just miss Terry and this is your way of dealing with it."

"Maybe."

Six months later

January was unseasonably cold for southeast Texas this year. Christmas had even brought a few snow flurries dancing through the air like wayward winter fairies. Alex pulled her flannel-lined field coat around her frame as she walked up the sidewalk toward the double glass doors of the post office.

"Morning there, Alex," Pastor Brian greeted her and held the door open while balancing a thick stack of magazines and manila envelopes.

"Thank you," she said, her words riding on the puffed condensate of her breath. He partially blocked her path into the post office.

"How are you? I know you've gone through a rough time."

Alex swallowed, centering herself. Part of her still grieved for the loss of Terry and the horses. It felt like her youth had been incinerated along with the place she had loved so much. But the other part was grateful for the catalyst that was about to push her life onto an unexpected path. She gripped the envelopes in her hand even tighter.

"I'm okay."

"Well, that's good to hear." He eyed her speculatively and readjusted the pile of mail in his arms.

"I'll see you on Sunday, sir," she said and entered the squat brown brick building before he could detain her any longer.

The light streamed through the glass enclosed interior, alighting the floor in a buttery square of sun that completely contradicted the frigid temperature outside. Her hands vibrated with adrenaline as she pulled open the handle to the outgoing mail slot with a creak. Inside the tray, she placed three identical white letter-sized envelopes. One to Texas University relinquishing her spot in the pre-vet program, one to Duke University accepting a spot in the freshman class of 2002 as a pre-med major, and one to an address in southern California.

She had rewritten the letter four different times. What could she say to her childhood best friend, her first love, her first heartbreak, that would suffice? Words meant nothing without actions. That's what he had told her when she told him her plans.

Duke had the best pre-med program in the entire country, and she had gotten in. She had tried to placate him with what was possible. That being across the country didn't have to mean goodbye, but in her soul, she knew that this wasn't who he was or what he wanted.

And then he had asked her to choose. He painted a beautiful picture: two small town kids at Texas University, living their dreams, seeing what happened after that.

But the edges of her reality felt charred. As charred as the remnants of Terry's barn. And the only way to heal was to put everything behind her. To start over. In a new place. With a new dream that ballooned so brilliantly, everything else was shoved into nonexistence. And so, she chose.

The last night she had seen him was New Year's Eve. He had told her he was leaving. For bootcamp. No fuss. No fanfare. He showed her a GED certificate and a fat envelope from the US Army. Like two similar charges, life was pulling them in completely opposite directions. Her to the East Coast and medical school. Him to the West Coast and the military. He had kissed her that night, slowly and fiercely, almost prayerfully. And then the next day he was gone. Maybe love was like that. Soul altering one minute and gone the next.

She repeated the last line of her letter as she closed the door to the outgoing mail with a clang.

Maybe dreams choose us, not the other way around. And this is what has chosen me.
Love always, Lex

TWENTY-EIGHT

Cole's Church, Texas, Summer 2011
Her mother's gentle hand prodded her awake. "Alex. Alex, we're home."

The white clapboard house looked the same except crisper and cleaner. And someone had repainted the shutters a powdery shade of blue. The porch swing hung lopsided from its frame, the wood faded and splintered. Two chocolate canines rocketed around the corner in pursuit of something furry that scurried up the ancient oak tree shading their driveway.

Alex didn't move, instead nestling her head farther into the crook of her arms to shield herself from the blinding sun.

"Jet lag?" her mom asked. "You'd think you'd be used to it. What with your hours at the hospital and all."

Alex mumbled an unintelligible response.

"When you're ready come on inside, I'm making spaghetti for dinner."

Peter ambled out of the house in faded jeans and a canvas work shirt, the bald spot on his head catching the late afternoon sunshine filtering through a canopy of oak leaves. He went straight to the back of the truck and lifted her suitcase over the side.

"I could have gotten that," Alex said, spurred out of her seat by guilt.

"Nope, no need," he huffed, clutching the roller bag to his chest. "Your mama says you're here to relax." He smiled then and any doubt Alex ever had about his sincerity faded into nonexistence.

Peter was quiet and steadfast and great for her mom. Until now, she had never imagined her mom wanting anything other than what she already had. She had never tilted the paradigm and seen her mom as a woman; a woman with dreams other than what she shared with the rest of the world or with Alex. Frowning at the thought, she watched Peter bang through the screen door then followed him inside.

There was something about dinner in her mom's house that settled her. Down to her very bones. The simple beauty of a vase of wildflowers in the center of a geometric array of floral placemats. The worn silverware and porcelain dishes with the equidistant cornflowers and the matching water glasses. A steaming pile of pasta with meat sauce covered her plate, a bowl of salad next to it. Reaching for her water glass, she sipped it, the familiar metallic tang of well water coating her palate. She swirled it around in her mouth, half believing that it would turn to wine if she willed it to.

"How is everything in London, honey?" her mom asked over the scraping of forks and soft whines of canines.

"It's good. Things are good."

"Have you found a job yet?"

"No." Alex shoved a bite of spaghetti in her mouth to ward off more questions.

"Well, I'm sure it's just a matter of time. Who in their right mind wouldn't want to hire you?"

"You'd be surprised."

The response earned her a confused stare as her mom chewed thoughtfully on her salad. Alex purposefully knocked a slice of bread off the table, which was gobbled up before it reached the floor. An aggressive wet nose nudged her ankle.

"Alexandra! Don't let them think they can eat from the table. I bet you don't let McCartney get away with that."

The apex of her heart tugged against her ribs at the mention of McCartney.

"There's no telling what Mary Lou is letting him get away with these days."

The sharpness in her mom's eyes softened. "Any chance of getting him over to London?"

"No. He's going to stay in Botswana with Mary Lou. Permanently."

"Why?"

"She's lonely and she adores him and, honestly Mom—don't look at me like that—I've been a terrible dog parent. I basically dropped him off at Mary Lou's in February and haven't spent any time with him since."

A palpable silence cloaked the table, layered with the guilt that came with hard choices.

Peter cleared his throat and took a swig of iced tea. "You plannin' on stayin' for the auction next weekend?"

Alex tucked her chin and swallowed. "I don't know yet. I told Ian I would be back on Friday and there's a flight that leaves early Friday morning."

"You don't want to see what happens to Terry's land?"

"I'm not sure, Mom."

"I heard there was some big developer gonna buy it," Peter said.

"Oh really?" Janie turned her attention to Peter and Alex quietly faded from the conversation and into her own head.

Sitting cross-legged on her childhood bed, she leaned over and released the shades on the window. The moon had started its ascension into black nothingness, a hint of fog blurring the edges of its perfect curves. A knock resounded on her door and then a hand pushed it open. Her mom waited in the doorframe, a cherry wood box tucked under her arm.

"What's that?"

Janie chewed on the inside of her mouth for a moment before answering. "It was your dad's. I found it at his house after he died last year." Janie held out the box and Alex recoiled.

"What's in it?" she asked warily.

"I'm not sure. Mementos. Maybe some photos. Anyway, I want you to look through it and see if there's anything you want to keep."

"Why would I want any of it?" A twitch developed under Alex's left eye.

"It's yours to do with as you please. Throw it all out if you want but maybe save the box for keepsakes. It was handmade."

Alex's hands closed around the smooth woodgrain and deposited it on the end of her bed.

"See you in the morning, honey."

"Night, Mom."

Janie gave her a searching glance as she pulled the door closed.

Alex's eyes flitted from one wall to the other to the box to a faded poster of Secretariat. Back to the box. Then to her dresser. Once it had been filled with childhood trinkets, school ribbons and birthday cards. They had all been cleared away and replaced by two framed photographs. One of Alex in her mid-twenties in a black and forest green regalia receiving her medical school diploma. The other of her and Ian on their wedding day, framed by the backdrop of cedars and the silver ribbon of a creek. Had it been only three months ago? In her mind, an age had passed. Why did time seem to move at different paces? Slow then faster. At a standstill then a whirlwind. But never at the pace she desired.

Before she could complete another thought, she was dialing his number.

"Alex?" His voice was gritty yet perfectly clear. He had answered on the second ring like he might have been waiting for her to call. Probably out in Montmatre until the wee hours.

"I miss you," she said, a raw, plaintive feeling claiming her chest and climbing up her throat. The tension that had been so thick and asphyxiating between them before she left London evaporated when she heard him chuckle softly. That deep, decadent laugh was a balm to her soul.

"Hold on. Let me go outside."

Fractured noise. Song lyrics behind hushed conversations. And then the opening and shutting of a door.

"Where are you?"

"A little jazz bar down the street from our hotel."

"Oh."

"How's Texas?"

Alex glanced around her room again and the space suddenly felt a million times too small. "Quiet. Hot."

He snickered into the phone the way he did when he was two bourbons in. "I know something else that's quiet and hot."

Her stomach fluttered. "Oh really?"

"Yes, but I seem to have lost it."

"You haven't lost it."

"Misplaced it then?"

"It's on a short-term loan. You'll get it back soon."

"I hope so," he whispered so quietly that she questioned that he had spoken at all.

She stilled, reaching across the distance with as much heartfelt emotion as she could muster, begging him, willing him, to feel it. To feel her. It brought tears to her eyes.

"How's Paris?"

"Busy. Stressful."

A taxi driver laid on the horn in the background.

"It sounds like you're having fun though."

"Trust me. After the day I've had, I've earned it."

Alex's stomach twisted into another knot. "What happened?"

"The foundation board met and decided we've grown too much in the last year."

"Isn't that a good thing?"

"It is, but it means they want me to step down from being chairman."

Alex sucked in a breath. "I'm so sorry, Ian. I know how much the foundation means to you."

She heard him sigh and imagined him hunched over, silhouetted by a gaslight lamp on a Parisienne street corner.

"It was inevitable. I don't have time to run the company and the foundation."

And be there for you. He didn't say the words, but they hung in the air and a twinge of guilt twisted through her.

"Who will run the foundation when you step down?"

"That," he said with enigmatic flare, "is the million-dollar question we'll be addressing tomorrow."

She stayed on the phone with Ian on his walk back to the hotel and while he readied for bed. She didn't want to hang up. Her finger hovered over the keypad of her phone long before she pressed end. And then, when he had begun to snore lightly, she imagined the scent of mint and bourbon on his exhaled breath and whispered "I love you" before hanging up.

After the vitality of late-night London, the quietude of the cozy ranch-style home made her restless. Her thoughts ballooned into the entirety of her bedroom space while the rest of the house slumbered. The rusted springs of her bed squawked in protest as she flipped onto her side and slid her feet down to the threadbare rug covering the honey-colored hardwood. She had come here for something. To find something. And she intended to find it, preferably before it found her.

Alex heard Peter snoring when she padded into the kitchen and began rummaging around in the cabinets. He didn't seem like much of a drinker, but then her hand closed around a smooth glass bottleneck hidden behind a cast iron skillet. Jackpot. Or Daniel's to be exact. Alex poured a finger's worth into a juice glass and carried it outside to the front porch along with the cherry wood box.

The creak of the porch swing in response to her weight cracked loudly through the air, splitting the sound of cicadas harmonizing somewhere in the dalisgrass. She took a swig of whiskey and coughed on the fumes before placing the glass on the armrest and pushing off with one foot. The rocking motion soothed her, settled her thoughts into the finely cut facets of her mind, until all that remained was the night on her skin.

Her index finger traced a deep scratch on the box's lid as she studied the woodgrain, red and swirling like beaded droplets of blood. She had no idea what she would find in this box. Not once did she remember seeing it in her parents' bedroom growing up.

Before she could change her mind, she flipped open the clasp. Her nose met with the scent of musty leather and pungent cedar. With trembling hands, she removed a yellowed newspaper clipping and unfolded it. Her parents stared back at her in grayscale. Her mom in a long-sleeved lace dress buttoned up to her neck. Her dad with a thin mustache in a dark suit, shaggy hair adorning a face lit up in a relaxed smile. She studied the photo. He looked happy. Not the miserable drunk she remembered.

Carefully folding up the thinning newspaper, she put it to the side. She removed the rest of the items. A gold wristwatch with water damage under the face. The green feather of a mallard duck. A school photograph of her in the first grade, her hair pulled back into a messy braid, a wide innocent smile minus her two front teeth.

In the very bottom, a pocketknife with the initials JRW rested atop a small leather-bound book that looked like a Bible. When she removed it, the book was smooth in her hand, the saddle-brown leather worn with age and the pages yellowed and flimsy. She flipped it over, her throat closing around a scream when she stared at the embossing. A backward B slashed in half with a horizontal line.

TWENTY-NINE

When the morning rays dusted her bedroom in a swirl of pink and gold, Alex sat against her iron headboard, knees tucked under her chin, feet tingling in protest from being in this position way too long. A shuffling of feet in the kitchen drew her attention and she crept out of her room, already fully clothed. Janie, the ends of her ginger bob wrapped in spongy pink curlers, scooped coffee into a white filter.

"Mornin', honey." She yawned, her unoccupied hand fluttering over her mouth. "Did you sleep okay?"

"Mmhmm," Alex lied, opening the fridge to remove a carton of orange juice.

"Good. I'm glad." Janie flipped the switch on the coffee pot and then pushed two pieces of bread into the toaster. "You want breakfast?"

"No thanks, Mom." Alex avoided her eyes, not entirely sure what she was trying to hide. Perhaps the festering of a terrible idea.

"What are your plans today?"

"Not much," she said quickly, evenly. "But I was wondering if I could borrow the truck?"

"Of course. Anything you need. Peter can drop me off and pick me up from work today."

Alex faltered a smile. "Thanks."

"Can you pick up some bread for me at the grocery store while you're out?"

"Sure, Mom." She reached out to swipe the keys from the hook, her stomach twisting in anticipation. "I'll see you later."

Purpose. Her foot pressed heavily onto the accelerator. Purpose to drive out discontent. To overpower failure. Purpose to lay the past to rest. With every twist and turn of Cedar Creek Road, she might have well been digging up a freshly laid corpse, scooping out the coarse dirt and letting the papery skin of her memories poke through. As the truck barreled past Terry's old place, she skidded to a halt in the middle of the road, sending a spray of loose gravel into the ditch.

From the open window, she peered through a copse of oak trees to the shiny glint of silver aluminum in the distance. No acrid scent of charred wood. No flames licking the heavens. Nothing but the sweet smell of freshly baled hay and the musk of undulates. A motley crew of sheep and goats clustered near the center of the pasture engrossed in chewing. She tried to recall the name of the family who had bought the place from Terry and rebuilt everything after the fire. From what she could see, they had done a nice job maintaining it.

Alex shifted into drive, a guttural moan escaping from the engine when she gunned it forward. She left the window down as she wound her way through sweet nothingness. Honeysuckle scented air urged her onward to where the road would fork, and she would veer to the right where the cedars became thicker and the undergrowth denser. A wide swathe of grass broke the tree line and she swerved into it, bouncing through holes dug by armadillos, spindly branches scraping the side of the truck with high pitched screeches.

When she came to a clearing, she slowed to a stop, throwing the truck into park and killing the engine. A giant oak stretched across the path, blocking anything except for a human or animal on foot. Like nature's soldier, it stood guard over the steep embankment that couldn't be seen from the road, an abrupt cutoff in the landscape that would land a person directly into the creek if they weren't careful.

She had brought Ian here once without telling him what it was. He hadn't needed to know that this stretch of land backed up to the old McCoy place. What would have become Terry's place. The church where they married was only a few miles down the road and the same creek that slid by in front of her ran under that wooden bridge where they said their vows. Where they became husband and wife. Lovers and partners for life.

She had driven him here in their rented car, a spontaneous stop on the way to the airport. He had loved this tree, marveled over it, and wondered how many years it had taken for it to grow this massive.

On their wedding day, Alex had released the convertible top to the car so they could admire the constellation of greenery pierced with shafts of springtime sun.

"I don't think I've ever been happier," Ian said hoarsely.

"Neither have I."

"Do you mean that?" He turned his head toward her, eyes as blue as the sky, resplendent with hope and longing.

"Of course. How could I not be? My life is a dream."

He traced the scalloped lace edge of her wedding gown, and she closed her eyes in a cloud of contented bliss. He slipped a finger underneath the neckline, tugging it down as he explored. She felt his hesitation, his uncertainty. They hadn't been together since his accident and their return from Mongolia. She had taken moments to pleasure him, of course. To tease him or coax him into her mouth or her hand, but, while his fractures were healing, she hadn't been brave enough to suggest anything else.

But that day had been different. Everything had been different.

She had thrown open the car door and stood in a pie slice of sunshine underneath the oak tree. And then she stripped. Watching Ian's face as she removed first her wedding gown and then her lacy underthings was like being worshipped with someone's eyes alone. His face had transformed from radiance to something feral when she finally slid a pair of lacy white panties to her ankles and tossed them to the side. She crooked a finger to summon him, but he was already exiting the car, striding forward on weakened but certain limbs.

She was a goddess of wind and water and earth. Something powerful and ancient and true as she stripped Ian of his clothes and then tugged him down onto her discarded wedding gown.

"I'll do everything," she had growled into his ear as he lay down. She threw one leg on either side of him, giving him no warning before she buried him deep inside her, as deep as physically possible and maybe even more. He had cried out, the sound of it licking pleasure up her spine. And she had moved ever so gently, squeezing and releasing, clenching her thighs to keep her weight off his healing legs as embers of fiery pleasure sparked from her middle. His hands reached out to grip her hips, urging them both into a rhythm that defied the wind.

When Alex exited the truck, she made her way past the spot where she and Ian had consummated the ground and stepped over a giant, overlapping network of tree roots to reach the riverbank. She sat down on a gnarled root that looked like an old woman's crooked finger. A gnat buzzed in her ear and somewhere across the creek a cow bellowed to its herd. She put her hands on either side of the ground, balancing on the knife's edge of the tree root.

This was why she had come. To remember instead of forgetting. Not just the fire, but who she was. Why she was. And the answer was in everything around her: in the roots of this centuries old oak tree grappling for a hold along a peaceful creek bank; in the earth that birthed her, grew her, made her as vibrant and resilient as the wildflowers that bloomed along its bank. She was tragedy. She was joy. She was Texas. And it was past time the demons were purged.

Walking along the creek was no small task. She went slowly, foothold after foothold, from tree to tree, until she reached a sharp bend in the creek. The water abruptly turned away from a fence that erupted from the earth in a sagging stretch of faded green aluminum and barbed wire. Stretching the wire apart with two hands, she wedged her body through the opening, feeling the sharp prick and subsequent tug on her shirt as she emerged on the other side.

The walk to the barn was short. As soon as she covered the first hundred feet of overgrown weeds and milk thistles, she glimpsed the peaked roof of a tired barn. The sole of her shoe crunched against a broken beer bottle. She frowned but kept going. The western wall of the barn sagged and groaned against the elements, its perimeter flanked by patches of thorned plants masquerading as bright yellow flowers.

When she drew closer, able to peer into the gaping mouth of the barn doors, she recoiled at the stench. A deer carcass hung from one of the rafters, spinning slowly through a hazy cloud of flies. Deep maroon splotches discolored the whisps of straw underfoot as well the dirt floor. Glass shards and discarded cigarette butts littered the grass around the barn's perimeter. She hurried past the lolling tongue and bulging, glassy eyes of the doe, her fur worn so thin that Alex could see the white crown of her skull. She dove deeper into the barn's interior noting the heavy cobwebs covering the rafters she had once cleaned. The sagging doors to unused horse stalls. A tack room with a rusted barrel blocking the door.

Exiting out the back, she took her first full breath in several minutes. Even the summer air couldn't clear her nasal passages of the smell of rotting flesh. A wave of nausea bent her in half. She hovered over her knees, focusing on the faded fibers of her denim jeans. Someone had been using this place for their own twisted pleasures. The thought ripped through her stomach like a poison.

When the waves of nausea passed, she cracked open an eye and let the ground shimmy into focus. The glint of metal caught her eye. She sent her hand to the ground and her fingers closed over a handful of discharged rifle shells. She examined the casings, slipping one into her pocket and then discarding the others into the grass. Her fingernails dug into her palms as she stalked back across the pasture.

When Alex climbed back into the truck, slamming the door behind her, the vibration cast the leatherbound book to the floorboard. She picked it up by the cover, dangling it away from her as if it would grow fangs and bite into the meat of her palm. She stared at the embossed mark on the cover—the mark of the sons of Brit. Whoever they were. Maybe they were a bunch of idiot redneck locals or sociopathic devil-worshipers. But somewhere in the deep and dark recesses of her memory, she knew it all had to be related. The threats. The fire. The reason this place had been abandoned. She settled the book into her lap and began thumbing through the yellowed pages filled with cramped print.

"Son of a bitch," she breathed as names and dates stared back at her. Weddings. Births. Funerals. It was a family tree dating all the way back to—she flipped to the first entry. Three men—brothers born in the year 1805. The brothers Powell. Born in Tennessee, they had joined Stephen F. Austin's original three hundred to settle on a hundred acres of land in southeast Texas.

She thumbed through the next several pages as familiar surnames appeared in a maze of genealogy: McNeil, Farfield, Cooper, McCoy, all names she recognized either from the cemetery or kids from school. No Powells appeared after 1945 when her father's uncle died in the war. The line ended like the fractured end of a tree branch. She scanned the last entry, filled in five years ago. The marriage of Earl McCoy to Jessica Randall.

Alex almost missed it, the ramshackle house hidden behind a forest of weeds, a rusted truck with a shattered rear window parked haphazard in the front yard. She crept along an unpaved shell road, past a shingled roof that sagged over a front porch littered with detritus: a pile of ratty towels, a gas can, a child's plastic car. She parked on the edge of the road just shy of a ditch half-full of murky water and backtracked to the leaning mailbox with McCoy spelled out in store-bought sticker letters. Her sneakers sunk into the saturated ground, announcing her arrival by the sucking sound made when she pulled them out. A dog's head reared up from the truck bed, a low growl followed by rapid-fire barking from between his black gums. Alex's heart rate kicked into a frantic gallop, and she froze.

"What's the matter with you, dog?"

A lady's voice screeched over the barking. Somewhere inside the house, a baby began to wail. A screen door popped open and a girl much younger than Alex emerged. A girl with skinny arms wearing a yellow tank top and denim cutoffs, a baby propped on one hip and a child fisting the hem of her shirt. She put a hand over her eyes to shield them from the afternoon sun. "You lost?"

Eyeing the dog whose fur was the color of the mud on her shoes, Alex inched forward. "No, I was looking for Earl and Jessica McCoy. Are you Jessica?"

"Why? Who wants to know?" She shifted the baby to her other hip. "You with those Jehovah's Witnesses?"

Alex shook her head. "No, I'm not with them."

"The courthouse then? Cuz I ain't seen Earl today."

Realization dawned and Alex took another few tentative steps forward. "I'm not here to cause you any trouble."

"Then what you want?"

Alex was close enough now that she was eye level with the child on the porch. A girl with curly blonde hair, unbrushed and wild with ringlets sprigging every which way. She offered a gentle wave, but the child looked up at her mom and whimpered. That's when Alex noticed the fresh, violaceous bruise stretching across her left cheek. Ice filled the back of her throat and she stuttered out her next words.

"I...I'm trying to get some information on a book that I found in my—" she paused, the word unfamiliar on her tongue, "—my dad's things. He died last year."

Jessica's eyes regarded Alex through slits, her mouth parting to reveal a large gap between her front teeth. "What'd you say your name was?"

"I didn't," Alex said. "But I'm Alex Wilde. My father was JR Wilde."

"He kin to Earl?"

Alex nodded and stepped up to the edge of the porch. "I think they were second cousins. On his mom's side."

She seemed to chew on the information before sidling away from the screen door, the young child scurrying to stay behind her legs. "Come on in, then. I got a few minutes before I need to get supper started."

The devastation of the house's exterior continued to the interior. A shag pea-green carpet had been ripped up in several places and was covered in empty soda cans, discarded clothing, and crushed cracker crumbs. Alex sat on the edge of a cushionless wicker chair across from Jessica, who plopped down on a dingy gray sofa that had once been the color of cream.

The little girl snatched a stuffed bear with missing eyes from the floor and scrambled onto the couch, plugging her thumb into her mouth. Jessica reached over and jerked it out. "I told you to stop that. That's fer babies and you ain't no baby no more."

Tears welled in the girl's eyes, soft brown doe-like eyes with long lashes. Alex couldn't tear her gaze from the handprint on her chubby cheek until the baby erupted in a hacking cough, his bare head turning lobster red from the effort. Twin streams of green mucus ran from his nostrils to his lips. Jessica wiped it away with the brush of her index finger.

"What did you mean to ask me?"

Alex cleared her throat around the ball of dread inside it. "I found a book in my father's things. A book with names and dates. When people died, when they got married and had babies. You and Earl are in there."

Jessica's eyebrows rose into the wrinkles on her forehead.

"This book has a symbol on the cover, a backwards B with a line straight through the middle. I was just curious what it meant and what the book—"

A pallor had replaced the pink hue of Jessica's cheeks, a defiance settling into the gray of her eyes. "I can't tell you nothin' about that."

The baby erupted into another coughing fit, and she juggled him in her arms, patting him on the back while he struggled to catch his

247

breath. This time his face turned a deathly shade of eggplant before he finished.

"You know, I'm a doctor. A doctor for kids," Alex said, leaning forward. "I could take a look at him if you want me to."

Jessica cut her gaze to Alex and continued her rhythmic patting between his shoulder blades.

"Has he been to a doctor?"

"You think I got money to take him?"

"No, I don't." Alex flicked her eyes to the kitchen where a cat was lapping at a bowl of cereal left on the table. "Has he been coughing for very long?" she asked, undeterred by the wariness Jessica wore like a shroud.

"About a week or so." Jessica bit her lip with her upper incisors. "But it ain't gettin' no better."

"Any fever?"

"I think so."

"Rash?"

"Not that I seen."

"Has your daughter been sick?"

"She been fine."

Alex reached out for the baby, scooping him onto her lap before Jessica could protest. One furrow appeared above his deep-set chocolate eyes, but no tears came, only curiosity. Jessica glanced between them and then twisted around to pull her daughter onto her lap.

"What happened to her face?" Alex asked coolly, her smooth expression hiding the adrenaline pulsing underneath her skin. Instead of answering, Jessica's face hardened into a mask that made her look decades older. Alex bent her head, inhaling the scents of grime and spilled formula when she pressed her ear to the baby's chest. He yanked on a tendril of her hair with sticky fingers and drew it to his mouth. She let him.

"His chest sounds congested, but I don't think it's pneumonia. He needs fluids and Tylenol when he gets fussy. And if you get into a warm shower with him, you can pat his back to get some of the mucus out."

Alex began working on disentangling her strands from a toothless mouth. When he began to fuss, she wrapped her arms around him and bounced her knee a few times, eliciting a short but hearty giggle.

"You're good with him." Jessica ducked her head and stared at her bare toes, the nails painted with chipped pink polish. "You got kids?"

"No. None that are my own, but I take care of a lot of kids in the hospital."

When Jessica hugged her daughter to her chest, Alex noticed the slump to her shoulders, the jut of her cheekbones and the scaphoid shape to her midsection.

"Look here, I can't help you much with that book, but I seen that mark before."

Alex reined in her emotions as tension built up her spine.

"I seen it on the inside of Earl's arm."

"Like a tattoo?"

"Yeah. It's on all of 'em."

"All of who?"

"Those hellraisers who think they own the county."

"Who?" Alex asked, the words already lit up like a neon sign in her brain.

"Those sons o' Brit."

THIRTY

Alex's skin prickled as she shifted in the wicker chair, beads of sweat collecting between her shoulder blades. The baby emitted a whine and reached for Jessica who slipped the little girl to the stained carpet so she could tuck him into her lap. His chubby hand tugged on the neckline of her top and a mound of flesh popped over the top and into his hungry bird mouth. The little girl curled up at her mother's feet, her head resting atop the stuffed bear, thumb back in her mouth. Her breath steadied and the bruise on her cheek moved up and down in time with her sucking.

"Who are they? Where are they from?" Alex hailed an assault of questions as Jessica ran a hand across her nose.

"They from all over. They think they're hot shit since most of 'em from families that settled here a long time ago. They have meetin's at night, like some secret society." She smiled and giggled to herself. "I followed my brother one time out to that land where they meet up, so I guess it ain't no secret no more."

"Where do they meet?"

"That old place on Cedar Creek that everybody done forgot about."

Terry's place. Alex's nails dug into her palms as she willed Jessica to keep talking.

"What do they do out there?"

"Man stuff, I guess. Drink whiskey. Shoot stuff. Mouth off about their women."

The little boy pulled away from Jessica's breast and fell into a coughing fit that spewed half-digested milk all over her exposed chest. "Dammit."

Alex jumped to her feet. "Can I get you a towel?"

"You best be goin'. I wouldn't go lookin' for those men if I were you." Her eyes shifted nervously toward Alex as if this was the first time she really saw her.

"Let's say I did. Where would I go?"

Jessica stood, slinging the baby onto her hip. "After work, they all meet up at that beer joint off Highway Thirty."

"Cooter's?"

"Yeah. That's the one."

With the truck idling at a T-intersection, Alex looked right then left then at the lazy red ball sinking into the horizon. Tonight, the sky was a mixture of reddish gold and warm candied orange. Toward the setting sun lay her mom's house, the fragrance of macaroni and cheese, and maybe, if she was lucky, a breeze to accompany her night on the porch swing. In the opposite direction lay a road paved with retribution and certain disaster. With adrenaline-soaked hands, she spun the wheel to the right and sped toward the red taillights beckoning her to join them on the highway.

The night was still early when she parked at the outer edge of a paved parking lot in front of a nondescript building with black siding and a black door. No windows that she could see. A single neon red sign hung from a peaked roof. Cooter's. At one point in the last decade the apostrophe had been snuffed out.

As the stars winked into existence, she wrangled with the voice in her head reminding her this was a terrible idea. She slumped down in her seat, waiting, watching. A few beat-up trucks swerved into the slots right next to the building, wedging a two-seater motorcycle between them. According to the sign posted next to the door, Monday was half price whiskey night.

A shrill ring from her phone skyrocketed her heart rate, her fingers shaking so thoroughly that she fumbled with it before answering.

"Hello?" she said, tucking the phone between her face and shoulder.

"Why do you sound like you're in a closet?"

"What?" She straightened abruptly at the sound of Ian's voice.

"What are you doing right now?" he asked suspiciously.

Alex willed smoothness into her voice. "Sitting out in my mom's truck and missing you." Neither was a lie.

"I miss you too."

She strained her ears to hear into the background of the phone, expecting a lively city or muffled laughter, but there was only silence.

"Where are you?"

"Home. I got back late from Paris."

"Oh." A part of her hated the thought of Ian being there alone between cold sheets. "How was the rest of the foundation meeting?"

"Interesting."

"Really? How so?"

"We spent an entire day discussing our current projects and the vision for the future, and I think we figured out what we need to keep our momentum going."

"That's fantastic, Ian. What is it?"

"You."

Alex stilled, gripping the steering wheel with one hand as a wave of confusion struck her in the face. "Me? What do I have to do with—"

"The board voted and decided they would like you to replace me as the chair of the Devall Foundation." He sounded resplendent, relieved even, like he had solved the puzzle of her future. Like he held the key to her career happiness and was dangling it in front of her. Only she didn't want it.

"Why me?"

He grunted as he flipped over in bed to change positions. "Because you're the perfect choice," he crooned. "You're an expert in pediatric medicine and global health not to mention you're the most selfless soul I've ever known."

The words sounded so pretty. For a moment, she let herself bask in adoration before uncertainty cast its shadow.

"I don't know. I have to think about it." The words soured her mouth even as she said them.

"What's there to think about? It solves everything."

A heated rush bloomed on her chest. "I don't know that it does."

"You'll have a job in London, an opportunity to travel and change the world. Isn't that what you want?"

"I do, but it means not being a real doctor."

She pictured Ian's life when they had met, shaking hands with dignitaries and posing for pictures at hospital openings. Watching as other people built the dreams she had once had for herself.

"Not in the traditional sense but—"

"It's just not what I pictured, Ian."

"I don't think you pictured any of this."

He meant him. He meant life with him. She hadn't pictured it, not at all. But it didn't mean she didn't want it. She blew some of the tightness out of her chest.

"What did *you* picture, Ian? That we would get married, and everything would fall magically into place. It never works like that."

"I knew we would figure it out. Being with you is what matters to me."

"And what if that meant changing everything else in your life? Would you do it?" Margaret's words flooded into Alex's consciousness. "Would you say no to a life in London? Would you say no to the Devall company? To your father?" Every single cell in her body quivered with tension as she gripped the phone to her ear.

"For you, I would." He spoke with gentle assurance. No hesitation. No explanation. *For you, I would.* Her stomach roiled with her own selfishness. "Are you asking me to?"

"What? No, I'm not asking you to do that."

Movement caught her eye. A group of men dressed in jeans covered in oil stains with trucker hats pulled low over their faces exited the red Bronco parked in front of her. She swallowed hard, squeezing swollen eyelids over watery eyes.

"This is a fantastic opportunity, Ian. I was just caught off guard and I need some time to think about it."

"Okay," he said evenly. "Friday. I have to tell them by Friday."

"I'll call you tomorrow, okay." She pressed end and stowed her phone in the glovebox in case Ian called back. "I love you," she whispered and climbed out of the truck.

The bar reeked of grime and sweat, long workdays, and even longer nights. A lone bartender, his entire head shaved clean except for a pointed goatee, towered behind the bar. Thick tree branch arms swiped a dirty towel across its stained surface. He reminded her of Jeff in stature but that's where the resemblance ended. And this place was no Ex-Pats.

When she emerged from the shadowed entryway, three stools and their accompanying bodies swiveled toward her, making quick, lewd assessments with their eyes. A single droplet of sweat careened lazily down her back. She wished she had worn anything other than a white t-shirt.

With robotic grace, she moved toward an empty barstool at the end and hopped onto the cracked leather. She could feel the eyes darting over her back, the exposed skin of her arms, her face. She ignored them all, except for the bartender. She met his gaze and motioned him over, noticing the inked teardrops dripping down one half of his face.

"You want somethin'?" he asked gruffly, a pair of gold teeth glinting at her beneath the overgrown facial hair.

"A drink," she replied, the moisture leeching out of her throat. What the hell had she been thinking?

"We got drinks." He leaned over, pursing his lips, and a splat of tobacco hit the bottom of a plastic cup.

"Whiskey?"

He curled his upper lip in approval and retrieved a bottle from under the bar. He slid over a glass covered in fingerprints and filled it half full.

"Thanks," she muttered, closing her mind to the infectious disease risk and throwing the glass to her lips. God, it tasted like car fumes and burnt corn. She stifled a cough and dabbed her mouth on the neckline of her shirt.

"Good, ain't it?" The chuckling voice came from her left. A gangly guy in his early twenties in tight jeans and an even tighter t-shirt. A giant belt buckle adorned his mid-section. He plopped down on the seat next to her and flipped his Farm and Ranch Supply cap around backward.

"Yeah." Alex feigned another sip. "It's real good."

"You waitin' on somebody?"

She nearly said yes but then she noticed his skinny forearm splayed over the bar and the blurry grayish-green edges of a tattoo.

"No," she said, studying his face, taking in the baby fat still present in his cheeks and the freckles over his nose. The eyes that were slightly too close together. Brown with bits of gold like a hayfield. He ducked his head shyly and jerked it to the side.

"My friends over yonder bet me twenty dollars I couldn't get you to come sit with us."

"Where are your friends?"

"Over there by the pool table."

Alex dared a look. The throng from the red Bronco. All carbon copies of the same person. One shorter. One taller. One wider. But all wearing the same clothes and the same superiorly stupid expression.

"Come on," Alex said, and his face lit with surprise when she gave him a wink. "Let's go get your twenty dollars."

Five pairs of eyes shifted toward her as she drew closer. As one of the taller ones bent over the pool table to take a shot, her eyes slid over his forearm and the backward B tattooed there. Jackpot.

A thick-middled guy in a Pearl Jam t-shirt gestured to a spindly wooden stool next to him but she shook her head, instead wrapping her hand around the wooden shaft of a pool stick. "Anybody want to play me at pool?"

Coarse laughter broke out as they watched her gather up the balls strewn over the green felt.

"I'll buy the beers," she added.

The laughter crescendoed along with a few whistles. The largest man in the group, almost as wide as he was tall, jerked the pool stick from his friend's hand.

"I'll play you."

His voice curdled Alex's blood. And for a second, his face became her father's. Dominant and leering. Merciless. She clenched her fist around the wood in her hand but forced her face to relax into a smile. "Should I break?"

"Why don't you get them beers first? Then you can do whatever you want."

His tongue darted over his lower lip like a reptile and in that instant, she wished she was a man. A six-foot man with shoulders as broad as a barn and a giant fist that would wipe the smirk right off his face.

When she returned a few moments later balancing a tray of beer bottles, he was bent over the pool table, eyes focused on a racked-up set of balls at the end. A giant clack resounded as the tightly packed triangle scattered and the broad man stood up to survey his work and accept a beer. She traded it for his pool stick, his sweat still clinging to the handle. It made her want to vomit.

Drowning out the room, the lecherous murmuring, the clank of bottles and stench of sweat, she focused only on the pristine white orb in front of her. "Side pocket," she whispered and struck. A cobalt blue ball zipped across the table and plunked into the intended hole. The men whooped behind her.

"Earl, you got yerself a shark."

Earl. She cocked a brow at Jessica's husband. He had no idea what kind of shark he had.

Two games of pool and twice as many rounds of beer later, most of the men had flushes creeping up their faces along with clumsy fingers and slurred words. Pearl Jam had run a hand along her backside at one point, and it had taken every ounce of her willpower not to whack him across the face with her stick. This game was becoming dangerous, and she needed to end it.

When the seat next to the youngest member of the group in the Farm and Ranch hat became vacant, she rocked onto the rickety stool. He put out a hand to steady her.

"Thanks," she said sweetly. "You know, I never asked your name."

"It's Curtis," he said, ducking his head down and staring into the mouth of his beer bottle.

"Curtis what?"

"Curtis McCoy."

"Did you grow up here?"

"Yep."

"Where?"

"Right past Cole's Church. In Cedarville."

"No way!" she exclaimed.

"You know where it is?"

"Of course." And then she added, "I like your tattoo. I have one too." She held up her inner forearm. Ian's name written in Cyrillic. Her heart liquefied at the sight of it.

"What's it mean?"

"It means fortune and glory," she lied. "How about yours?"

"Oh." The shade of pink in his cheeks deepened and he twirled the beer bottle in his hands. "It's a secret."

"I love secrets," Alex whispered.

"It's the mark for our—" He twisted around both directions to see if anyone was listening. "For the sons of Brit."

"What are the sons of Brit?"

"A special society we belong to."

"Oh wow. How do you get in?"

"Not just anybody can. You got to be related to the founders."

"You sound important."

"Me, naw. Earl there, he's the boss. I just got initiated last year."

"What was that like?"

A cloud descended over his squinty eyes and he tightened his jaw. "They take us out to the meetin' place, and we gotta kill somethin' with our bare hands and then eat it."

"That sounds...disgusting." Alex wrinkled her nose. "Where can you even do that around here?"

"Over off Cedar Creek."

"The old McCoy place? I thought somebody owned that."

"No, ma'am. That's S.O.B. land. Always has been. Always will be."

"What you guys talkin' about?"

Stale breath blew across Alex's face. It was now or never.

"Curtis was just telling me about the sons of Brit."

Earl's jaw dropped open in surprise and Curtis began coughing violently.

"That right?" He jutted his unshaven chin toward Curtis' cowering silhouette. "You been runnin' yer mouth, boy?"

The words were slurred. Sloppy. Alex noticed the deepening crimson lines running through the whites of his eyes. He squinted them at Alex.

"What'd you say yer name was, girl?"

"I didn't," Alex said evenly, her eyes leveling with his muddy brown ones.

Over Earl's shoulder, a man dressed in a jacket despite the summer heat caught her attention as he stood from the end of the bar, towering above everyone else.

"Don't be smart with me," he threatened, and her eyes snapped back to his face.

"My name is Alex."

"You from 'round here?"

"Yes."

"You don't sound like it."

"I've been away for a while."

"Who you kin to?"

Her skin crawled with the lie that wound its way out of her mouth. "Teresa Hawthorne." His face contorted into a mask of cold fury. "Do you know her?"

"I heard of her."

"Then you know what happened to her."

"What I heard is she drunk herself silly and burned down her own barn. Nearly killed herself."

"Except that I was there that night," Alex said coldly. "And I know for damn sure she didn't burn down the barn."

He leaned in, inches from her face, so close that Alex could see the rhythmic tic of his jaw muscle. "You can't prove nuthin'. Can she boys?" He stepped back and roared in laughter. Roared so loud that Alex thought her ears would split open from the noise.

"You're right. I can't." Alex nodded to each of the men in turn, allowing her lip to curl up in a smile. "But that land, Terry's land, is not yours and you will never set foot on it again."

"How you gone manage that?" He laughed again, hollow and grating. The rest of the men shifted nervously and cast their eyes to the sawdust floor.

"I don't have to manage anything. It's not your land."

Earl stepped back and scoffed, his tone dropping an octave. "It ain't yours neither. You best not be threatenin' me. That'll be the last thing you ever do."

Nervousness lapped in Alex's midsection, but she pushed it down. She'd been raised with abuse and cruelty. They would not win. Not anymore. Her fear was palpable but so was her resolve. She stood to leave, brushing past Earl's sweat-soaked thorax. A hand snaked out and curled itself inside her waistband.

"Who said you was goin' anywheres?"

Alex reached into her pocket for her phone, her hand filling up an empty pocket. *Damn.* She left it in the truck. "Let go of me."

He sneered at her and tightened his grip. She knew he could smell her fear, her adrenaline. The fight or flight response pulsed through her arteries as her pupils dilated and her breathing quickened.

"I'd do what she said."

The voice was low. Menacing. Commanding. It came from a figure that stood in the shadows beyond the light fixture over the pool table. The man stood at least a head taller than everyone in the room and had shed his jacket to reveal the rippling muscles of his chest and forearms. As he stepped forward, a length of auburn hair flopped over onto his forehead, onto a face covered in a carpet of facial hair with sea green eyes that dared these men to challenge him.

When Earl loosened his grip, Alex scurried away, reaching for the hand stretching toward her. Warm, strong fingers closed around her wrist.

"Hello, Lex."

THIRTY-ONE

"What on God's green earth were you doin' in there with those fuckers?"

Justin had practically carried her to the truck, her body limp from the adrenaline coursing through it. Alex didn't answer, her mind buzzing like bees in a hive. Once they made it to the sanctuary of the truck cab, she let the bees loose.

"It doesn't matter. I can't believe you're here. I thought you were overseas."

She leaned over to throw her arms around his neck, the coarse hairs of his beard abrading her cheek, the pungent vapors of his exhaled breath stinging her nasal passages.

"It's good to see you," Alex said against the skin of his neck.

"It's good to see you too," he said slowly, leaning back to slump against the headrest, his knees wedged under the glovebox.

"Seriously though, what are you doing here?"

"You first," he said.

She sighed through her nose, tucking one foot under her opposite knee. "I'm in town visiting my mom and I found something in my dad's old stuff." She paused to press her fist into her teeth. Justin watched her in absolute stillness. "You remember when Terry's barn burned down?"

He dipped his chin once. His eyes were darker than she remembered. Twin abysses of green that were glacier-like as they slid over her face.

"I found a book with the names of those bastards that were threatening her."

"And you thought you'd march right over here and bring 'em to justice." The corner of his mouth twitched.

259

A giggle rose in her throat, a chaotic giggle that split her lips apart. "Something like that. It sounds totally stupid when you put it that way."

"It was totally stupid. I know some of those guys. They're trouble, Lex. Like, been in the pen trouble."

"But they took someone's life away. They can't just get away with it. You should see what they did to her land."

A dark pair of eyebrows drew up in an arch. "You've been out there?"

"Yeah, earlier today."

"I thought you were smarter than this, Lex. Aren't you some famous doctor now?" His eyelids formed slits as he gave her knee a shove.

"No." Her face heated. How could she explain that she was a doctor with no job? No patients. No purpose. "Your turn," she challenged.

Justin rubbed a hand along his facial hair, a spectrum of brown and reddish gold strands. She'd never seen his face anything but smooth and angular. The beard was so thick it muted his bone structure.

"What's with the beard?"

His eyes tightened, their color flattening to a matte green that contrasted with the blooming blood vessels in his sclera.

"It makes it harder to pick us out from the crowd."

"In Afghanistan?"

"Yep."

He continued rubbing along his jaw, his eyes shifting from her face to the building in front of them and then to the shadowed highway behind them.

"Will you be home for a while?" Alex asked, a strange feeling fisting her heart.

"Yeah, I will. I've earned it after my last four tours."

"Was it as bad as everyone says?"

"It was worse."

Everything about him was so much harder than she remembered. His voice. His eyes. Every inch of pure muscle from his neck down to his calves. But it was the eyes that bothered her the most. The waves of joy and mischief had been replaced by a still, flat calm. Perceptive and anticipatory. Protective and perhaps even predatory.

"You look...different."

His lips twitched briefly as he flexed his pectoral muscles. "How so?"

"You look like—" She scanned his face again, her eyes snagging on the lips that were once as familiar as her own. "A yeti."

A laugh burst out of his throat. He looked surprised at the noise, as if he hadn't laughed that way for a very long time.

"What? You don't like my beard?" He grabbed her hand and rubbed her palm along its surface. The tickling sensation made her squirm, and she pulled her hand back to her chest.

"Not really."

The intermittent wheezes of their laughter echoed around them until a light flashed from inside the bar. The front door swung open, and Earl stumbled out, followed closely by his cronies.

"Start the truck," Justin commanded, "and let's get outta here."

Alex didn't waste time thinking or asking questions. She revved the engine and exited the way she had come, swerving the truck onto the feeder road.

"Turn here," Justin said and she obeyed.

"Where are we going?"

"Shortcut."

"Where's your truck parked?"

"Back at the bar."

"Don't you need it?"

"Nah, I'll get it tomorrow. You can drop me at my house if you still know where I live."

"Of course, I know."

Next to her, he slumped in the passenger seat, cheek plastered against the window. She concentrated on driving as they were swallowed up by the night and a comfortable silence. Alex wound through a thick forest of trees lined with barbed wire, popping out on the cutoff to Justin's house.

"Just like old times," he said as the truck slowed to a stop in his grandparent's driveway.

Alex squinted when he heaved open the door and the interior light flipped on.

"Thanks for the ride," he mumbled as one leg slid to the ground.

Alex reached out and wrapped her fingers around his bicep. "Why were you in that bar tonight?"

He stilled then shifted away from her until he was swallowed up by the shadows.

"I had my reasons just like you had yours. 'Night, Lex."

He was gone before she could complain that his answer wasn't an answer at all.

"Chief Richardson will see you now."

Alex peeled herself from the lime green vinyl seat, replacing the dogeared copy of *Good Housekeeping* on the scratched surface of a coffee table. The whir of a fan vibrated through the small office space, and as she passed by its perch atop a metal filing cabinet, a puff of air brushed the hair sticking to her right temple.

"Sorry it's so dang hot in here. AC's not workin' right," said the receptionist between smacks of gum.

"It's okay," Alex replied, wishing she had opted for shorts instead of jeans.

"Charlie, you in there?" A hand with red press-on nails pounded on the frosted glass that read "Chief of Police, Cole's Church."

"Come on in," a thin, reedy voice shouted through the door.

The receptionist ran a hand through her short, highlighted layers then twisted the knob and ushered Alex inside. A man with thinning sandy hair was seated behind a desk piled with manila file folders and covered in paperclips. His arms were thin and lily white, his abdomen soft and protruding. He gestured to an upholstered office chair in the corner before steepling his fingers on top of the largest file folder.

"What can I do for you, Miss Wilde?"

As Alex sat, she assessed his features, finely boned with a thin mustache gracing his upper lip. He looked like a boy playing dress up in a police uniform, except for his eyes. They were steel gray, flat and disinterested.

"I want to ask about a case from 1997."

"A case that old is public record," he said smoothly.

"I already know what's in the public record, but I have a question. If new information was uncovered, could charges be brought against someone?"

"Depends on the crime, dear, and the statute of limitations."

She cringed at the word *dear*, intended not to endear but to demean.

"What kind of case you talkin' about?"

"There was a barn fire here in Cole's Church on July 4, 1997. The owner was inside when it happened, and she was left severely impaired. She died a few months ago after living in a facility for years with a feeding tube and no quality of life." Alex barred her mind against the images her words created and clenched her middle around its gnawing queasiness. "Before the fire happened, she was being threatened by some people who called themselves the sons of Brit."

"Never heard of 'em," he interjected.

"I think they caused the fire."

He pushed away from the desk's edge with his palms, his eyes two glittering daggers in a mask of nonchalance. "You got proof?"

"No, but, if you bring them in for questioning—"

One half of his face twitched violently, and he cocked his head. "I got a total of four policeman for an entire county. You think I got time for somethin' like this?"

"I think you could make time if you wanted to."

"Miss Wilde, I don't appreciate that tone." He turned his attention to the pile on his desk, shuffling it around with no definite purpose. "You finished?"

A lick of flame propelled Alex from her seat and she strode out the glass door with black lettering. "Not in the slightest."

Cole's Church had one of some things and none of a lot of things. One place to get burgers. One grocery store. One stoplight. One gas station. Alex braked a little too hard as she pulled in next to the only open gas pump. She glanced at her phone. Lunchtime. Her stomach growled in time with the truck guzzling gasoline. This place had changed hands many times over her lifetime. She remembered one summer when it had served snocones, big mounds of frost tinted with the most outrageous colors. And then in high school it became a gas station/pizza parlor combo with pizza so greasy that she and Justin had to press it between a handful of paper towels before stuffing it in their mouths.

Now it had been bought out by some convenience store chain with a wall of refrigerated drinks and any snack food she could imagine. She didn't recognize any of the people behind the counter when she went inside to pay. Somehow the anonymity felt wrong.

By the time she pulled into her driveway, dark clouds had begun to gather, squeezing the sunshine from the afternoon. She put on her shorts and running shoes anyway. The absence of the sun took the edge off the day and Alex focused on breathing. In. Out. With every breath cycle, she loosened the net on her snarled thoughts. Coming to Texas had been a way of distracting herself. To escape from the uncomfortable drama of her real life.

But now that she was here, this life seemed much too real. And things that she had buried under layers of ambition and success and saving the world wouldn't stay buried any longer. Growing up here had seemed like a steppingstone. Something she would plant a foot on until she leaped into her real life. But now she found herself wanting to straddle both sides of the river because this life was real too. Maybe even more real than her life in London.

She imbibed the scent of freshly cut grass. Felt the light pattering of misty rain on her nose and the country lane beneath her feet. It was real. And it was home.

When she passed Justin's house, he was sitting on the porch in Grandma Robbins' white rocker, hat pulled low over his face, legs extending about a mile from his body and crossed at the ankles. She waved but he didn't wave back. By the time she turned around on her route and passed the house again, he was gone.

"You forgot my loaf of bread," Janie chided that night while Alex set the table for supper.

"Huh?" she said, glancing at a text from Ian on her phone.

I miss your beautiful face.

"My bread," said Janie more firmly as she fashioned a sandwich from smoked turkey slices and a hot dog bun.

"Oh geez, Mom. I'm so sorry." Guilt flashed through her. "I can go get some now."

"No, honey. It's dinnertime. No need for you to—"

Alex laid a hand on her freckled forearm. "I want to, Mom. I'm not super hungry tonight."

Back in the truck, she drove toward town, the sun setting in a brilliant purple haze behind her. She dialed Ian, but then realized it was midnight in London and hung up before it had rung more than twice. She parked in the rear of the lot and slipped in the sliding glass doors, a baseball hat pulled low over her forehead. Not that she minded if people recognized her, but she didn't feel like talking. Their small-town grocery store was a hotbed of ladies seeking out bits of gossip as juicy as a Sunday ham.

Other than Justin, no one she knew had seen her at Cooter's last night. The last thing she needed was Janie finding out. She dodged past the meat counter through a serpentine line of people waiting on their cuts of beef and scurried down the bread aisle. After tucking a loaf of bread under one arm, she took two steps before colliding with a muscled bicep inside an olive-green sleeve He didn't even glance down.

"You just can't seem to help yourself," he mused, reaching out a hand to yank her ponytail.

"Trust me I can." She batted his hand away. "What are you doing here? Are you following me?"

He looked at her in mock exasperation. "And if I was?"

"I would tell you not to." Which was a lie. She knew Justin could see right through it. His face smoothed.

"I'm shopping." With his other arm, he brought forth a red plastic basket.

"Beer and banana Moon Pies?"

"Yep."

"Since when did Stanley's start selling beer?"

"Five years ago."

"Oh." Alex shifted and realized she was smashing the bread with her hands. "Is that your dinner?"

"Yep." He turned to go, tight muscles of his back coiling as he strode down the aisle, the reddish gold strands of his hair glinting under the fluorescent lights. "You comin'?"

She followed the red taillights of his truck into the heart of Cole's Church through a neighborhood and then to the back of the library. Without waiting for her to park, he exited the truck and walked off the asphalt into a thicket of grass. Alex scrambled after him, her feet wrestling through a constellation of weeds before landing on a dirt path she hadn't known existed.

"Where are you going?" she asked, stumbling behind his graceful stride.

"You'll see," he crooned, one hand swinging the beer and the other stuffing a Moon Pie into his face. The moon cast a silvery light on their footsteps as they walked along a curated trail through the brush and undergrowth. When the vegetation thinned out, Alex could make out the silhouettes of a slide and swing set.

"I didn't know there was a path between the back of the elementary school and the library."

"They made it a few years ago. I hear they're going to name it after this girl who used to live here and spend all her time surrounded by books."

"Shut up." Alex shoved him forcefully from behind, but he merely chuckled as he barely rocked forward on his toes. When they reached a fallen tree, its roots exposed and twisted as if they still groped for the earth, Justin settled onto the ground, pressing his back against the trunk. Alex heard the hiss of a seal being broken.

"Want one?" He turned and offered the bottle.

"You can't drink on school property. It's against the law."

"I'll just add it to the list of laws I've already broken."

He turned and guzzled the beer. His melancholy tugged at Alex's heart. She sat down in the grass next to him and opened her own bottle. "Can I have a Moon Pie, too?"

At some point during the evening the chronic fog blanketing their town dispersed to reveal a crisp black swathe of night studded generously with stars. A breeze blew through every now and again, causing the swings to sway eerily on rusted chains. A throaty frog belched a lullaby nearby as the rest of the world fell into an easy sleep. Lights blinked off in the surrounding neighborhoods, thrusting them into a comfortable dark. A darkness where anything could be said.

"I bet you have to be really brave to do what you do," Alex mused, her head leaning against smooth bark.

"Brave or just really stupid," he mumbled.

"You have to watch people die. I know what that's like."

He grunted but didn't say anything for a while.

"My last two tours were hard." She heard him gulp another mouthful of beer and sigh. "I don't sleep anymore. Not unless I drink until I pass out."

"What do you see when you close your eyes?"

"Soldiers. Civilians. Our faces. Their faces."

"Are you going back?"

"No, I did back-to-back tours and now I'm gettin' out."

"What will you do?"

"I don't know. Maybe I'll get a dog or find a nice girl to settle down with."

Alex laughed but the words rubbed against an ache that cracked open inside her chest. "Women are suckers for men in uniform. At least, that's what I hear."

"I heard you got married."

"I did."

"Does he make you happy?"

"He does."

"Then why are you here and not with him?"

"It's complicated. I needed to get away for a while. Figure some things out."

"Sounds about right."

"What does that mean?"

Justin didn't answer right away, and Alex heard the hiss of another bottle being opened. "Isn't that why you left Cole's Church?"

"There was nothing left for me here," Alex whispered hoarsely.

"There was plenty left for you, Lex. You just didn't want to see it."

"Neither did you."

"I did see it. I saw *you*. I've always seen you."

Alex didn't think she was breathing anymore.

"I had my reasons, but I shouldn't have left either," he said.

She hoped the frog drowned out the uptick of her pulse and that the dark hid her face. *Then why did you?* She tried to ask the question, but fear gripped her throat. She wasn't sure she wanted to know the answer anyway.

Justin grunted to his feet, squatting to sweep the grass with his bare hand. "Timing's a bitch, I guess."

Alex opened her mouth to respond but Justin's stream of cursing broke the mood.

"Son of a—what the hell?"

He picked up his right arm and even in the dark, Alex could see the steady stream of blood dripping from his inner forearm and forming a black oval in the grass.

"It's not that bad," he slurred when Alex pushed him into the passenger side of her mom's truck.

She gripped his slippery fingers and jerked his arm toward her in the dim overhead light. A curvilinear gash on his inner forearm welled with blood, fileted open by a vicious edge of glass.

"Hello, I'm Doctor Wilde. Nice to meet you," she snarked, daggering him a look. "It *is* that bad. You need stitches."

"You think we get stitches in the military? We're lucky to get clean water and some duct tape."

"Fine, but if this gets infected, you'll probably lose the function of your right hand which I'm guessing a helicopter pilot is required to have."

He sighed tucking his chin so far onto his chest that his beard covered the logo on his t-shirt.

"Where we goin' then, Dr. Wilde?"

THIRTY-TWO

Years had passed. Decades even. Yet the waiting room of the Cole's Church Community Hospital looked the same as the day Justin had carried her in here with a broken foot after the fire. The same dingy white floor and pea-green vinyl furniture. The same smell of old skin and disinfectant. She approached the starched white uniform behind the triage desk.

"Excuse me, I have a friend who needs a lac sutured." She gestured to Justin whose arm was wrapped in a makeshift bandage of blue paper towels they had found in Janie's truck. The woman handed Alex a clipboard.

"Fill out these forms. I'll take him on back and you can meet us in room two."

Alex glanced down at the packet of paperwork—standard consent and insurance information. "Oh, I'm not his—"

Justin put up a finger to silence her then reached around to his back pocket with his good arm and withdrew a leather wallet.

"Here. I can't write, not without bleeding all over their forms. Just sign it and we can get this over with."

Taking the wallet and the clipboard, Alex plopped into one of the cleaner looking chairs and began scrawling his name onto various lines. In the wallet, she found his driver's license, which had expired, a military ID, credit cards, and a wad of cash. She stuffed her fingers deep inside searching for his medical insurance card, but instead fished out a scrap of folded paper. Blue lined notebook paper that had crinkled over time, the torn edges softened with age. Shaking, she unfolded it and stared at a page filled with her handwriting and a date of January 1998.

Dear Justin,
You were always more than my friend. You were my protector. My first love.
My first heartbreak. Yes, I love you. I hope you never doubted it. And I hope
that wherever and whenever you think of me, you think of a girl who loves
you. I am so sorry that I wasn't ready to give you my heart, but I don't have
the luxury of making promises to anyone right now. My heart is broken but
healing, and I don't know when or how it will ever become whole. What I
do know is that the healing needs to happen far away from here. From
everyone who hurt me. From everyone who loved me. Because achieving my
dreams—that will be the thing that puts me back together again.
Maybe dreams choose us, not the other way around and this is what has
chosen me.
Love always, Lex

He had kept it. All this time. All these years. Through God knew how many cities and countries and life changes. Hastily, she refolded the letter and replaced it in his wallet, along with the rest of the contents. A strange nostalgia gripped her, like a specter, gesturing ghostly hands down the path not taken. She paused for a moment to see what images would materialize in her mind's eye. An alternate future. But as the blurry became vivid, like images in a developing photograph, she was interrupted by a brusque voice.

"Miss? He's askin' for you."

"I'm coming." Shoving the clipboard into the woman's pudgy hands, she edged past her and down the hallway.

Justin was lying on a stretcher, his eyes closed, his face underneath the scraggly beard glistening with a sheen of sweat. The nurse had draped his arm across a metal surgical table and covered the wound with a fresh square of sterile gauze. Crimson had soaked through the dressing and two linear streams ran down his arm. Alex cupped his cheek with her palm.

"How are you feeling?"

"Not drunk enough."

"Does it hurt much?"

"I've had worse." One green eye slowly opened, its bleary surface vacant and tired.

The nurse, dingy gray hair clinging to her scalp, limped into the room. "Just so you know, it's gonna be a while. Dr. Wesley is on call tonight, and he's in Cedarville deliverin' a set o' twins."

Alex crossed her arms across her chest. "How long?"

The nurse shrugged, her lips twisting up in a grimace. "Never can tell." She yanked the curtain closed behind her, the clattering of the rings grating on Alex's nerves.

Pacing back and forth a few times, Alex surveyed the contents of the room and then began pulling open drawers and opening cabinets.

"What are you doing?" Justin groaned, flopping his good forearm over his face.

"How do you feel about someone who's had a few beers sewing up your arm?"

The lighting was terrible, even with the flashlight from her phone trained on the wound. In sterile gloves and a mask, Alex probed the area, pushing a lobulated piece of fat tissue back into the hole. Burnt orange rivulets of betadine had dried on the inner surface of Justin's arm. Alex reapproximated the tissue, tilting her head one way and then the other.

"It's a clean lac. I think it will go back together nicely but you'll probably have a scar." She perched on the edge of a rolling stool and picked up a syringe of lidocaine, squirting a few drops out of the end before directing it to the edges of the laceration.

"What's that?"

"It's just lidocaine, a numbing medicine."

"I don't want it," he said flatly.

Alex sighed heavily through her nose. "Don't be a baby. It stings but then you'll be numb when I start suturing."

"I've spent the last two years being numb, Lex. No more."

She swallowed her retort, the words turning to ash in her mouth then sliding down her throat. Instead, she nodded tightly and willed away a prick of tears. "Okay then. I'll let you know when I'm sticking."

Using a pair of sterile forceps to close the wound edges, she thrust in the curved needle like a hawk's talon through skin and tissue. She kept going, creating a row of neat sutures, her hands throwing surgical knots then clipping the ends. Justin remained still, his breathing even and deep, occasionally emitting a grunt but nothing more.

"Last one," she murmured, pulling the final corners of skin together then surveying her work. It didn't look half bad. She applied a sterile bandage and had rolled over to the trash can to toss the used supplies when she heard Justin clear his throat.

"There was a raid one night. I flew some guys in and we took all kinds of fire the minute we landed. I took a bullet in the shoulder." He reached up and tugged down the neck of his shirt, an ugly scar covering most of his deltoid, framed by the black lines of a tattoo. "I was lucky though. Not all the boys made it back that night. By the time I landed, I had lost so much blood that I passed out and didn't wake up until days later."

Alex snapped off her gloves and moved closer to him, sliding a hand onto the scar. His bare skin was smooth and comfortably warm. "I wish I could fix this one too." She didn't mean the physical scar.

"You have enough of your own without worrying about mine."

He took her hand, pressing it to his face. Her thumb drifted over the corner of his mouth. His eyes closed and he rested the weight of his head into her grip. And for a moment, the travails of a soldier, the pain and grief of a hero, of a man she had once loved, had shrunk down to fit into the palm of her hand.

Behind them, the ambulance bay doors popped opened, and a gush of night air blew the privacy curtain aside. Alex shifted her eyes to the stretcher clattering over the metal grate of the entryway. Two medics in navy blue uniforms took turns squeezing a rubber bag attached to a mask. A mask too large for the small figure underneath it. With calm purpose propelling her forward, she dropped her hand from Justin's face and closed it around the canary yellow metal of the stretcher.

She glanced at the illuminated light sources above her. Unlike the rest of the hospital, this room had been updated since she had been here last time. When she had watched from the doorway as people pushed on Terry's chest and injected her with medication. A shiver traveled down her spine before she turned her attention back to the child.

Blonde curly hair matted with blood framed a pixie-like face, a nose sprinkled with freckles. A faint bruise was visible along her right cheek bone. The medic's booming voice drowned out the roaring in Alex's ears.

"We have a three-year-old female status post blunt trauma to the head found unresponsive at the scene. Breathing is shallow and pulse is present. No response to sternal rub."

Alex positioned herself at the head of the bed, taking over the bag mask from the younger medic. "Any other injuries?"

"We're not sure. She was laid out on the front porch when we arrived."

"Does she have an IV?" Alex fired.

"Yeah, we were able to get a twenty gauge in the right AC."

"Are you the doctor?" The older medic stared at her quizzically.

"Um..." She pressed her lips together while adjusting the mask on the girl's face.

The gray haired nurse squeezed her middle between the two medics to wrap a blood pressure cuff around the girl's limp arm. "She ain't the doctor."

"I'm not the doctor in this hospital but I am a doctor. An ICU doctor for kids."

"You don't got privileges here," barked the nurse.

"I know, but I'm the only one here who can help this girl." She lasered a look at each of them in turn. "Unless you all want to watch her die."

The older medic who was tall with a thick head of salt and pepper hair met her eyes. "What do you need, doc?"

Although the supplies were scant, Alex dug through a cabinet until she found a working laryngoscope and breathing tube that would fit in the girl's airway. The medics stayed to help and between the four of them—herself, two eager medics and a surly-faced nurse—EKG stickers were placed, and sedation medicines were drawn up. The girl had done little more than moan a few times. She didn't even try to bat Alex away when her eyelids were peeled open for a pupillary exam. Two chocolate drops with round black centers.

"Her pupils are equal but really sluggish. Let's get this show on the road." Alex's mind and body went to a place of familiarity. A universe where she was the master. "Push the fentanyl."

As she instructed the younger medic, she became vaguely aware of a towering silhouette leaning against the wall near the doorway. She slid in the breathing tube through a mouth full of mucus and blood then squeezed the bag a few times to evaluate the rise of her chest. She motioned the older medic to the head of the bed.

"Can you tape the tube and bag her while I finish my exam?"

"Sure thing, doc." He winked as he took over the airway.

Alex started from top to bottom, running her fingers over the boggy swelling underneath the blonde ringlets and then the blue-green bruise over her cheek. When she lifted the girl's shirt, her body was covered in welts from the slap of a leather belt. A fresh burn the size of a dime disrupted the pink skin of her forearm. Cold fury exploded in her chest and pulsed through her.

"Fran." Alex looked up at the hawkish eyes of the nurse, her color sallow in the fluorescent light. "Can you do me a favor and call the police?"

As the nurse hurried off as quick as she could go on one good leg, Alex flicked her eyes up to the monitor.

"The heart rate is dropping. I don't like it," she barked. She pointed at the fresh-faced medic. "I need you to call a helicopter so we can get her transferred to the children's trauma center in Houston."

"I'm on it." He pulled out a phone and began dialing.

Alex began yanking open drawers to the crash cart and throwing boxes of syringes on the bed.

"Can I do anything to help?"

A murmur in her ear. A timbre that sent a vibration of calm through her senses. She turned to Justin's perceptive gaze.

"Yes. I need you to keep eyes on the monitor for me while I draw up these meds. Let me know if the heart rate drops below seventy or the saturations drop below ninety."

"Okay." He nodded and took up a post at the end of the bed, feet apart and arms crossed, not diverting his eyes from the constant stream of vital signs. The stance of a soldier who now relished in having a purpose.

After starting another IV, Alex administered a cocktail of medications to support the girl's blood pressure. She was poised to stick the smooth skin of her wrist for some labs when a giant commotion erupted outside the door.

"Where's my baby girl?"

Jessica McCoy, followed closely by a beet-faced Earl, burst through the doors so hard that they hit the plaster with a resounding crack. As wild as a feral cat, she darted her eyes around the room from the medic to Justin and then stopped at Alex.

"You! What are you doin' to my baby?"

Alex calmly placed the needle and syringe on the bed and stood between the couple and her patient.

"My name is Dr. Wilde. I specialize in treating very, very sick children and I just happened to be in the ER with my friend—" she gestured to Justin's figure looming over them from the opposite side of the bed, "—when your daughter was brought in by the ambulance."

"What's wrong with her?" Jessica's speech was garbled, her words separated by sobs. Earl had yet to meet her eyes.

"She suffered an injury to her brain. I can't be sure the extent of the damage, but I had to put in a breathing tube because she wasn't breathing on her own. I've called the helicopter to take her to the children's hospital in Houston."

"I don't understand." Jessica made a move toward the child, holding out her arms. "She was fine today. I ran down to the convenient store and when I got back, she just fell out on the ground and started shakin'." Jessica peered at Alex through thick gloppy mascara and ground her teeth together. "What's wrong with her?"

Alex took an extra-deep breath, letting every ounce of calm settle deep inside her and fill her with words. Gentle words. The right words. But how was it ever right to tell someone that their child had been beaten almost to death? She steeled herself and mentally forged a wall between herself and everyone in the room.

"Your daughter has a head injury as well as a burn on her hand and multiple bruises all over her body that were caused by someone."

Earl's eyes snapped to hers, flaring first with rage then recognition. "What you mean someone?"

"I mean that another person caused these injuries."

"That's not possible. She was with me all day." Jessica rubbed her forearm across her dripping nose.

"Who stayed with her when you left for the store?"

Jessica's eyes cut to Earl and a low growl started in his chest.

"I'm warnin' you. If anythin' happens to her, it'll be your fault and you won't live to see another day," he bellowed into the sterile atmosphere.

As thick hairy arms reached toward her, Alex pressed into the floor beneath her feet, waiting for the impact. It never came. Earl's head snapped backward as a fist connected with his nose, an arc of blood spurting toward the ceiling. He staggered side to side as Justin pulled his fist back into his chest.

The doors burst open again as Fran bustled in on the coattails of Chief Richardson who surveyed the room with cold interest until he spied the child on the stretcher, her exposed body covered in bruises and healing burns. And then he reached for his handcuffs. "I need to speak with whoever's in charge."

His eyes sought out the gray-haired medic, but the medic pointed at Alex. "That'd be the doc over there."

Chief Richardson regarded her with new interest.

"Dr. Alex Wilde." She stuck out a hand, grasping the policeman's slim, paper-white fingers in her own. The pencil thin mustache on his lip twitched.

"Doctor, huh? And you the one carin' for this little girl?"

"I am," Alex said, watching Earl try to staunch the blood dripping from his nose.

"Then do you mind tellin' me what happened?"

"She was beaten," Alex said, swallowing past a lump in her throat. Justin put a hand on her back to steady her. "Her injuries are consistent with child abuse—multiple bruises in various stages, brain injury that she may not recover from, burn marks on her hand."

"And who is responsible for this?"

"We believe it was Earl McCoy, her father," Alex stated calmly.

"You can't prove nothin'," Earl sputtered, a fresh stream of blood leaking from one nostril.

"Of course, I can," Alex said smoothly. "You were left alone with a child and now that child has injuries consistent with non-accidental trauma."

Chief Richardson made a move toward Earl, like one would a rabid dog, slow and purposeful.

"You ain't no expert," he screamed as the sound of helicopter blades thundered overhead.

"Actually, I am."

"You willin' to come down to the station for a formal statement, Dr. Wilde?" asked the Chief as he pushed Earl against the wall and handcuffed his wrists.

"Absolutely."

The sound of helicopter blades thundering overhead drowned out the chief's next words.

"Earl McCoy, you are under arrest for..."

THIRTY-THREE

When Alex schlepped into the kitchen the next morning, Janie was violently whisking a half dozen eggs, punctate droplets of orange splattering the countertop next to her.

"Next time I send you for bread, remind me to remind you to let your mother know if you aren't going to come back."

A sizzle split the air in half when the eggs hit the frying pan.

"I'm sorry, Mom." Alex wrapped her arms around her mother's thin shoulders and pressed her chin on top of her sponge rollers. "I ran into Justin and then we ended up in the emergency room—"

"Yes, I know." Twin crimson splotches stained Janie's cheeks. "I had to find out from Mrs. Robbins when she called me late last night."

"I'm sorry, Mom. It won't happen again."

Janie blew breath from pursed lips then took a sip of coffee. "I know you can take care of yourself, but I'm still your mother and I'll always be looking out for you."

"I know, Mom. I know." She held onto her mother until the burnt smell of eggs wafted from the stove.

When Alex stepped into the police station for the second time in a week, a familiar wet heat greeted her. The wind from the box fan propped up on the windowsill failed to lift the wisps of hair melded to her forehead. Even the faded beige wall was dripping sweat. Gum smacked between the molars of the woman behind the front desk.

"Sorry. We still ain't got this thing fixed."

"It's fine." Alex smiled, adjusting the rolled-up sleeves of her button down.

The lady fanned a folded-up copy of *US Weekly* against her

cleavage. "It's hotter 'n all get-out in here." She stood up, still fanning herself, and slung on her purse. "The chief is in his office sweatin' like a pig. If he asks, you tell him I went down the street for a Coke."

"I'll do that," Alex promised, unsticking the front of her shirt from her skin. When she made it down the hall past a set of aluminum folding chairs and a topsy turvy filing cabinet, she reached up to knock on the frosted glass door with black stenciled lettering.

"It's open. Come on in."

Chief Richardson glanced up from his desk. He had unbuttoned the top two buttons of his navy uniform, showing a triangle of worn white t-shirt. His temples were damp with sweat and his mouth held in a thin line, but there was a brightness to his eyes that Alex hadn't seen the first time.

"Take a seat, Dr. Wilde."

"You can call me, Alex." She perched on the edge of the upcycled office furniture and crossed her legs at the ankles.

"For the purpose of this meeting," he said evenly, "you will be Dr. Wilde and I will be Chief Richardson." His expression softened before he said, "But then after that, you can call me Charlie." He picked up a sheet of paper between two outstretched hands, his eyes scanning the page. "I read your statement. Anything you'd like to change before we add this to evidence?"

"No. I stand by every word."

"You'll be willing to testify in a court of law?"

"I will."

Pressing his lips together, he nodded in approval. "How's the girl?"

"I called the hospital this morning and she's in the ICU. Her head CT showed a bleed around the brain, but luckily they were able to drain it. She had some other injuries, a few healing fractures and bruises, but nothing too major."

"Is she gonna make it?"

"She will, but she'll need a long time to recover." Alex cleared her throat as a bird settled in a tree branch outside the window. "Where's Earl? Is he still in jail?"

Chief Richardson placed a stack of papers face down in a pile and leaned back in his chair with a smug expression. "I convinced the judge to hold him without bail. It turns out in addition to last night's charges, he was wanted for assault, driving under the influence, and unpaid parking tickets."

"He deserves to rot in a jail cell for the rest of his days."

"Between you and me, Alex, if I have anything to say about it, he will."

When did her dreams become decisions? When did her decisions become new dreams? At what point had the momentum of life sent her aloft into the stratosphere to meet the next unexpected gust of wind?

Alex stared upward through closed lids, the wind caressing her face as gently as her mother's fingertips. The rising moon whispered a lullaby as the silent water beneath her feet rippled in time to the slow thump of her heart. She remained unmoving, barely feeling the weathered wood against her spine. Utterly calm. Without need of anything except the air swirling in and out of her lungs. An inner pearl of perfect clarity nestling in her chest.

"You belong out here."

Alex's abdominals contracted and her hair trailed behind her in a sweeping river of chocolate as she sat up. Her eyes fluttered open. "How did you know where I was?"

Justin shrugged, folding up his legs to sit down beside her on the wooden bridge.

"Am I that predictable?" she teased.

"Sometimes." He flashed her a wry grin. "Other times not so much. Like last night...that was...you were amazing."

The dormant wings of her heart fluttered as she let sweet victory slide over her.

"I have to admit. It felt good."

"What part?"

"Fighting for kids who can't fight for themselves."

His eyes. They were the perfect shade of seafoam green. The color of the ocean right as it crested. They studied her, moving past the skin of her face, her parted lips, her throat into somewhere deeper. Somewhere remote and vulnerable. Into the same part of her that held the precious kernel of her future.

"Why did you leave?" she whispered.

"Lex..."

She reached over and took his hand into both of hers, sandwiching his scars and calluses between her smoothness.

"Why?"

His chest heaved once before he brought her hands to his lips and kissed one of her knuckles. "Because I finally saw it."

"What did you see?"

"You, Lex. How special you are. What you were meant to become in this life. We were just lucky to get you for the time we had you."

"I'm the lucky one. I never could have become who I was meant to be without all of this." *Without you.*

Words hung between them. Decades of words not spoken and never would be. All drifting silently past then catching air. They were sitting close enough that she could feel his breath on her cheek, the vibration of his heart through his hands, and suddenly the silence begot awkwardness. Justin let go of her to hoist his body onto the rail and fling his legs over the side of the bridge.

"What now, Lex?"

"Everything in my life has always felt so right—medicine, working in Botswana, Ian." Her heart lurched when she said his name. "But this—all of this—it feels right too."

"You could do a lot of good here. For the kids, I mean."

"I know."

"And it would be good for you too. To be with the people you love. That love you."

"I know."

Justin twisted toward her, the sun catching the reddish gold in his hair, a wide smile between his cheeks. And suddenly they were seventeen again with an entire world of adventure and possibility waiting for them.

"So, what'll it be, Lex? Roots or wings?"

An owl flapped overhead, its wings spreading as it glided past before diving into the trees.

"I'd like to think," Alex mused, "that I can have both."

Alex lingered in her mom's driveway, enjoying the safety of the truck cab before she had to leap onto the ground with two feet, setting in motion the next chapter of her life. She yanked on the doorhandle before she could change her mind.

Inside the house, she crept to her room but didn't turn on the light. The gentle glow from her window creating a slice of moonlight on her bed was enough. She put her phone to her ear and dialed.

"Did I wake you?"

"No, I was just about to leave for the office."

"Do you have a minute?"

"For you, always."

Ian's voice did something to her, stirred her in a place remote and quiet that only he belonged.

"I need to tell you a story," she said, her voice wavering. "One summer, when I was seventeen..."

It took more than a minute, but he listened intently, only now and then adjusting his breathing to reflect his emotions. When Alex finished, overwhelming relief swam behind her eyes despite the arcing tension on the other end of the phone.

"Why are you telling me this now?"

"I needed you to know because everything that happened that summer is the reason I became the person I am. And it's time I did something to honor where I came from."

"You want to be home?" His voice vibrated with uncertainty.

"Of course, I do. Texas is my home but," she paused, her breath hitching as she struggled for words, "so are you. Everything here was my past. And you are my future. But I think to be happy, I need both in my life." Ian took a breath to speak but she cut him off in a torrent of words. "I want to take the position."

"The foundation position?"

She nodded excitedly even though the only being that could possibly see her was the owl sitting in the tree outside her window.

"Yes. I want to chair the Devall Foundation."

"I wasn't expecting that," Ian breathed.

"Me neither," Alex gulped. "When you asked me, I didn't think I would ever say yes."

"You can't imagine how much I wanted you to. What changed your mind?"

"I was reminded of how to dream, and I started understanding, maybe for the first time, that I could take this life and do something truly great for a lot of people. That somewhere inside me there was a scared little girl who became a warrior, and now she wants to fight for those who can't fight for themselves."

"God, I love you."

"I love you, too." Alex bit her lip and was answered by pounding in her chest. "Can I ask you a favor?"

"Anything."

"As the new foundation chair, I already know the first thing I want to do."

"Of course you do."

"But I need a bit of a loan."

"Baby, just say the word. Whatever you need, it's yours."

"Okay. Thank you."

A crystalline tear dripped over her chin and onto her outstretched leg, catching starlight as it fell.

"My turn for a question." His voice had dropped an octave. Somber and thoughtful. "Did you love him?"

"Justin?"

"Yeah."

"I did. I still do. But not enough to change my life for him."

THIRTY-FOUR

The day of the annual Brazos County auction dawned amid a barrage of summer showers as August wept its hello. And then sometime midday, it stopped, and the clouds parted to reveal a blistering sun that turned the air into fine steam.

Alex woke early, a live wire of anticipation coursing through her. She had packed the night before, stuffing her suitcase to the point of bursting with trinkets from home and a carefully wrapped loaf of banana nut bread that her mom was sending to Ian. *Ian.* By tonight she would be on a plane headed back to London. Something that didn't seem so daunting now that she had an anchor, a foothold, in her hometown. And somehow that made navigating life's ocean less perilous.

Her phone pinged and she glanced down at it.

Thought you would want to see this. Love you.

When she clicked on the link, a glossy image of her taken in Botswana last year filled the entire screen of her phone. She read the caption. "Dr. Alexandra Wilde named chairwoman of the Devall Foundation." An article followed with a brief history of the foundation and a quote from Ian as well as from George: "I can think of no one more qualified in heart or fortitude to lead us into the future." The rest of the words on the page blurred behind a curtain of her tears.

Yesterday she and her mom had driven up to Houston. When they entered the brightly lit hospital room, Jessica was seated at her daughter's bedside, her thumb rubbing circles onto a tiny hand. Alex surveyed the bedside monitor, noting the proper tempo and frequency of the green spikes and red bumps, before tiptoeing to the bedside.

"Hi, Jessica."

Her dirty blonde hair had been pulled into a knot on top of her head and she still wore the same tank top and denim shorts from several nights ago. Her face was pale and smeared with mascara from the path of dried tears. She squinted at Alex.

"Do you remember me from the other night?"

Jessica nodded and scrubbed a hand over her face then over the seat of her shorts as she stood up. "Course I do. You want somethin'?"

Alex wrapped an arm around her mom to bring her forward. "We came to check on you and Emma Jean. How is she?"

Jessica shifted her eyes to her daughter and then back to Alex. "She hasn't woke up yet."

"I'm sure they're keeping her heavily sedated," Alex said gently. "It takes time for brain injury to heal."

Jessica sniffled as a fresh tear leaked out the corner of one eye. She used a grimy finger to wipe it away. "I just can't believe all this..."

"It's not your fault."

Her eyes deviated upward in what seemed like an appeal for mercy and she gave a harsh laugh. "Ain't it though?"

Alex moved to sit on the bed below Emma's feet and placed a hand on Jessica's bony shoulder. "What you did saved her. If you hadn't recognized that something was wrong and called the ambulance, she would have died. You saved her," Alex repeated firmly, willing Jessica to meet her eyes. "And I imagine you will never let anyone hurt her ever again."

Jessica's chin quivered and her mouth opened but nothing came out. Janie stepped over and unhooked an overflowing tote bag from her shoulder. "We brought you a few things."

"I don't need—"

"Now it was no trouble. Just a few things that will make your stay here more pleasant. From one survivor to another." Janie began unpacking the bag as Jessica exclaimed over the contents.

Alex took Emma's hand. "You're going to be fine," she whispered, "because you're young and you're strong and most importantly you're loved." Alex could have sworn her eyelids fluttered in response.

Janie poked her head into Alex's room, the sound of sizzling bacon crackling through the air. "Good! You're up. What time do you want to head over to the auction?"

Alex shrugged. "Whatever time you think, Mom."

"Well, I want to get a good seat near the action so how about right after lunch?"

Alex couldn't stop the grin from happening. "Sure. Sounds good."

"There's a lot of people interested in Terry's land," she continued. "I was in the store yesterday and Mabel Merriweather told me some guy from California wants to turn it into a bed and breakfast. Can you imagine?"

While Janie prattled on and fussed with a pair of socks discarded under the rug, Alex feigned listening while she plotted.

Music blared from a set of speakers, a downhome beat with plenty of slide guitar, as Alex waited in line underneath a tri-colored banner. Men in straw cowboy hats and plaid shirts tucked tightly into starched blue jeans greeted one another with handshakes and slaps on the back. The women faded away from the clusters of guffawing cowboys and formed their own tight knit circles balancing handbags and children between exchanges of gossip. Alex hung back on purpose, letting Peter direct her mother inside while she loitered at the entrance.

When it was her turn, she stepped up to a long rectangular table draped in crisp white cloth, her heart nearly jumping out of her throat.

"Name?" boomed a deep throated man in a bolo tie.

"Alexandra Wilde."

His eyes glanced upward. "You kin to Gary Wilde?"

"Uh, no, I don't think so," Alex answered.

"Alrighty then. We got numbers twenty-seven, fifty-two, and thirteen left." He gestured to the circles stamped with numerals and hot glued to popsicle sticks.

"I'll take thirteen."

"You sure? You not worried about bad luck?"

"Thirteen *is* my lucky number." Alex smiled broadly and accepted the auction paddle, tucking it in her blue shoulder bag.

A wall of muscle leaned against the entrance to the sand-filled arena when Alex rounded the corner. Arms folded over his chest, eyes bright and face clean shaven, he looked exactly as she remembered once upon a time. His face lit into a smile at the sight of her and he fell into step as she walked past.

"Fancy seeing you here," he drawled.

"I'm just following someone's advice."

"What advice is that?"

"To be a part of where I came from."

"Sounds like a really smart guy. Handsome too, I bet."

"Don't forget arrogant." She used her index finger to poke him in the ribs.

Justin chuckled and threw an arm over her shoulders. "I see your mom over there," he said, pointing at Janie who was involved in an animated discussion with a lady in a giant pink Stetson.

"I'm actually going to sit over there." Alex cocked her head toward the section reserved for buyers. Justin raised his brows at her.

"What are you about to do, Lex?"

"You'll see. Want to join me?"

The auctioneer was a stooped bald man who was so bowlegged he tottered when he walked. His boots thudded on each wooden step as he ascended the auction platform, the voices in the crowd ceasing with every step. The sound system squawked as he adjusted the microphone toward his lips.

"Ladies and gentlemen," he said smoothly, gently, like a spring waterfall into a river. "The first item up for auction will be a wedding dress from the late nineteenth century. Now who'll give me..." His voice rose and the crowd sat transfixed at his tempo, his perfect timing and enunciation. "Sold to the lady in the pink cowboy hat."

For the next hour and a half, each time the gavel struck, the crowd erupted in a composite score of clapping and whistling. Boot stomping and whooping. A vintage car sold for some exorbitant amount to a suited gentleman holding a cell phone to his ear. A 1920's engagement ring went for a small sum as well as an intricately carved leather saddle.

Alex's palms left sweat stains on the pages of her program when she flipped through to locate the blurb on Terry's property. Twenty-nine acres of waterfront property in the heart of Brazos County.

"Are you really gonna do this?" Justin hissed as the gavel fell again. Her eyes never left the stage.

"Yes," she hissed back.

"How in the hell—"

She batted a hand toward his face to silence him.

"Next up," boomed the auctioneer, "we have a prime piece of property along Cedar Creek, a real beauty fit for horses, livestock, or whatever you folks can dream up."

Alex's insides were so tight that she thought her guts might twist into a knot.

"Now who'll start me at three hundred thousand..."

A man in a gray suit with slicked back hair raised his paddle. Alex darted a look from him to an upscale cowboy in a black felt hat who raised his in response.

"I got three fifty give me four...give me four."

Gray suit raised his arm, his face betraying no emotion, and black felt hat rose again as well.

"Who'll give me five...lookin' for five..." The auctioneer ping ponged his sharp eyes between the two men.

"Put your hand up," Justin whispered as Alex held up five fingers.

"Whoa there, we got five from the lady in red..."

Alex heard the murmurs sweep through the crowd, a few craning their necks to get a glimpse of her. Black hat wiped his brow and shook his head. The perceptive eyes of the auctioneer swung to the gray suit. His mouth moved against the receiver of his phone, and he held up six fingers. "Six, I got six..."

Alex gritted her teeth and honed her gaze on the man at the podium. His mouth moved with the cadence of his words and suddenly she was astride her chestnut horse at a gallop, hooves pounding, breath mixing with the early morning dew. Her heart thumped once, slowly, assuredly, and she held up seven fingers.

"Seven! Going once..." The auctioneer glanced at gray suit who faltered. "Going twice...Sold to the lady with the number thirteen."

The entire arena exploded with thunderous noise as everyone jumped to their feet. She was pulled into the solidity of Justin's side as he wrapped an arm around her, shaking her like a ragdoll. The very best part, though, was catching the stunned expression on Janie's face.

The sky had turned a brilliant shade of tropical orange by the time Alex arrived at the private hangar. A silver jet waited to whisk her away into the sunset, even though part of her would remain here, in her small Texas town where she grew up. She had a place here now, a purpose, and she would be back soon. She had told Justin as much.

After the fanfare had died down, she had filled out the paperwork for the land sale under Justin's watchful eye.

"I didn't see this coming."

Alex smiled as she signed her name to the last page of the thick packet and handed it to the man in the bolo tie. "I didn't either, until two nights ago."

"What do you plan on doing with it?"

A smile beholden to all manner of secrets lightened her face as she straightened from the table. She rose on tiptoe to reach Justin's ear and repeated, in a whisper, the plan she had presented in an emergency board meeting yesterday over speakerphone.

"How are you gonna keep those Brit bastards away?"

"I was thinking," Alex mused, a smile playing on her lips, "of finding a very intimidating ex-military officer to watch over it for me."

Her eyes focused on his mid-section and the fibers in his shirt while he shifted from one leg to the other. He cleared his throat before resting his hands on her shoulders. She looked upward to a pair of seafoam green eyes cresting with hope and resolve.

"It would be my greatest honor."

The airplane engines were already whirring by the time she settled into her seat. She reached into her blue shoulder bag for her phone, instead finding an envelope wedged in the side pocket with her name on it. She unfolded the piece of notebook paper inside.

Lex,

We don't often meet someone who settles in our soul like you settled in mine. And for the longest, I didn't understand the purpose in it, but I'm starting to. Thank you for giving me something new to believe in...to fight for. I'm a better person because of you. We all are. I used to think that I was just the dream you didn't choose, but maybe you were choosing me all along and things worked out exactly as they should have.

Love always,
Justin

She read it twice, and then, folding it into a tiny square, placed it carefully into the crevice of her wallet.

Alex must have dozed off some time during the trans-Atlantic flight across a black ocean through an even blacker night. When she opened her eyes, the sun shone brilliantly through the oval window, piercing through the opaque film covering her corneas. *Ian.* He was out there somewhere past the tarmac and the shiny communications tower. Waiting. For her.

The taxi to the unloading area seemed to take forever and each bump in the asphalt jolted Alex's nerves. Her eyes scanned the horizon for the midnight-colored sedan and Mark in his driving regalia. But it was empty apart from the glittering roadway. When she exited the plane and took a deep breath, the air was lighter, already cooler with the impending autumn chill. Not the heavy warmth of southeast Texas. But over time, it too would become as familiar as the rich Texas humidity, as the noise and smog of Philadelphia, as the dust-laden freshness of Botswana.

In the distance, she saw a car turn into the one-way lane between hangars. A vintage sportscar painted sky blue barreled toward her. A fine spray of pebbles became airborne when it skidded to a stop and Ian jumped out of the driver's seat. One minute she was gawking at his deft handling of the car and the next she was being crushed into his warm chest.

Sensation overpowered everything else as she clutched at the material of his shirt and inhaled his spice and leather scent. She wriggled out of his embrace to throw her arms around his neck and meet him with furious lips, parting only to draw a ragged breath and then continue. His fingers wound through her hair, and she clawed at him to bring their bodies closer. When she was with him, nothing else existed.

He shuddered under her touch, dragging his tongue over the roof of her mouth and sucking on her bottom lip before tucking her into the place between his neck and his shoulder. Fluttering layers of his hair tickled her cheek, like the brush of raven's wings.

"I missed you."

"I missed you too."

Alex felt the vibration of her phone in her shoulder bag and ignored it. She reluctantly pulled back from the delectable proximity of his jawline to meet his eyes. Eyes as blue and limitless as the sky.

"Ian," she breathed. "Thank you. Going to Texas was exactly what I needed and the land, it means everything to me. I didn't even realize how much until now."

He wiped a tear from her cheek with his thumb. Gently. Reverently.

"And you mean everything to me."

Her bag continued to buzz like a pesky insect as he led her around to the passenger door and opened it with a flourish. "Where to, my lady?"

Making love to her husband in a vintage Corvette for the entire air crew to see was more than tempting. Instead, she sighed and ran a hand down his chest to curl her fingers inside the waistband of his jeans.

"Take me home."

When she watched his pupils dilate amidst the transfixed awe on his face, a rush of heat warmed her from the inside.

"I'm so glad I drove the Corvette."

Alex giggled and settled into the supple cream leather. When Ian revved the motor and spun out of the parking lot, she laughed, rocking along with the car's momentum as they took the turn onto the expressway. Alex rolled down the window, desperate for a fresh brush of air on her cheeks, a cool verbena scent with a tinge of sea salt. She clutched her bag to her chest and when it vibrated for a third time, she dug her phone out of its recesses.

"Ian," she said sharply. "We need to get to St. Mary's." Her knuckles whitened as they clenched around her phone. "Rox is in labor."

THIRTY-FIVE

As soon as Ian pulled into a parking spot, Alex pushed open the door and planted her feet on the concrete.

"Did she tell you which room?" Ian huffed as he quickened his stride.

"Three-oh-three," Alex gasped and entered a bank of elevators.

"Is it time for the baby to come?" Ian asked and Alex glanced quickly at her digital calendar.

Rox was thirty-seven weeks exactly.

"It's a few weeks early but yeah, it's time."

When the elevator dinged, Alex took off like a lit charge for the nurses' station. A finely boned woman with close cropped flaming orange hair peered at her over a computer monitor.

"Can I help you?"

Alex licked her papery lips. "I'm here to see Roxanne Clarke-Brizido. I'm her...sister."

"I don't think so," the lady snipped. "No one except actual family is allowed back. Hospital policy."

Of course it would be this way in a hospital renowned for delivering the squalling infants of celebrities, past and present queens included. Ian shouldered past her and locked eyes with the middle-aged woman.

"What my wife means is that Nic and Rox are as close as we have to family. And we're certain that they would appreciate our support right now."

Alex stayed obediently quiet while the woman was hypnotized by Ian's overproductive charm. She shifted in her seat and then hardened her eyes on the computer.

"I'll need to get your names. Hospital policy."

The door of number three-oh-three was open a crack and Alex knocked gently before pushing it open farther.

"Rox?" Alex wasn't sure what she expected—nail biting, sheet gripping, tortured groans and grunts—but it wasn't the sight of Nic reading a magazine and Rox applying a coat of pink polish to her nails. Her hair was swept up into a top knot, delicate strands escaping down the back of her neck. Her face, though moon-shaped from pregnancy, was resplendent in a full accoutrement of makeup. When she noticed the pair in the doorway, her smile stretched the entire width of her face.

"Alex! Ian!" Putting down her polish, she motioned them over. Alex started forward and sunk carefully onto the bed next to her. "I'm not going to break," she squealed, pulling Alex into a fierce hug.

Alex's gaze fell to the elastic band around Rox's middle as her ears picked up the steady blips on the attached monitor. "Everything okay?"

"She asked for her epidural as soon as we got here. Since then she's been as cool as a cucumber." Nic folded up his magazine and stood to clap Ian on the back.

Rox glared in their direction. "There's no point in suffering through this part."

Nic's adoring look softened Rox's glare, and he walked over to rub her back in wide protective circles. "Of course not. I love you, mama."

Rox tipped up her chin so he could plant a kiss on her pink lips then shoved him away with a manicured hand. "I love you too. Now go make yourself useful and bring me another Sprite, extra ice."

"For my queen, anything." Nic bowed before shoving Ian through the doorway and back out into the hall.

When they were gone, Alex turned to Rox. "I could have gotten you a drink."

"Oh please. It was just an excuse to get some alone time with you. So how was Texas?"

"It was...good. And exactly what I needed."

Alex knew the words were vague, intentionally so, but how could she sum up a journey that had taken her over a decade to make? Rox eyed her, the light from the hospital ceiling bringing out the gold in her irises, like flecks of metal.

"If you say so, I believe you. I'm glad," she continued. "I was worried about you there for a while."

"Why is that?"

Rox chewed her lip, contemplating her words. "I was sure you would decide that you couldn't fit into Ian's life here in London."

The sentence punched her in the gut with its truth.

"You've got a wild side, a restless side, and it's what makes you absolutely brilliant, but it means you have trouble staying grounded."

Alex let the words settle, accepting them for what they were. Perhaps the next best thing to looking at herself in the mirror.

"I didn't want to be grounded. Ever," she admitted. "But then being in Texas made me remember the root of who I was. Who I am. It helped me find purpose in a life that I didn't necessarily choose but that chose me."

"But will you be happy?"

"With Ian?"

"With everything? Ian, his lifestyle, the family drama, your work, your future."

"I will be. Because life isn't meant to be lived any other way."

The empty spaces between monitor beeps got longer and Rox gripped her back.

"Are you okay?"

"I think," she said between gasps of breath, "it's time for me to push."

"Are you sure? How can you tell?" Alex asked and then felt a wave of incredible stupidity. Of course, she was sure.

Rox cut her eyes to Alex. "Get Nic."

Alex tore through the hospital breezeway, weaving past labor and delivery nurses in petal pink scrubs and a trolley full of neatly folded linens. A rim of sweat crowned her forehead and her hands were shaking by the time she found Nic and Ian in a cafe downstairs sipping coffee. With one glance at her face, Nic abandoned his mug and a delectable chocolate croissant, hastily wiping his hands down the front of his track pants.

No words were exchanged. Instead, the trio jogged toward the elevator and Nic pushed the up arrow. Then they waited and waited. Nic fidgeted. Ian coughed nervously and Alex glanced around wildly.

"Stairs," she said, pointing to a corridor at the rear of the hospital lobby. Each of them took off at a jog, Nic outpacing them easily by the time they ascended the stairs. By the time Alex and Ian burst through the stairwell door on the third floor, they only caught a glimpse of Nic's shoes as he rounded the corner to Rox's room.

"Best of luck, brother," Ian whispered and turned to Alex. "Shall we?" He cocked his head toward a glass door labeled in feminine script. *Waiting room.*

Alex settled onto a couch bathed in mid-morning sunshine, tilting her head against the stiff tapestry cushion and indulging in a moment of perfect stillness. Ian scooted next to her until their torsos aligned. Her arm tingled when it met with his bare skin.

"How long do you think it'll take?" he asked, genuinely curious.

"Babies come when they're ready," she yawned, "but I don't imagine it will take too long. Rox isn't the patient type."

She felt the shudder of Ian's silent chuckle. Lulled by the sound of his breathing and the endearing warmth of the sun, she skated on the edge of dreaming and wakefulness. Maybe this had all been a dream. A foray into an alternate universe and when she awoke, it would be the middle of a rainstorm in her Philadelphia apartment.

She would wake up and life would be good but not great. It would be the life she dreamed of but not one she had never imagined. It would be a singular path forward instead of constantly grappling with the past and churning toward the future. It would be rootless and restless. It would be free. But freedom always came with a price.

"Alex." His voice was elegant and smooth and richly soft. She thought she was dreaming until fingers intertwined with hers and she heard her name again. "Alex?"

"I'm here," she murmured.

"I need to know something."

"Mmhmm."

For one more luxurious second, she soaked in pre-slumber bliss before her eyelids fluttered open. Ian's nose was an inch from her face.

"Why did you need to go to Texas?"

A complicated question deserved a reverent answer and she mulled over her words carefully, feeling out any rough edges before they left her lips.

"I think—" her tongue brushed over the puckered skin of her lower lip, "—that I felt out of place in life. In my life with you. Like a piece that just wouldn't fit no matter how I angled it. And I thought that if I wanted to understand how I ended up here, I needed to understand how it started and revisit the decision that pushed me off one life trajectory onto another."

"Med school?"

"Yeah, but it was more than that. I buried the past, Ian, as deep as it would go. Once I left Cole's Church, I never spoke of my childhood again. Of my father, of that fire and what it cost me. I thought that was the only way to move forward—to survive—but I was wrong."

He squeezed her hand but said nothing, giving her the space to keep unraveling her thoughts.

"I didn't just leave behind the people that I despised. I left behind the people that I loved too. People that befriended me, cared for me, loved me." Her voice cracked as she continued. "And going back there, actually seeing it for what it was, I realized that like it or not, it made me. That place is part of who I am at my very core, and I didn't choose it. Sometimes I didn't even want it, but it chose me and I'm grateful. And it turns out that the past is not so different from my future."

"In what way?"

"It's not a life that I would have chosen."

Ian tensed, the worry swelling behind his eyes.

"But I'm grateful that it chose me. That you chose me."

"I will always choose you."

"And I will always choose us."

"What about your doctor life?"

Alex expected a piece of her heart to cave in at the question but strange enough, it didn't.

"I went into medicine to fight for those who couldn't fight for themselves, and I plan to keep doing that, however I can, whether it's in a hospital or under a tree or as part of the foundation."

She knew a thin film of tears had coaxed themselves over her eyes. She didn't care. Ian's warm lips found the center of her forehead and warmed it with a kiss. A kiss laden with promise.

"I think you should call your mother." The words left her lips before she realized it and Ian pulled back from her.

"Why?"

"I think, in her own way, she was trying to look out for you when she took me to lunch. I think she's trying to make up for the past."

Ian grunted but didn't disagree, which Alex took as a good sign.

"She loved you once." Alex stroked his furrowed brow with her index finger. "She could again."

Instead of replying, he leaned forward and kissed her, roving over her lips until she was breathless.

When the door to the waiting room burst open with a buoyant Nic, hands flapping in all directions, Alex and Ian sat up as a unit, her drowsiness completely obliterated.

"What?" she stammered.

Nic waved them toward the door he had propped open with an extra-large sneaker. "Roxanne and I would like you to come meet our baby girl."

Alex bolted to the door, Ian closely behind her, but checked her momentum to a slow crawl once she reached number three-oh-three, now covered in a paper stork with a pink bow around its neck. The room was warm, the air almost honeyed, when she entered and heard the faint mewling of a baby. Rox's golden hair was plastered to her forehead with a glistening crown of sweat. Alex thought she had never looked more beautiful. Without disrupting the wrapped bundle in her arms, she motioned Alex over to the bed.

"Come over and say hello."

Her face was nothing short of angelic, a set of perfect lips under a shapely nose, a few tufts of dark hair visible at the edge of her knitted hat. Alex curled her fingers around Rox's forearm, and the baby popped her eyes open, milky gray irises that would probably darken into a chestnut brown in the next few months. She had a galaxy of stars in the depths of those eyes and lashes like spun silk.

"Hi, little one."

Rox adjusted her so she was nearly upright. "We would like to introduce Aria Alexandra Brizido. Aria meet your Auntie Alex." Alex felt the weight of Ian's hands on her shoulders. "And your Uncle Ian." Rox looked past Alex with a devilish grin. "Would you like to hold her?"

Ian grew still. Alex felt him stop breathing.

"Me?"

"Of course, you. Alex will be holding her plenty in the very near future and we thought you needed the first turn." Rox shared a sly smile with Nic.

Ian stepped next to Alex, hands outstretched so that she could guide them under the baby's head and bottom. She looked so tiny in his sinewy arms against his broad chest, her eyes regarding everything with unexpected quiet.

The vision of Ian locking eyes with a baby, shifting his weight so that he rocked her, soothing her in his deep throaty voice, did something to Alex. Something crushing that flayed her open and made parts of her ache. She slid a hand over her lower abdomen to support whatever throbbing was happening deep inside her. She knew that Rox was watching and probably internally congratulating herself.

It was nearly evening when she and Ian finally collapsed into the car. After too many pictures and retrieving Rox's favorite Indian takeout, they left the new parents to rest and revel in the emotional letdown of participating in a miracle. When the car doors clanked shut, Ian paused over the ignition with the keys in his hand.

"That was—"

"I know," Alex finished.

The throbbing yearning inside her had built over the past few hours—the past few months really—and begged to be unleashed. Alex sent a hand over to Ian's leg where her fingers traced gentle lines up his thigh muscles. Upward and upward into the crease of his jeans and then higher still, underneath his shirt where she could finger the lower ridge of his abdominals. He stuffed the key into the ignition with a giant smirk and a cocked brow.

"I'll have us home in less than fifteen minutes."

"Maybe," Alex said, popping the button of his jeans, "I can't wait that long."

THIRTY-SIX

Cole's Church, Texas, December 2011

"There you go." Alex tipped her head upward. "Just like that. Keep your back straight and your hands quiet." Her grip tightened on the leather reins as she glanced back at the swaying figure of a young girl with curly tendrils of hair the color of straw dancing in the light winter breeze. Her boots slogged through the shifting sand and the pony next to her quivered his nostrils at the overpowering scent of evergreens. When they reached the gate, Alex dropped the reins and reached her arms up the fuzzy chestnut sides to lift the girl to the ground.

Despite the solemnity of her brown eyes, her lips lifted in a crooked smile. "Can I come back tomorrow?"

Alex squatted, reaching with her thumb to rub a smudge of dirt from the girl's cheek. Easily removed. Unlike the bruises that would always linger under her skin. Or the scar on her temple, hidden by a patch of spiky blonde hair.

"Of course you can."

Alex ushered the girl through the gate with a gentle hand between her shoulder blades. The girl skipped across the grass to her mother who waited beside a beat-up gray sedan. Alex raised a hand and Jessica nodded in greeting as she opened the car door, her complexion brighter, her posture straighter. While they sped down the driveway, her fingers snuck up to scratch the starred forehead of the compact chestnut horse next to her. The clearing of a feminine throat snapped her to attention.

"Dr. Wilde, I'm sorry to interrupt, but I have a few things to ask you before tonight."

Alex rolled her eyes in mock chagrin. "Charlotte, we've been working together for months. Please start calling me Alex."

The full-figured girl next to her with flat brown hair pulled into a low ponytail, clutched her laptop tighter to her chest and shifted her weight, the hem of her gray slacks dragging over the grass.

"Okay," she sighed, pushing her tortoise shell glasses higher onto her nose. "Before the dedication tonight, you have a phone meeting with the minister of health in Mongolia about your visit to the children's hospital next month and then the Uhuru Elephant Reserve is still waiting for a reply on whether or not you and Mr. Devall will be attending their gala in March..." Her voice trailed off as Alex's mind wandered elsewhere.

The last few months had been a veritable blur. Settling into the role of Devall Foundation Chairwoman had required her to fill some very large, very formidable, shoes. She hadn't pretended to know what she was doing when she had stepped into the cheerfully decorated office space for the first time a few months ago. Yet the entire cadre of office staff had paused in their conversations to greet her. Some with enthusiastic handshakes. Others with hugs, like Rachel and Lydia, whom she had known since her time in Botswana.

With Lydia's help, she had quickly learned the basics and was well on her way to mastering the complicated spreadsheets of the various charities supported by the foundation. The office merely served as a landing zone for the actual work happening on the ground. She and Ian had spent the first part of October in Botswana and celebrated Thanksgiving with a quick trip to Nepal, where she had spent two glorious days teaching advanced pediatric resuscitation to a local group of pediatric specialists.

"And the catering should be delivered no later than five so we need to have the tables and tent completely set up no later than four..."

Quivering lips reached over to nibble on her outstretched hand. She used her fingertips to push away the velvety muzzle.

"That all sounds fine, Charlotte."

"I have a few more things to check off the list..."

Alex stared pointedly at her assistant. "I trust you. Probably even more than I trust myself to decide the seating arrangement or the wine list or the way the napkins should be folded."

Charlotte ducked her head and adjusted her glasses. "Of course, Doctor...Alex." Her pale face relaxed into a smile that showed a few of her top teeth.

Over Charlotte's head, a hand waved at her from the gaping

mouth of the barn. "I'll see you around four, Charlotte. Is that okay?" she said, tugging the pony along a dirt path toward the stalls. When she looked back, her capable assistant was already engrossed in a phone call, furiously taking notes with a number two pencil.

"Love what you've done with the place," Alex said, grinning as as she surveyed Justin's sweat-soaked t-shirt and characteristic upturned grin, no longer hidden behind a mask of melancholy.

He tugged off his gloves and leaned against the forest green backdrop of a pair of barn doors. Alex peered around him, the scent of fresh straw and horse musk striking her full in the face. A *clippety clop* of hooves resounded against concrete then a whicker of protest as a stall door was slid into place. A pale freckled hand reached out for the leather reins she was clutching, and she handed them over, her palm running along the burnished copper backside as the pony was led inside. Justin glanced up at the towering structure, two stories of stalls and office space and a giant storeroom.

"She's a beauty," he said and then cleared his throat.

A silence settled over them, light and far from awkward. Silence as simple and pure as the wind ruffling the tufted ends of Alex's braid.

"I couldn't have done this without you."

"Of course not," he scoffed but then looked away. Alex followed his gaze toward the riding ring enclosed by a glossy black wooden fence.

"Are you happy?" she asked. "Being back here?"

"Happy as a clam."

"No, I mean it." Alex balled up a fist and socked him in the arm.

"It's home. It'll always be home."

"Yeah, I know what you mean."

"What about you?"

"What *about* me?"

"Are you happy?" He toyed with the finger on his suede glove before meeting her eyes.

"Why are you asking me that?"

"Because I want to make sure you left here to live the life you always dreamed of, not just because you were running from something."

Alex nodded in understanding. "Fair question. I *was* running from something, but at the same time toward something."

"And now?"

"And now I'm right back where I started."

Justin regarded her with intent, soulful eyes, haunted eyes that were just now seeing life again. Beauty again. "You are so far from where you started."

And she was. Somewhere along the way, the broken shards of her heart had mended. Soldered back together by purpose and then by sacrifice and then by love. And she was just starting to understand what her dreams really looked like. They were a life where fear was irrelevant. Where she could serve and protect and save the innocent lives cast into her path. They looked like the sunset from the back of a horse. They looked like a mother's face when she found out her child was going to be okay. They looked like the ocean's sky contained in the spheres of a perfect set of eyes that belonged to the man who owned her heart.

Sometimes the end of a story was actually the beginning.

"So are you," she said, blowing Justin a kiss as she strolled toward the gravel drive. When she reached the end, she ran her hand along an iron gate, cooled by the impending winter chill, and tugged it open to let a jet black sedan pass through. Her fingers trailed the gentle script of the sign hanging on the front: The Teresa Hawthorne School of Therapeutic Riding.

"We would like to welcome everyone this evening to the official opening of the Devall Foundation's latest project." Alex parted her lips in a deliberate pause and surveyed the outdoor tent, simple yet stylish, a few strands of lights artfully criss-crossed above the guests' heads. Round tables covered in white cloths dotted the enclosure, the faces seated around them illuminated by the flickers of candlelight. Flames danced on a winter's breeze and matched the warmth Alex felt inside her chest as she picked out the individual faces: her mom and Peter sitting with Natalie and Mrs. Ashwell; Justin and his grandparents; Doctor Z, a shock of gray hair flopped over onto the neat horizontal lines on his forehead; a few of the teachers from the high school and the mayor, her bright red hair cut in a trendy shag. Chief Richardson, out of uniform for once, leaned over to whisper something to his pregnant wife.

Her eyes swept over the table at the far back of the tent. Charlotte in a black cocktail dress busily snapped photographs with her phone and a few of the foundation committee members tipped their glasses toward her. She took a breath and continued.

"The construction of this riding school will bring an opportunity to the community of Cole's Church that has never before existed. Adults and children suffering from various forms of trauma will find a safe place here. A place to heal and animals ready to help them deal with their pain." Alex cleared her throat, her heartrate picking up in cadence, pounding her from the inside like a set of hooves.

"When I was a little girl, I unfortunately experienced abuse at the hands of my father. I was lucky enough to have people in my life who cared about me." Her eyes flickered over her mother and then came to rest on Justin's auburn head. "And I had the horses. Without them, I wouldn't be the person you see in front of you today."

A thin film of tears blurred her vision and the rest of her words got caught in the rapidly accumulating lump in the back of her throat. Silence fell, punctuated by a few coughs and a creaking of chairs. A steady palm came to rest against her back as a figure in a slim cut navy blazer filled up the space beside her.

"Those of you who know my wife well realize that modesty is her biggest flaw."

Laughter ebbed and surged in a symphony of chuckling.

"You're late," Alex whispered, tipping up her chin to kiss Ian on the cheek.

"I know. Who knew this place was completely off the grid of any GPS?" His hand wrapped around her waist and pulled her into his side. "Forgive me?"

She threaded her fingers through his and tilted her head to rest on his shoulder. Ian's voice rang over the crowd. "Everyone please join me in raising a glass to the Teresa Hawthorne School of Therapeutic Riding and the new chair of the Devall Foundation, Dr. Alex Wilde."

Applause erupted followed by high pitched whistles and the clanking of beer bottles against glassware. Alex settled back into herself, relief flooding into the soles of her high-heeled shoes. A few servers began sifting between the tables, unloading trays of plated barbecue dinners and baskets of buttered bread. Bent heads, some with straw cowboy hats, became engrossed in soft conversation. In the background a speaker started up with the first chords of a twangy country song. A reed-thin woman in leggings and black boots approached her, dark hair curling around her ears. Her arms reached out for a quick embrace and Alex leaned close enough to smell her floral perfume. Her lips split into a smile between apple red cheeks as she pulled back.

"Great party," she exclaimed.

"Thanks," Alex said and made space next to her for Ian.

"Ian, this is Gwen. She's going to be managing the barn and teaching a few of the classes."

"Nice to meet you," he said smoothly as she grabbed his outstretched hand in a tight grip.

"Likewise," she said.

There was something smooth and solid about her. Alex had known the first minute of their meeting that she would be the perfect person to run this place in her absence. When Gwen faded into the background, swept into conversation by a cadre of cowboys, a growing crowd stood behind her, waiting their turn to offer congratulations. One after the other, they offered a handshake or more frequently a hug and a reference for how they knew her.

"I remember when you were in high school..."

"I've known your mom for years..."

"I used to teach you at Sunday school..."

And on and on until only one tall silhouette remained.

"Ian, this is Justin, my best friend from high school. Justin, this is my husband, Ian."

The two men regarded one another carefully, speculatively, as if inspecting for any flaw, any chink, that would prove they were unworthy of her.

"Nice to finally meet you." Ian put out a hand that was immediately swallowed up by Justin's.

"You, too."

"Alex was lucky to have someone like you growing up."

"We were lucky to have her." Justin's eyes brightened.

Silence ensued and Alex thought her heart might lodge in her throat and choke her.

Justin grinned and pulled his hand away only to clap Ian on the shoulder with it. "Think you can convince her to stick around for a while?"

"You know Alex. She does what she wants when she wants."

She narrowed her eyes at both of them as they shared an unexpected laugh.

"Just so you know, I will be here this entire week working in the new pediatric clinic at the local hospital."

"I hope you improved your sewing since then." Justin held up his arm for Alex to see the crescent shaped scar on his forearm.

"I could have done a better job if someone had kept still instead of jerking every time I poked."

"She took a thorn out of my hand once," Ian added, "after pouring my good bourbon all over it."

Laughter rumbled up from two chests and part of her didn't mind at all that it was at her expense. It sliced through the tension like a knife through hot butter.

"You a bourbon, guy?" Justin eyed Ian with new interest.

"Absolutely."

"Come on then. You gotta try some stuff I have behind the bar."

Before trailing behind Justin, Ian wrapped a protective arm around Alex's waist, pulling her close before releasing her. Alex also didn't miss the kiss he planted squarely on her lips.

If she closed her eyes against the starlight, she could almost smell the ocean from here. It traveled on the same wind that licked the coast then blew inland to settle between the creek and a row of cedars older than her. She sat on the bank of the creek, the party unfolding behind her in a storm of light and music. But it was the quiet that had always called to her. Seduced her. Befriended her. And she sat in it now, wrapped in its perfection, listening to the gentle ripples of the creek below, cushioned by a sloping stretch of earth. She felt full. Full of the contentment offered after hardship and pain and sacrifice. A contentment that chased away fear and uncertainty until there was no room for anything else except love and life.

"I thought I might find you out here."

"Oh really?"

Alex tipped up her chin to meet Ian's lips, warm despite the night's chill, and spiced with bourbon. He settled onto the grass next to her, his brow furrowing when she studied his face.

"What?" she asked.

"I don't think I've ever seen you look more alive."

She smiled, knowing it was true. "I am," she admitted. "I never dreamed life could be so—"

"Full," Ian finished.

"Yeah. I love you," she whispered into his mouth, right before tasting the bourbon that lingered there.

"A question," he interjected between kissing the underside of her jaw, "have you ever had life changing sex beside a creek?"

Heat coursed through her middle and she bit her lip. "Put that

ABOUT THE AUTHOR

HK Jacobs is native to a small town in Texas that gave her both roots and wings. She holds a Doctor of Medicine from Baylor College of Medicine and a Master of Public Health from the University of Texas. She is a board certified pediatric critical care physician whose passion is traveling the globe caring for seriously ill children in low-middle income countries. She currently resides in Texas, where she continues to balance the many roles in her life—mother, physician, humanitarian, dreamer, and author.

Made in the USA
Columbia, SC
16 May 2022